"Sophie, about the kiss—"

"You don't have to say anything. I was upset, and so were you. It was a mistake. I'm sorry. It won't happen again. You know, I should probably get going—"

Liam grabbed her hand before she could take off. "Wait. You have nothing to apologize for. I just don't think a relationship right now is a good idea for either of us."

She frowned. "A relationship? How did we go from a kiss to a relationship?"

He didn't have a clue. He wasn't thinking. He couldn't. Every ounce of blood from his head had gone south.

PRAISE FOR DEBBIE MASON AND THE HARMONY HARBOR SERIES

"Debbie Mason writes romance like none other."
—FreshFiction.com

"I've never met a Debbie Mason story that I didn't enjoy."
—KeeperBookshelf.com

"I'm telling you right now, if you haven't yet read a book by Debbie Mason you don't know what you're missing."
—RomancingtheReaders.blogspot.com

"It's not just romance. It's grief and mourning, guilt and truth, second chances and revelations."
—WrittenLoveReviews.blogspot.com

"Mason always makes me smile and touches my heart in the most unexpected and wonderful ways."
—HerdingCats-BurningSoup.com

"No one writes heartful small town romance like Debbie Mason, and I always count the days until the next book!"
—TheManyFacesofRomance.blogspot.com

"Wow, do these books bring the feels. Deep emotion, heart-tugging romance, and a touch of suspense make them hard to put down…"
—TheRomanceDish.com

Also by Debbie Mason

The Highland Falls series
Summer on Honeysuckle Ridge

Christmas on Reindeer Road

Falling in Love on Willow Creek

A Wedding on Honeysuckle Ridge (short story)

The Harmony Harbor series
Mistletoe Cottage

Christmas with an Angel (short story)

Starlight Bridge

Primrose Lane

Sugarplum Way

Driftwood Cove

Sandpiper Shore

The Corner of Holly and Ivy

Barefoot Beach

Christmas in Harmony Harbor

The Christmas, Colorado series
The Trouble with Christmas

Christmas in July

It Happened at Christmas

Wedding Bells in Christmas

Snowbound at Christmas

Kiss Me in Christmas

Happy Ever After in Christmas

Marry Me at Christmas (short story)

Miracle at Christmas (novella)

One Night in Christmas (novella)

Mistletoe Cottage

DEBBIE MASON

A Harmony Harbor Novel

FOREVER

NEW YORK   BOSTON

Forever
Hachette Book Group
1290 Avenue of the Americas, New York, NY 10104
read-forever.com
twitter.com/readforeverpub

Originally published in mass market and ebook by Forever in October 2016
Reissued: October 2021

Forever is an imprint of Grand Central Publishing. The Forever name and logo are trademarks of Hachette Book Group, Inc.

The publisher is not responsible for websites (or their content) that are not owned by the publisher.

The Hachette Speakers Bureau provides a wide range of authors for speaking events. To find out more, go to www.hachettespeakersbureau.com or call (866) 376-6591.

ISBNs: 978-1-5387-3797-2 (mass market), 978-1-4555-3718-1 (ebook)

Printed in the United States of America

OPM

10 9 8 7 6 5 4 3 2 1

Acknowledgments

Many thanks to my editor Alex Logan for allowing me the creative freedom to follow my vision for this book and the new series. She not only works tirelessly on behalf of my books, but she also makes each one so much better with her creative insights. To the dedicated sales, marketing, production, and art departments at Grand Central/Forever, thank you so much for all your efforts on behalf of my books. They're greatly appreciated. I'm also grateful to my daughter Jess for reading the book through its many stages, and to my agent Pamela Harty for always being there when I need her.

My heartfelt thanks to Vanessa Kelly and Allison Van Diepen for all their support and encouragement. I'm so lucky to have you both in my life.

To Sharon and Scott LeClair, thank you for being the best sister and brother I could ask for. Love you both.

Thanks also to my mom and her friends for providing the inspiration for the Widows Club in Harmony Harbor. You're not as quirky as the members in Harmony, but you're just

just as wonderful and fun. You're proof that seventy really is the new fifty.

To my wonderful husband, amazing children, and adorable granddaughters, I couldn't do what I do without your love and support. Thank you. You guys are my world.

To the readers who have been on this journey with me since the release of the first book in the Christmas, Colorado, series, thank you so very much for sticking with me. Your support and your lovely reviews, e-mails, Facebook posts, and tweets mean the world to me. I hope you enjoy hanging out with the Gallaghers of Harmony Harbor as much as you did the McBrides of Christmas, Colorado.

Chapter One

♥

Sirens wailed, the fire engines' red and white lights bouncing off the clapboard Colonials on Main Street. People strolling along the tree-lined sidewalk turned to watch the rigs careen around a corner while cars veered to the side of the road. Ladder Engine 1 and Engine 6 were headed west of Harmony Harbor to Greystone Manor.

Three hours earlier, Liam Gallagher had been heading home to Boston. He'd stopped by the station to say goodbye to his father, Fire Chief Colin Gallagher, on the way out of town. But, because he loved his old man, who had put up with Liam for the past month, he'd made his first mistake. He'd let his dad convince him to stay another day. Taking his father up on his challenge had been a bigger one. Under the watchful eyes of the three men who knew him about as well as he knew himself, Liam would be battling his first fire in more than five weeks. Built in the early nineteenth century and modeled after a medieval castle, Greystone Manor was a firefighter's worst nightmare. And over the last month, Liam had been battling one of his own.

The chief disconnected his cell phone call and shifted to face Liam and Marco DiRossi, Liam's childhood best friend. The rest of the crew followed behind in the ladder engine. Fergus MacLeod, a burly beast of a man with russet hair and beard who'd known Liam since he was in diapers, blasted the horn at three-second intervals to clear the intersection up ahead. Liam's father raised his voice to be heard. "Manor's full of smoke, but the sprinklers haven't kicked in. Lights went out, and the generator took longer than it should to come on. A couple of guests sustained minor injuries evacuating—"

"GG and Grams?" Liam asked, unable to conceal the anxiety in his voice. He wasn't worried his father would misconstrue the reason for it or reprimand him for interrupting his brief. Liam's great-grandmother Colleen owned and operated Greystone with the help of her daughter-in-law and Liam's grandmother, Kitty.

He'd never understood what had possessed his great-grandmother to turn the manor into a hotel. If it had been up to him, she would have sold out years ago. Especially now that his grandfather Ronan was no longer there to help run the place. Liam hoped she'd be more open to the idea after tonight.

"Jasper got GG out, but your grandmother, a woman, and a young child are still inside. They can't find the little girl. Kitty and the woman refuse to leave without her." His father looked at Marco. "Jasper says she's your sister, son. And the little girl is her daughter, your niece."

Liam blew out a silent whistle. *Sophie DiRossi*. He hadn't thought about her in years, and there'd been a time when she'd been all he thought about. He glanced at Marco, who sat in the jump seat across from him.

Beneath an inch of dark scruff, Marco's jaw tightened. "Jasper's gotta be mistaken, Chief. Sophie and her kid live in LA. She hasn't been home since she left."

"Just wanted to give you a heads-up in case it's true," his father said then glanced at Liam and lifted his chin at Marco before facing forward.

Everyone in Harmony Harbor knew how the DiRossis felt about Sophie and her mother's defection. Within six months of Sophie and her mother taking off, the oldest of the DiRossi siblings, Lucas, had left Harmony Harbor, and a year later, their father, Giovanni, remarried and moved to Italy.

"You okay?" Liam asked his best friend.

Marco took off his helmet to stab his fingers through his dark hair. "Jasper has to be wrong. There's no way it's Sophie."

If Jasper said it was Sophie, Liam had no doubt that it was. Nothing got past the old man—a fact Liam, his brothers, and cousins could attest to. Jasper, or Jeeves as the Gallagher grandchildren referred to him, had been at Greystone for as long as any of them could remember. A tall beanpole of a man with stiff, overly proper manners, he ruled the manor and the Gallagher family with an iron fist hidden inside a velvet glove.

Since Marco knew Jasper almost as well as Liam, either his friend was in denial or he held a grudge longer than Liam had given him credit for. Noting the angry bounce of Marco's right leg, he was going with the latter. Then again…"They'll be okay, buddy. We'll find your niece. Get them out of there."

"Yeah, yeah, I know. What I don't know is why the hell she's here. After eight years, she just shows up out of the blue…" With a white-knuckled grip on his helmet, Marco gave his head an angry shake.

So Liam had been right after all. "I don't get it. Aren't you happy she's finally come home?"

"Give me a break. You have no idea what her leaving did to my family. For two years, we never heard a word from her. Now we're lucky if she calls a couple times a year. And for the amount of time she talks, you'd think we were putting a trace on her phone calls."

"So, what, you don't believe in second chances? Don't be a hothead and blow it. At least you still have a sister." Liam sensed his father glancing his way and Fergus's eyes on him in the rearview mirror.

"You're right. Sorry, I didn't think."

Fergus blasted the horn as he drove beneath a vine-covered stone arch, past the iron gates leading into the estate. The headlights and emergency lights sliced through the gloom of the late October night and Liam leaned forward. What got his attention wasn't the sprawling mansion built of local granite or the people scattering from where they'd been standing on the circular drive. It was the white smoke billowing from the manor's entrance. He opened the door as the engine rolled to a stop and smelled the air—chemicals, not burning wood. "There's no fire," Liam said to his father as he jumped onto the asphalt.

"Not yet, but could be electrical. Breathing apparatus on, Liam," his father called after him.

Liam raised his gloved hand, indicating he heard him as he jogged to where Jasper was leading Kitty from the manor. "You okay, Grams?" he asked once he reached them.

She nodded through a coughing fit.

He rubbed her arm and looked at Jasper. "Sophie and the little girl still inside?"

Jasper gave him a clipped nod. "We'd gone through most of the upper and main floors before Miss Kitty was overcome."

"All right. Go let Dad check you both over," Liam said as he started into the building then pivoted when it hit him what he was smelling. "Jasper, you didn't have the fog machine going, did you?"

"Certainly not, Master Liam. As your father directed, I expressly forbade Miss Kitty and Madame from using it this Halloween."

Since *Madame* didn't like to be told what she could or couldn't do, Liam didn't rule out the possibility that Colleen and a fog machine were behind the smoke. As he walked into the entryway, he tapped the switch on his helmet twice. The beam of light cut through the haze, providing him with a 180-degree view. He jogged across the lobby, calling for Sophie while trying to get an idea where the smoke originated from. He spotted what he believed was the point of origin at the same time he heard someone cough.

A woman with long, dark hair stumbled out of one of the sitting rooms. "Sophie, it's Liam." He tipped up his helmet as he closed the distance between them.

She lowered a denim jacket from where she'd held it over her mouth and nose. Her face was pale, her golden brown eyes red-rimmed. She looked exhausted and utterly terrified. "My little girl. I can't find my little girl. You have to help me—" She started coughing again.

"I'll find her, Sophie. But you need to—" He broke off as a second beam of light joined his. "Marco, get her out of here," he ordered his best friend.

Marco nodded, his expression unreadable as he reached for his sister.

She pulled away from her brother and frantically shook her head. "No, I can't go. I have to help you find her. You don't—"

Her brother cut her off. "Dammit, Soph, don't be stubborn. We'll find her, but you have to—"

"No, no, you don't understand. She's terrified of fire…of firemen. And she can't…" Her voice broke on a sob. Liam saw the herculean effort it took for her to regain control, but she did, and then she finished what she'd been about to say. "She can't talk."

He and Marco shared a glance. Their job just got a whole lot harder. "Sophie, I'll take off the breathing apparatus and my helm—"

"Like hell you will," his father said through his com. Marco said the same thing beside him.

Liam knew the reason for their concern and ignored them. He couldn't think about that now. Couldn't let the memory of the warehouse fire into his head. "I'm going to find your little girl. What's her name?"

She held his gaze as though she believed him and swiped at her eyes. "Mia. Her name's Mia." Overcome by another coughing fit, Sophie struggled to take the knapsack off her shoulder. Waving off his offer to help, she dug around inside and pulled out a pink pig with a singed ear. "We had a fire at our apartment in LA. Other than Mia, Peppa Pig is pretty much the only thing that survived. It might help if you show her…" Sophie bit her bottom lip then handed him the stuffed animal. "Please, Liam, please find her. She's all I have."

He slipped the pink pig into his pocket. "Right now it doesn't look like we're dealing with a fire. She'll be okay, Sophie. I'll find her," he promised.

"Jesus, Soph. Why didn't you call us? Why didn't…"

Liam didn't waste time waiting for Sophie to answer her brother. He jogged toward the door behind the grand staircase. It led to the basement, a place that had featured prominently in his nightmares as a little kid. Probably because his older brothers and cousins had traumatized him with stories about the long-dead pirates that haunted the narrow passageways and secret tunnels. If the upper floors had already been searched, it's possible he'd find Mia down here.

Smoke billowed through the partially open door, and Liam adjusted his breathing apparatus before opening it wide. As soon as he did, he was hit by a thick wall of smoke. The beam of light cut through the fog and illuminated the spiral staircase.

Liam started down the stairs and the stone walls closed in around him, transporting him to a wide-open space filled with movement and noise. Voices came over his radio—yelling, the rapid repeat of gunshots. Faint at first, and then the gunfire became louder. *Get down. Get down.* He belly-crawled to where Billy lay in the middle of the floor, laser beams zinging overhead from one side of the warehouse to the other. Shouting. Everyone shouting. A bullet shattered the concrete an inch from his head, and then another one…

Something repeatedly bumped his leg, getting harder with each jab, and the flashback started to fade. Liam looked down. A pair of small blue eyes stared up at him. It was a black cat. It took a moment for his head to clear and get his bearings. He wasn't in Boston; he was on the stairs at Greystone.

Someone yelled over the radio. "Liam, are you all right? Liam, goddammit, answer me."

"Good. I'm good, Chief. I'm in the basement. Must have played havoc with the com," he lied to his father, who must already suspect what Liam had been denying. He was so far from good it wasn't funny. "Found the problem," he said as he reached the bottom of the stairs.

To his left, barely visible behind cardboard boxes piled

precariously close, sat two overheating commercial fog machines. They were damn lucky the units hadn't caused a fire. He reported his findings to his father over the com at the same time Marco thundered down the stairs.

When he reached the bottom, Marco searched Liam's face and stabbed an angry, gloved finger in his chest. "Get your head out of your ass, Gallagher, before I do it for you."

"I know. I know. But now's not the time to—" He broke off and frowned down at the cat head-butting his leg. For a second, Liam was afraid he'd zoned out again. But, no, Marco would have seen it coming on and shook him out of it. The cat meowed and looked toward the tunnels. Liam didn't read minds, cat or human, but somehow he knew this was about Mia. As though the cat sensed he'd clued in, he took off. Liam ran after him.

"Where do you think you're going?" Marco called out.

"To find Mia," he shouted back. His voice sounded like he'd been hacking up a lung. Maybe he had been during the flashback. Though now wasn't the time to think about those missing minutes and what they would have meant had they been battling an actual blaze. He'd beat himself up over it later.

As he made his way deeper into the tunnels, the smoke wasn't as bad. He pulled off his breathing apparatus, stopping briefly to remove the tank and rest it carefully against the damp stone wall. He thought he'd lost the cat until he heard an impatient meow up ahead. The beam of light from Liam's helmet caught the end of the cat's tail just before it disappeared down a narrow passageway.

As soon as Liam rounded the corner, he spotted the little girl. Sophie's daughter sat with her back to the wall, her forehead resting on denim-clad knees that were pressed to her chest. She slowly raised her head and blinked into the bright light.

"Hey, Mia." He didn't want to frighten her and crouched a couple yards away. Then he took off his helmet and set it on the ground, angling it so the light didn't hit her in the eyes. He smiled. "I'm Liam Gallagher, a friend of your uncle Marco. Your mommy too. I've known her since she was a little girl not much older than you are."

She scuttled away from him then came to her feet, her eyes darting from left to right. His chest tightened. He recognized the look on her face, the wide-eyed panic and fear of someone who'd suffered a trauma. He should know, since after tonight, he could no longer deny he'd suffered the same. "Your mommy gave me"—he wracked his brain for the pig's name—"Porky." She looked at him. "Peppy the pig?"

The faintest hint of a smile touched her adorable heart-shaped face. "Do you want your pig?" he asked, reaching in his pocket.

She gave her head a quick shake, and Liam withdrew his hand from his pocket. He got it. The singed ear was a reminder of what she and her stuffed animal had been through. "You don't have to be frightened, sweetheart. There wasn't a fire, just a lot of smoke from the fog machines." Within minutes, there might have been a fire. But looking at Mia, he couldn't let his mind go there. Couldn't think of her down here trapped and alone. "I know you're scared, and you don't know me, but your mommy's worried about you, so whaddya say we get out of here?"

She looked down, her long, dark hair shielding her face, but not enough to hide the slight flush pinking her cheeks. He frowned and followed her gaze, wondering what…He briefly closed his eyes. She'd wet her pants.

He cleared his throat. "Mia. Sweetheart." Her big blue

eyes flitted to his face then darted away. "If I tell you a secret, do you promise not to tell anyone?" She glanced at him then gave him a hesitant nod. "Okay, I'm holding you to that. When I was around your age…Now that I think about it, I was way older. Like ten." He'd been five. "My brothers and cousins brought me down here to hunt for buried treasure. We had flashlights and shovels, and while we were digging, they told ghost stories. Really spooky ones. And then they turned the flashlights off. They left me down here for hours all by myself in the dark. I was so scared, I wet my pants." That part was true. "So you see, you have nothing to be embarrassed about. Happens to the best of us," he said with a smile, and shrugged out of his jacket, holding it open for her. "You can put this on, and no one will know. It'll be our secret. Sound good?" He'd find a way to tell Sophie without embarrassing Mia.

She took a couple hesitant steps toward him. "Thatta girl," he said, and leaned over to wrap the jacket around her tiny, delicate frame. "It's pretty long. Is it okay if I pick you up so you don't trip?" She nodded, and he lifted her into his arms. "You know what? You're as brave as any firefighter I know, so you should probably wear this." He put his helmet on her head, grinning when she disappeared beneath it. He tipped it up. "There you are."

She rewarded him with a smile that lit up her face and wrapped around his heart, squeezing tight.

"Mia DiRossi, you're going to be a heartbreaker just like your mother."

Chapter Two

♥

Sophie DiRossi stood alone in the shadow of the beech tree with her arms wrapped around her waist, staring at the manor's smoke-filled entrance, willing Mia to appear. It felt like she'd been standing here for an eternity. She'd left Harmony Harbor because of her daughter, and she'd come back for the same reason. If she'd had a crystal ball, she would have kept driving. Only she'd run out of gas, and she didn't have any money or anywhere else to go. It's how she'd ended up at Greystone. The last place she wanted to be.

A large, dark form took shape in the smoke and drew her attention. She squinted, wondering if it was her imagination. Then Liam stepped out of the haze with her daughter in his arms, and a cheer went up from the crowd. Sophie's legs buckled, relief weakening the tight reins that had held her emotions in check the entire arduous drive from California to Massachusetts's North Shore.

All the worry, fear, and guilt she'd tried to hide from Mia over the past three weeks bubbled up inside Sophie and ex-

ploded in a torrent of tears and noisy sobs. She stood there
like a blubbering idiot, helpless to get herself under control.
Covering her mouth with both hands only served to muffle
the wracking, body-heaving sobs.

It was like she was channeling her passionate and emotional Italian grandmother. That thought alone should have
been enough to put an end to Sophie's cringe-worthy performance, but she was afraid it was about to get worse when
she sensed the crowd looking her way and a half-hysterical
giggle escaped from between her fingers.

And then Liam was there, pulling her against his muscled
chest. His arm across her back was firm and supportive, his
big hand gentle as he stroked her hair. As he held both her
and her daughter in his arms, Sophie leaned into him, soak-
ing up every ounce of his warmth and comfort. She couldn't
remember the last time someone had held her like this. The
last time someone had told her everything was going to be
okay, and she believed them.

He whispered the words against her hair—the pull of his
deep, gravelly voice stronger than the urgent one in her head
demanding she release the man she once prayed would notice her. He was a Gallagher—a danger, not a balm. But it
had been so long since she'd had someone to lean on that
she couldn't bring herself to let him go. She wanted to experience the feeling of being safe and protected for just a
little longer. Her brief reprieve was cut short when the strong
smell of ammonia invaded her nostrils.

She lifted her head and glanced at Mia then raised her
questioning gaze to Liam. Her heart skipped a beat when
she met his eyes. If she'd been asking the question out loud,
the words wouldn't have made it out of her mouth. Shock
and a healthy dose of feminine appreciation would have held
them hostage. With her panic over Mia and the smoke in the

manor, Sophie hadn't registered just how tall and broad he'd become. She didn't remember his eyes being that deep, compassionate blue. Or his face with its chiseled angles being so breath-stealingly beautiful beneath his thick, wavy black hair, his nose strong and bold above his full, sensuous lips. Her blatant study of Liam ended the moment he gave her an almost imperceptible nod. Her little girl had been terrified and wet her pants.

Sophie's view of Liam's handsome face blurred as tears once again flooded her eyes. If she hadn't caught Mia staring at her from under the helmet just then, Sophie would have subjected her audience to another ugly cry. But that wide-eyed, worried look on her daughter's face was all it took for Sophie to pull herself together. Too bad she hadn't thought of that a few minutes ago.

She stepped away from Liam and turned her head, giving her eyes and nose a quick wipe on the sleeve of her black hoodie before looking up at him with a self-conscious smile. "I'm sorry. I don't know what came over me. I should be thanking you, and instead I cried all…" She went to touch the damp spot on his T-shirt but quickly jerked her hand away, afraid she might be tempted to pet his rock-hard pecs or fall into his arms again. "Sorry, we've been on the road for six days, and I haven't gotten much sleep. And then when Mia—"

Liam ducked his head to look her in the eyes, a slight smile touching his perfect lips.

"Sophie, you don't have to be embarrassed. Does she, Mia?"

Her daughter looked like she was about to nod—*Yes, she does*—but then glanced at Liam and shook her head.

Sophie winced at Mia's initial reaction. "Thanks, but it was a pretty epic meltdown. I don't usually fall apart like that." And make a complete and utter spectacle of herself, she thought, as she lifted Mia's hand to her lips and kissed her soft palm. "You okay, baby?" she asked, hesitating before rubbing her daughter's fine-boned fingers against her cheek. These days Mia rarely let Sophie display any kind of motherly affection, and she took advantage of the moment, holding Mia's hand against her face.

What she wouldn't give to have her daughter back. The little girl who spent more time singing than talking, who giggled and made jokes and loved to play make-believe and kiss and cuddle her mother. Sophie squeezed her eyes tight to keep the tears at bay. She had to knock off the emotional crap. She'd embarrassed her daughter enough for one day.

Mia pulled back her hand and nodded. Sophie wondered what Liam thought of her daughter's chilly reception to her affection. But he was looking past her, his broad shoulders rising on a deep, inward breath.

"Liam, paramedics are waiting to check you over," his father called out.

Picking up on the tension in Chief Gallagher's voice, Sophie glanced over her shoulder. Liam's father was a tall and handsome man. Like his son, he was one of the to-serve-and-protect Gallaghers—calm and quietly commanding. But the way he was dragging his hand over his thick head of gray hair didn't seem the least bit calm. He appeared upset with his son.

She looked up at Liam. "Is there something wrong?"

"No, nothing." He smiled at Mia as he handed her off to Sophie. "I'll take this." He carefully removed the helmet from her daughter's head. "But you better keep my jacket. Temperature's dropped, and we don't want you catching a cold." He winked at Mia then looked at Sophie. "Wasn't under the best of circumstances, but it was good seeing you.

Marco should be finished in there shortly. Take care. You too, sweetheart." He lightly tapped his finger on her daughter's small, upturned nose before moving to walk away.

"Liam, wait." Sophie reached for his hand. He turned, and she slipped her hand into his. His fingers were calloused, warm, and strong. "Thank you for finding Mia. For…" Unable to mention the pants-wetting episode without embarrassing her daughter, Sophie said, "Thank you for everything you did for us tonight."

He gave her fingers a light squeeze. "Just doing my job, Soph."

"I doubt comforting hysterical women is in your job description." He'd done more than comfort her; he hadn't judged her. And he'd made her daughter feel safe. He had no idea what an incredible feat that was.

"You'd be surprised." He smiled as he extricated his fingers from hers. "I better get going."

Well, that was embarrassing. She hadn't realized how tight she'd been holding on. "Oh, right, sorry. Bye," she said, sounding a little disappointed even to her own ears. She shouldn't be. She should be relieved he was walking away without commenting on Mia's Gallagher-blue eyes or asking questions about why Sophie had come home and why her daughter had been happier in his arms than hers. The only reason she could think of for her disappointment was that Liam had been a friendly, familiar face.

Not that familiar, she thought, as he walked away and she got her first good look at the way he filled out his navy T-shirt, at the corded muscles of his arms and the breadth of his shoulders, his wide back tapering to meet turnout pants held up by suspenders. Her memories of him were of a handsome boy, but now he was all man. An incredibly gorgeous man with a body…

Sophie blinked, surprised at the direction of her thoughts, by the warm flutter in her stomach. She couldn't remember the last man who gave her butterflies. Between trying to eke out a living and taking care of her daughter, she hadn't had time for a love life. She'd been like the pet hamster in Mia's classroom—constantly running on the wheel of life, trying to get ahead. Instead she'd been trapped and going in circles. Until the fire at their apartment had stopped the wheel, and they'd both fallen off.

Only this time, Liam had been there to catch them, to save them, to...*Whoa, where the heck had that come from?* Sophie rolled her eyes. Fantasies were fine for seven-year-olds but they were dangerous for a twenty-six-year-old woman starting over. She didn't have time for a man. She had to focus on repairing her relationship with her daughter and building them a good life. A better one than they'd left behind. And the last man she should be fantasizing about was a Gallagher.

Maybe she should have shared that with her daughter, she thought when Mia wriggled out of her arms and set off determinedly after Liam, his tan-colored jacket with the strips of neon-yellow tape dragging behind her daughter like a bride's train.

"Mia baby, come back here. We have to wait for Uncle Marco," Sophie called out, sighing when Mia ignored her. After her crying jag, Sophie had hoped to stay right where she was. Far away from the crowd gathered near the ambulances and fire engines. She wanted to avoid Colleen and Kitty. The less contact she had with the two older women the better.

When Sophie's car broke down five miles outside of town, she'd decided it was safer to cut through the Gallaghers' five-thousand-acre estate rather than walk on the side of the road at night. If it wasn't Halloween, it probably would have been. But she and Mia had stumbled out of the woods and ended smack dab in the middle of the Gallaghers' haunted tour—a Harmony Harbor institution. One that Sophie had taken part in over the years. Mostly tagging along after Marco and Liam. Back then, Sophie had been half in love with her brother's best friend. After years of trying to get Liam to notice her, though, she'd given up. Then his older and, in Sophie's then-teenage mind, more exciting and sophisticated cousin, Michael Gallagher, came to town.

Liam looked over his shoulder. The lights from the emergency vehicles cast his face in shadows and light. She made out a flash of white teeth when he smiled and held out a hand to her daughter. He glanced at Sophie and lifted a broad shoulder. "Might not be a bad idea to have her checked over."

No, it was a good idea. There hadn't been a fire, but there'd been enough smoke to irritate her daughter's already sensitive lungs. Sophie nodded as she started toward them.

"Just a precaution, Sophie," Liam said, as though he sensed she was beating herself up for not thinking to get Mia checked out herself. Either that or he was worried she'd have another meltdown. He didn't know her anymore. He didn't know that, other than the night she was arrested and thought she'd never see her daughter again, Sophie never broke down. She didn't cry or whine or complain either. She took life's blows on the chin and moved on. Until tonight, she hadn't realized how tired she was of moving on, of putting on a brave face.

Kitty Gallagher walked toward Sophie. An elegant, older woman with white-blond hair that framed her classically beautiful face, Liam's grandmother wore hunter-green rubber boots, a Mackintosh jacket the same color, and a sympathetic look in her blue eyes. Kitty had been lovely and kind to Sophie and Mia, insisting they join them at the manor for some Halloween treats. If Sophie hadn't seen the hint of a smile on her daughter's face as she held and petted the Gallaghers' black cat, she would have politely refused the invitation. It had been a mistake not to. One more to add to an ever-growing list.

Kitty looped her arm through Sophie's. "Don't worry. Liam's a registered EMT. If he'd been the least bit concerned about Mia, he would have run her over to the paramedics straightaway," the older woman said in a soft, lilting voice.

The knot in Sophie's chest loosened at Kitty's reassurance. Though it tightened again as she watched Liam walk toward the ambulance with her daughter's tiny, trusting hand in his.

"It appears my grandson has become a hero in your daughter's eyes, Sophie," Kitty said with a fond smile.

For a few brief moments, Sophie had felt the same. But now, more than ever, she wished she'd been the one to find her daughter. What she wouldn't give to have Mia look at her like she was her hero. "I'm not surprised. He was wonderful with her."

"He has a way of putting everyone at ease, our Liam does. But I think there may be more to it than that. I think Mia recognized a kindred spirit."

Sophie stopped abruptly, the force of the movement jerking the older woman backward. "Sorry." She reached out to steady Kitty while berating herself for overreacting. She hadn't seen any signs earlier that either Kitty or Colleen had been the least bit suspicious that Mia was one of theirs. If Kitty had been, Sophie's reaction just now might have tipped her hand.

"Sorry," she apologized again, pointing to a puddle. "I

thought it was black ice. I didn't want you to slip." She stifled a groan at her excuse. Honestly, if she was going to stay in Harmony Harbor for more than a few days, she had to become a better liar. Rosa, her grandmother, would see through her in a heartbeat. And the next words out of Kitty's mouth made Sophie wonder if she had too.

"None of us can afford to slip, can we, dear?" She held Sophie's gaze for a brief moment then gave her a winsome smile. "You don't have to worry about me. I come from good Irish stock. Strong bones and constitution."

Fear buzzed through Sophie, making it difficult to think. She wasn't sure if Kitty's remark had been innocent or a warning that she knew her secret. She wanted to run to the back of the ambulance where Liam had just placed her daughter, scoop up Mia, and spirit her away. Before she followed through with the thought, Kitty nodded at Mia, who scooted over to make room for Liam beside her. "My grandson sees it, too, I think. But of course he would."

Sophie's throat closed with panic. She'd lost her chance to escape. Kitty would confront her now.

"I should probably explain before you think I'm just a fanciful old woman. Both Liam and Mia were recently traumatized in a fire. It's a connection they share. One I think they recognize in each other."

Sophie's shoulders sagged in relief, and she was able to breathe again. It took a little longer to actually form a coherent thought. When she was finally able to, she asked, "What happened to Liam?" while at the same time searching for some outward sign of his trauma.

He was making faces at Mia as he blew into a tube that measured his lung capacity. His antics earned him a small smile from her daughter. He had no idea how big a deal that was. Over the past several weeks, Sophie had become well acquainted with a similar plastic cylinder. Getting Mia to submit to tests of any kind had been trying, but that one in particular…

Sophie drew her gaze from her daughter and Liam when Kitty answered her question. "They responded to a four-alarm fire at a warehouse and ended up in the middle of a gang turf war. Liam was shot trying to rescue his friend, a fellow firefighter, who sadly died. Despite his own injuries, Liam saved two other men."

She wondered if that's why Chief Gallagher and her brother had been angry when Liam spoke about removing his breathing apparatus. Which he'd done for Mia. Sophie knew this because her daughter had been wearing his BA when he'd carried her out of the manor. Something she was able to recollect now thanks to hindsight. Obviously her meltdown had been long enough that he'd been able to remove the equipment before taking Sophie into his arms.

A tiny shiver accompanied the warm fuzzies at the thought. Liam Gallagher had once held a special place in her heart. It was kind of scary to think that he'd come close to reclaiming it in less than a couple hours back in Harmony Harbor.

Kitty continued, lowering her voice as they drew closer to the ambulance. "He refuses to talk about that night. And heaven help you if you suggest his actions were heroic. His father's worried about him, and so am I."

"He seems fine," Sophie said, thinking of his commanding presence when she'd first seen him in the manor. His reassuring calm and confidence.

Kitty raised an eyebrow. "So does Mia."

Sophie'd had no choice but to share with Liam's great-grandmother and grandmother why Mia didn't speak, so Kitty was well aware that Sophie's daughter was far from fine. But she didn't get the chance to acknowledge that the older woman made a good point. The female paramedic was at that moment attempting to check her daughter's lung capacity.

With a mutinous expression on her face, Mia crossed her arms and pressed her lips together. Sophie caught the look of surprise on Liam's face. People were always surprised when Mia, who looked like an angel, displayed the stubbornness of a mule.

"You take care of Mia, dear. I have to speak to my son before my mother-in-law tries to convince him I'm the one who turned on the fog machines. It would be just like her to throw me under the bus." Kitty lifted her chin to where Colin Gallagher stood a few feet away with the Gallagher matriarch and her right-hand man, Jasper.

Sophie moved toward the ambulance. "Excuse me," she said to the paramedic, and crouched in front of her daughter. "Mia, look at Mommy." Her daughter doggedly stared at her sparkly blue tennis shoes, swinging them back and forth. "Baby, you're okay. You won't have to go back to the hospital, I promise." Usually that would be enough to get her daughter to acquiesce. But Mia didn't seem as worried about a return visit to the hospital—maybe because they were no longer in LA. If Sophie didn't need the reassurance her daughter was okay, she'd probably cave. She cast an apologetic glance at Liam before saying, "They just have to check to make sure that Mr. Gallagher did his job and protected you from the smoke. You don't want him to get in trouble, do you?"

Mia stopped swinging her feet and looked up from under her long lashes at Liam. She shook her head and obediently opened her mouth for the paramedic.

Liam held Sophie's gaze. "Thanks, Mia, but you don't

have to worry about Mr. Gallagher. My dad won't get in trouble. He's been chief for as long as there's been a fire station in Harmony Harbor."

Sophie wasn't sure if he was giving her a shot because she'd called him Mr. Gallagher or because she'd lied to her daughter. He'd always been a stickler for the truth. Liam and Marco had gotten into trouble at least once a week when they were younger thanks to Liam's unwillingness to lie. It'd driven her brother nuts.

She twisted her hand around her wrist, thinking of the lies she'd told so far and how many more she'd have to tell in the future to protect herself and her daughter. Obviously she was projecting. Liam would understand that she'd been using him as an excuse to get Mia to comply with the paramedics. But when Mia pinned Sophie with a look she knew all too well, she was feeling less than kindly disposed to her daughter's hero.

"Not quite that long, son," his father said dryly.

Liam shrugged. She wasn't sure if he meant the dismissive gesture for her scowl or his father's sarcasm.

The paramedic removed the tube from Mia's mouth and smiled. "All good. In the normal range." Her daughter jumped off the back of the ambulance, and Liam went to stand up. "Oh no you don't," the thirtysomething brunette said to Liam. "Lift your shirt, hot stuff, and let me have a look."

Liam laughed. "Yeah, not happening. I'm good, Kris."

"So I've heard." She gave him a flirty wink. Then, with gloved fingers, motioned for him to lift his T-shirt. "Your dad asked me to check you out. Don't be embarrassed if you got a little flabby while you were convalescing. We won't tell anyone, will we, Daff?" she said to the other paramedic who approached the ambulance.

"My lips are sealed. Just hang on a sec, and I'll give you a hand." The woman grinned as she started to unload her supplies in the ambulance.

Sophie's irritation with Liam for Mia's reproachful look faded at the reminder he'd been shot.

"You two so hard up you're getting unsuspecting men to strip for you now? You know, there's a club—" He winced as though remembering Mia was there and hanging on his every word.

Sophie needed to know he was okay and intervened. "Liam, maybe you should let them check you over. You were carrying Mia, and with all your equipment…"

"Soph, Mia probably weighs—" Giving his head a slight, frustrated shake, he tugged up his T-shirt. "Happy now?"

Sophie hoped his question wasn't directed at her. She doubted she could respond even if she wanted to. And it wasn't because of the small, puckered scar on the left side of his stomach. The ridges of taut muscle and a tantalizing, narrow trail of dark hair that disappeared beneath his turnout pants were messing with her head…and other parts of her anatomy. Parts that hadn't been messed with in a long time.

The paramedics moved in, spoiling the sigh-inducing view. Sophie leaned to the left.

Kris glanced over her shoulder with a knowing grin. "Looks pretty good, don't you think?" the paramedic asked Sophie.

"Yes." The word came out as an embarrassing croak, and she cleared her throat. "Really, really good."

Chapter Three

♥

Sophie glanced in the rearview mirror as she drove the gas-guzzling, white Cadillac past Greystone's open gates. Liam and his perfect abs were getting into the fire truck. She was pretty sure her face had gone the same color as the engine when she'd shared her personal opinion of his chiseled six-pack. She couldn't say what his reaction had been to her embarrassing croak or equally embarrassing *"Really, really good."* Marco had shown up and Liam had jumped at the chance to get out of there, accompanying her brother to retrieve Sophie's car. A brother who'd made it clear she had some explaining to do.

Marco, who sat in the passenger seat, kept glancing back at Mia. "So what happened to the kid? Why doesn't she talk?"

"Marco!" One of the toughest things about living in LA had been how much she'd missed her family, particularly her brothers. But at Marco's insensitive question, she was beginning to wonder if she'd idealized them over the past eight years.

"What? It's a legitimate question."

"Yes, when we're alone. And stop calling her 'kid.' Her name's Mia," Sophie whispered, meeting her daughter's eyes in the rearview mirror. She faked a bright smile. "You okay, baby?"

"Seriously? She's been sitting in pee for the last hour. How do you think she is?"

Sophie shot him an I-don't-believe-you glare.

He had the good sense to look sheepish. "It's okay, kid. No biggie. Your mother used to wet the bed. Didn't you, Chunk?" Marco rubbed Sophie's head.

She grinded her teeth and pushed her hair from her eyes. "We don't say things like that."

"How come?"

Sophie didn't bother sharing her opinion on words that promote a negative body image. Marco wouldn't get it. Moreover, he wouldn't care. Which made the prospect of living under the same roof as her brother and grandmother worrisome at best. Rosa didn't have a filter either. "Did you let Nonna know we were coming?"

Sophie worried the inside of her bottom lip, hoping he didn't ask why she hadn't. Her cell phone had run out of minutes two days before, and she didn't have any room on her credit card to top it up. But that excuse wouldn't fly with her brother, and she didn't want to tell him the truth; she'd been afraid they wouldn't want her and Mia.

"Nope, Harmony Harbor's grapevine was working overtime. She called me when Liam and I were getting gas for your car. Pretty sweet ride, sister mine. You must be doing well in Cali-forn-i-ay."

Sophie winced. She may have embellished a bit on her

phone calls home. In her defense, she didn't want them to worry about her. "It's not mine. It belongs to Mom's boyfriend."

Her brother's teasing expression faded. "Does it now. And how is Mother Dearest?"

She wasn't Tina's biggest fan at the moment, but Sophie had legitimate reasons for her problems with her mother. All Tina had done to Marco was leave Harmony Harbor and their father. But, in her brother's eyes, Tina was responsible for tearing their family apart. The reason Lucas had joined the military and basically disappeared from their lives. Kind of like Sophie had for eight years. So she supposed she didn't have a right to pass judgment on Marco and his hostility toward Tina. After all, he'd been the one left behind to take care of Rosa and the deli.

Like always, though, Sophie felt the need to come to her mother's defense. Maybe because in a way she was defending her own actions. "Might be time to bury the hatchet, brother mine. Dad seems pretty happy with his new family." Ouch, that had come out a little sharper than she'd intended.

Her brother opened his mouth, glanced back at Mia then closed it with a noncommittal grunt. Sophie realized he'd never mentioned if Rosa was happy about them being in town. "So what did Nonna say?" she asked, steeling herself for his response.

"Seeing as how she hasn't seen you in eight years and her arch nemesis saw you first, what do you think?"

Her fingers tightened on the steering wheel. Kitty and Rosa's long-standing feud was the stuff of legends in Harmony Harbor. No one seemed to know what had happened between the two older women, but they couldn't be in the same room without sparks flying. Rosa was the worst. If she had her way, she'd run the Gallaghers out of town. Little tough to do seeing as they were Harmony Harbor royalty. The feud between her grandmother and Kitty had been one of the reasons why Sophie had left town with her mother when she'd found out she was pregnant.

"It's not like I could help where my car broke down," she defended herself as she drove past the town hall and copper-domed clock tower situated on the hill overlooking the harbor with its rugged shoreline. She used to spend her summers exploring the hidden coves and salt marshes, hanging out at the sandy beaches and hunting for sea glass.

She took a moment to absorb the view that she'd taken for granted for eighteen years. She didn't realize until that moment how much she'd missed her hometown. Founded in the early seventeenth century by William Gallagher, Harmony Harbor was steeped in maritime history. Its twisty, narrow streets were lined with homes once owned by sea captains and merchants—Colonials, Cape Cods, and Victorians. The family-owned boutiques, art galleries, pubs, and gift shops were housed in quaint sea-foam-green and ocean-blue clapboards on Main Street.

But even more than the scenic beauty of Harmony Harbor, she'd missed the friendly, relaxed atmosphere…and her grandmother. She twisted her hands on the wheel and glanced at her brother. "Aside from us ending up at Greystone, is Nonna at least happy we're here?" she asked as she turned down the familiar street.

Marco lifted his chin. "See for yourself."

Her grandmother paced the brick sidewalk in front of DiRossi's Fine Foods, the Italian grocery store and deli that Rosa had started as a single mother of three preschoolers. Which pretty much made her a rock star in Sophie's eyes.

Over her navy dress and white apron, her grandmother

wore a pink sweater, her hands gripping the edges tight, a pair of pink fuzzy slippers on her feet. "She looks good," Sophie said past the lump in her throat.

"Yeah, she does," her brother agreed with a fond smile.

As a young woman, Rosa DiRossi had been movie-star beautiful. In Sophie's mind, she still was at seventy-three. Her cheekbones were high and prominent, just like her proud Roman nose. Her eyes were dark and exotic with lashes so long you'd think they were fake. She wore her dark, curly hair loose and to her shoulders. The curls were natural, the color...not so much. It suited her, though.

"Still a pain in the *culo*," her brother added as Sophie pulled in front of the red Colonial that housed the deli on the main floor and the DiRossi family apartment above.

At least her brother said *ass* in Italian. Maybe she wouldn't have to warn him about his language after all.

"Jesus, Ma!" he yelled at their grandmother when she yanked the back car door open before they'd come to a full stop.

Rosa cuffed him on the back of his head. "There's a bambina. Watch your mouth," she said then pressed her hands to her chest and stared at Mia, her eyes shiny and wet. Sophie blinked back tears of her own and got out of the car, walking around to where her grandmother stood murmuring, "*Molto bella*. She has the face of an angel." Rosa lifted the gold crucifix she wore at her neck to her lips and kissed it then held out her arms. "Come, come to your nonna, bambina."

"I have to help Mia out of her booster seat, Nonna. The seat belt is finicky."

Her grandmother straightened and slowly turned, her dark eyes roaming Sophie's face before she pulled her in for a fierce hug. "It's been too long, *bella*. Too, too long."

"I know, Nonna," Sophie said, hanging on just as tight.

She sniffed into her grandmother's neck, breathing in the familiar scent of lemons.

Rosa pulled back and took Sophie's face in her hands. "You're home now. That's all that matters, *sì*?"

Everything inside Sophie went weak at her grandmother's easy acceptance. They were welcome here. They had a home, and they were safe. "*Sì*." Before she went to take Mia out of the car, Sophie thought it best to warn her grandmother or she'd no doubt comment on the smell. She whispered what had happened at the manor.

Rosa flung her hands in the air. "Poor bambina. What was Kitty thinking? Fog machines! Foolish old woman."

Afraid her grandmother would ask too many questions in front of Mia, Sophie looked at her brother, nudging her head in her daughter's direction and touching her mouth. Her brother sighed then nodded. He'd tell Rosa that Mia didn't speak. Sophie would explain why to them later.

As she fought with the seat belt, Mia leaned around her. She stared at Rosa, who was half talking, half yelling at Marco in Italian, her hands moving as fast as her mouth.

Sophie smiled. "You'll get used to her, baby."

Rosa frowned when Sophie placed Mia on the sidewalk. "What do you feed her? She's too small. Too skinny."

Sophie had invented a fake father for Mia. A father with beautiful blue eyes who'd died a month before their daughter's birth. She'd told the story so often to Mia and her mother, and anyone else who asked, that Sophie had almost come to believe it herself. Her mother had been so caught up in herself that it hadn't been difficult to convince her that Mia was two months premature. But here in Harmony Harbor, that two-month difference might not be enough.

Sophie put her hand behind her back and crossed her fingers. "She's only six, Nonna. I wasn't much bigger than she is at six."

Mia narrowed her eyes at Sophie and crossed her arms. Sophie winced. She'd have to figure out a way to explain the lie to her daughter, but right now, her grandmother was a bigger concern. Rosa's gaze sharpened as she looked closer at Mia; then she lifted her eyes to Sophie and gave her a brisk nod. "*Sì*."

In that brief moment of silent exchange, it felt like her grandmother had uncovered Sophie's secret, and they'd made a bargain that it would stay that way.

Sophie left the small, cramped bedroom that she and Mia had shared last night to retrieve her contacts from the counter in the bathroom. She'd taken them out before her shower that morning. She lifted the towel beside the sink then bent to search the floor, her eyes landing on the wastebasket. She groaned. Her grandmother had thrown them out, and Sophie didn't have another pair. She was farsighted and needed them. It looked like she'd be wearing her glasses for the foreseeable future.

"Nonna," she began as she walked into the kitchen. Her heart practically stopped at the sight of her daughter at the gas stove. She raced across the pale yellow linoleum floor and grabbed Mia off the chair, hugging her tight to her chest. "What were you thinking?" she yelled at her grandmother. "I told you what happened. I told you—" Mia looked at her, her small face pale, her blue eyes wide, and Sophie choked down the rest of her panicked outburst. Weak-kneed, she moved to the kitchen table and sat down with Mia on her lap.

Rosa looked at her like she was crazy. "What's the matter with you? I'm right here. We were heating up soup for lunch." She threw up her hands and turned back to the stove.

Sophie couldn't believe her grandmother didn't understand why she was upset. Once Mia had been bathed, fed, and tucked into bed last night, Sophie had sat at this very table and told her grandmother and brother what had happened. Sure, she'd left out some details—like that her mother had left Mia alone and that Sophie had been arrested for child endangerment. Unwilling to give Rosa and Marco another reason to hate her mother, she'd told them the sitter hadn't shown up. As for the arrest, she didn't want to upset or worry them.

But Rosa knew the most important detail of all—that Mia had accidently burned down their apartment and nearly lost her life trying to bake a cake. She'd wanted to surprise Sophie. To celebrate Sophie finishing her hotel management degree. Every morning in the month leading up to the big day, Mia'd check off the calendar on the fridge, and they'd do a silly little dance around the postage stamp–sized kitchen.

It was the day their lives should have changed for the better, but obviously it hadn't worked out that way. The police had pulled Sophie out of her final exam and arrested her because Tina hadn't been at the apartment when Mia got home from school like she'd promised. She'd been at a hot yoga class.

Sophie pressed her face into Mia's hair, breathing in the sweet scent in order to calm her racing heart. Mia didn't squirm and wriggle to get away. "Sorry, baby," she whispered, loosening her hold to stroke her daughter's hair. She glanced at her grandmother's stiff back. She wore her pink slippers, navy dress, and white apron, talking to herself in Italian as she stirred the big pot of potato, kale, and sausage soup.

Her grandmother didn't understand Sophie's fears, and

she wouldn't try. Mia didn't inherit her stubbornness from the Gallaghers. Oh no, she got her mule-headedness from the most obstinate woman Sophie had ever known. Now, as a mother, Sophie could almost sympathize with her own. It couldn't have been easy living and working with Rosa day in and day out...or being married to Rosa's son. However, until the night Tina had announced she was leaving, Sophie had thought her parents had the perfect marriage. It's why the divorce had hit her so hard. But from the vantage point of distance and maturity, she could see the signs had been there all along.

Mia wriggled out of Sophie's arms and hopped off her lap. The powder-blue, sparkly leggings she wore under her *Frozen* T-shirt bagged at her knees as she walked to the refrigerator. Sophie needed a job. With her first paycheck, she'd buy her daughter clothes that fit and that were better suited to the North Shore's climate than LA's. She stood up and tightened the belt of her grandmother's robe, adding clothes for herself to the list. At least for work. She could make do with the one pair of jeans and two sweatshirts she'd bought at Goodwill before they left California.

She went to her grandmother and wrapped her arms around her waist. "Sorry, Nonna. I shouldn't have yelled at you. It's just when I saw Mia so close to the flame under the burner..." She kissed her grandmother's cheek.

Mia's eyes flicked to Sophie; then she took a flyer off the harvest gold refrigerator and went back to the table.

Her grandmother put down the wooden spoon and patted Sophie's face. "You eat. You feel better, *sì?*"

Of course, because food was a magic cure-all in Rosa's eyes. Sophie smiled, reaching past her grandmother for the yellow soup bowls. "Do you have time to eat with us?"

"You think I'm going to work on your first day home with

the bambina? I called Louisa and Sylvia. They're good girls. I trust them."

Sophie chewed on her bottom lip, casting a sidelong glance at her grandmother, who bent to take a loaf of bread from the oven. She cleared her throat, hating to ask for anything more, but she didn't really have a choice. At least if she worked at the deli, she could keep Mia with her. "Nonna, are you hiring?"

"No. Your brother, he's worse than Giovanni. Cut, cut, cut the expenses. That's all he does." She made slashing motions with her hand then frowned. "*Perché?*"

Sophie forced a smile, ladling soup for Mia into the bowl. "No reason," she responded to her grandmother's *why*. "I just thought, if you needed help, I could work a few hours for you."

Rosa waved a dismissive hand. "You need to rest, get some meat on your skinny bones." She glanced over her shoulder at Mia then raised her eyebrows at Sophie and tapped her fingers and thumb together to mime talking. "Spend time with your bambina."

The idea of spending time with Mia outside of a car sounded wonderful. Sophie couldn't remember the last time she'd had a real holiday. Maybe it's what they both needed. They had food and a roof over their heads. She fingered the twenty-four-carat-gold St. Peter's medal at her neck. Her grandmother had given it to Sophie the morning of her Confirmation. It's the only thing she had left to pawn. If she shopped carefully…

She walked to the table with Mia's bowl of soup. "You have to let me contribute something, Nonna. I don't feel right—"

"Don't talk foolish," her grandmother said, placing the bread she was slicing into a basket.

No one ever won an argument with Rosa, so Sophie let it go for now. "I'm just going to move this until after you eat," she told Mia, picking up the flyer to set the bowl in front of her.

Sophie glanced at the paper. There was something familiar about the stone cottage in the photo. The surrounding trees and exterior were decorated for Christmas. As were the living and dining rooms featured in two smaller interior shots below. Old Mia would have been squealing with delight. She loved Christmas.

At the reminder of the upcoming holidays, Sophie's heart squeezed. She'd never been able to spoil Mia like she'd wanted to, but unless she got a job, Santa would be skipping their house altogether. At least this year they would be spending the holiday with family.

Mia tapped the flyer and looked up at Sophie with a hopeful gleam in her eyes. Other than with Liam and the Gallaghers' black cat, it had been weeks since she'd seen anything besides fear and distrust in her daughter's eyes. It felt like a breakthrough, and Sophie's heart lightened. "It's a pretty cottage, isn't it? Look, there's even an Elf on the Shelf." She bit her lip. She probably shouldn't have pointed out the elf in the pink skirt sitting on a mantel above a cozy stone fireplace. Mia had gotten her elf at the staff Christmas party last year and named it Trina. Trina had been lost in the fire along with the rest of their Christmas decorations.

Mia pursed her lips and shook her head, taking the flyer from Sophie. She turned it over and tapped again.

"Sit," Rosa said, placing a bowl of steaming soup in front of Sophie and the basket of bread on the table. She glanced at the flyer. "It's a raffle. Half the proceeds go to Greystone. The other half to Mothers Against Drunk Driving."

Now Sophie knew why the cottage looked familiar. "This

is Kitty and Ronan's cottage, isn't it?" The couple had begun their married life in the cottage before moving into the manor when Ronan's father died. A ten-minute walk west of Greystone were several cottages and bungalows. They were rented to guests or used by the extended Gallagher family when they came to visit.

"*Sì*," her grandmother said, her voice tight, and then she rolled her eyes. "They named it Mistletoe Cottage for the raffle."

Sophie read the rules. "You bought a ticket?" she asked, unable to keep the surprise from her voice. Not only would the raffle benefit Rosa's arch nemesis, the ticket cost a hundred dollars. A small fortune in her frugal grandmother's eyes.

Rosa shrugged. "Mothers Against Drunk Driving is a good cause. And the publicity, it's good for the manor. They need all the publicity they can get."

Sophie imagined MADD was an organization near and dear to the Gallaghers' hearts. Liam had lost his mother and sister in a car accident. Eyewitnesses had claimed the driver of the car that hit them was drunk. But neither the car nor driver had ever been found. Kitty hadn't lost only her daughter-in-law and granddaughter in the accident; she'd lost her husband too. Grief stricken, Ronan had suffered a fatal heart attack two days after Mary and Riley Gallagher's funeral.

"Mrs. Gallagher mentioned business is down. She thought it might have something to do with the new hotel in Bridgeport." Colleen had cornered Sophie in the sitting room at the manor last night, seeking advice. She'd overheard Sophie telling Kitty that she'd left her job at a hotel in LA. Somehow they'd missed the part that Sophie had been a maid at the hotel, not the manager. And she hadn't actually *left* her job. She'd been fired when she'd refused to leave Mia's hospital bedside.

A few minutes into Sophie and Colleen's conversation, someone had spotted smoke. It was then that Sophie discovered that Mia, who'd been eating a pumpkin cupcake and playing with the cat seconds before, was gone.

Rosa made an *eh* gesture with her hands. "It's not the hotel. They're losing business because they're *stupidi*. Ronan dies, and they…" Her grandmother mimicked a wailing, prostrate woman.

"Nonna!" She supposed she shouldn't be surprised by her grandmother's lack of empathy. She'd had no choice but to pick up the pieces and make a life for her three small children when her husband died. Rosa wasn't exactly a sympathetic woman to begin with.

"What? It's true. No conferences and weddings booked at the manor in all that time. Businesses in town, we depend on them. Now the mayor, she's trying to get them to sell. A developer, he wants to buy the estate, tear everything down, and put up condos. Condos. Bah!"

Sophie couldn't imagine Harmony Harbor without Greystone standing sentry on the rocks above the harbor. She'd worked part-time at the manor when she was in high school. It was the one time Tina had stood up to Rosa. Not that her grandmother had made it easy for Sophie. Despite that, she'd loved working at Greystone. It was the reason she'd decided to go into hotel management. With its turrets, stone walls, and richly appointed rooms, it had been like working in a fairy-tale castle. Only her own fairy tale hadn't turned out as she'd planned. Her Gallagher prince had turned into a frog.

But that one mistake had given Sophie her greatest gift—Mia. Her daughter was all that mattered. She drew herself back to the present and the conversation. "Colleen won't sell," she said. At least it hadn't sounded like she would the night before.

Rosa rubbed her thumb and fingers together. "No, but the kids, they'll want the money."

Sophie was distracted by Mia tapping the flyer again and giving her a hopeful nod. She wished she could give her daughter the answer she wanted to hear. "Sorry, baby, but Mommy doesn't have a hundred dollars." Realizing what she'd inadvertently revealed to her grandmother, Sophie briefly closed her eyes. She opened them to see Rosa staring at her. The insistent ringing of the phone saved Sophie from coming up with a response. Her grandmother pushed back from the table with a look on her face that suggested Sophie's reprieve would be short-lived.

Rosa answered the phone. *"Sì."* She frowned. "Who is this?" Her eyes shot to Sophie then to Mia. *"Un momento."*

"Mia, come with Nonna. I'll show you my ticket for the raffle." As her daughter jumped off the chair, Rosa bent down and whispered to Sophie, "The lady, she says she's with the Department of Child Welfare."

Sophie waited for the door to her grandmother's bedroom to close before picking up the phone. *Don't panic. Stay calm.* "Hi, Mrs. Whitmore. I was just about to call you."

"I've been trying to reach you since yesterday to set up your at-home visit, Sophie. Your mother gave me this number. We should have been informed you were going out of state. I think I made that very clear at our initial meeting."

"Yes, yes, you did." Sophie's knuckles whitened as she clenched the phone. "Like I said, I planned to contact you. I decided it was best for Mia and me to move back home to Harmony Harbor. I have family here and a good support system. It's a small town, and rent will be cheaper."

"I see. Did you share your plans with your mother? Because she seems to think you're returning to LA."

"No, Mrs. Whitmore, I didn't. Is that a problem too?"

"Sophie, I'm not the enemy."

"Really? 'Cause it kind of feels like you are. The charges were dropped, Mrs. Whitmore. I'm a good mom. I don't do drugs or go to bars or have men back to my apartment. Mia is the most important thing in the world to me. I would never intentionally put her in danger. All I was trying to do was make a better life for us. That's all I was trying to do." The fight went out of her, and she sagged against the wall.

"Sophie, our preliminary investigation supports everything you've just said. We got back glowing reports from your roommates, coworkers, and the woman who provided before and after school care for Mia. But because of the circumstances, we're legally required to do a follow-up visit. I'm going to transfer your file to the Massachusetts Department of Child Welfare. Is this the number where you can be reached?"

"Yes, I'm staying with my grandmother until I find a place of our own."

"All right. You should expect to receive a call from them within the next month. That should give you plenty of time to get settled and find steady employment before your follow-up visit. How is Mia? Any more nightmares?"

"No, she hasn't had any more nightmares." After yesterday's episode at Greystone, Sophie'd been surprised she hadn't. No doubt she had Liam and his comforting presence to thank for that. Sophie wished she had someone to comfort her now. If anyone from Children's Services found out what had happened at the manor, she'd have another red flag on her file. She'd thought that by coming to Harmony Harbor, she'd at least escape child welfare and the threat that they'd take her daughter away.

After answering the rest of Mrs. Whitmore's questions, the caseworker wished Sophie good luck and said goodbye.

Sophie hung up the phone and rested her forehead against the wall. Strong, firm hands took her by the shoulders and turned her around. "This time you tell me the whole story, *bella*. Sit."

"Mia..."

"She's good. She's watching the TV." Her grandmother bent down and pulled a bottle of red wine from the bottom cupboard.

"Nonna, I'm not drinking at noon."

"It's for me," she said, pouring herself a juice glass full. She sat beside Sophie at the table, and this time she didn't leave anything out.

Her grandmother swore in Italian, cursing out interfering government agencies and Sophie's no-good mother. Sophie didn't have the energy to make excuses for Tina. Once her grandmother got her temper under control, she said, "I'll make some phone calls. See if anyone—" The phone rang, cutting her off.

Sophie's heart pounded. "What if it's—"

Rosa tossed back her wine and got up from the table, patting Sophie's shoulder as she reached for the phone. "Leave it to your nonna. I will take care of them. *Sì*," she snapped into the receiver then frowned and nodded. "She is. Oh. All right, I will tell her. An hour? *Sì*. She will be there."

Sophie twisted the red-checkered tablecloth between her fingers. "Who was it?"

"Colleen Gallagher. She wants to meet with you. I think she's going to offer you a job. The manager's position."

As much as Sophie needed a job, she couldn't work at Greystone.

Rosa returned to her chair and glanced at her bedroom, nodding slowly. "Two birds, one stone. You're a smart girl. You'll turn Greystone around, and the child welfare people, they will be happy. Good job, steady job. It's good. It will work."

Her grandmother was right. If Greystone was owned by anyone other than the Gallaghers, Sophie would jump at the opportunity. As it was, she hesitated. First off, she knew Rosa. She'd only be able to set aside her feud with Kitty for so long. Then there was Sophie's biggest fear—running into Michael. "I don't know, Nonna. Maybe I should—"

"You rarely see the Gallagher grandchildren at Greystone," Rosa said conversationally. "I don't remember the last time Michael was in town."

Sophie's eyes shot to her grandmother. Rosa patted her hand. "Don't worry, *bella*. No one will take Mia from us. Colleen offers you the job, you say *sì*."

Chapter Four

♥

The couple making out on the couch decided it for Liam; he was heading home to Boston. He'd begun to suspect his dad had a thing for the attractive, fiftysomething redhead who lived across the street. From the looks of it, he'd been right. Maggie Stewart was a bit of a mystery woman. No one really knew her story, other than that she was an artist and had moved to town to buy a high-end art gallery a couple years earlier.

GG probably did. She knew everyone's story. And Maggie belonged to the Widows Club. A club his great-grandmother had founded years before. If anything was going on in Harmony Harbor, you could bet they were behind it.

As Liam went to backtrack up the stairs to his bedroom, a floorboard creaked. His father and Maggie broke apart like a pair of guilty teenagers.

"Hey, son." His father straightened his navy uniform shirt, his face flushing a dull red. "You have a good night?"

It was a question his father asked him every morning.
With that same searching look in his piercing blue eyes. He
didn't want to know if Liam had a good night. He wanted
to know if it was nightmare-free. It hadn't been. Which may
be the reason Liam said, "Yep, but apparently not as good
as your morning. You might want to—" He rubbed his lips
with his thumb. If the flattening of his father's mouth was
any indication, the chief probably wished Liam had kept his
closed. He might have, but it was a little disconcerting seeing his dad wearing red lipstick. "It's not really your color.
Looks great on you, though, Maggie."

Fiddling with the gold bangles on her wrist, Maggie
glanced from his father to Liam, and gave him a self-conscious
smile. "I probably should be going. I just wanted to drop off
some muffins and check on you both."

He shouldn't have let his frustration get the better of him.
His jab at his father had embarrassed Maggie. "Don't leave
on my account." Liam glanced at the stack of muffins on the
platter and picked one up. "These look…great," he said in
an effort to make up for his smart-ass remark. Because they
didn't. They were the oddest-looking muffins he'd ever seen.
They were burnt orange with what looked like melted ched-
dar cheese on top.

His father leaned back out of Maggie's line of sight and
gave his head an almost imperceptible shake.

But his warning came too late because Liam had already
taken a bite. "Umm, really good," he said at the same time
looking around for something to put out the fire in his
mouth. "I'm going to get a glass of milk. Anyone else want
one?"

Maggie beamed. "Oh good. It's a new recipe I've been
experimenting with for my next coffee klatch. I was worried
I'd added too much cayenne," she called after him.

Maggie attended a weekly morning meeting with the Widows Club. All of whom, as far as he knew, were over seventy. Other than Maggie, of course. So he should probably tell her the truth. But no way was he going to be the one to dim the wide smile on her face. He'd leave that to his father.

There was a solid *thunk* on the front door, and their golden retriever started barking. "Cut it out, Miller," his father said when the dog kept it up.

"Shush now. I'm just getting the newspaper, my beautiful boy," Maggie said, and Miller immediately stopped barking. Their dog was stupid in love with Maggie.

Liam had just poured a glass of milk and was in the process of guzzling it down when she called out, "Liam, you made the front page of the *Harmony Harbor Gazette*. Oh, that's so sweet. Look, Colin, it says, 'Gallant Gallagher strikes again. Harmony's local hero rescues the damsels in distress.'"

Liam choked on the milk, spilling it down the front of his Boston Fire Department sweatshirt. He wiped at the damp spot as he walked into the living room. "Thought journalists were supposed to print fact not fiction. Old Lady Harte should retire."

"She has. Her grandchildren Poppy and Byron have taken over the paper. And I for one think they're doing an incredible job."

"I agree with Liam. They've turned it into a gossip rag. Chief Benson threatened to throw them in jail last week for interfering in a case," his father said, referring to Harmony Harbor's chief of police.

Maggie lifted a shoulder. "They're doing something right. Circulation has increased by thirty-five percent, and they just took over in September. It's because of Poppy and Byron that the raffle is doing so well. Ask Colleen and Kitty if you don't believe me," she added when his dad raised a skeptical eyebrow. "If more grandchildren stepped up to the plate and took over the family businesses in town, it would give Harmony Harbor the boost it sorely needs."

Since Liam was one of the grandchildren she was obviously referring to, he ignored her. He'd heard it before. The Widows Club had the same mission statement as GG and Kitty. Maggie went back to looking at the paper. "This child is absolutely beautiful. I wonder if her mother would let me paint her? How are they, by the way?"

She handed Liam the paper. He doubted Sophie would be any happier than he was by the coverage. They'd featured a photo of him carrying Mia out of the manor and one with Sophie in his arms. The angle of the shot clearly captured her meltdown. He could still see her standing there in the glow of the emergency lights with tears streaming down her beautiful face.

He hadn't gotten a good look at her in the smoke-filled manor. It hadn't been the time to take in the changes to the woman he once thought he was in love with. She was still as pretty as he remembered, but what surprised him was how worn out and fragile she looked. Hard to tell with the oversized sweatshirt she had on, but from the feel of her pressed against him, she was less curvy than he remembered. And those golden brown eyes of hers practically swallowed her pale face.

"Liam?" Maggie prompted.

"Huh?" Oh, right, she'd asked him how they were doing. "Good, I think. Mia didn't suffer any ill effects from the smoke." But after Marco had called Liam with an update last night and filled him in about the fire in LA, he imagined it brought back too many memories for sleep to come easily. Especially for Sophie. Now that he thought about it, the changes in her weren't a surprise. She had to have been as traumatized as Mia.

Though he sympathized with her now, when Marco first told him Mia had been alone at the time of the fire…Yeah, he hadn't been so sympathetic then. All he could see were those big, blue eyes in that adorable, little face looking at him like he was her hero. She'd made him want to slay dragons for her. He'd had to remind himself that Sophie wasn't the bad guy. She was a single mother trying to do her best for her little girl. It wasn't her fault the sitter had been a no-show. Still, he couldn't ignore the nagging voice in his head that wondered why she hadn't phoned and checked on the babysitter and Mia. He was being unfair; he knew that. It went with the job, he supposed.

"Son, you're zoning out. Did you get any sleep at all last night?"

Liam tossed the newspaper on the coffee table. "I'm not zoning out. Just thinking about Mia. The kid's been through a lot."

"So has Sophie. I was concerned about her, but a couple minutes in your arms and she calmed right down," his father said with a grin.

He should have known his dad would find a way to get back at him for his earlier jab.

"Am I missing something?" Maggie asked as she picked up the paper to study the photo.

"No, it's just Dad being—"

"Liam used to have a—"

"You know what? I'm outta here. Should have been on the road an hour ago." Liam headed for the stairs before his father put him in the crosshairs of Maggie and the matchmaking Widows Club.

"On the road to where?" his father asked.

He stopped and turned. "Boston." At the concern tightening his father's face, Liam sighed. "Dad, I talked to Captain Harris last night and told him I needed another week or so to work through things. I can do that there. It'll be good for me to hang out at the station." He wasn't exactly sure that was true. No doubt he'd be hit with a barrage of memories as soon as he walked through the doors. Memories of that night... and Billy.

Liam caught the silent exchange between his father and Maggie before she said, "I should probably get going." She leaned toward his father then glanced at Liam and stood up. Tossing one end of her brightly colored shawl over her shoulder, she headed for the door. Miller whined, and she went over and gave him a quick rubdown, her long, pumpkin-orange, fringed skirt making a puddle on the floor. "I'll see you later, my beautiful boy." She looked at Liam as she came to her feet. "I know it's not my place, but as some- one who's grown very fond of you, I hope you'll listen to your dad. Call me later, Colin."

"Bye, Maggie," his father said, his eyes coming back to Liam once she'd closed the door.

"What's she talking about? Or do I even want to know?"

"I talked to Harris this morning, and we—"

"Come again?"

"Just hear me out. I suggested to Harris that you work for me for a couple weeks. He thought it was a good idea, and so do I." He raised his hand when Liam opened his mouth to argue. "Think about it. We're a smaller station. It's not like you're going to be dealing with four-alarm fires like you would be with BFD. Marco, Fergus, and I will have your back. The three of us know what you've been dealing with. We'll help you work through it. You have a good crew at Thirty-Nine, son, but it's not the same."

There was some truth to what his father said. Liam got

along well with everyone at Ladder Company 39, but he wasn't overly close to anyone. He'd go out with them for a beer, catch a football or hockey game, but other than that, he kept everyone at arm's length. They'd have his back, but if he had a flashback like he did last night, they wouldn't trust him to have theirs. And they'd be right.

As though his father sensed he'd made his point, he continued. "Besides that, I need an extra set of eyes at Greystone. Something's going on at the manor."

"Do you mean with Grams and GG?" It wouldn't be a surprise if there was. Kitty and Colleen had never really gotten along. Things had gotten worse since his grandfather was no longer there to play peacemaker.

"Not sure. Both Kitty and Jasper swear they had nothing to do with the fog machines being turned on, and GG says the same thing. But her memory isn't what it used to be, and none of the staff has admitted to turning them on." His father pinched the bridge of his nose between his thumb and forefinger, his tell that he was tired or had a stress headache coming on.

His dad didn't need the constant hassle of running interference at Greystone. He had enough on his plate at the station. *And with me,* Liam thought guiltily. He hadn't made it easy on his father these past few weeks. Granted, the chief constantly worrying and checking on him had worn thin. But it came from a good place, even if he seemed to forget Liam was an adult now. "GG should accept the offer from the developer and sell out."

His father let his hand fall to his side. "I don't understand you boys. Greystone and the estate have been in our family for more than seven generations. She's protecting our heritage, your heritage. Your grandfather would roll over in his grave if he heard you talk like that."

48 Debbie Mason

"Come on, Dad. They're too old to take care of a place that size. And the money—"

"Talk like that in front of GG and she'll take her cane to you. You kids have no respect for history. It's not all about money, you know."

His great-grandmother and grandfather had lived in the past and celebrated it every chance they got. Ronan Gallagher had been a renowned historian. He'd been writing a book about Greystone and the family before he died—all the stories he'd told them as kids. Ronan had loved the estate almost as much as he'd loved Kitty and his family. GG was the same. Supposedly she'd begun writing a book about Harmony Harbor when she turned a hundred. She was pretty secretive about it, so no one knew if it was true or not. But as far as the money...

"Maybe you should tell that to Uncle Sean. He'd sell out in a heartbeat," Liam said, referring to his father's older brother.

"Only because of his social-climbing wife."

"Don't hold back. Tell me how you really feel about Aunt Maura."

His father snorted a laugh. "You always were a wiseass."

"Yeah, about that. Sorry for what I said earlier. I didn't mean to embarrass Maggie." Now it looked like he'd succeeded in embarrassing his father again. "It's been seven years, Dad. Mom would want you to move on with your life. She'd want you to be happy," he said, forcing the emotion from his voice. It was something he'd heard his mother say after losing a close friend. Still didn't make it any easier to say to his dad. But he needed to hear it. "So do we; Maggie's great."

His father ran his finger under his collar. "She is. She's a very nice woman. But it's not like that...We're not..."

"Okay, good to know. I didn't want to cramp your style, so I thought, if I'm sticking around for another week, I'd move into the manor. But if you and Maggie aren't—"

"That might not be a bad idea." His father's eyes narrowed when Liam grinned. "Not for me, for your grandmother and GG. If you're there, you can keep a closer eye on them and the staff. I'll give you a day or two before I put you on rotation."

"I'm sure I'll be able to keep myself occupied. GG probably has a to-do list a mile long. I'll check out the generator and electrical while I'm at it."

"I'm sure you'll have plenty to keep you busy, son. But it may not be GG giving you the orders. She's planning on offering Sophie DiRossi the manager's job."

As Sophie got out of the car, she tugged on the hem of the black skirt her grandmother had lent her, praying the safety pin holding it up didn't pop open. There hadn't been much they could do to improve the fit of the white polyester blouse with the bow at its neck or the clunky black shoes she wore. As Rosa had informed Sophie when she'd asked if she had another pair, beggars couldn't afford to be choosers. Like she needed the reminder. Sophie hoped her meeting with Colleen went better than being dressed for it by her grandmother.

A cool ocean breeze sent bright yellow and red leaves tumbling across Greystone's parking lot. Rosa's black, all-weather coat snapped and flapped against Sophie's ankles as she opened the back car door. The wind carried with it the smell of brine and the familiar sounds of seagulls and the waves crashing against the rocks of Kismet Cove.

Sophie's hair whipped across her face as she leaned in to fight with the buckle of Mia's recently cleaned booster seat and stuck to the red lipstick her grandmother had insisted she wear to compensate for the dark shadows under her eyes. Apparently she looked like death warmed over. Between her outfit and her grandmother's assessment of her looks, Sophie wasn't feeling exactly confident about her upcoming interview. And then there was the matter of Mia.

Nothing Sophie or her grandmother did or said could convince Mia to stay with Rosa. Maybe she'd picked up on Sophie's own anxiety. These days, she wasn't comfortable leaving her daughter with anyone, despite the risks of having Mia around the Gallagher matriarch. She probably should be including any Gallagher, but she had a feeling Colleen was the most dangerous of them all. Sophie was hoping, if Colleen offered her the job, she'd allow Mia to come to work with her. At least for a week or two until they got settled.

Removing the strands of hair from her lips, Sophie smiled at her daughter as she helped her out of the car. "You're not nervous about coming back here, are you?" Mia managed to project her disdain for the question with her silent stare. "So you're good?" That got her a nod. *Great.* Sophie closed the door. "No running off this time, Mia. You have to stay with Mommy. This interview is really important." Her chest constricted as she thought about how important it was.

She took Mia's hand in hers, tightening her grip when her daughter tried to pull away. Sophie ignored Mia's peeved expression and walked across the parking lot to the flagstone path. When they rounded the side of the manor, they were met by a dark-haired woman smoking a cigarette. She wore a black, lace-up vest over a scooped white blouse and an emerald-green flounced skirt that reached her knees. Sophie smiled at the woman at the same time wondering what Irish holiday fell in November.

"Sophie." The woman smiled, dropped her cigarette, and

ground it into the garden soil with the heel of her shoe. Sophie couldn't help but notice that they were as ugly as hers. When the woman moved closer, she had a sudden flash of recognition. It was her cousin. Her second cousin, really. But she looked nothing like the woman Sophie remembered. The saying "a shadow of her former self" rang true for Ava DiRossi.

"Ava." Sophie covered her shock with a wide smile and gave her cousin a warm hug. As a young girl, Sophie had idolized Ava. With her mass of long, ebony-black curls, exquisite bone structure, and gorgeous green eyes, her cousin had been the most beautiful girl in Harmony Harbor. But it wasn't just her looks; Ava had been full of life—passionate, sexy, smart, with a heart as big as her personality.

Her cousin pulled back and smiled. "It's been so long. You're all grown up now. Auntie Rosa called this morning to say you were in town. I was hoping I'd get to see you. This must be your daughter."

Sophie nodded, hoping her grandmother had also told Ava that Mia didn't speak. "Mia, this is your cousin Ava. Can you shake her hand?"

Ava smiled at Mia and crouched beside her. "Maybe a hug instead?" her cousin asked with a touch of the old Ava in her voice and smile.

As her daughter stepped into her cousin's arms, Sophie wondered what had happened to the girl she remembered. The girl who'd loved and married Griffin Gallagher at eighteen. Sophie was ten years younger than her cousin and didn't really know all the details about what had happened back then. Griffin had been in the military, training to become a Navy SEAL, and Ava had gone to Northeastern to become a nurse practitioner. Even though they were separated by distance, they'd seemed happy. Then Ava had divorced him and quit school. No one seemed to know why.

Ava held Mia close, stroking her hair with a faraway look in her eyes. Then she blinked and forced a smile for Sophie as she released Mia and stood. Since Sophie was a pro at the fake smile and hiding her feelings, she could recognize when someone else was doing the same. She wondered what her cousin was hiding.

"So what are you two doing at Greystone? Have you come for tea?"

"A job. I have an interview with Mrs. Gallagher. Is there something special going on today?" she asked, thinking that would explain the costume her cousin wore.

Ava frowned then followed the direction of Sophie's gaze and sighed. "No, the costumes were Kitty's idea. She was going for the full Irish experience—music, food, and dress. We're lucky she didn't dress us as leprechauns. You should see your grandmother when I walk by the shop after work." Ava did an impression of Rosa's "What's the matter with you?" complete with hand gestures.

Mia was watching Ava with a tiny smile on her face. Her cousin winked. "Your nonna is crazy, but a good crazy." Her expression grew serious when she glanced at Sophie and lowered her voice. "Do Jasper and Kitty know about the interview?"

"I'm not sure. Why?" Sophie asked as they continued down the path to the manor's entrance.

Ava lifted her skirt and arched an eyebrow. "The full Irish experience is part of Kitty's plan to prove to Colleen she's ready to take over Greystone. Let's face it. Colleen's a hundred and four. It's not like she'll live forever. And Jasper, he's devoted to Kitty. If Colleen does offer you a job, and you take it, he won't make it easy for you, Sophie."

That wasn't exactly a surprise. Sophie remembered Jasper from when she'd worked at Greystone. But she hadn't realized she'd be stepping on Kitty's toes. Sophie glanced at Mia and thought about the social worker's phone call. "I'm not as easy to intimidate as I was at seventeen. If Colleen offers me the manager's position, he'll be working for me."

"Speak of the devil," Ava murmured as she pushed open the manor's heavy oak door. "It's too bad Auntie Rosa and I didn't know your plans nine days ago. We could have started a novena for you."

The tall, silver-haired man looked down his long, narrow nose at her cousin. "You're five minutes over your allotted time for break. It will be coming out of your paycheck." He sniffed. "And you smell of smoke. I suggest you quit that filthy habit."

There was a part of Sophie that agreed with him. At least when it came to her cousin smoking. The man was beyond rude, though. She half expected Ava to call him out on his behavior; that was something the old Ava would have done. Instead, her cousin meekly nodded, briefly touching Sophie's arm before walking away with her head down, her once long and lustrous hair pulled back in a lank ponytail. Sophie couldn't help but wonder if working at Greystone had anything to do with the changes in her cousin.

"You're late. Madame is waiting for you in the study."

Angry at the thought that this man might have had something to do with breaking her cousin's spirit, Sophie met his pale-blue eyes, held them, and said in a tone as clipped as his, "Mrs. Gallagher's aware I'd be late. Come on, Mia."

She took her daughter's hand and glanced at the lobby. Last night, the lighting had been soft and subdued, and she'd been too nervous and tired to really take in the changes to Greystone. It was still as grandly beautiful as she remembered with its soaring ceilings, majestic stone fireplace, and elegant staircase, but there were small signs that time had taken its toll. Notably, there wasn't a guest in sight.

If she got the job, Sophie would have her work cut out for her. The first to go would be the new uniforms, though she'd noticed Jasper wore the same dark suit he always did. Maybe she'd dress *him* as a leprechaun. But she forgot all about Jasper when she and Mia reached the study down the hall from the entryway.

A rush of nerves caused Sophie's heart to pound. Eight years earlier, she'd stood outside this very door. Only it hadn't been completely closed like it was now. Through the small gap, she'd seen Michael and his mother, Maura Gallagher.

Sophie hadn't heard from him since the night they'd made love at Kismet Cove. He'd told her he loved her, and she'd told him she loved him too. So she hadn't understood what was going on. Until she'd overheard Maura and Michael's conversation in the study.

"I don't know what GG told you, but you're getting worked up for no reason, Mother. It was nothing. Just a summer fling. It's over."

"I'm relieved to hear that, but really, Michael, you could have made a better choice for a summer companion. It's such a cliché. The wealthy grandson and the maid. If that's not bad enough, the girl is a DiRossi."

"You don't know me very well if you think I've had only one *summer companion, Mother,"* Michael said, his tone snide. *"And you seem to be forgetting that Griffin was married to a DiRossi."*

Maura Gallagher gave a disdainful sniff. "Yes, and look how well that turned out. If you plan on following in your father's footsteps and becoming governor someday, you need to give more thought to who you're seen with."

"I'm twenty-four. I'm not looking to settle down."

"Your father and I have high hopes for you, darling. We don't intend to let you throw them away on some trashy, little upstart from Harmony Harbor."

"Don't worry, Mother. Your dreams for me are safe."

"Don't be sarcastic. I'm just looking out for your best interests. I've known girls like Sophie DiRossi. She'll probably have three children before she's twenty-one and work as a maid the rest of her life. Girls like her have no drive or ambition. Unless it's to trap a man like you into marriage."

So maybe it hadn't been working at the manor that was behind Sophie's dream to manage a hotel after all. Maybe it had been the memory of Maura Gallagher's damning prediction. It didn't matter. Sophie couldn't do this. But when Mia tugged on her hand and she looked into her daughter's eyes, Sophie knew she didn't have a choice.

She forced a smile and let go of Mia's hand to rub her damp palms on her skirt. She took a couple deep breaths and was about to raise her hand to knock…when the safety pin in her skirt let go at the same time the door to the study opened to reveal Liam Gallagher.

Chapter Five

♥

Sophie didn't know if it was because of her recent trip back to the past, but for a brief moment, looking into Liam's blue eyes was like looking into Michael's. She shouldn't be surprised. The Gallagher boys all bore a striking resemblance to one another. With Michael and Liam, it had been even more pronounced. But Michael had been a smooth-talking jerk, and Liam…

The open end of the pin jabbed her in the waist and cut off the thought. Her eyes widened both in pain and horror as the pin kept moving and her skirt slid down her hips. She grabbed the waistband to hold it up in the front while twisting to keep the fabric away from her back, pushing her hips forward to stop the pin's downward slide. It didn't work, and she pushed her hips to the right and then to the left.

"Interesting dance moves, Soph. Guess you're pretty excited about your job interview," Liam said with a hint of laughter in his voice.

"I'm not dancing. I'm having a wardrobe malfunction," Sophie informed him from between clenched teeth.

His eyes moved over her, and he opened his mouth.

"Liam, what the bejaysus are you doing out there? I don't have all day," Colleen Gallagher called from the study. "Send the girl in."

"Give me a minute, GG. I want to talk to Sophie. Why don't you go in and visit with Simon, Mia?" Her daughter stared at him. "Your friend, the cat. They finally gave him a name."

"*We* didn't. Your grandmother did. And a foolish one it is, if you ask me. I don't know why I agreed to keep the damn thing anyway. Black cats are bad luck, and he's snotty. He acts like he's lord of the manor. What are you waiting for, child? Come in, come in."

Obviously the older woman's cantankerous tone of voice didn't faze Mia because she walked right into the study. Liam closed the door and took Sophie by the arm to pull her into an alcove, causing her to loosen her hold on her skirt.

"No, don't…Ow."

He held up his hands and took a step back with a wary expression on his handsome face. "Maybe you better tell me what the problem is."

"Okay, but don't laugh. I had to borrow clothes from Rosa for the interview, and they're too big. So we pinned the skirt…"

"Gotcha. How about you take off your coat and—" he began as he moved behind her.

"I can't. My skirt will fall off if I do." She heard what sounded like a snort of laughter and looked over her shoulder. "You're not supposed to laugh."

He crouched behind her, his eyes glinting with amusement. "I'm not. I'll just…" He lifted the hem of her coat and disappeared beneath it. "Ah, it's a little dark under here. Whereabouts is the pin?"

That was an easy enough question to answer. She knew exactly where the pin was—it was stabbing her left butt cheek. But with Liam's hand resting on her hip while the other one skimmed over the back of her skirt, she was having a difficult time staying focused. All she could think was that Liam Gallagher, who'd once played the starring role in her teenage fantasies, was touching her butt. "Where it shouldn't be," she finally managed to say, reaching back to show him. She ended up hitting him on the head instead.

"Hey, I'm doing my best not to touch your ass, but it's kind of—"

"May I ask what you're doing, Master Liam?"

Jasper was like a wraith. You never saw or heard him coming. He'd appear out of nowhere. Sophie wanted a do-over. This day was turning out worse than she'd expected. And that had been pretty bad.

Liam's messy, dark hair appeared from under her coat. "Maybe you could—"

Was he seriously going to ask for Jasper's help? Sophie drew her foot back and lightly kicked Liam in the shin. He raised his gaze to hers, lifting an eyebrow. She gave him a do-it-and-die look.

He grinned. "All good here, Jeeves. My hammer got caught in the hem of Sophie's coat."

"In the future, I'd suggest you be more careful with your *tools* around Miss DiRossi, Master Liam," the older man said, spearing Sophie with his ice-blue gaze. His mouth pressed in a thin line of disapproval as he walked away.

Sophie's cheeks heated. She knew exactly what Jasper meant. In the eyes of Colleen's right-hand man and confidant, a DiRossi would never be good enough for a Gallagher.

Just like Michael's mother, he perceived Sophie as a threat to the family's good name.

There was a part of Sophie that wanted to stand up for herself, tell him that she'd had the opportunity to trap a Gallagher and hadn't. Tell him what she thought of his opinion of girls like her. But she wouldn't. She'd sacrificed too much to keep Mia's father a secret, and it had nothing to do with pride. Her greatest fear had been that with their money and connections, Michael and his parents would have forced Sophie to give up Mia or taken her daughter from her.

She bowed her head, letting her hair fall forward in an attempt to cover her reaction to Jasper's jab. "Maybe I should just—" she began before Liam cut her off.

"Let go of your skirt, and I'll—"

"But—"

"Trust me, okay?"

"Okay," she said, and did as he asked, because that was one thing she'd always known. She could trust Liam. He wasn't like his cousin. Neither was his family. The summer Gallaghers were different from the Gallaghers of Harmony Harbor.

"This might get a little awkward," Liam said as he pulled the fabric away from her body. "The skirt's big, but it's not that big, so I'll apologize for any inappropriate touching now."

Her embarrassed laugh morphed into a moan when his hand slid between the skirt and her backside. His warm fingers brushed against body parts that no man had touched in a very long time.

He cleared his throat. "Got it. Now what do you want me to do?"

She cleared her throat too. "Thank you. Would you mind repinning it?"

With his hand holding the skirt in place, he came to his feet. "There's too much fabric. It'll just reopen. I have a better idea. Hold your skirt."

She grabbed the fabric at the same time he let go. He came to stand in front of her and lifted the bottom of his navy sweatshirt. She looked up at him. "You're a lot bigger than me, but your sweatshirt won't be long enough to cover my...What I mean is, if you're thinking I can wear your sweatshirt as a dress, it won't work."

He smiled as he undid his belt. "I'm not letting you go into a meeting with GG and Kitty wearing a sweatshirt. Not when you went to all this trouble to look professional." He pulled his brown belt from the loops. "Let's try this." He stepped closer, putting his arms around her. She could smell soap and fabric softener, the heat of his body enveloping her as he positioned the belt around her waist. She was tempted to wrap her arms around his and lean on him for just a minute...or two. "Okay, maybe you better take it from here," he said, his voice gruff as he threaded the end through the buckle.

Afraid he'd read in her eyes what she was feeling, she kept her head down and focused on the belt. "Thank you," she murmured, pulling it way past the last notch.

"Hang on." He took a screwdriver from his tan suede toolbelt.

"No, don't make another hole for me. I'll just tie it."

"It's not a big deal, Soph. This way you know it won't come loose."

That was the problem. It kind of was a big deal because it meant all those tempting muscles were just a whisper away. She looked down at his bent head as he worked the screwdriver through the leather. His dark hair was thick, the ends curling slightly where they met the neckband of his sweatshirt. Her fingers itched to run wild through those lustrous black strands. His knuckles pressed lightly into her stomach as he held the belt in place, and more inappropriate thoughts started filling her head. She sucked in a breath.

He glanced up at her and frowned. "You okay?"

No, she wasn't okay. The chastity belt she'd put on her libido had discovered the key. And that key was apparently Liam. "Good, really, really good." Oh, good Lord, was her face turning as red as it felt? "Um, Colleen's probably wondering what happened to me, so if you could—"

"You're good to go," he said, and stepped back, returning his screwdriver to his toolbelt.

Maybe that was the problem. She'd always had a thing for a guy who worked with his hands. Who was she trying to kid? She'd always had a thing for Liam and apparently some of those feelings were still there. "Thank you. I really appreciate your help. I'll get your belt and your jacket back to you as soon as I wash it. If Mia and I keep it up, you won't have any clothes left," she said in an attempt to lighten the mood then realized he might take it the wrong way. It didn't help that she was now picturing him naked. She covered her face. "Pretend I didn't say anything."

"You're welcome, Sophie." He took her hand from her face and placed the pin in her palm. "You might want to disinfect the scratch when you get home."

She nodded. "Thanks. I will. I guess I better get in there." She looked at the door and squared her shoulders.

"Soph, about the job. Are you sure—"

"Kitty and Jasper don't want Colleen to hire me, do they?"

"If GG wants to hire you, no one will be able to stop her." He shoved his hands in the front pockets of his jeans. "So you really do want the job?"

"It's not so much want, as need, Liam." She lifted her chin. "I'm well qualified for the position. I'd do a good job. It's not like—"

"You don't have to get defensive. I'm sure you would. It's just…never mind. Good luck." He opened the door for her.

Mia sat cross-legged on the area rug at the foot of Kitty Gallagher's chair with the cat in her arms. Her daughter's face was flushed, her eyes bright with what looked to be unshed tears.

Kitty put down her knitting to glare at her mother-in-law. "Leave the child be. She'll talk when she wants to."

Colleen Gallagher sat behind a large, formidable mahogany desk wearing a white blouse with a bow at the neck. It looked an awful lot like the one Sophie currently had on. The older woman's short hair was wispy, her heavy upper lids making her eyes appear small in her round face. Though faded with age, the blue eyes of the Gallaghers' matriarch were sharp and probing as they moved from Liam to Sophie. "I just asked—"

"You've been peppering her with questions for…Look, here's Sophie and Liam. Come in, my dear."

She never should have left Mia alone with them. She hurried to her daughter and cupped her face. "Are you okay, baby?"

"Don't coddle the child. Of course she's fine. Now sit down and let's get this interview over with."

That didn't sound promising, but at the moment, Sophie didn't care whether she got the job or not.

"Soph, why don't I take Mia with me? Helga should be taking the cookies out of the oven for tea about now," Liam said.

She gave him a grateful smile. "Would you like to go with Liam and get some cookies, Mia?" She didn't know why she even bothered to ask. Mia released the cat and jumped to her feet. Sophie followed her to Liam's side. She chewed on her bottom lip and glanced at her daughter sliding her hand into Liam's. "You're not going to eat the cookies in the kitchen, are you?" she asked, nervous about Mia being around the industrial ovens.

"Yeah…" He looked at her more closely. "No, we'll eat in the dining room with the guests."

"Thank you," she said on a sigh of relief.

"Don't worry about GG. She's all bark and no bite."

"I heard that," his great-grandmother said.

"You were meant to. And you and I are going to have words later."

"Just get your chores done, and we won't."

"This has nothing to do with *chores*, and you know it."

She shrugged. "Bring me some soda biscuits when you return with the child. The ones with raisins. Oh, and take your grandmother with you."

"I'm staying right where I am, thank you very much. Take a seat, dear," Kitty said to Sophie.

Liam shot his great-grandmother a warning look before closing the door behind him and Mia. Colleen rolled her eyes. Sophie wasn't sure if the eye roll was meant for Kitty or Liam. She took her seat across from the older woman.

"All right, let's get the paperwork out of the way, and then you can tell us how you plan to turn Greystone around." Colleen handed Sophie several papers.

Sophie drew her glasses from the top of her head and put them on to study the contract. She looked up at Colleen. "You mean I'm hired? For the manager's position?"

"Of course I do. Why do you think I was asking you all those questions last night? You've got nothing to hide, do you? No outstanding warrants or a record?"

Other than Mia and the arrest, she didn't. "No, no, I don't."

"Any problems with drugs or drinking?"

"No, neither."

"Fine then. You're hired." She rolled a pen across the desk. "We'll start you at forty-five thousand a year."

Sophie looked up from the paper.

"I suppose that's lower than you were expecting, but we don't have much room in the budget to maneuver right now. We can structure some kind of bonus at a later date."

If she'd finished her degree, Sophie would have been earning closer to seventy-five thousand, but she hadn't expected the salary at Greystone to be that high. It was higher than her previous job in LA. Which of course it would be since she'd been a maid. She was about to reassure Colleen when the older woman added, "You get free room and board. There's a two-bedroom apartment over the carriage house that you can use."

A small spurt of excitement and hope ignited inside Sophie. She couldn't remember how long it had been since she'd felt either emotion. At least when it came to her career and future. What Liam made her feel earlier didn't count. Well, it shouldn't. She really had to stop thinking about him.

Colleen must have mistaken her silence for disappointment because she sighed and said, "I was afraid it wouldn't be enough. What do you—"

"No, I'm more than happy with the offer, Mrs. Gallagher. I really am. There's just one problem."

"No more Mrs. Gallagher. Reminds me of my mother-in-law. The woman would have stolen the blessing from the holy water. Besides, it makes me feel old. Call me Colleen. Now, tell me what the problem is, and we'll solve it."

Sophie pressed her lips together to hold back a laugh.

Kitty, with a smile playing on her lips, bent her head over her knitting. "It's about Mia. I know it's a lot to ask and terribly unprofessional, but I was hoping, for the first week or two at least, that I can bring her with me to work. I'll make sure she doesn't bother the guests. She's very quiet—"

"Of course she is. The child doesn't speak."

"Yes, about that. The child psychologist recommended that we don't pressure Mia. She—"

"What did I tell you, Mother Gallagher? You shouldn't have been badgering the child like you were."

"Oh, be quiet over there and get back to your knitting. If you ask me, there's a great deal of sense outside that psychologist's head."

Sophie thought Colleen was agreeing with her, until she realized what she'd actually said. "Mrs....Colleen, Mia suffered—"

The older woman waved her hand. "Fine, I'll not say another word about it. You can keep the child with you for as long as you like."

Tears of gratitude welled in Sophie's eyes. With free room and board, she wouldn't be living paycheck to paycheck, struggling to put food on the table and clothes on her daughter's back. The job was exactly what she'd been hoping for when she'd started her degree. There was only one problem, but she pushed it away. If Colleen and Kitty hadn't guessed Mia's parentage by now, they never would. She blinked the moisture from her eyes. "Thank you. I promise, she won't interfere with me doing my job."

"Good. Now let's get down to business. I've got the mayor and that realtor gal breathing down my neck, and they've lit a fire under my grandchildren. All anyone thinks about nowadays is the almighty dollar."

"Colin doesn't. It's Maura and Tara who are the problem." Kitty looked at Sophie and explained, "Tara is my son Daniel's wife. Maura put a bug in Tara's ear. They're as thick as thieves those two are."

Colleen snorted. "She's his third wife…or is it his fourth? I've lost—"

"You know darn well she's his third wife." Self-consciously, Kitty lifted a shoulder and said to Sophie, "He has a bit of the wanderlust. He's an archaeologist. They're living in Ireland at the moment."

"No excuse for him not to visit. We rarely see the boy. Barely know his girls," Colleen grumbled then waved a dismissive hand. "Doesn't matter. I took care of that problem months ago. But I want to prove to the mayor that she doesn't need a bunch of high-end condos to revitalize the economy in Harmony Harbor. If I don't put a stop to this nonsense, she'll try and steal someone else's property out from under them. We're going to bring the manor and the town back to what they were in their heyday. And you're going to tell us how to do that, Sophie DiRossi. So what's the plan?"

Kitty moved to the chair beside Sophie. She glanced at her mother-in-law when Colleen sighed then smiled at Sophie. "I have some ideas that I think will—"

"For the love of all that is holy, Kitty. Give your brain a rest. The return of the Irish didn't work."

"It wasn't as successful as I had hoped, but I also came up with the idea to raffle off the cottage, and it's doing very well. I think my new idea will too. Pirates." She made a ta-da motion with her hands. When both Colleen and Sophie stayed silent, she did it again.

Sophie cleared the nervous laughter from her voice before speaking. "I think that's a great idea"—Colleen stared at her with her mouth half open—"for a theme night or even a weekend," she added at the look of disappointment on Kitty's face. "Once I've had a chance to go over occupancy rates in the last two years, the discounts, rebates, and override commissions you have in place with your distributors, as well as evaluate the manor's online presence and guests' feedback on TripAdvisor and Google Plus, I'll be able to give you a detailed plan of action."

Kitty and Colleen stared at her.

"Is something wrong?"

Colleen grinned. "You're the answer to my prayers, Sophie DiRossi. That's what you are. You've taken a weight off my shoulders already. I don't have to worry about Greystone with you at the helm. Kitty and I've done our best, but our hearts haven't been in it since we lost Ronan, Mary, and Riley."

"Don't worry, Colleen. There's a lot we can do right away to motivate the staff and revitalize Greystone. The raffle's a great start, but I'd like to come up with something in the next week to lift the manor's profile in a wider market. Something that would draw attention from media outlets in Boston is what I'm looking for."

Colleen and Kitty shared a look.

"Do you have an idea how we can do that?" Sophie asked. It was important that both Kitty and Colleen felt like they were a part of the changes. They might be happy with her taking over now, but she didn't want them to start resenting her. Greystone wasn't just a hotel; it was their home.

"We had the perfect opportunity two months ago, but we had to pass. We didn't have the energy to deal with everything Bethany was demanding. It's a shame, though. A high-society wedding like that would have put us back on the map. If you'd only come home earlier, we would have jumped at the chance, dear," Kitty said.

Sophie was disappointed too. A high-profile wedding would have been just what they needed to jump-start cash flow.

Colleen's eyes roamed Sophie's face, and then she gave a decisive nod and picked up the phone. "Don't count us out yet, ladies. I have a feeling this is kismet. Michael, my boy, it's GG. About your wedding…"

Chapter Six

♥

Liam had two rules in his playbook that he hadn't broken since he'd made the list after losing his mother and sister—keep it light and keep it simple. If you don't get attached, you don't get hurt. So for a guy who'd perfected the art of staying uninvolved, Liam knew he was in trouble the moment he offered to help out Sophie and take Mia with him. He shouldn't be surprised. If there was one person in this world guaranteed to throw him off his game, it was Sophie DiRossi.

When his dad told him GG planned to offer Sophie the manager's position, that should have been Liam's cue to get the hell out of Dodge. But no, the thought of going back to Ladder Company 39 before he got his head straight had worried him more than seeing Sophie again. Seeing her might have been okay. His hand up her skirt and his fingers skimming over an ass that was as shapely and perfect as he remembered…Yeah, so far from okay it wasn't funny. Then he'd gone and made it worse by wrapping his belt around a

waist his hand could span, standing close enough to see the
yellow flecks in her golden brown eyes and smell her sweet
vanilla scent.

But it had always been more than Sophie's pretty face, gorgeous eyes, and curvy body that had turned him on. She'd
had this incredible warmth and energy about her that sucked
people in. She never stopped doing and dreaming and made
everyone around her feel like they could move mountains.
Which meant trouble of another kind. If there was anyone
who could convince GG and Kitty that they could turn Greystone around, it was Sophie. With her cheering them on, they
wouldn't listen to reason or his very real concerns.

Just before he'd left his great-grandmother's study to see
Sophie dancing outside the door, he'd laid out his concerns
about the generator. It needed to be replaced. And that was
just one of many things that needed to be either replaced or
repaired. Greystone was the mother of all money pits.

If he was lucky, they wouldn't be able to afford the going
rate for a hotel manager, and Sophie would refuse the job.
Maybe then they'd listen to him and accept the developer's
offer. He closed the study door. Mia tugged on his hand,
reminding him that Sophie had more than herself to think
about. She had a little girl to support. GG might not be able
to offer the going rate, but there weren't many jobs available
in town that would pay better. Clearly luck was not something he had a lot of these days.

Mia smiled up at him, her small fingers tightening around
his. Yep, out of luck and in trouble. She'd be about as tough
to resist as her mother. At the thought, he considered returning Mia to the study, but she was happily skipping alongside
him, and he didn't have the heart to disappoint her. Apparently GG's attempts to browbeat Mia into speaking bothered
Sophie more than her daughter.

"Careful, sweetheart," he said as she hopped down the steps leading into the lobby with its timber-vaulted ceiling and gray slate floor. An attractive woman with shoulder-length hair the color of a copper penny looked up from where she sat in one of the brown leather wingback chairs beside the massive stone fireplace and smiled.

Liam returned her smile. He'd seen her around but hadn't been formally introduced. Dana something. GG and Kitty were constantly singing the woman's praises. She'd decorated the cottage for the raffle and had been a paying guest at the manor since the beginning of September. And paying guests were few and far between these days. As evidenced by the nearly empty lobby. Other than Dana, there was an older man sitting at the bar. A woman Liam didn't recognize sat behind the reception desk filing her nails. He wondered if Sophie had any idea what she was getting herself into.

"Okay, Mia, let's get you those cookies," Liam said, and started toward the dining room. He didn't get far.

Mia stood staring at the grand staircase with its red runner. The door to the basement was behind the staircase, so he was worried that she was thinking about being lost in the tunnels the night before. Liam crouched beside her. "We're going to the dining room. It's over there"—he gestured to the far right of the lobby—"nowhere near the basement."

She shook her head and dragged him to where a brass easel held a laminated poster advertising the raffle. He took it off the stand and stood it on the floor in front of her. The poster was bigger than she was. She beamed up at him and tapped on the stone cottage decorated for Christmas. He imagined the holiday decorations were the draw. His sister had been the same. Riley had loved everything about Christmas. Days before they'd lost her, she'd cut the top off an

evergreen and put it in her room. By then, she'd been playing carols for a month.

His sister's love of all things Christmas had been the
reason Riley and his mom were on the road that night. It
was the second week in October, and they were headed
to Boston for some early Christmas shopping. Riley and
his mom had planned to make it a family affair. He and
his brothers had been home to celebrate his dad's birthday.
His mom and sister had been disappointed when Liam, his
brothers, and his father bowed out. It was a decision each
of them had lived to regret. If they'd been in the car, they
could have saved them.

He pushed the memories aside. "The cottage is a short
walk from here. Maybe your mom will take you to see it."

She pointed to herself and then at the cottage.

He took in the lightweight sweater she wore over her
T-shirt. "You're not really dressed for a walk today, sweetheart."

She repeated the gestures more emphatically this time, as
though Liam were a little slow on the uptake.

He scratched his chin. He'd never liked charades. "You
like the cottage?" She placed her hands over her heart and
nodded. "Okay, you *love* the cottage." She nodded enthusiastically. Now they were getting somewhere. He glanced
around. When he didn't see any sign of Jasper, he handed the
poster to Mia. "There you go. Now let's get some cookies.
I'm starved." She didn't move. "Sorry, it's too big for you
to carry, isn't it?" He tucked the poster under his arm and
headed for the dining room…without Mia. He turned. Her
arms were crossed, her eyebrows drawn inward, her mouth
bunched up. At that moment, Liam kind of empathized with
GG. He was tempted to say, *Just tell me what you want, kid,*
but he didn't want to upset either Mia or her mother. Be-

sides, if he was frustrated, he could only imagine how the little girl felt.

He walked back to her. At a loss at what to do, he replaced the poster on the easel. Dana glanced their way. She held up a magazine and moved her hand as though writing. *Thanks,* he mouthed. He didn't think Mia was old enough to write, but right about now, he was willing to try anything. He dug out a pencil and small pad of paper from the pouch in his toolbelt and held them up. "Why don't we go sit in the dining room, and you can draw me a picture of what you want?"

She gazed longingly at the easel, but nodded. As they walked into the almost-empty dining room, he immediately spotted another problem. Hazel Winters, Harmony Harbor's mayor, and local realtor Paige Townsend were seated at a table by the back wall of windows.

He pulled out a chair at the table nearest the door. "We'll sit here, Mia."

With the pad and pencil clutched to her chest, she turned in a circle, taking in the space. He supposed through the eyes of a little girl, it was pretty impressive. Housed in one of the mansion's four turrets, the dining room was an octagon. She wouldn't notice that the Persian carpet was threadbare or that there were nicks in the dark wood paneling that covered the bottom half of the walls. The red damask wallpaper covering the upper half had seen better days too.

"Hey, Erin," he said to a twentysomething blonde pushing the dessert cart their way. She gave him a flirtatious smile.

"Hey there, hot stuff. Haven't seen you here for a while. Who's your little friend? Hi there, cutie."

Mia didn't look up. Her tongue sticking out the side of her mouth, she chewed on it while drawing her picture.

"Mia. She's shy," he said in order to stave off any questions about why she didn't speak. He wondered how Sophie handled all the questions. Had to be tough explaining to everyone she met about the fire. "How long have Paige and Hazel been here?"

"Long enough to interrogate Jasper and the other staff about last night. Sounds like they think Colleen will be more open to an offer now." She gave him a worried look. "You don't think she'll sell, do you?"

A sane person would. "No, your job's safe for now, Erin. Hey, have you heard any of the staff talking about the fog machines?" Jasper and his grandmother had already questioned the staff, but Liam had to give it another shot. If Erin knew something, she'd tell him.

"Would you go out with me if I told you who did it?" she asked with an impish grin.

He liked Erin. She was a pretty woman and exactly the type he typically dated—she wasn't looking for a serious relationship. But she worked at Greystone, and staff was off-limits. Something his parents and grandparents had drilled into their heads. It was a good rule. Too bad his cousin hadn't abided by it that long-ago summer. But Michael never thought rules applied to him. At least back then.

Mia stopped drawing, her eyes flicking from Liam to Erin.

"Sorry, I already have a cookie date." The side of Mia's mouth turned up in a small smile. "Besides, I don't want you to lose your job. I'm pretty sure, if you read the small print in your contract, there's a no-dating-a-Gallagher clause."

She laughed then glanced over her shoulder toward the kitchen. "I better serve you or I'll never hear the end of it from Helga," she said, referring to the cook who'd been with Greystone for as long as Liam could remember.

"So, you never did tell me if one of the staff was responsible for turning on the fog machines."

Glancing at the kitchen again, Erin placed a platter of assorted cookies and cakes on the table. "Coffee?" He nodded. Once she'd retrieved the pot off the cart, she lowered her voice and poured his coffee. "Weekend staff isn't around, but everyone thinks Kitty did it. You know how she is. She wants everything to be a big event." She made a face and held out her skirt. "Case in point. Hey, did you hear Colleen's interviewing Sophie DiRossi for the manager's position? Jasper isn't happy. He said—"

Liam cut her off. He had a fairly good idea what Jasper thought of Sophie. Any DiRossi for that matter. "Erin, Mia is Sophie's daughter."

"Oh...ah…Really? I thought she was one of your relatives." She shrugged. "Guess it's those blue eyes. Do you want a chocolate milk or orange juice, cutie?"

Mia looked at him.

"Chocolate milk?" he asked, and she nodded.

"She really is shy," Erin said as she poured Mia's milk then placed the glass in front of her. "Hey, didn't Sophie go out with your cousin Michael back in the day? Guess she didn't have a problem breaking the no-Gallagher-dating clause."

No, she didn't. Which wouldn't have been a problem if Liam had been the Gallagher she'd wanted to date, but he'd missed his chance. He was five years older than Sophie. And being a guy who followed the rules and was also her brother's best friend, he'd been waiting until she grew up to ask her out. He'd missed out by one day. The night of her eighteenth birthday, his cousin asked her out. "They're the reason GG added the clause."

"Miss," a man a few tables over called.

"Be right with you, sir." Erin smiled then said to Liam, "I think you've been spotted." She nodded in the direction of Hazel and Paige's table.

"Thanks for the warning," he said, though it wasn't as if he could leave. Mia hadn't finished her cookies and milk yet. But maybe it was for the best. He'd get rid of Hazel and Paige before GG ran into them. They'd just get her riled up, and she didn't need the stress. Doc Bishop had called last week to tell his dad he was worried about her blood pressure. Which was the reason Liam hadn't forced the issue of the generator with her. He'd talk to his dad instead. And add to his stress level. Right about now, Liam was missing his drama-free life in Boston.

Mia slid the pad of paper across the table. She'd drawn three stick people and what appeared to be Mistletoe Cottage. He smiled and pointed to the tallest of the stick people. "Is this me?" She nodded shyly and took a bite of her cookie. "And this is you and your mommy?" he guessed. She'd added long hair to both, and the one in the middle was short. That earned him another nod. "You want the three of us to go for a walk to the cottage?"

She shook her head, and he held back a sigh. He'd been doing well up until then. She put down her cookie and took the pad of paper from him, flipping to the next page. He blinked. She'd written *tickit* and *Mia* beside what he imagined was supposed to be a raffle ticket. The first thought that came to mind was that she wanted to win the cottage so that the three of them could live there. He quickly banished the idea before it took hold.

Before he thought about how much he'd once loved Sophie and how, if things had turned out differently, Mia would be his and they might have been living happily ever after in the stone cottage in the woods. Obviously the banishing thing wasn't working out as he'd planned. And for a guy who kept his life simple and entanglement free, that was kind of scary. A family wasn't in the cards for him. He refocused on the paper. His imagination was working overtime. Mia hardly knew him. "Okay, I get it now. You want me to buy a raffle ticket for you so you and your mommy can win Mistletoe Cottage, right?"

He didn't know how to break it to her that staff and family members weren't allowed to enter the raffle, but he didn't get the chance. Hazel and Paige arrived at their table. "Oh my, is this the adorable child who was trapped in the fire?" the heavyset mayor in her brown wool suit asked. Hazel went to stroke her hair and Mia ducked away from her hand.

"There wasn't a fire, and she wasn't trapped," Liam said. He'd known Hazel since he was a kid. She was a nice woman and had been mayor of Harmony Harbor for at least a decade, but she had a tendency not to think before she spoke.

"I do hope her mother isn't going to sue. Poor Colleen has enough to worry about with all the bad press," Paige Townsend said with fake sympathy, tucking a strand of silver-blond hair behind her ear. He'd gone to school with Paige. Her family owned a frozen seafood plant in town, and she'd lorded it over the kids in school. He had a feeling she hadn't changed.

"Not sure what you're talking about, Paige. There wasn't any bad press. It's okay, eat your cookie, sweetheart."

Paige looked down her nose at him. Tall and well put together, she'd be attractive if she were a nicer person. "Obviously you haven't been online. People are raising concerns for the town's safety." She waved her hand. "But it's a moot point. My client has authorized me to make Colleen an offer she won't be able to refuse."

Even though Liam wished that were true, he knew it wasn't. He also felt the need to come to the manor's defense

for GG's sake. He wouldn't put it past Paige to start an online campaign against Greystone. "Paige—"

"Well, would you look who's come to call," GG said,
standing hunched over her cane at the entrance to the dining
room. Her greeting as much as her toothy smile surprised
Liam. Simon wasn't as friendly. He sat beside GG's feet,
hissing at Hazel and Paige. "Should have known how fast
good news travels in Harmony Harbor. Sophie girl, get over
here so I can introduce you to the mayor." She waved Sophie
forward.

Liam didn't know what was going on, but from Sophie's
expression, it was anything but good news. Her face was
pale, her movements jerky as she repeatedly twisted her
hand around her wrist.

"Hazel, meet our new manager. She ran a five-star hotel
in LA."

Sophie stared at GG. "Colleen, I—"

Kitty came up beside Sophie and whispered in her ear
then patted her shoulder. GG kept talking as though Sophie
hadn't said a word. "Did I mention it was a two-star hotel
before she got a hold of it? The plans she has for
Greystone…took her three hours to lay everything out for
us. We're going to be bigger and better than ever, Hazel. And
we're kicking off the—"

Liam shook his head. They'd been in there twenty minutes at most. His grandfather used to say no one had kissed
the Blarney Stone more often than GG.

"I'm sure Ms. DiRossi has good intentions, Colleen, but
as they say, talk is cheap. Now"—Paige opened her purse
and pulled out an envelope—"you can take this to the bank.
My client has authorized me to make you a generous offer."

"Póg mo thóin," GG muttered.

Kitty pressed her fingers to her mouth. Not in horror, because GG told a lot of people to kiss her ass. More likely she was trying to hold back a laugh at the stunned expression on Paige's face.

"Now, Colleen, there's no need to be—" Hazel began.

"Put a sock in it. You're both ruining my moment. We're hosting one of the highest-profile weddings of the season. My great-grandson Michael and his fiancée, Bethany Adams, will be married at Greystone on Christmas Eve. Folks will know Greystone is back in the wedding business now."

If possible, Sophie looked paler than she had before. The only reason Liam could come up with to explain her reaction was that she was still in love with his cousin.

"Oh yes, Sophie my girl, I know your secret," Colleen murmured as she slowly made her way from the dining room to the elevator beside the atrium. She knew everyone's secrets. There wasn't a person in Harmony Harbor who didn't have one. Along with the history of the town, she'd recorded them all in a leather-bound book. She'd called it *The Secret Keeper of Harmony Harbor*. Now, if she could only find the damn thing. Her memory wasn't what it used to be. She didn't mention it to Colin, but she was worried she'd been the one who turned on the fog machines and had forgotten that she did so.

A dull ache under her ribs forced her to stop a moment to catch her breath. She leaned heavily on her cane. The pain was coming more frequently these days. The excitement probably didn't help. Or maybe it was guilt that she'd meddled in her great-grandson and Sophie's affairs. Colleen's meddling had gotten her into trouble in the past. Truth be told, it nearly cost her the love of her son and husband. She thought back to that morning fifty years earlier. Had it really been that long? Bejaysus, she was old.

She rubbed her chest. She'd stopped meddling from that morning on…mostly. No doubt there would be hell to pay before this sorted itself out too. But she'd known the moment she saw Sophie and Mia what she had to do. It was…kismet. Sophie had arrived in Harmony Harbor just when Colleen needed her most. She'd kept tabs on Sophie when she was in California and knew exactly what the girl was made of. Smart, resourceful, and hardworking, Sophie had what it would take to turn Greystone's fortunes around.

Once Michael saw her again and met his daughter, he'd spend more time in Harmony Harbor. Which meant Bethany would eventually get tired of playing second fiddle to Michael's daughter and divorce him. Leaving Sophie to run the manor with Colleen's great-grandson at her side. Michael loved Greystone as much as Colleen. He'd protect the Gallagher legacy.

The door to the elevator slid open, and the black cat slunk inside. Colleen didn't have the energy to shoo him away and followed. She leaned against the brass rail for support. The pain expanded in her chest, and she couldn't breathe. She dropped her cane, frantically tugging at the top buttons on her blouse. They popped off, pinging against the walls of the elevator. She tried to call for help as she slid to the floor, but only a moan escaped from her mouth. Slumped against the wall, unable to lift her head from her shoulder, she watched the cat pad to her side. The animal's blue eyes suddenly seemed familiar and arresting. He rubbed his head against her cheek, the rumble of his purr and the softness of his fur calming the panic that had all but overwhelmed her moments before. Then, with one last look at her, Simon leaped from the elevator just before the door slid shut.

Chapter Seven

♥

So this is it, Colleen thought as her field of vision narrowed to pinpricks of light. Instead of pain, she was filled with a warm lethargy and acceptance. She was dying. She wasn't afraid. At a hundred and four, she'd been living on borrowed time. She was at peace. Soon she'd be reunited with her husband and children and all those who'd gone before her. In some ways, living for so long had seemed more penance than gift.

She made out the pounding of feet coming toward the elevator. Suddenly cool air and light filled the space, and she found herself cradled in strong arms before being gently laid on the floor. "You're going to be all right, GG. I've got you. Stay with me."

Aw, Liam my boy, I would save you from this if I could. You'll count me among those you couldn't save, won't you, child?

The boy needed the love of a good woman to mend his broken heart. But after the loss of his mother and sister, he

was afraid to love. Afraid to let anyone in. His brothers were
the same.

"The paramedics are on the way, Liam. Tell me what you
need me to do."

She recognized that voice. Soft but with an underlying
strength, compassionate and kind. It was Sophie. Now there
was a woman…Once again Colleen was overcome with
panic. She'd forgotten something. Something important. But
before she could tease the answer from her unreliable memory, her vision cleared. Liam's hands were pressed to her
chest, Sophie kneeling at his side. Colleen frowned. She was
floating above them. She heard a meow and looked down.
Simon stared up at her.

"So you can see me, can you?" she said, surprised to find
she had a voice.

No one below her reacted. They were focused on trying
to revive her. A commotion outside the elevator drew her attention. Ava pushed her way through the crowd to kneel at
Colleen's side across from Liam and Sophie, her voice was
calm and professional, reassuring. Liam's shoulders relaxed.
He was no longer in this battle alone.

*Oh, but of course the girl would know what to do,
wouldn't she? She'd left college only months before receiving her nursing degree.* Ava's secrets had stolen her joy, her
life and love, Colleen thought sadly. *I should have broken
my vow before now. Meddled sooner. Told Griffin…*Colleen
felt jumpy and anxious again. What had she forgotten? Meddling, it had to do with meddling. She was sure of it and just
as sure that somehow she'd made a hash of things. But her
worries disappeared when a warm, shimmering light beck-
oned from outside the elevator. She floated through the doors
to the atrium. The golden light glistened through the wall
of windows facing Kismet Cove, the white-capped waves

crashing against the rocks, the harbor in the distance, the deep blue ocean beyond.

Colleen smiled. It was time to go home. Filled with joy and anticipation, she moved toward the welcoming light, anxious to be reunited with her loved ones. She turned for one last fond look at those she'd leave behind. Her grandson Colin had arrived with the paramedics. They were preparing to load her body onto the gurney, but Liam refused to give up and waved them off. Ava across from him worked just as diligently to save her.

"It's time for me to go," Colleen whispered with a hint of regret. Worried how they'd fare without her, she asked the good Lord to bless her family by reciting an old Irish prayer: "May God give you…for every storm, a rainbow; for every tear, a smile; for every care, a promise; and a blessing in each trial. For every problem life sends, a faithful friend to share; for every sigh, a sweet song; and an answer for each prayer."

The words comforted her, and she floated toward the light. But at an insistent meow, she looked back to see Mia clutching Simon to her chest. The little girl looked up at Colleen, and her heart that had stopped beating gave a panicked thump. And not because she realized that the child could see her. Oh no, it was like someone was hammering on Colleen's brain, telling her to remember, telling her that she had indeed made a terrible mistake. Her meddling was going to hurt the ones she loved and put Greystone at risk. She couldn't leave until she'd discovered what she'd done wrong and made it right.

She floated to the gurney and tried to jump back into her body. She sailed through herself and ended up underneath the stretcher. She shook off the odd sensation to try again. But this time she backed farther away to get a running start…and once again whooshed through her body. As she sat beneath the gurney, she sensed someone watching her and turned. Crouching a few feet from the stretcher, Mia stared at her. The child glanced at the adults who were once again trying to revive Colleen and put Simon down.

Mia crawled between the legs of the paramedics. *Do it again,* she mouthed, and pointed above her at the gurney.

Colleen nodded and came to her feet. Her head and shoulders went through her stomach. "Clear," a paramedic said, and pressed the paddles to Colleen's chest. Her body jolted, and she ended up beneath the stretcher again.

"Ah well, child. It appears my time here is truly up."

A small frown pleated Mia's brow, her eyes focused on Colleen's lips. She couldn't hear her. With a fond smile, Colleen reached out to touch Mia's cheek in farewell, and her hand went through the child's face. Mia giggled. Colleen frowned. To her mind, if the child could laugh, she should be able to talk. She hadn't gotten anywhere with Mia earlier. There was no sense trying again. She couldn't hear her anyway. Sophie would have to sort it out.

Colleen waved and floated back to the atrium in search of the light. It was no longer there. The welcome mat to heaven had been rolled up. She felt a pang of regret. Perhaps it was for the best. If she had unleashed a storm with her meddling, she'd have the chance to make things right before facing her maker…and her husband and son.

She floated back to the gurney and stood behind Mia, who once again held Simon in her arms. "Time of death, fifteen hundred hours," the paramedic pronounced.

Colleen thought it rather ironic that she'd died on All Saints' Day. She was hardly a saint. She had her secrets too. But if she wanted to be ready the next time heaven rolled out the welcome mat, she had work to do. She had to find her book.

Sophie retrieved a tray of pizzelles and biscotti from the backseat of the Cadillac at the same time her grandmother picked up one piled high with zeppole and pignoli. Rosa had been baking for the past three days. From the amount of food piling up in the manor's kitchen, so had half the town.

Her grandmother hip-checked the passenger side door shut. "What do I know. I've only raised three children and you and your brothers."

Rosa was ticked at Sophie for refusing to bring Mia to the wake tonight. "She's been traumatized enough in the past week, Nonna. She saw Colleen die. She doesn't need to see her lying in an open casket." Not to mention being terrified the first night they'd arrived. At this rate, Mia would never speak.

Rosa rolled her eyes as Sophie joined her on the walkway. The wake was being held at Greystone as per Colleen's wishes. "She wanted to come. It would have been good for her. It shows respect. Ah well, she'll come to the funeral then."

Oddly enough, Mia *had* wanted to come. Her reaction to seeing Colleen die had been odd too. She hadn't been as upset as Sophie had expected her to be, and that worried her. Mia had put up such a fuss when she found out Sophie planned to leave her behind with Marco, that she'd been tempted to give in. Neither her grandmother nor her daughter had any idea how hard it was for Sophie not to bring Mia with her. But she wanted to protect her daughter like she hadn't been able to the day of the fire at their apartment and the day she got lost in Greystone's tunnels. Mia was just beginning to get over her nightmares. She wouldn't add another one to them.

"We'll see," Sophie said, even as her stomach clenched, rebelling at the thought of bringing Mia to the funeral. Michael and his family would be there. It was bad enough she'd have to attend.

Rosa adjusted the tray in her arms. "You baby the child."

Something her grandmother had told Sophie at least three times a day since they'd moved in. Now with her job at Greystone and the apartment that went with it in limbo, Sophie would have to continue biting her tongue.

"She's only sev…six. She's been through a lot."

"Ah, Michael. *Stupida*. I forgot. Better she didn't come tonight."

It still surprised Sophie every time her grandmother did that. Brought up Mia's father without asking anything more. It was just accepted. Something they'd deal with together. "Kitty says they're not coming tonight. They had a prior commitment. They'll be here in the morning." There would be another brief visitation before the funeral at noon tomorrow.

"You can't avoid him forever, *bella*. If they have their wedding here—"

"I don't even know if I still have the job, Nonna." She prayed that she did. Though in light of Colleen dying, she felt guilty for thinking about herself. "No one will know what's going to happen to Greystone until after the funeral. The Gallaghers are meeting with the lawyer then. And despite what Colleen told Hazel and Paige, Michael didn't agree to have the wedding here until he cleared it with his fiancée." Which was the only reason Sophie hadn't run from the office that day. But with the threat of Children's Services' impending visit hanging over her head, it was something she'd have to deal with. The job was too good to pass up.

"Colleen, she was a smart old lady. She will have made arrangements to protect Greystone." She glanced at Sophie. "You be sure they pay you for the time you put in."

Sophie had come to Greystone the morning after Colleen had died as though she had the job. Kitty had seemed glad to have her help organizing the upcoming wake and funeral. "I'm sure they will," she said as they reached the heavy, dark wood doors. Sophie noticed the black ribbons tied to the iron knockers and sighed. She understood Greystone was in mourning, but Colin and Kitty had agreed that Colleen wouldn't want the guests to feel uncomfortable and leave.

"I'll make sure they do. I'll talk to that old bag of bones," Rosa said, referring, Sophie knew, to Jasper.

Balancing the tray against the door frame, Sophie opened it. "No, you won't. Behave, Nonna. Kitty and Jasper are having a difficult time." Sophie reminded herself of the same thing every time Jasper countermanded one of her requests to the staff or vetoed her suggestions. He'd been with the Gallaghers for decades, so obviously he was feeling Colleen's loss. Even though Sophie suspected he'd treat her exactly the same way if she actually got the job. Something else to look forward to.

"What? You don't think I know that?" Rosa asked as she sashayed through the doors. Her grandmother had bought a new black dress for the occasion and spent the last hour in the bathroom doing her hair and makeup. In Harmony Harbor, wakes and funerals counted as a social event. Sophie hadn't spent much time on herself, but her grandmother had bought her a new dress too. Black, of course. Sophie loved the long-sleeved, wraparound knit dress just the same. She hadn't had a new dress in years.

"Ladies." Jasper nodded from where he stood in front of the elaborate spray of white roses intertwined with sprigs of shamrocks on the round table. As soon as Sophie stepped inside, she was hit by warm air dripping with the heavy scent of flowers, notably lilies. She'd be surprised if In Bloom, the flower shop in town, hadn't run out of stock. There wasn't a flat surface in the manor that didn't hold a floral arrangement.

Rosa thrust the tray at Jasper. "Sorry for your loss. She was a good, good woman. She will be missed."

"She will. Thank you," Jasper said as he accepted the tray.

"I will miss her myself, you know. She was good to me." Rosa opened her oversized purse and pulled out a handful of tissues to dab under her eyes. She sniffed. "Good for our town and for—"

Sophie heard the warble rising in her grandmother's voice and cut her off. "You should join your friends and Kitty in the sitting room, Nonna." There was a private viewing for the Widows Club for one hour prior to the wake opening to the public.

Jasper sent Sophie what appeared to be a relieved glance. Since his default facial expression was disapproval, at least where she was concerned, he'd obviously seen Rosa in her position as official keener before. Although from the sounds echoing off the lobby's cathedral ceiling, she had some competition.

"*Sì. Sì,*" her grandmother said, talking to herself in Italian as she made her way down the steps. Jasper's gaze followed Rosa across the lobby to the sitting room, and he gave his head an almost imperceptible shake.

"You can leave the tray on the table, Jasper. I have to make a phone call. I'll take the tray to the sitting room once I'm finished."

He opened his mouth to say something, then closed it

when a group of older women arrived. Sophie headed for the study to call her brother in private. She didn't think Kitty would mind. They'd organized the wake and funeral from there the past two days. As soon as she walked inside and closed the door behind her, she realized she wasn't alone.

The room was dark, except for the light from the green lamp that pooled on the desk and from the quarter moon streaming through the window where Liam stood. His back was to her, the black, well-cut suit he wore emphasizing his broad shoulders and long legs. His dark, wavy hair curled damply at the collar of his white shirt. She hadn't seen him since the day he'd worked valiantly to save his great-grandmother. She'd heard he'd been at the fire station to free up his father so the chief could spend time with Kitty.

Liam glanced over his shoulder, and she caught a brief glimpse of his perfect white teeth. He'd been Sophie's pet project back in the day. She'd studied him, could read every nuance of his face, his smile. She'd only ever gotten the tamped-down version of the charming but wicked smile he'd given the other girls in town. She got the one without heat. The one that said *You're cute but annoying.*

"Hey, Soph." His voice was like his smile…quiet.

"Sorry, I didn't mean to disturb you. Are you okay?" she asked as she made room for the tray on the desk.

"I'm good. How are you doing? How's Mia?"

She walked to his side and touched his arm, feeling the tension in his bicep. The same tension that hardened his chiseled profile. She wished she had the words to take some of his sorrow away. Instead she lifted on her toes to kiss his clean-shaven cheek. His skin smelled spicy and was warm against her lips. "We're good. I'm sorry for your loss. I didn't get a chance to tell you the other day." She glanced at the old-fashioned crystal tumbler in his hand. There was

a decanter of amber liquid sitting on the window ledge in
front of him. "Are you sure you're okay? You know you did
everything you possibly could to save her, don't you?" She
couldn't imagine how difficult it had been for him to work
on his great-grandmother, but he'd been amazing. He hadn't
hesitated or given up. Outwardly he'd appeared calm and
quietly confident.

He lifted the decanter and raised an eyebrow. "Have a
drink with me?"

"I shouldn't. I'm driving."

"Small glass. We'll drink a toast to GG."

She nodded and walked to the globe that served as a bar.
She retrieved a glass and handed it to him, watching as the
amber liquid splashed into the crystal. It looked delicate in
his large, capable hand. "Thank you." She lifted the glass
and touched it to his. "To Colleen, a woman who will live
forever in the hearts of everyone in Harmony Harbor."

He smiled. "There'll be no forgetting her. She was a force
to be reckoned with. To GG," he said, and they both took a
drink.

The whiskey burned a path down Sophie's throat, and she
choked. She waved a hand in front of her face. "That's, ah,
potent stuff."

Liam smiled and took the glass from her, setting it beside
the decanter. "You need some water?"

"No, I'm okay. What about you? Is there anything I can
get for you? I know this must be really hard for you, losing
Colleen."

"She was a hundred and four, Soph. We didn't expect her
to live forever."

"You seem so sad. I was worried...I thought maybe—"

"GG was an amazing woman. Greystone won't be the same
without her, and we'll all miss her, but I was thinking about

my granddad, mother, and sister." He looked out the window and took another drink. "They were waked here too. Mom and Riley then a few days after their funeral, Granddad."

"I'm so sorry, Liam. It must have been devastating for all of you to lose them like you did. I don't know if you got it, but I sent you a card."

"I did." He glanced at her. "I thought you'd come home or call."

She'd known the card wasn't enough when she'd sent it. He was her brother's best friend. She'd practically grown up with him and knew his mother well. Mary Gallagher had been a kind woman with an easy laugh and a warm smile for everyone she met. "I didn't have the money to fly home, Liam." She didn't add that, even if she had, she wouldn't have come home no matter how much she'd wanted to, and she did. More than any of them would ever know. "I didn't even have enough money to make a long-distance call."

He turned to face her, his brow furrowed, and put down his glass. "I thought you were living with your mother."

"No, she wanted me to give up Mia. We had a fight, and I moved out." Pregnant, broke, and alone, she'd never been more terrified in her life.

Her luck changed the next day when she got a job at a run-down motel. The pay wasn't great, and the work wasn't easy, but Doris, the tough-talking, chain-smoking owner, took Sophie under her wing. Tina waltzed back into Sophie's life a few months later. Doris had called Tina the night Mia was born. But she couldn't tell Liam any of this because Mia had been almost six months old the day Tina told Sophie about the tragedy that struck his family.

"Jesus, Soph, all you had to do was call your family. They would have—"

He had no idea how many times she'd picked up the

phone. "You weren't there the night my mom and I left, Liam. They practically disowned me."

"You should have called me then. I would have sent you the money. Jesus, if I knew it was that bad, I would have come and got you myself."

She looked away. She couldn't let him see how much his words meant to her. "Why would you? I—"

"Why? Because I was in love with you. I would have done anything for you back then."

She stared at him as the blood rushed from her head, leaving her weak-kneed and off balance. It couldn't be true. She didn't want it to be true. "W-why would you say something like that? You didn't even know I existed." She was surprised she sounded so calm when all she wanted to do was yell at him. Tell him to take it back. Because if there was any truth to what he said, any truth at all…

His laugh was rough. "Seriously? You didn't think I knew you existed? When I'd come home from school, it was you I spent time with, no one else. I took you surfing and fishing, combed the beaches for sea glass with you for hours, and you didn't think I was interested? Give me a break."

"Yes, you hung out with me and we spent a lot of time together, but not once did you ever look at me the way you did Arianna Summers, Mackenzie Ryan, and Lacy Bishop. You didn't flirt with me or—"

"No way was I going to make a move on you. You were sixteen, and I was twenty-one, and you were my best friend's baby sister. But you had to have known."

"How? How was I supposed to know?" Fighting back bitter tears, she flattened her palms on his chest and pushed him. If he would have given her the slightest hint he had feelings for her, she would have waited. She wouldn't have dated his cousin. She wouldn't have…

"Hey, why are you mad at me? I was trying to be a good guy and do the honorable thing. I was waiting until you turned eighteen."

"Thank you. Thank you so much for thinking for me, Liam. For not giving me any say in the matter. I was young, but I wasn't stupid." She pushed him again and swore at him in Italian. "I loved you. I loved you, you big idiot."

He stared at her and slowly shook his head. "No, you loved Michael. You told me you did. It wasn't me."

"No, I—" She swallowed the words that would give everything away. "Before Michael, it was only you, always you, Liam."

Several emotions crossed his face at once. She imagined he felt the same as she did moments ago—shocked, angry...bereft. He turned and picked up his glass, tossing back the amber liquid as he stared out the window. "It doesn't matter. It was a long time ago. But, Soph, the past has to stay in the past. I saw how you reacted when GG announced that Michael and Bethany were getting married here. You're still in love with him. They'll be here tomorrow—"

"What are you talking about? I'm not in love with him. I don't know why you'd say—"

"Really? So why did you look like you were about to faint? If you weren't upset that he was getting married, why were you doing this?" He put down the glass and took her hand, circling her wrist with his fingers, twisting them around and around.

He saw too much. She had to think of a believable excuse, but she was afraid he'd see through a lie. So she'd tell him the truth. Just not about Mia. Liam would never forgive her for keeping her daughter a secret from his cousin. Family meant everything to him. The Gallaghers were loyal through and through. They might have their disagreements, but they had each other's backs. They always had. "Trust me, I'm not in love with Michael. I don't want anything to do with him." She went to tug her hand from his, but he held on.

His thumb absently traced her scar; then he frowned and turned over her wrist. "What's this?"

She hesitated then reluctantly admitted, "I was arrested the day of the fire. The police dragged me out of my final exam and charged me with child neglect and endangerment. The officer who put the handcuffs on me wasn't gentle. I went a little crazy when they told me that Mia was in the hospital. I fought them. I tried to get away. I—"

He interrupted her, his fingers tightening around her wrist. "So you lied to Marco about the sitter being a no-show? You actually left Mia on her own and went to class?"

"How can you even ask me that? You know me." She jerked her hand from his, unconsciously curling her fingers around her wrist.

"Hey, I didn't mean to upset you." He took her hand and gently rubbed the scar. "I'm sorry, Soph. You're right, I do know you. Tell me what happened."

She looked out the window to the courtyard, tracing the outline of a tree with her finger on the glass. Anything to put off talking about what happened again. It was bad enough she had to live with it forever. But she felt Liam watching her and knew his patience would only last for so long. If there was anyone she wanted to know the truth, it was him. "It was my last exam to get my degree. My regular sitter, a neighbor in the building, had to go out of town for a family emergency. My friends were working, and there was no one else, so I asked my mother. I called and reminded her the night before and again that morning. I was late getting off work and had to take a bus route I wasn't familiar with. I was panicked, afraid I'd miss my exam, and didn't call Mia until I'd almost reached the school. My mother wasn't there. I called her cell. Her hot yoga class had run late. She was completely unfazed that Mia was on her own. She told me to relax, that she'd be there in ten minutes. I didn't trust her and called one of my friends. I was on the other side of town, and even if I took a taxi, it would have taken me at least forty minutes to get home. My friend, we were roommates, told me she'd go right away and not to worry and take the exam. She and my mom got there at the same time. It was almost too late." She looked up at Liam. "You can't tell Marco. Rosa knows, and that's bad enough. But Marco would tell Lucas, and they'd never forgive my mom."

"Can you?"

"I don't know." A waft of cold air brushed against her back, and she shivered.

Liam let go of her hand and drew her into his arms. "I'm sorry, Soph. So damn sorry you and Mia had to go through that. But it's over now. You're—"

"It's not over."

He drew back to look down at her. "What do you mean?"

"Just before the interview with Colleen, I got a call from Child Protective Services. They weren't happy I left the state before my in-home visit. My file has been transferred to a caseworker here. What if I don't live up to their expectations, Liam? What if they take Mia from—"

"Look at me. No one is going to take Mia from you." He cupped her face with his hands, ducking to meet her eyes. "Let me help you. I think I know someone I can talk to for you. And if I don't, I'm sure my dad does. Will you trust me to do this for you?"

"Yes, I trust you. I always did," she managed to say past the lump in her throat.

"I wish I would have known how you felt about me eight years ago."

"Me too." Sophie wasn't sure if she reached up on her toes or if he lowered his head. If he meant to comfort her or if she was seeking it when their lips met. The kiss was tentative, soft, and sweetly tender. But when his hands moved from her face and into her hair, and she moved hers between them to curl into his jacket, the kiss changed. She tasted the whiskey in his warm mouth, and he explored hers with a raw passion that made her moan and…

There was a heavy thud, like something had fallen. Sophia and Liam jerked apart at the same time the study door opened.

Chapter Eight

♥

Unable to take his eyes off the woman he'd just kissed, Liam blinked against the light that suddenly flooded the study. He'd kissed Sophie and made her moan one night years before. Instead of drinking his granddad's hundred-year-old whiskey, she'd been drinking cheap wine. But to Liam she'd tasted of sweet ambrosia and victory. He'd won the heart of the girl he loved. Or so he'd thought. If only she'd told him then what she had tonight—that she'd loved *him*. That one word would have changed his world and hers. She lifted her heavy-lidded eyes to his, desire slowly fading as reality and Jasper intruded.

The old man stood in the doorway with his mouth compressed and his eyes narrowed. It was an expression he'd directed at Liam more times than he cared to remember. At least when he was young. He didn't have only parents and grandparents to keep him on the straight and narrow; he had Jeeves. The Gallagher family watchdog.

"Your grandmother and Miss Kitty are waiting for you in the drawing room, Miss DiRossi."

Her eyes flicking from Liam to Jasper, Sophie said, "Thank you. I'll be right there. I have a call to make."

"My apologies. I presumed you would have made your call by now."

Sophie stiffened and lifted her chin. "Apology accepted. I'll be with them in a moment," she said, a note of dismissal in her voice.

Liam wondered if Jasper could tell that, beneath the bravado, Sophie was embarrassed to be caught in a compromising position. To anyone else, a kiss wouldn't be considered compromising or a position. But to a woman who hoped to manage Greystone and a man whose employee handbook dated back to the dark ages, it was. Now, if Jasper hadn't interrupted them…

Maybe he owed the old man his thanks, Liam thought as his eyes were drawn back to the dark-haired beauty in a black dress that hugged her curves. She wasn't the girl he remembered. Too many years had passed. Too many things left unsaid. If he told her now, he risked losing her trust. He wanted her to trust him. Whether she'd admit it or not, she needed his help—for her own sake and Mia's. Due to her misplaced sense of loyalty to her mother, she wouldn't tell Marco, and her grandmother wouldn't know how to help her, but Liam did.

She waited until Jasper left the room before taking her cell phone from the pocket of her coat. "I have to call Marco."

"Do you want me to leave?"

"No, of course not. I'm just checking on Mia." She turned to the window and spoke to her brother.

Liam bent down and picked up the book that had fallen

to the floor, placing it on the desk. He smiled when Sophie cursed out Marco in Italian. "Problem?" he asked once she returned her phone to her pocket.

"I told him Mia can watch *Casper*, and what does he put on? *Halloween Five*. She's…six, and he's got her watching horror movies. If that doesn't give her nightmares, the pop, candy apples, and popcorn will. He's thirty-one going on fifteen."

Liam struggled to hold back a laugh. His best friend was an idiot, but he had his back. "Most guys are. Betcha he ends up being Mia's favorite babysitter."

"No, that would be you. I think you're the reason she put up such a fuss about coming tonight."

He liked the kid…a lot, and he liked kissing her mother a lot too. But he and Sophie had a complicated past, and gorgeous single moms with adorable daughters were not in his wheelhouse. The rules in his playbook might not be as old as the ones in Jasper's handbook, but they were as non-negotiable. A relationship with Sophie would be the polar opposite of keeping it easy and simple. There was nothing simple or easy about Sophie DiRossi.

"Liam, did I say something wrong?"

"No…" He rubbed his jaw. "Soph, about the kiss—"

"You don't have to say anything. I was upset, and so were you. It was a mistake. I'm sorry. It won't happen again. You know, I should probably get going. Rosa—"

He grabbed her hand before she took off. "Wait. You have nothing to apologize for. I just don't think a relationship right now is a good idea for either of us."

She frowned. "A relationship? How did we go from a kiss to a relationship?"

He didn't have a clue. "That's not what I meant to say. Okay, so maybe I thought seeing that you're a single mother, you wouldn't be looking for just a good time. You're not, are you?"

"I'm a healthy twenty-six-year-old who hasn't had sex in six years. So what do you think?"

He wasn't thinking. He couldn't. Every ounce of blood from his head had gone south.

She started to laugh. "You should see your face. I've shocked you, haven't I? I'm sorry. I don't know what made me say that. Other than that it's true, I guess. Don't worry. I'm not going to compromise your honor, Liam. I'm just tired and stressed. I have a daughter to think about, and a life to rebuild." She glanced at the door. "You don't think Jasper will tell Kitty about us, do you?"

Did she really expect him to be able to speak right now? She was staring up at him with an anxious look in her big eyes, so obviously she did. He jammed his hands in his pant pockets and tried to surreptitiously adjust himself while clearing his throat. "No, there's nothing to tell. He didn't see anything."

"He acted as though he did."

"He always looks like that. Don't let him get to you....Listen, I was serious about helping you with Protective Services."

"If you want to help me, the best thing you can do for me is make sure I keep my job here."

Now that could be a problem. Before he could come up with a way not to give her too much hope or steal it away, her phone beeped.

"Sorry, it might be Marco." She retrieved her cell from her pocket, looked at the screen, sighed then answered. "Yes, Nonna. I'm coming—" She glanced at Liam.

Worried that his inward groan at the thought of Sophie and orgasms hadn't been so inaudible after all, he walked casually to the desk and grabbed a cookie. He stuffed it in his mouth.

"No. It's a private viewing for the Widows Club, and I'm not…You what? *Sì. Sì.* I'm—" She glanced at Liam again. He picked up another cookie. "I'll be right there." She shrugged out of her coat. When she turned to lay it over the back of the chair, Liam promptly choked on the cookie. The dress hugged the lush curves of an ass that his fingers had brushed against only a few days before.

She glanced over her shoulder. "Are you okay? Do you need some water?"

No, he needed a cold shower and to stay as far away as possible from Sophie. "I'm good."

Jasper reappeared in the study two minutes after she'd rushed off. The old man eyed Liam as he took another cookie. "Ah, I see."

"What do you see, Jeeves?"

"A man who'd best have a care. You stand to lose more than you stand to gain, Master Liam."

Sophie had just passed the reception desk when she realized she'd forgotten the cookies. Which shouldn't have come as a surprise since she'd lost her head and her filter. *I haven't had sex in six years,* she mimicked herself. Honestly, what had she been thinking to say that to Liam of all people? It was that kiss, the feel of his…*Oh, would you stop?* she berated herself. She had enough to deal with without getting herself all hot and bothered thinking about Liam. Thanks to her grandmother, she was now an honorary member of the Widows Club. Honorary because she hadn't been married to Mia's fake father who fake died.

She consoled herself with the thought that surely she'd met her quota of stress-inducing events for the day. Hopefully she'd be able to take fifteen minutes to sit in a corner and relax with a cup of coffee. But she was barely ten feet from the drawing room when the wailing and keening she'd heard earlier started up again. Earplugs...all she needed was earplugs and she'd zone out in a secluded corner of the sitting room. She turned to head for the reception desk and was nearly run over by a bald-headed man—his face red—pushing a television on a stand toward the sitting room.

"Sorry, my dear." He stopped to rub his sweaty brow with a white hankie then offered his hand. "George Wilcox."

"Sophie DiRossi."

"Ah, just the young woman I was looking for. I'm the Gallagher family's attorney. I"—he looked around and lowered his voice—"Kitty tells me that Colleen had every confidence in you, my dear. She felt certain you could turn the manor's fortunes around."

"Thank you. Greystone won't be the same without her. But I'm not sure I still have a job, Mr. Wilcox."

"You do. Obviously I can't share with you the contents of the will, but it is imperative that you do whatever you can to show a profit as quickly as possible. The mayor and that realtor aren't about to give up. I've been fielding calls from Paige Townsend for the past two days. The woman has no respect for the dead."

Sophie's relief that she had the job was tempered by the knowledge that Paige was hovering in the wings. Looking for any opportunity to swoop in and steal Greystone out from under the Gallaghers. Sophie owed it to Colleen, and to Kitty, not to let her get away with it. Which meant they needed to host Michael's wedding. "I appreciate the opportunity and Colleen's faith in me. I won't let her down, Mr. Wilcox."

"I'm glad to hear it. It's up to us to see her wishes are

fulfilled. I'll contact you once the Gallaghers have been apprised of the situation. Any changes or upgrades to the manor will be cleared through me. Some monies have been set aside, but not enough for any major renovations. Let's hope Michael and Bethany decide to hold their wedding here. I'll try to guilt them into it tomorrow." He winked. "Now, Colleen taped a final message for the Widows Club. Would you mind helping me?"

"Of course." Sophie took hold of the opposite side of the stand, and they wheeled it into the dark-paneled room. Colleen's rosewood casket sat open beneath a window framed by heavy red velvet drapes with tiered stands of floral arrangements at either end. The four rows of chairs forming a semicircle around the casket were mostly filled. Two older women knelt side by side on the kneeler.

Apparently they were trying to outdo each other's show of grief. One would wail, and the other would wail louder. Mr. Wilcox grimaced as he situated the television a couple feet from the head of Colleen's casket. The older woman was dressed in a somber navy jacket, skirt, and white blouse, a silver rosary intertwined through her white-gloved fingers.

Sophie's gaze moved to Colleen's face, and she did a double take. Kitty should have prepared her mother-in-law for the wake, Sophie thought as she took in Colleen's rosy red cheeks on her otherwise pallid face, her eyebrows darkened to frame her blue-shadowed lids. The short silver waves that had once framed her face were tightly curled.

"Ladies, Colleen left a final message for you. I'll leave you to your privacy," Mr. Wilcox said, drawing Sophie's attention from Colleen. He handed her the remote. "I'll be at the bar if you need me." He looked more than a little relieved to get out of there when several women started to cry. Sure enough, Rosa was one of them. Sophie was tempted to follow Mr. Wilcox to the bar.

"Sophie dear, not all the ladies have arrived. We'll give them a few more minutes," Kitty said from where she sat surrounded by her friends. The new matriarch of Harmony Harbor and the Gallagher clan seemed to be holding up well under her grief. She looked elegant in a black pantsuit trimmed with black jet beads. Her makeup, unlike Colleen's, was tasteful and her hair elegantly coiffed.

At the aroma of freshly brewed coffee coming from the other side of the room, Sophie made a beeline for the long banquet table loaded down with pastries and sandwiches. From the corner of her eye, she noticed Ava hovering outside the doors to the sitting room. Her cousin wore a gray sweater over a shapeless black dress with her long hair scraped back from her pale face. Ava spotted Sophie and hurried to her side. "I'm so glad you're here," her cousin whispered.

Despite seeing Ava every day, Sophie still found it difficult to get used to the changes in her. It was like her cousin did her best to look unattractive. But she couldn't disguise her exquisite bone structure or stunning green eyes. Sophie smiled. "I'm surprised you're here, but I'm glad you are."

Ava tugged the sleeves of her sweater over her hands and curled her fingers around the gray wool. "They made an exception for me. I'm pretty sure Colleen badgered them into submission. She decided I needed a social outlet. I'm the token divorcée."

Sophie could tell her cousin would rather be anywhere else but here, but she thought it was sweet that Colleen had invited Ava to join the Widows Club. Even though Ava had divorced her great-grandson, Colleen had been looking out for her in her own way.

They got their coffees and found two empty seats to the

left of the table. "I got the job," Sophie whispered once they were seated.

Ava squeezed her hand. "I'm so glad. Please tell me we don't have to wear the costumes anymore."

"They'll be the first to go. I don't want to step on anyone's toes, though. I was hoping you'd help me out. Be my eyes and ears."

Ava nodded, her gaze darting around the room. "I keep to myself, but I hear things. There's already been some chatter. I'm sure it will die down once they know they still have their jobs. At least for now. Did Colleen leave the manor to Kitty?"

"I'm not sure, but she'd be the most likely choice. Mr. Wilcox is talking to the family tomorrow after the funeral."

"We better hope it is Kitty. If Colleen left Greystone to her grandchildren, Colin will be outvoted. Maura and Tara will push to sell," Ava said, her knee bouncing.

"Are you okay? You seem nervous."

"Griffin's arriving tonight. Kitty asked me to make up his room. Or I should say *their* room. His wife will be joining him."

Poor Ava. Sophie's problems were nothing compared to hers. At least she wasn't in love with Michael, and he had no idea Mia was his. "Really? I thought they divorced a couple years ago."

"They did. I guess they've reconciled. *Non mi importa*," she added when Sophie cast her a concerned glance. Ava might say she didn't care, but Sophie didn't believe her.

Dana Templeton looked their way as she entered the room and gave them a wan smile. Sophie had made a point of introducing herself to the tall, willowy redhead the other day.

Ava leaned into Sophie. "She's hiding from someone."

"Why would you say that?"

"She's wearing a wig. She has other ones in her room, colored contacts too."

"Maybe she's sick?"

"In the head, *sì*. The medication that woman takes, it's a wonder she can walk and talk." She shrugged. "Ah well, everyone has their *accidenti*."

Her cousin was right. They all had their crap to deal with. Sophie made a mental note to keep a close eye on Dana. The last thing Greystone needed was another death. Sophie crossed herself.

"Auntie Rosa is rubbing off on you," Ava said with a smile then glanced at the entrance to the sitting room. "This should be interesting. Here comes Maggie." She nodded at an attractive fiftysomething redhead wearing a vibrant eggplant-colored cape over an ankle-length skirt two shades lighter paired with fringed boots. A multitude of colorful bangles jangled on her arm when she waved to the women with one hand while pulling a cart behind her. On the cart, there appeared to be a framed picture wrapped in black fabric. "Colleen commissioned her to paint a portrait of her. Look at Kitty's face."

"Why does she look…panicked?"

"Maggie's famous for her nudes. She owns an art gallery in town called Impressions. Very chichi."

"She wouldn't paint a hundred-and-four-year-old woman in the buff. Would she?"

"If anyone would, it would be Maggie. You'll like her. I doubt she did, though. Rumor has it she's dating Colin, and the Gallagher men are prudes."

If that was true, Sophie could only imagine what Liam thought when she overshared about her sex life. She wondered if Ava noticed what was surely Sophie's now-red face. But her cousin was focused on the drama unfolding across the room. Kitty appeared to be trying to talk Maggie out of displaying the painting with several of her friends backing her up.

"You've seen my work before, Kitty. I don't know what you're worried—" Maggie began as she took the painting off the cart.

Kitty grabbed hold of one end, and the two women started a tug-of-war. "Yes, I have, and that's what I'm worried about. I can't have a naked portrait of—"

Rosa got up from her chair. "*Basta!* Enough! You must honor Colleen's wishes."

"Thank you, Rosa," Maggie said, retrieving her painting from Kitty.

"*Prego.*" Rosa straightened her dress as though she'd been in a fight. Then she walked to Maggie's side to help her remove the seascape that hung on the wall.

"Okay, everyone, close your eyes. Not you, Rosa. I need your help," Maggie said.

Sophie closed her eyes along with the other women. She heard Maggie and Rosa whispering. There was a dull clunk, a few muttered Italian curse words, and then, "*Molto bella.* Look, ladies, look what Maggie has created. It is a masterpiece."

Sophie opened her eyes at her grandmother's reverent tone. Maggie had painted the manor at sunset. The angle was such that you were looking down on Greystone with Kismet Cove, the lighthouse, and the harbor in the background. Sophie didn't see any sign of Colleen until she lifted her eyes to the orange and red dappled sky. There she was, watching over her legacy like a guardian angel. And not just Colleen. Behind her were smaller images of the family members who'd gone before her. Sophie made out Ronan, Mary, and a little girl she assumed was Riley.

Her grandmother was right. The painting was beautiful, magical, and whimsical. The artist was not only incredibly talented, but she also clearly knew and loved her subjects.

Her cousin sniffed beside her, wiping her eyes on the sleeve of her sweater. Sophie slid her arm around Ava's shoulders. Her cousin had worked at Greystone for almost a decade, and she'd been a Gallagher for three years. In her heart, maybe she still was.

"I'll miss her. I didn't realize until now how much," Ava said on a broken whisper.

Sophie gave her cousin's shoulder a comforting squeeze.

"Kitty?" Maggie said, playing with her bangles. "What do you think?"

Seemingly overcome with emotion, Kitty pressed a hand to her mouth and shook her head. The mourners got up from their chairs and moved closer to inspect the painting and much oohing and aahing ensued. They made room for Kitty when she finally pulled herself together. She stared at the painting, raising a finger as though to touch each of her loved ones. Then she turned to face Maggie, her cheeks damp with tears. "I don't know what to say. I never expected anything like this. It's a precious gift, Maggie. You're a gift. I know it's not enough, but thank you."

Pretty much all the women started to cry again. Though it was hard to tell if her grandmother was one of them. Rosa stood with her back to the room staring at the painting. When she finally turned around, she swiped at her eyes and said, "Sophie, our hour is nearly up. Colleen's message."

Once the women had shifted their chairs to get a better view of the television, Sophie pressed the remote. Colleen's voice was muffled. A heavy oak dresser with a mirror filled the screen. Colleen was visible in the mirror, her face the picture of frustration as she moved the hand-held video camera around and a stone wall appeared, and then a window.

Laughter filled the room. "She never did figure out how to use a camera, or her phone," someone said.

Colleen's nose and eyes filled the screen. "Hello, can you hear me?" She held the camera out from her face. "Jaysus, who the hell is that? Is that me?" She touched her face. "I guess it is. Why was I doing this anyway? Oh right." She leaned closer to the screen again and shouted, "If you're watching this, I've gone to meet my maker. I'll be with my loved ones now. Not that I don't love all of you, I do…or I did." She waved her hand. "You know what I mean. Anyway, I want you to carry on when I'm gone. Finish what we started. We need the younger generation to come home to Harmony Harbor. I've done my part." She grinned. "Batten down the hatches, ladies. It's going to be a bumpy ride."

She held up a brown leather-bound book. "This is the real reason I've recorded this message for you. I've about finished my memoir, *The Secret Keeper of Harmony Harbor*. I've written down all of the town's secrets, yours and mine too." There was an audible gasp from the audience, and the women moved to the edge of their seats, Sophie included. If she'd been wrong and Colleen had known her secret…

Several of their voices rose above a whisper. Someone shushed them. "I wouldn't want it to fall into the wrong hands, so it's probably best if I tell you where I've hidden—" The screen filled with static.

Rosa waved her arms, yelling, "Sophie, hurry, fix it!"

"Yes, dear God, fix it. We can't lose her now," someone else yelled.

"I'm trying." Sophie stood up and moved closer to the television.

Ava grabbed the remote from her, aiming it at the TV and frantically pressing buttons. Nothing worked; the static got worse, and then the screen went black.

"Maybe it was the cat. See him? He's sitting right there," another woman called out, pointing to where Simon sat at the foot of the stand, watching them with a bored expression on his face.

While everyone yelled suggestions at Ava, Sophie took advantage of the distraction and edged toward the door. She walked casually from the sitting room and then sprinted for the stairs. Colleen had made the video in her bedroom; Sophie was sure of it.

She ran up the stairs to the second floor and down the hall, taking the next set of stairs to the third floor. Out of breath by the time she reached the circular staircase leading to the tower, she paused for a minute and leaned on the brass rail. She should have taken the elevator. At the sound of running feet two floors below her, she pushed on. If Colleen had known about Mia, Sophie had too much to lose if someone discovered the book before she did.

She reached the upper landing where gold-framed Gallagher family portraits graced the stone walls. The entire fourth floor was reserved for Kitty's and Colleen's suites. From her time working at the manor, Sophie knew that the walnut-colored studded door she now stood in front of led to Colleen's. She hesitated, feeling uncomfortable invading the older woman's private space. With a whispered apology, Sophie opened the door. After all, Colleen wanted them to find the book.

The scent of roses wafted past Sophie's nose as she entered the room. A crystal vase overflowing with rainbow-colored roses stood on the nightstand beside the dark wood canopied bed, a book lying open on the red-and-gold bedspread. Sophie's heart raced as she turned it over—disappointed to discover it was a book of poetry and not Colleen's memoir. Her gaze flitted over the Gothic style leaded windows that overlooked the gardens, the oil painting of the harbor hanging over the unused fireplace with the wrought-iron branch of candles standing in front of it, to the sitting area.

Shelves of books lined the walls while others were piled haphazardly on the antique tables on either side of a well-worn love seat, additional stacks creating small towers on the hardwood floor. A cluttered feminine desk sat in the center of the area rug with a spectacular view of the ocean through the French doors that led onto a stone balcony. One of the doors was slightly ajar, letting in the sound of waves hitting the rocks, and the cool breeze, which ruffled the red-leafed vines climbing the balcony walls.

Rubbing her arms against the chill, Sophie moved to the door and closed it. As she did, she scanned the rows of books on the shelves, searching for a binding similar to the one Colleen had held up. But there was no sign of the brown leather-bound book. At the sound of running feet on the tower stairs, she raced to the door to lock it. She was too late. Ava and Dana burst into the room, breathless and flushed.

"Did you find it?" Ava asked, her eyes frantically searching the room.

Sophie opened her mouth to answer at the same time Rosa, Kitty, and Maggie shoved their way inside, sending Ava and Dana stumbling toward the bed. Unlike Sophie, her grandmother, Kitty, and Maggie had no compunction invading Colleen's space. Neither did the rest of the Widows Club, who arrived a few minutes later. Books flew off the shelves, clothes out of the dresser drawers, papers out of the desk. Sophie joined her grandmother to search under the bed.

"Look for loose floorboards," Rosa directed, cursing when she bumped her head on the bed frame.

"It's okay, Nonna. This is my problem, not yours. I'll—"

Her grandmother's eyes flicked to Sophie, a touch of pink coloring her prominent cheekbones. She went back to trying to pry the floorboards loose as though Sophie hadn't spoken. It was then that she realized her grandmother didn't want to find the book to protect Sophie's secret; Rosa had one of her own. Just like every woman in this room.

Twenty minutes later, she and her grandmother crawled out from beneath the bed. They had nothing but broken fingernails and dust bunnies covering their black dresses to show for their efforts.

A woman with steel-gray curls entered the room holding up a mangled videotape. "We won't be getting anything off this. It's fried."

An hour later, Kitty voiced what everyone else had deduced by that time. "The book isn't here."

Chapter Nine

♥

Sophie had managed to find a parking spot across the road from the church. Probably because her grandmother had insisted they arrive thirty minutes before the funeral. If Sophie had gone to work this morning, that would have been a problem, but she'd called in sick. After learning about Colleen's memoir and being unable to find it, she'd spent half the night tossing and turning and hadn't been up for an early morning face-to-face with Michael and Maura Gallagher. She'd considered skipping the funeral and reception afterward altogether.

But she'd been thinking more clearly following a hot shower and several cups of coffee and had given herself a mental kick in the pants. She needed the job, and if she had any hope at all of turning Greystone's fortunes around, she needed Michael and Bethany to choose the manor as the venue for their wedding. They needed the publicity to attract the attention of the numerous wedding and event planners Kitty and Colleen had turned away over the past seven years.

Even though Colleen's infamous memoir could lead to Sophie's downfall, she wanted to prove that Colleen's faith in her hadn't been misplaced.

Before they left for the church, Sophie had called to tell Jasper she was feeling better, and she'd be there to handle the reception. To which she received a snotty "Perhaps it would be best if you stayed at home, Miss DiRossi. At least until you're fully recovered."

He had no idea how much she'd like to do just that. The day promised to be as dark and foreboding as the weather. A light drizzle fell from the slate-gray clouds hanging above the spire of the brick church.

"Careful, Mia," Sophie warned her daughter, gripping her hand a little tighter as they started across the road. The temperature was steadily dropping, and she was worried Mia would slip. One of Rosa's friends had dug up some of her granddaughter's old clothes and given them to Mia. Black shoes, tights, a jumper, and a white blouse that she wore beneath a red velvet coat with a Peter Pan collar.

Rosa tilted her black umbrella to give Sophie a smug smile. "She's excited to go to the funeral, aren't you, bambina?"

Mia nodded, tugging at Sophie's hand to hurry her along.

Sophie didn't understand why her grandmother thought a seven-year-old being excited to attend a funeral was a good thing. It struck Sophie as odd and worrisome. The only reason she could come up with for her daughter's ebullient mood was that Mia wanted to see Liam. Or maybe thanks to Marco's choice of movies, and the fire, nothing frightened her, and she'd developed a taste for the macabre.

"You have to be quiet…," Sophie began then sighed; obviously that wasn't a problem. "Sit still and be respectful in church, baby."

Her grandmother's eyes narrowed when they reached the sidewalk. "You didn't take her to church in Hollywood?"

Sophie wasn't up for a lecture and was about to say that of course she did, when Mia shook her head at the same time slanting a glance from under her long lashes at Sophie. She was beginning to think her daughter took pleasure in throwing her under the bus. "There wasn't a church in our area," she defended herself.

Rosa pursed her lips. "You will come to church with Nonna from now on, bambina. You're in second grade, *sì* ? You will have your Reconciliation and First Communion next year. We'll—"

"First." Sophie cleared her throat. "She's in first grade."

Mia tugged her hand from Sophie and waved two fingers at her and then at her great-grandmother.

"Ah, we may have a *problema*," Rosa said with a grimace.

Ya think? Sophie wanted to say, but instead forced a smile for her ticked-off daughter. "We'll talk about it when we get home." Only they weren't going home right away because they were going to the reception at the manor. Of course her grandmother wouldn't miss that. And her brother, who cooked as well as Rosa, had agreed to help out at the reception. So Sophie had no choice but to bring Mia with her. Which meant her problems were increasing at an alarming rate.

They walked up the steps to the church doors. A priest wearing white vestments greeted her grandmother warmly as they entered the vestibule. Sophie was relieved to see it wasn't Father Garibaldi. Short and thickset with dark eyes that seemed to see through to your soul, he'd been old school—all fire and brimstone. Sophie spent most of her teenage years convinced she was going to hell.

Rosa introduced them to Father O'Malley. "Welcome to

Immaculate Conception," he said. He looked to be in his
midthirties. He was handsome with curly brown hair, and his
hazel eyes were kind behind his wire-framed glasses.

"Sophie, she used to go to church here. They've just
moved back to Harmony Harbor. We'll be here every Sun-
day." Rosa glanced at Sophie. "She'll be at confession on
Saturday—"

"Nonna." Sophie gave the priest a self-conscious smile.
"It's nice to meet you, Father O'Malley. We should probably
take a seat."

His eyes crinkled at the corners with what looked to be
amusement. "It's nice to meet you, too, Sophie. And you,
Mia."

They walked into the nave. The main part of the church
smelled of lilies and furniture polish. "Honestly, Nonna, did
you have—" Sophie began.

"What? Confession is good for your soul. Maybe it would
be good for you to—"

"Not today, okay?" The day was going to be difficult
enough without her grandmother making Sophie feel as
though she wore a scarlet *S* on her forehead. She wasn't that
bad. She didn't believe God would punish her for having sex
before she was married or being an unwed mother. The lies,
though…Yes, the lies might be a problem. They kept growing, compounding.

All she was trying to do was protect Mia, and, yes, herself. Sadly, those same lies she'd been telling to protect her
daughter were driving them apart. At this point, if Mia found
out Michael was her father, she'd probably leave Sophie
without a backward glance. Her chest grew tight with panic
at the thought. If she lost her daughter, Sophie didn't know
how she'd go on.

Her grandmother shrugged and dipped her fingers in the

font, blessing herself with holy water. Sophie did the same. She picked up Mia, dipping her small fingers in the holy water and teaching her to make the sign of the cross. Mostly because she needed to hold her in her arms. Sophie pressed her face into the soft, silky waves, smelling the lingering scent of baby shampoo. She'd made a mess of everything, and she didn't have a clue how to make things right.

Her grandmother started down the blue-carpeted aisle toward the front of the church. "Nonna," Sophie called out to her in a half-whisper. The pews were beginning to fill up. She recognized several local business owners and a couple of people she'd gone to school with, and smiled. Mia wriggled out of her arms. Sophie put her down, grabbing her hand before she took off after Rosa. "Nonna," she tried again, waving at her grandmother, who'd stopped to chat with several members of the Widows Club.

"We'll sit here," Sophie told Mia, ushering her daughter to the dark oak pew at the back. She wanted to be as far from the Gallagher family as possible. Surprisingly, Mia didn't argue and took her place closest to the aisle.

Her grandmother walked toward them, making an *eh* gesture with her hands. "What are you doing back here? Come, I found us a seat at the front."

Sophie nodded at Mia. "If we have to leave, we won't disturb anyone." It wasn't really a lie.

Her grandmother cast one last longing look toward the front of the church before taking her seat between Sophie and Mia. Rosa pulled down the padded kneeler. "Come, you pray with Nonna."

Watching her grandmother patiently teach her daughter to pray, Sophie was overcome with guilt. She'd forced Rosa, a God-fearing woman, into the untenable position of lying for her. Sophie joined them on the kneeler. She needed a way out of this mess. They'd just sat back on the bench when Ava arrived. Her cousin had exchanged her gray sweater of last night for a black trench coat that looked like it could wrap around her twice. Her grandmother clicked her tongue. "There's nothing left of that girl." When Ava joined them, Rosa asked, "Where's Gino?"

Rosa had been married to Gino's older brother, Antonio. Gino had been a commercial fisherman; his legs had been crushed in an accident on the boat six months after Ava had divorced Griffin. Gino was confined to a wheelchair, and Ava had been taking care of him ever since. Rosa, never one to keep her opinion to herself, blamed Gino for working Ava to the bone.

Her cousin took a seat beside Sophie. "He's not feeling well. The damp weather is hard on him."

"Weather." Rosa made a disparaging sound in her throat. "He drinks too much."

Sophie nudged her grandmother.

"What? It's true. Look at you, *cara*," Rosa said to Ava. "You are skin and bones. You want me to talk to him? I'll talk to him. Give him a piece of my mind, I tell you."

"I'm good, Auntie Rosa. I'm coming down with something, that's all."

Rosa snorted. "Just like Sophie. The two of you never should have gotten involved with a Gallagher. I warned you about that family, but do either of you listen? Oh no, you both—"

"Nonna, keep your voice down." Sophie practically had to sit on her hands to keep from covering her grandmother's mouth. In Italian, she reminded Rosa about little ears. Sophie didn't know why she'd ever shared her secret with her grandmother. The stress must have caused her to lose her mind.

"What Gallagher is she talking about?" Ava whispered to Sophie.

She glanced at her grandmother, who'd taken a child's prayer book from her purse to give to Mia. If Michael and Bethany ended up having their wedding at Greystone, Sophie would need an ally. "I'll tell you later. Did Griffin arrive with his wife last night?" Sophie had left the manor not long after their futile search of Colleen's rooms. The funeral home's staff had managed the wake.

"I was finishing up their room when they got there." She made an embarrassed sound in her throat. "I don't think he knew who I was. His wife asked me for more towels."

Sophie briefly closed her eyes. She could only imagine how Griffin and his wife's interaction with Ava had made her feel. The same way Sophie had felt the day she'd overheard Michael and his mother in the study—like she was nothing. Sophie didn't know Griffin's wife, but she did know him. Unlike Michael's parents, Griffin's were down-to-earth and had brought up their children to be respectful and kind. But her cousin had been the one to ask Griffin for a divorce, and twenty years as a Navy SEAL might have changed the man Sophie remembered.

She closed her hand over her cousin's and gave it a light squeeze. "I'm sorry. They won't be here for long. I overheard Kitty tell Jasper they're leaving tomorrow. Don't help out at the reception. Go home and get some rest."

Sophie had asked Ava to help prepare the food for the reception the day after Colleen had died. She'd had an ulterior motive for the request. She'd approached Helga, who'd run the manor's kitchen for the last five decades, with some ideas to freshen up the outdated menu, as well as suggesting what should be served at the reception following the funeral. Helga had shut her down and basically thrown her out of her kitchen. If that was all it was, Sophie could probably find a way to work with the older woman.

But outdated menus and a temperamental chef weren't her only problems. Sophie had been fielding complaints from guests about the food for the past two days. They were sending their meals back to the kitchen uneaten. The waste was out of control and costly. Which is why Sophie had been playing with the idea of leasing out the space to an independent restaurateur. It was the perfect way to cut costs while guaranteeing their guests a pleasant dining experience. And she had the perfect candidate in mind—her cousin.

"It's more peaceful at the manor. I'm helping out in the kitchen. It's not like I'll run into him." Ava bowed her head and picked at a loose button on her trench coat. "You'd think it wouldn't be so hard to see him after all this time," she murmured.

If her cousin wasn't stuck in a rut, if she actually started living again, it wouldn't be so hard. As a little girl, Sophie remembered Ava cooking in her grandmother's kitchen, laughing and dancing, filled with passion and life. She wanted to see that girl again. Other than Rosa, no one could cook like Ava. Besides Marco, Ava was the only one Rosa allowed in her kitchen.

As the organist began to play "Be Not Afraid," the staff from the manor filed into the church, taking up three pews in the middle section to their right. Mia leaned over the benches' armrest to get a better view. Sophie reached past her grandmother to tug on Mia's coat. "Sit down, baby."

Then Marco, looking handsome in his dress uniform, walked in with a large contingent of firefighters. He lifted his chin in greeting before following his coworkers. They took up the pews in front of the manor's staff, just behind where the Gallagher family would be seated. Sophie stiffened at the sound of voices coming from the vestibule as the organist transitioned to "Here I Am, Lord."

The Gallagher family had arrived.

She glanced at Ava. If possible, she was paler than when she'd joined them in the pew. Sophie imagined she looked the same as she prepared to see Michael for the first time. The congregation came to their feet as Colleen's six grandsons wheeled the casket into the aisle.

Michael stood on the left, staring straight ahead, as tall, dark, and handsome as she remembered. Griffin was on his right, the tallest and broadest of Colleen's great-grandsons. Fairer than his brothers and cousins, he took after his mother. Liam was in the middle across from his brother Aidan. Michael's brothers brought up the rear.

Father O'Malley, with an altar boy and girl behind him, placed the white baptismal cloth on the casket and said the blessing. Liam stood so close to their pew that his black coat brushed against it. Before Sophie could stop her, Mia tugged on his coat. Liam looked down at her daughter and winked; then he glanced at Sophie. Her eyes got caught up in his warm Gallagher-blue gaze, and her mouth went dry. Despite that telling reaction, it would have been safer if she kept looking into his eyes. But it seemed, when it came to Liam, self-preservation was no longer her number one priority. She let her gaze drift to his full, sensuous lips, remembering how they'd felt on hers. His mouth tipped up at the corner, and she dropped her gaze to her feet, almost positive he knew what she'd been thinking.

She should have kept them there because, as they began wheeling the casket down the aisle, Kitty, with Colin and Jasper on either side of her, led the Gallagher family procession past them. They were followed by Michael's parents, Maura and Sean. The former governor, who was as handsome as his sons, nodded at several people he obviously knew. Maura, her chin-length hair the color of her mink coat, stared straight ahead with her nose in the air. Her features were sharp and untouched by age. She looked the same as she had the day Sophie overheard her talking to her son in the study.

As the three women walking behind Maura and Sean came into view, Ava stiffened beside Sophie. They were all beautiful, their hair various shades of blond. Sophie assumed they were Griffin's and Aidan's ex-wives and Michael's fiancée. The woman with streaky blond hair and a long side bang glanced at Ava. Dark, judgmental eyebrows rose above her assessing brown eyes. Sophie took her cousin's hand and stared back at the woman who was obviously Griffin's ex-wife.

"You don't have to help out today, Ava," she whispered to her cousin when the last of the family members took their seats, and they took theirs.

Rosa lightly pinched Sophie's thigh. "No. She is a DiRossi. She has nothing to be ashamed of."

"Oh, but I do," Sophie thought she heard Ava say.

She didn't get the chance to question her cousin as the funeral mass began. Throughout the service, she kept a vigilant eye on Mia, relieved and a little surprised by how well her daughter was behaving. Though she supposed she shouldn't be. Mia had always been well behaved. Though these days Sophie never knew what to expect from her. Fifteen minutes later, her daughter proved her right.

After receiving Communion, Liam and his brothers walked to stand near the casket, and, as per Colleen's request, the three men began to sing "Amazing Grace" a capella. The men's deep, baritone voices were as beautiful as they were. Liam and his brothers had a band when they were younger and had developed quite a following on the local bar scene. Listening to them now, she could understand why. By the time they finished, there wasn't a dry eye in the church.

Her grandmother gave Sophie and Ava the evil eye when they refused to go up and receive Communion. She took Mia with her. While they stood in line, Sophie overheard Rosa telling Mia to place her hands over her chest and the priest would give her a blessing. What she forgot to explain to Mia is that you don't drop your great-grandmother's hand, get on your hands and knees, and crawl under the casket.

Frozen in horror, Sophie watched as her grandmother got down on her hands and knees to try and coax Mia from under the casket. Father O'Malley and the altar girl and boy tried to do the same. As the entire congregation shifted in their pews, craning their necks to get a better view, including Michael and his parents, Sophie slunk down on the bench. A bench that was now shaking because Ava was laughing so hard behind her hand. As if her daughter hadn't made enough of a spectacle of them, Sophie started laughing too. The more she tried to stop, the worse it got. Through eyes filled with tears of laughter, she watched Liam walk to the casket. He crouched down, said something to Mia, and she immediately crawled out. Sophie couldn't see what was going on because he had her daughter in front of him, but it appeared that Father O'Malley was giving her the blessing.

People turned to stare at Sophie and Ava because, while Liam had the situation in hand, they didn't. Walking back with Mia's hand in his, Liam looked at Sophie, his eyes warm and amused. He smiled and winked when he lifted Mia onto the bench. "Don't worry," he said. "Happens to the best of us."

As he walked away, Ava leaned into Sophie, her voice still cracking with laughter. "Is that your Gallagher?"

Sophie said, "I wish he was."

Chapter Ten

♥

Liam leaned against the bar in the manor's lobby, flanked by his brothers Griffin and Aidan. He couldn't remember the last time they'd been together. His brothers rarely came back to Harmony Harbor. If you asked them, they'd tell you it was because they lived out of state and were busy with their chosen careers. Even Liam, who lived less than an hour away, used the same excuse. Well, up until last month he had. His father and grandmother had basically kidnapped him the day he'd been released from the hospital.

People looking from the outside in might think the reason the Gallagher brothers didn't come home was because they didn't love their dad or each other, but that wasn't the case. It was easier to stay away than confront their grief and guilt over the loss of their mother and sister, than deal with it head-on.

Out of all of them, their brother Finn was the only one who had a legitimate excuse. He spent most of his time in far-off countries volunteering with Doctors Without

Borders. At that moment, he was in Central Africa. It's why he couldn't make it home for GG's funeral. Finn had always been an adrenaline junkie—the more dangerous the job the better. All four of them were. They'd obviously inherited the gene from their father. Only these days, Liam's thrill-seeking gene seemed to have gone missing. He took a pull on his beer at the thought.

"Sound mind and body, my eye, George!" A woman's strident voice came from the room they'd just left.

"Poor Aunt Maura, she isn't taking it too well, is she?" Griffin said, the dimple showing up in his cheek belying his pretense at sympathy. None of them were particularly fond of their aunt.

"I'm not worried about her, but I am concerned for Mr. Wilcox. We'll draw straws, see who goes and rescues him," Aidan suggested with a grin, grabbing a handful off the bar.

"They're all the same size, dumbass. How about rock, paper, scissors?" Griffin suggested.

His brothers were more buddy-buddy than they'd been in each other's company for a long time. It was a nice change, but it was also weird. They weren't acting like themselves. Maybe because they'd just discovered they'd inherited Greystone and the estate. GG had skipped over Kitty and her grandsons, leaving it to her great-grandchildren. Which meant they'd all be multimillionaires if they sold out. Only problem was, it had to be a unanimous decision. All ten of them had to agree to sell. It looked like they already had one dissenter—his cousin Michael. Uncle Daniel's three girls were wild cards too. No one seemed to know where they were. His uncle was off on a dig somewhere and couldn't be reached. Until they attained a consensus, GG had appointed Mr. Wilcox as the trustee.

"Let me guess. The flask you two were passing around

in the limo wasn't filled with hot cocoa," Liam said as they headed to the dining room where the reception was being held.

"He always was a smart kid, wasn't he, Griffin?" Aidan asked.

"Don't judge, baby brother. If you'd brought along your ex-wives, you'd be drinking too."

Aidan snorted a laugh at Griffin's response.

Liam could understand Aidan's ex driving him to drink. Harper was a coldhearted bitch. They'd divorced the year before, and she'd refused every custody arrangement his brother proposed. As a psychiatrist, she knew what buttons to push and whose strings to pull. Granted, his brother's job as an undercover DEA agent made it easy for her. But Griffin and his ex…"I thought you and Lexi were good."

Griffin and his wife's split two years before had been amicable, or so Liam had thought. He liked Lexi. As far as the family was concerned, she'd saved Griffin. As a military cop, she could handle his brother, who wasn't always easy to handle.

"Most of the time we are. Just not here." His brother took a swallow of his beer, his eyes scanning the dining room.

"Yeah, guess having your *two* ex-wives under the same roof—"

Griffin cut him off with a look then nodded at the dining room. Liam knew he'd made a mistake razzing his brother when he spotted Sophie in a black dress serving coffee to Kitty, his father, and Maggie. Nothing had been sacred in the house on Breakwater Way, including Liam's crush on Sophie.

"So…Sophie DiRossi's back in town and running the manor. How's that working out for you, little brother?"

"Real good if she likes him as much as her little girl

seems to." Aidan grinned, obviously referring to Mia and her disappearing act at the church. Liam found himself smiling. And not just at the memory of Mia under the casket. He was thinking of Sophie giggling uncontrollably. It was the first glimpse of the happy, carefree girl he'd fallen in love with. Though he imagined it wasn't much fun for Sophie at the time. He remembered what it was like to have something strike you as funny in church. Usually it was Finn who'd start it, and Liam would be the one sent to his room when they got home.

Aidan's grin faded as something or someone caught his attention at one of the tables. "I don't know why the hell I gave in to her. Liam, you better give Sophie a heads-up. Harper was asking questions about her little girl and found out she doesn't speak. Between that and the episode at the church, she's probably pulled out her copy of the *DSM-5* from her purse."

Liam followed the direction of his brother's gaze. Mia sat at a table coloring with Aidan's six-year-old daughter, Ella Rose, while Harper looked on. Rosa sat at the table beside them with several members of the Widows Club.

Griffin frowned. "The kid doesn't talk?"

"No, and it's not a big deal. She's been through a lot, okay? They both have," Liam said. Then realizing neither of his brothers knew what he was talking about, he told them what happened in LA.

His brothers exchanged a look, one he recognized.

They knew him too damn well. Knew that the moment a woman started to want more than a good time, Liam was out the door. But he hadn't sounded like he was out the door when he was talking about Sophie and Mia. More like invested and overly protective. So it was probably best not to call them on it. Especially seeing as how he'd been thinking a lot about her the past few days. It was hard not to. The kiss they'd shared and Sophie's revelation she'd been in love with him, too, was going to make it even more difficult to get her out of his head. He'd caught himself wondering about testing the waters to see if her feelings for him were still there.

Today, at the church, he thought they might be. From his own reaction to her, he knew he felt more than a passing attraction. If she didn't have Mia, he'd think about asking her out, see where it went. But long-term relationships and happily-ever-afters weren't in the cards for the Gallaghers of Harmony Harbor. If he needed proof of that, all he had to do was look at his older brothers. So it was best to keep both Mia and Sophie at arm's length. First he had to warn her about Harper. The last thing Sophie needed was the psychiatrist sending up red flags.

"Tell Harper to back off and mind her own business. I don't know why you brought her. She and GG couldn't stand each other," Liam said.

"Baby bro is right again, Aidan. GG always was a good judge of character. Too bad she won't be around to help you pick out your next bride."

Aidan scowled at Griffin. "That won't be a problem, seeing as how I have no plans to marry again. And FYI, she liked *both* of your wives, wiseass."

Griffin flipped off Aidan.

"I'll talk to Harper and tell her to back off, Liam. The only way she'd let me bring Ella Rose home is if she came along. She doesn't believe children should attend wakes or funerals, and she was afraid I'd go against her wishes."

Which explained why Erin had been babysitting Liam's niece last night and this morning. One more strike against Sophie.

"The woman just tunes me out, but I'll give it my best shot," Aidan said, and walked down the steps into the dining room.

"I'm not ready to go in there just yet. Let's wait out the eulogies. I saw Michael's three-page speech. He's been taking lessons from his father." Griffin leaned against the door and pointed his beer bottle at Mia. "I think your new best friend just spotted you."

The little girl had a wide smile on her face and was waving, but it wasn't at Liam. He looked behind him. No one was there.

Griffin rubbed his arms. "It's freezing in here. The faster we sell this place the better. It's a mausoleum. Hey, what did you do that for?"

"Do what?" Liam asked, waving at Mia, who was actually waving at him now.

"Whack me on the back of the head."

"I didn't touch you." He narrowed his eyes at his brother. "How much have you had to drink?" After they'd lost their mom and Riley, Griffin drank too much. Until he met Lexi, who'd arrested him after he'd been in a fight at a bar.

Griffin rubbed the back of his head. "Don't start on me. I'm good."

Liam removed the beer bottle from his brother's hand and flagged down a passing waiter. "Let's keep it that way. Thanks," he said to the waiter, handing him both bottles.

"Careful, little brother. I might start asking questions you don't want to answer. Like why aren't you back at Ladder Company Thirty-Nine? Lost your mojo?"

"Always good to catch up with you, Griffin. I'll talk to you later."

His brother grabbed his arm as Liam started to walk away. "Sorry, that was uncalled for. I guess I'm testier than usual."

Griffin shoved his hands into the pockets of his black suit pants, rocking on his heels. "I saw Ava last night. I swear to God, Liam, I would have walked by her on the street and not known who she was. What's going on with her?"

"You've been home since you two divorced, Griffin. You must have seen her—"

His brother shook his head. "Only from a distance."

"Believe it or not, since Sophie's come home, Ava looks better than she did. GG and Grams have been worrying about her for years. GG got her to join the Widows Club in hopes it would bring her out of her shell."

"I'm not dead yet," his brother muttered.

"You've been divorced from her for more than a decade. Why the sudden concern?" He eyed his brother. "You still have feelings for her?"

"Not the way you're implying, but we were married for three years. You don't just shut your feelings off. I'm concerned about her, that's all."

His brother had left something out. Ava DiRossi had been the love of Griffin's life. He'd been in love with her all through high school. "That concern have anything to do with you and Lexi splitting up?"

Griffin glanced at his ex-wife. Lexi had joined Kitty, Colin, and Maggie at the table. "If you asked Lex right now, she'd probably say it was. But no, I loved Lex. Still do. She's my best friend."

"Just what a woman wants to hear."

"I liked you better when you kept your opinions to yourself. So you going to tell me why you're not back at Thirty-Nine?"

As a Navy SEAL, his brother would understand what he was dealing with. Probably better than Liam did. "Working through stuff. I'll get there."

Griffin's eyes narrowed at Liam, searching his face. "I know I haven't been there for you since Mom and Riley died. All you have to do is pick up the phone."

"Thanks. Same goes. I miss us, miss how we used to be as a family."

"Yeah, me too. How's Dad doing?"

"Good. Probably be better if he admitted he has feelings for Maggie." His brother stiffened beside him. "I've gotten to know her better this past month, Griff. She's a nice lady. She'd be good for Dad."

"I know. I wasn't—" His brother stopped talking when their aunt Maura walked by. She acknowledged them by lifting her pointed chin.

"Hey, boys, you doing okay?" their uncle Sean asked, coming up between them to pat them both on the backs.

"Sean, do you hear your son? He's just announced that he and Bethany are holding their wedding at Greystone because it was your grandmother's dying wish. I swear to God, I could happily wring Mr. Wilcox's neck for telling him that. Look at this place. There's…" She stiffened and narrowed her eyes at Griffin and Liam then looked down at the black cat by her feet before saying to her husband, "Get in there and put a stop to this nonsense."

"Jaysus, stay single, boys," their uncle murmured. Then louder, "Coming, Maura."

"Always did feel sorry for Uncle Sean. Sounds like good advice for the Gallagher boys. Too bad Michael didn't listen to him. Did you meet Bethany?" Griffin asked.

"Yeah, she makes Harper seem almost angelic." When they were younger, Liam and Finn teamed up with Michael against their older brothers and cousins. They'd been best of friends until his cousin had stolen Sophie from him. But Liam had stopped carrying a grudge several years back, and he hung out every couple of months with his cousin. Michael was a successful assistant district attorney in Boston with plans to follow in his father's footsteps. That, Liam suspected, was the reason his cousin was marrying Bethany, whose wealthy blue blood family had the connections to make his dream come true. Or maybe Liam was just being cynical.

Griffin snorted. "We probably should get in there. Dad and Lexi have been giving us the stink eye for the past five minutes." They walked in to the sound of applause and cheering. The people from town had risen to their feet. "Looks like the golden boy is the hero of Harmony Harbor."

Liam glanced at Sophie, wondering if Michael was her hero too. His cousin had just handed her the means to reestablish Greystone as a wedding destination.

"Girl, bring me a coffee." His aunt Maura flagged Sophie down then took a second glance. "You're one of those DiRossis, aren't you?"

"You gonna take her out, or am I?" Griffin muttered.

Liam didn't respond. He was already halfway to Sophie's side. "I'll take care of the coffee," he said when he reached her.

"It's okay. I've got it. Besides, you're not the hired help. I am." She winced. "Sorry, I shouldn't have said that. She just…"

"I know. She makes us all crazy. Don't let her get to you. She's upset that Michael and Bethany are having their wedding here. And, Soph"—he took the coffeepot from her—"I'm sure you're happy about that, but fair warning, you're gonna have your hands full with Bethany."

She wouldn't meet his eyes, turning instead to pick up another carafe. "I'm sure it will be fine." She didn't sound convinced. If he read her wrong—and she really did think it was going to be a cake walk—she got a rude awakening when they reached his aunt's table.

"Liam, for goodness' sake, put that down before you spill the coffee." Maura looked at the platinum blonde across the table from her. "This is exactly what I'm talking about, Bethany. They don't even have enough help to handle Colleen's reception."

Liam opened his mouth to defend Sophie, but she gave her head an almost imperceptible shake. Unwittingly, he had probably made matters worse by trying to help out, so he did as she asked.

Sophie gave his aunt a tight smile. "This has been, as I'm sure you're aware, a difficult time for the staff. They were very close to Colleen, and I felt they should be allowed to properly mourn her."

Maura crossed her arms and raised an eyebrow. "You? Who are you to make such decisions?"

Sophie lifted her chin. "The manager." She put down the carafe and extended her hand to Bethany. "I look forward to working with you, Ms. Adams. I was hoping we could have a preliminary meeting before you leave."

Bethany looked Sophie up and down. "You? Don't you mean with your wedding planner?"

"Oh no, Ms. Adams. You're marrying a Gallagher. I wouldn't think of passing you on to anyone else. I'll be taking care of the details personally to ensure your wedding is perfect."

Bethany moved her head back and forth before nodding. "Yes, now that I think about it, I prefer that you do. I went through a wedding planner and two of her assistants at the last venue. It was a nightmare. I'll speak to Michael and get back to you with a time we can meet before we leave."

"Perfect." Sophie moved the salt and pepper shakers from

the middle of the table and set down the carafe. "Someone will be by to bring you a fresh pot when you need it."

Liam held back a smile. Sophie obviously had experience dealing with women like his aunt and Bethany. She didn't need him to come to her defense. At least that's what he was thinking until he heard Harper call out, "Ms. DiRossi." And his brother mutter, "For Chrissakes, Harper. Leave it alone."

As they moved away from his aunt's table, Sophie went to take the pot from him. "Liam, I'm perfectly capable of handling your family. You don't have to follow me around."

"You were great with Maura and Bethany, but I'm not sure you can handle this member of the family. Aidan's ex-wife Harper is a psychiatrist. She's been asking questions about Mia."

Sophie's hands dropped to her sides, the color leaching from her face. "What kind of questions?"

He placed his hand on her lower back. "Let's get out of the way," he said, and guided her to a quiet corner at the back of the room.

"Liam, what's going on? You're scaring me."

"Relax, it's just about Mia not—"

"Excuse me, Liam." Harper nudged him aside and extended her hand to Sophie. "I'm Dr. Granger. Perhaps you've heard of me?"

"No, I'm afraid I haven't. What can I do for you, Dr. Granger?"

"Liam, do you mind? I'd like to speak with Ms. DiRossi privately."

"Actually, I do mind. The middle of the reception to honor my great-grandmother who just passed away isn't exactly private, now, is it?"

"Liam's right. I'm a little busy at the moment. Perhaps we can arrange to speak later?"

"Well, if you're too busy to speak about your daughter's issues…"

Sophie stiffened. "My daughter is recovering from a trauma. I've consulted with one of the best child psychologists in LA, and I'm quite aware what to expect and how to help her with her recovery."

"I'm not sure I'd agree. I was at the funeral and have been observing Mia ever since. I'm concerned. As I understand it, she's had several major upheavals in the past weeks that I believe have had a negative impact on her recovery. Mia needs stability, Ms. DiRossi. She needs to feel safe and secure."

"Which is why we moved back to Harmony Harbor. I appreciate your concern, but I have guests to see to. If you'll excuse me."

Liam watched as Sophie wove her way through the tables to reach Mia. She crouched beside her daughter's chair with a wide smile, as though her exchange with Harper hadn't shaken her. Liam knew better. He'd seen the panic in her eyes before she'd banked it. His brother leaned toward Sophie and said something. Probably apologizing for his ex and trying to reassure her. Liam turned back to Harper. "Stay out of it."

She raised her manicured hands as if the matter was now out of them. "As a psychiatrist and a mother, I have an obligation to file a report with the authorities if I believe a child is at risk."

"Be careful, Harper. Two can play at that game."

"Are you threatening me?"

"Damn straight I am. You cause problems for Sophie, and I'll cause them for you. My brother doesn't see through you, but I do. You're using Ella Rose to get back at him for divorcing you." He cocked his head. "Is it just me or does Ella Rose seem pale to you? Maybe a little withdrawn?"

"How dare you! You have no idea who you're dealing with."

He smiled. "Neither do you. But if you don't get your head out of your ass and grant my brother shared custody, you'll find out."

She gave a dismissive sniff and strode to her table. Sophie, as though sensing her approach, picked up Mia and walked to the kitchen with her in her arms.

Liam's threat hadn't been an idle one. The distance between him and his brothers had gone on long enough. They now fought their battles alone instead of together like they used to. It was about time they had each other's backs again. Right now, Aidan needed them. Liam didn't trust the sanctimonious, high-and-mighty Harper.

Michael, who'd been talking to his mother and fiancée, looked over when Harper stormed off. He raised his eyebrows at Liam then said something to Bethany and stood up. As his cousin made his way to where he stood at the back of the room, Liam knew he'd found the answer to Sophie's problem. Even though everything inside him rebelled at the thought. He wanted to be the one who solved her problems, and he knew why.

By asking his cousin for help on Sophie's behalf, in all likelihood, Michael would slay her dragons and become her hero. Liam pushed the thought back to where it belonged—in the past. He wasn't twenty-three, and he was no longer in competition for Sophie's affections. He was over his crush. And just to make sure, because his subconscious and other parts of his anatomy were calling him a liar, he looked over at his brothers to remind himself what happened when you let passion overrule your brain. It worked. What worked even better was seeing Mia and Sophie walk out of the kitchen carrying trays of cookies. This was about them, not him. He would do whatever he had to protect them.

Michael leaned against the wall beside Liam. "What did you do to piss off Harper, buddy? Tell her it was about time she got her head out of her ass and grant Aidan shared custody?"

"How do you do that? You got bionic ears or something?"

Michael grinned. "It's what I would have told her, and you and I always did think alike. Great minds and all that."

"Yeah, well, right now it's your great mind I need. I have a favor to ask."

"You got it. Anything you need. All for one and one for all, remember? Us Gallaghers stick together."

He did remember. Back in the day, they were all thick as thieves. But just like Liam and his brothers, they'd grown apart. "Okay, Cape Crusader, I appreciate it. But this might prove to be a tough one, even for you. Do you remember Sophie DiRossi?"

"Gorgeous brunette with big eyes and a rockin' bod? Yeah, might have a faint memory of her. She was sweet. What about her?"

Liam gritted his teeth. His memory of why he and his cousin weren't as close as they'd once been wasn't as faint as Michael's memory of Sophie. Liam reminded himself this wasn't about him and relaxed his hands that had balled into fists. "She's managing the manor. She's moved back to Harmony Harbor with her daughter, and she's having a problem with Child Protective Services."

"Wait a minute—" Michael looked around the room, and his eyes widened. "That's Sophie's kid? Jesus, how old was she when she had her?"

"Nineteen, I think. Her name's Mia. Sophie hasn't had it easy, Mike. She could use a break," he said then told his cousin everything that had happened to her in LA, including her arrest. When he finished, he added, "This falls under client privilege. I don't want anyone else to know about the arrest."

"You know me better than that," Michael said, every inch the lawyer now. "Just from what you've told me, sounds like they're going through the motions, and Sophie won't have to deal with CPS after they've done her in-home visit. I can vouch for her and make that go away if you want me to. Do you have the name of her caseworker?"

"Might be best if you talk to Soph. Sophie." Liam waved her over. "Thanks, Mike. I really appreciate you handling this."

"Anything for you, buddy. You know that." He turned to smile at Sophie when she approached and extended his hand. "Nice to see you again. It's been a long time."

Liam frowned and looked around the room, wondering if he'd missed something. Sophie had lost all the color in her face and her hand appeared to be trembling when she shook Michael's. "Nice to see you, too, Michael. Is there a problem?" She looked from his cousin to Liam at the same time twisting her right hand around her left wrist.

"No, Liam asked me to look into your case for you. I'm sorry what you and your little girl went through, Sophie. The last thing you need is CPS breathing down your neck. I'll take care of that for you. All I need is your caseworker's name, and I can handle it from there."

"Thank you. That's very kind of you to offer…" she said while staring at Liam.

Okay, he knew that expression on her face, and it wasn't good. If looks could kill, he was a dead man. He didn't have a clue what he'd done wrong.

She continued. "I have it handled." She shot another furious look at Liam before giving his cousin a tight smile. "I look forward to working with you and Bethany on your wedding. Thank you for agreeing to change venues. At this late date, I can't imagine that was easy for you. I hope you know how much we appreciate it."

"If you change your mind, just give me a call. I really don't mind, Sophie," his cousin said then glanced in his fiancée's direction. "About our last venue…" He loosened his tie. "They kind of fired us. Bethany wants our wedding to be perfect, and she can be a little…What the hell, you'll be working with her. She's turned into a bridezilla. It's not her fault. My mother and hers are making her crazy."

"Don't worry, we'll do everything we can to make planning your big day more fun than stressful for Bethany. We really are honored to be hosting your wedding. It means a lot to all of us here at Greystone."

"Anything for the Save Greystone team. Now we just have to get my cousins on board. Including this guy right here."

Chapter Eleven

♥

No good deed goes unpunished, was the thought running through Liam's head when his cousin outed him. So much for his nostalgic memories of cousinly bonds.

"At least now we know who's Team Greystone and who isn't," Sophie said. She rewarded the Cape Crusader with a sweet smile and shot Liam another death glare before heading for the kitchen. The force with which she slapped her hand on the door and pushed it open made him wince. No doubt about it, he was in her bad book. "Thanks a lot, pal," he muttered at his cousin.

"What did I…" A slow smile curved Michael's lips. "So it's like that, is it?" His cousin waggled his eyebrows and stuck out his hand. "Welcome to Team Greystone."

"I'm not Team Greystone, and you know why I'm not. There's no way—"

"Save the explanation for your girlfriend. But before you do, I suggest you work on your closing argument." With a smug look on his face, Michael turned to walk away.

"She's not my…" He didn't bother finishing the sentence. Michael wouldn't hear him anyway. He was whistling "Going to the Chapel."

Marco, wearing a white, double-breasted jacket and checkered pants, came out of the kitchen. He whipped off his hairnet at the same time as he searched the dining room. When his eyes landed on Liam, he stalked toward him.

He jabbed his finger in Liam's chest. "What did you say to upset my sister?"

"Which time? She was mad at me right from the get-go, and I have no idea why. I was…What did she say I said?"

"I haven't got a clue. That's why I'm asking you. She's banging around in the kitchen, and she's going to deflate my chocolate soufflé." His eyes narrowed at Liam, who pressed his lips together to keep from laughing. "One laugh out of you, and I'll never make you another pie. Now start from the beginning. She's upset, and I want to know why."

"If you'd stop talking about your soufflé and tell me what she said, I'd have a starting point."

"Okay, wise guy, you figure it out. We ask what's wrong, and this is what we get. Liam, he…sniff, sniff. Liam, he…hiccough sob. Liam, he…Rinse and repeat."

Liam winced and began walking toward the kitchen. "Don't worry. I'll talk to her and make it right. Seriously, bro, I thought I was doing her a favor."

"How so?"

"You know, with Child Protective…" He trailed off at the stunned look on Marco's face. "You didn't know, did you?" The only thing he remembered Sophie telling him to keep quiet about was her mother's involvement the day of the fire. He had to calm Marco down before he stormed into the kitchen demanding answers. "Relax, okay? There's nothing to worry about. Michael says they'll do one home visit, and that'll be it. She's a good mother, Marco. You know that. She has nothing to worry about. They had no grounds to arrest her in the first…" *Aw, hell.* "Wait. Marco!" He made a grab for the back of his best friend's jacket and grabbed air instead. Several people at the tables nearest him turned to stare. He faked a smile then grimaced when Marco reached the kitchen and flung open the door, swearing at his sister in Italian. Loudly.

Griffin was sitting back in his chair with his arms crossed and a grin on his face. Probably because swearing Italians brought back memories of his own fights with Ava. Liam waved at him to get his attention and mouthed, *Music.* Since his brother had personal experience with an upset DiRossi, he'd know just how loud to crank it. Liam did one more sweep of the room. Harper and Ella Rose were gone, and Mia was with her grandmother, who looked like she was about to get up. Liam shook his head, indicating everything was okay.

With the dining room under control, he walked to what he imagined was the out-of-control kitchen. He ducked in time to avoid getting beaned by a stainless steel pot that came sailing at his head. None of the DiRossis had thrown it. The cook did. "Out! Out of my kitchen now! All of you!"

Liam held up his hands. "Ava and Marco are just helping out for today, Helga. They'll get out of your hair as soon as the reception's over."

"Ha! A lot you know." The older woman pointed at Sophie, who'd bent down to pick up a broken plate. "She's trying to steal my kitchen out from under me."

Hands on his hips, Marco stood over his sister. "You tell my best friend, but you don't think I have a right to know that you were arrested, Sophie? Arrested!"

Ava stood in the corner, her long hair piled on top of her head. "Marco, leave her alone. I'm sure there's—"

Helga crossed her arms and nodded. "I knew there was something off about that one. You should fire her. Fire the whole lot of them." She plunked a pot on the stove to make her point.

Marco rushed to the oven and opened it. "*Una vecchietta grinzosa!* You ruined my soufflé."

"No one wants your snotty soufflé anyway."

Liam ignored the escalating war of words between Marco and Helga and focused on the woman throwing the broken plate in the trash. She was too pale and too quiet. "Soph, I didn't—"

She opened the walk-in cooler, got inside, and slammed the door.

Ava narrowed her eyes at him, jerking her thumb at the cooler. "Fix it."

Easy for her to say. Liam didn't know what he'd done wrong. Apart from sharing with her brother that she got arrested and, thanks to his cousin, that he wasn't a member of Team Greystone. He opened the door and walked inside. "Soph—" She threw a head of lettuce at him. He caught it and put it on the shelf. "Look, I know you're—" She threw another head, which he also caught. "Okay, can you stop with the—" He ducked as a bunch of carrots hit the door behind him. Now he was ticked and stalked toward her. "Stop it. Now." Closing his fingers around her wrist, he moved into her, pressing her against the back wall with carrots dangling over her head. "All right, that's better." Only it wasn't because he was so close that her body was pressed against his, and when she moved…"Stay still. I'm not letting you go till you hear me out."

She lifted her big, luminous eyes. "Why? Why did you do it?"

The look of betrayal in her gaze gutted him. "Swear to God, Soph. I had no idea you didn't tell Marco about the arrest. I promised I wouldn't say anything to him about your mother's involvement, and I didn't—"

The cooler door swung open. "What about my mother? And what the hell are you doing with my—"

Liam took the carrots from Sophie's hand and flung them at Marco's head. "Stay out of it."

Ava grabbed her cousin and pulled him back, shutting the cooler door.

Liam looked down at Sophie. "Will you come with me someplace private so I can explain why I did what I did?"

When she nodded, he released the breath he'd been holding and went to step back. He couldn't; he was stuck.

He was about to try again when Sophie fisted her hands in the lapels of his suit coat. "Don't move. My chain's caught on the button of your shirt." She swore in Italian and wriggled to maneuver her hands between them. She froze, her eyes lifting to his.

"Sorry, it's cold in here, but it's not that cold. And hearing you swear in Italian turns me on."

"Don't make jokes, Liam. This isn't funny."

"I'm telling you the truth, Soph. I'm not trying to be funny. I was only trying to help you when I told Michael. I'd never do anything to intentionally hurt you. Here, let me try." The longer they were plastered against each other like this, the harder it became to remember why he wanted to keep Sophie at arm's length. To think about anything other than kissing her. But his brilliant idea to help loosen the chain only served to increase his desire to have his mouth on hers. As he moved his hands between them, his knuckles brushed against her warm, silky skin and the voluptuous curves of her breasts.

A low breathy moan escaped from her, and she caught her full bottom lip between her teeth. He had to distract her, and not just because she was obviously embarrassed by her response to him. He was perilously close to forgetting why a relationship with Sophie was a bad idea. "Tell me why you're mad at me. It'll help you focus on something else besides…" He cleared his throat.

"I'm not thinking about kissing you or having sex with you, if that's what you're insinuating."

Obviously they were both in denial. She wanted him as much as he wanted her. He dipped his head and nipped her earlobe. "Liar."

She shivered. "Fine. But it's not you. It could be anyone. No sex for six years, remember?"

"Nope, totally forgot about that. Thanks for the reminder, though. My fingers are too big. You try again." It was an excuse. He needed his hands free to lift her chin so he could look into her eyes. To prove she was feeling what he was. To be able to hold her gaze and have her tell him what he did wrong so he could make it right.

Moving his hands into her thick, dark hair, he tipped her face up. "Michael's a lawyer, Soph. A good one. He's an assistant district attorney, which means he knows people who can help you."

"I didn't want your help or his. I told you that, Liam. The only thing I asked was that you help me keep my job. You're not going to, are you?"

"Of course I will. I'll do anything you need me to do to ensure Michael and Bethany have a great wedding. I won't sabotage you. For as long as Greystone remains open, I'll support you as much as I can. But I can't vote to keep Greystone in the family. I'm sorry if that's not the answer you want to hear."

"You know it's not. For argument's sake, let's say we can convince nine out of ten of the Gallaghers to keep the estate. Will you make it unanimous?"

"Yes." It was an easy answer. He knew she had no hope of winning over his brothers. But when she rewarded him with a wide smile, he was almost tempted to give her the answer she really wanted and throw in with the Cape Crusader. "Am I forgiven?"

She bowed her head and went back to work on the tangled gold chain then nodded. "Yes, I shouldn't have put you in the position of lying to my brother. I'm sorry. I know you meant well with Michael too. It's just"—she lifted a shoulder—"I'm used to taking care of Mia myself. I don't like asking for help."

"I get that. I won't interfere again unless you ask me to. Sound good?"

"Really good."

"Really, really good?" he asked, thinking back to the night she arrived at Greystone and her comment to Kris.

She rolled her eyes. "Yes, Liam, you have very impressive abs. No sex in six years, remember?"

"You know, it might make this easier if you don't keep reminding me of that. I think I have an idea that will help you untangle the chain. You need to go at it from a better angle." He placed his hands under her ass and lifted her up. "Wrap your legs around me."

"Like this?"

"Oh, yeah, just like that." Any hope he'd had of keeping his life simple and uncomplicated vanished the moment Sophie wrapped her long, toned legs around his waist. He moved one hand up her back and under her hair to her nape. "You mind if I keep myself occupied while you work on the chain?"

"What did you have in mind?" From the warm glint in her eyes and her sultry smile, she knew exactly what he had in mind.

"This," he said, and kissed her how he'd been wanting to since the night in the study. But it wasn't the same. It wasn't tender or gentle. It was…

A woman cursed outside the cooler. In Italian. Liam jerked back.

Sophie, her beautiful face flushed and her lips damp, gave him an impish grin. "So I guess my grandmother cursing in Italian doesn't have the same effect on you as I do," she said as she unwound her legs from his waist and slid down his body.

"Good—" He broke off at the sound of the cooler door opening and Rosa yelling at Sophie in Italian. Nope, not at Sophie, at him. He didn't understand what she was saying, but he definitely heard her spit out *Gallagher*. There was a lot of contempt behind the word too—a couple of curse words even. Those he did understand. "Mrs. DiRossi…" At the flash of fiery temper in Sophie's grandmother's eyes, he closed his mouth. He didn't know what to say that wouldn't make the situation worse.

"Nonna, it's not what you think. My chain's caught on Liam's button. We were just trying to—"

Rosa muttered something in Italian, and then said, "Give me a knife."

Behind her, his supposed best friend grinned. "Coming right up."

Liam swung his gaze back to Sophie, but he didn't get a chance to say anything because Rosa was suddenly beside them with a knife in her hand. It looked sharp. Really sharp.

"Now, Mrs. DiRossi, you know me. I would never—"

Rosa lifted the knife, the light from the bulb overhead

glinting off the blade. Liam placed his hands protectively over his groin. He could have sworn he heard Sophie laugh, but he wasn't sure because he was too busy praying. Rosa sliced the button off his shirt in one expert stroke.

Now that he could breathe and think clearly again, he decided a relationship between him and Sophie wouldn't only be difficult and complicated; it might also be dangerous.

An hour after the reception ended, someone knocked on the study door. Sophie looked up from the computer screen. "Come in." She winced, too sultry. If it was Liam as she hoped, he'd know she'd been fantasizing about him instead of working on her ideas to present to Michael and Bethany. The couple hadn't had time to meet with her today, but they'd scheduled an appointment for next weekend.

Ava peeked her head around the door. "You have a minute?"

"Sure. Come in," she said, managing to keep the disappointment from her voice. "Everything okay?"

"I was worried about you." She took the seat across from Sophie. Ava still had on her chef's uniform, her waist-length hair piled on her head. She looked good, Sophie thought. Better than she did when Sophie first arrived in Harmony Harbor. Maybe her plan would work after all.

"It was a bit of a crazy afternoon, but I think it went well, don't you?"

"*Sì*. Kitty was pleased. She stopped by the kitchen to let me know. Helga was another story. But that's not what I meant. You were upset, Sophie. And not just a little upset. Whatever Liam said"—she gave Sophie a pointed look—"or did, seemed to help. I just want you to know I'm here for you."

Sophie's cheeks warmed. It wasn't only the memory of

making out in the cooler with Liam that caused the heated flush. It was embarrassment over how she'd reacted to him telling Michael. It wasn't his fault. She was the one with the guilty conscience, with something to hide. The only thing Liam had been guilty of was trying to help, to protect her and Mia. "He did help."

"I'm sure Auntie Rosa will be pleased to hear that," her cousin said, the touch of a smirk on her lips.

"I was a little nervous when she came at him with the knife." Sophie laughed at the memory of Liam's expression when he covered himself. "So was Liam."

"He had good reason to be." Ava smiled then twisted the gold chain at her neck. "At the church this morning, you said you wished he was the Gallagher Auntie Rosa referred to. But he's not. Is…Is it Griffin?"

"No, oh God no. Of course it's not, Ava. It's…" She paused. Today was crazier in more ways than one. She'd had to acknowledge the feelings she had for Liam were no longer the ones she had as a girl. Obviously she was as attracted to him as she'd always been, which wasn't a surprise. He was even more handsome than she remembered, taller, broader, stronger…just more.

But she'd been a teenager with virtually no life experience when she had a crush on him. Now she was a woman with an abundance of it, most of it far from fabulous. She recognized a good man when she saw one, an honorable man, a kind man, a man who did the right thing always. A man who was sweet and caring and protective of Sophie *and* her daughter. He was the real deal, and her feelings were beginning to feel real too. And that was scary…

"It's Michael," she admitted to her cousin, because she needed someone to talk to. Someone closer to her own age who would understand, and hopefully be honest with her.

Sophie wasn't sure she was doing the right thing anymore. Michael had seemed different, less full of himself and arrogant. Kind, really. Supportive like Liam. So now the guilt that she'd kept a good man from knowing his daughter was beginning to outweigh her need to protect them both.

"What happened, Sophie? Did he hurt you?" Ava's hands were clasped tightly in her lap. Her face was pale and pinched, her expression anxious. Something dark and troubled swirled in her eyes.

"No, of course not." Sophie placed her elbows on the desk and cupped her face in her hands. She looked at her cousin. "I've never told anyone this before."

"Tell me, Sophie, please."

She nodded, stacking the papers on her desk as she worked up the courage to finally tell the story to someone. Like ripping off a bandage, she decided the best thing to do was jump right in. "I ran into Michael the night I went out with a bunch of friends to celebrate my eighteenth birthday. Everyone knew us in town, so we went to a bar in Bridgeport. We started drinking and acting stupid. They were teasing me because I was the only virgin in our group. They dared me to lose my virginity to the next guy who walked in the bar. I wasn't going to. I was going to come up with an excuse, and then the next guy walked in, and it was Liam. The guy I'd been crushing on since I was fourteen. So I took it as a sign and took the bet. Only once I walked over, I realized it wasn't Liam. It was Michael. He seemed so mature and sexy." Sophie covered her face. "I can't believe how stupid I was back then. I'm going to lock Mia up from sixteen to twenty-one."

"We were all stupid, Sophie. Some of us more stupid than others. You were just a kid. Michael was what, twenty-four?"

"He was, but I knew what I was doing. I didn't sleep with him that night. But his age was one of the reasons that I eventually did. I figured a twenty-four-year-old wasn't going to be happy with a girlfriend who'd only go to first base. Second, eventually. It was pathetic. I wanted to be like my friends. I wanted a boyfriend. I was in love with the idea of being in love. Michael was smart and handsome and reminded me of Liam with his Gallagher-blue eyes. Only he didn't treat me like a kid. He seemed to really like me. But first-time sex isn't as romantic as the movies and books make it out to be. So I spent most of July trying to avoid having it again while hanging on to my smart, sexy, older boyfriend."

Sophie stopped and reached for her mug of coffee. Stalling, she took a sip. This was the hard part. The part where her cousin would undoubtedly judge her and find her lacking. "Do you remember the big party Michael organized at Greystone that summer?"

"Vaguely. I think I remember Jasper complaining about the mess the next morning."

"It got out of hand. So did I. I drank way too much and got sloppy and emotional. I was afraid Michael didn't love me anymore...I thought I saw him kissing another girl and took off to Kismet Cove. Another brilliant move on my part. I was lucky I didn't kill myself. It was so dark, I couldn't see my hand in front of my face. Plus, by that time, I was officially wasted.

"Anyway, Michael came after me. I, ah, threw myself at him." She released a self-conscious laugh at the memory. "The poor guy probably didn't know what hit him. I spent half the summer avoiding sex, and then I basically tore off our clothes and jumped his bones." She cleared her throat. "That's the night Mia was conceived."

Ava stared at her. "But I thought…Mia is Michael's daughter?"

"Yes, I…" She glanced at the door. It was still closed, but she could have sworn she heard someone on the other side. "Did you hear that?"

"No. But I'm used to the noises. This place creaks and groans all the time. Don't worry, it was probably just a draft." Ava rubbed her arms. "It's freezing in here."

"I'll turn up the heat." Sophie got up and adjusted the thermostat. Instead of returning to the chair behind the desk, she walked to the window.

"Sophie, please don't think I'm judging you, but why didn't you tell Michael when you found out?"

"I probably would have if I hadn't overheard him talking to his mother two days after the night at Kismet Cove. Right here in this room." She repeated the conversation he'd had with his mother.

"Quello che una cagna," Ava said, shaking her head.

Sophie agreed with her cousin. Maura was a bitch, and from what Sophie had seen and heard today, she hadn't changed. Which was one of the reasons Sophie still didn't want to tell Michael. "That's why I left with my mother for California. Left everyone I loved behind because I was afraid they'd hate me and I'd make things worse between Nonna and the Gallaghers. When things got really bad in LA and I was desperate, I nearly broke down and called Michael. But I was afraid they'd force me to give up Mia or take her from me. She was all I had."

"How bad did things get, Sophie?"

She pressed her forehead against the cold pane of glass and told her cousin everything. About the lonely nights, the constant struggle to put food on the table and pay the bills, working at the hotel during the day and studying all night.

The bank had foreclosed on Doris the day after Mia's third birthday. Doris went to live with her sister in Utah, and Sophie had to start over again. She found a job at a boutique hotel. The pay was better, but she no longer had a room at the motel or the ability to keep Mia with her while she worked. By the time she paid for childcare and rent there wasn't much left at the end of the month. But there were good times too. She had friends, and she had Mia. She told Ava how Mia had been before the fire, and she told her about the fire and being arrested.

Ava came up behind her and wrapped Sophie in her arms. "I'm sorry. I'm sorry your life in LA was so difficult. But I admire you, Sophie. I admire you for working so hard to provide a good life for your daughter and never giving up. I'm glad you came home. You belong here. It will be better now."

"In some ways, it is better, but in other ways, it's worse. I'm lying to everyone. And Mia knows it. I don't know what to do."

"What are you afraid of?"

"That I'll lose her. That Michael and his mother will take her from me. That Bethany will hate her. That Liam will hate me for keeping Mia from Michael."

"Ah."

"Ah? What does that mean?"

"You have feelings for Liam."

She thought about him following her around with the coffeepot, trying to protect her from Maura and Harper. "I do. I'm just not sure what they are." Or maybe she was afraid that she was.

"We should have listened to Auntie Rosa and stayed away from the Gallagher boys. She always said no good would come from a Gallagher and DiRossi union."

"Do you have any idea what happened between them?"

She shook her head. "All I know is that the feud began in the early seventeen hundreds when William Gallagher destroyed Marcello DiRossi's shipbuilding business. I'm not sure what happened between Rosa and Kitty, but I think it had something to do with Ronan."

"But Kitty and Colleen have been so good to you. To me too. And here we are trying to save Greystone."

"And your daughter is both a DiRossi and a Gallagher, and this is her legacy."

"Meow."

Sophie nearly jumped out of her skin when Simon wound his way around her legs. She pressed a hand to her pounding heart. "How did he…"

Her eyes shot to the study door. It was open.

Chapter Twelve

♥

Y ou scared the bejaysus out of me, Simon. I thought I was about to have a bloody heart attack." As soon as the words were out of her mouth, Colleen chuckled. "Not that it would matter, I suppose, seeing that I'm already dead. Or am I undead? Haven't quite figured all this out yet." Colleen frowned at the cat purring and winding his way around Ava's and Sophie's legs. "How did you get in here? You haven't developed a talent for going through closed doors now, have…" Colleen's gaze flicked to the study's door. It was open. "Jesus, Mary, and Joseph, someone let you in!"

She'd been so caught up in Sophie's story, she hadn't noticed they had company. If she had, she would have warned the girls by pushing a book off the desk. Same as she'd done the night of the wake when Sophie and Liam were having a snog in here. Seemed to be quite a bit of snogging going on between those two. But that was the least of her worries. If someone had been eavesdropping…"We're in a pickle now, Sophie my girl. That we are." It wasn't the right time for the news to come out. Colleen wanted to wait until after the wedding.

"Come on, laddie. It's time for us to do some investigating. Find out who was listening in." She headed for the door, turning back when Simon didn't follow her—too busy cozying up to the girls. "Leg man, are you? I'll leave you to it later, but right now I need your help. Step lively, Tom Cat. There's a spy to be found."

Colleen walked through the door. It gave her a shiver every time she did, but she was getting better at this ghost gig. At least there was no more of that floating nonsense. And every once in a while she'd been able to make her presence known. Like she'd done with Griffin. The boy deserved a good whack upside the head talking about Greystone the way that he did. No matter, if Colleen had anything to do with it, Ava would change his mind.

Oh yes, Colleen knew exactly what she was doing when she left the estate and manor to her great-grandchildren. She just needed time for her plans for their love lives to come to fruition. She was canny when it came to choosing the ones they were meant to be with. Sooner or later her great-grandchildren would all be back in Harmony Harbor where they belonged, and Greystone would continue to be a shining beacon of hope and a link to the past.

"All right now, show me who let you in." Simon stared at her. "Oh for the love of all that is holy, did you pay no mind to who opened the door for you?"

Someone talking in the library drew her attention from Simon. She walked a little way down the hall, entering the room to see Paige Townsend dressed all in black. As though she gave a flying fig about Colleen's demise. The woman made herself at home sitting in Ronan's favorite wingback chair by the window. Every wall, right up to the third story, was covered with dark oak shelves lined with books. They'd been collected by generations of Gallaghers; some were priceless and some well-worn favorites. Colleen wondered if perhaps she'd hidden her memoir here. She was about to scan the shelves when she picked up on Paige's conversation.

"Yes, well, it wasn't my fault her great-grandson found the fog machines before they set the boxes on fire. Even without a fire, I expected her family to encourage Colleen to sell. I know I did, sir. I need more time…How was I supposed to know she'd drop dead before she signed? How long…Well, there's only one holdout, so I'd say the odds are looking up. All we need to do is convince Michael Gallagher to sell."

The woman made a face, as though she didn't relish sharing the next bit of news. "We may have a slight problem, though. Today he announced he's having his wedding at the manor. I know, I'm not happy about it either, sir. The last thing we need is for the new manager to generate more publicity and income for Greystone. Sabotage the wedding?" The realtor tipped her head back and looked up at the ceiling. "Of course I'm up for it. Yes, I'll be in touch."

She disconnected. "Arrogant ass. If I didn't need the money, I'd tell him to find someone else to do his dirty work. What are you looking at, cat? Shoo, get out of here."

"It's you who best be leaving," Colleen said, and went to push the ladder to give the woman the fright she sorely deserved. Colleen's hand passed through the brass rail. She tried again with the same result. It was no use. She must have used too much energy whacking Griffin earlier. Simon hissed at Paige and jumped on the woman's lap. The realtor shrieked and leaped off the chair.

Colleen smiled as Paige rushed past her. "Well done, Simon. At least we know she wasn't the one spying on Ava and Sophie. If she had been, she'd know exactly how to sabotage the wedding."

Following the realtor out of the library, Colleen checked the alcoves and hidey-holes as she went. No one was about. Paige headed for the bar where her partner in crime, Hazel, chatted up Colleen's attorney.

George patted his flushed face with a hankie. "Give it up, Hazel. Colleen was of sound mind when she had me draw up her will, and I'd advise you not to stir up trouble." He narrowed his eyes at Paige. "And you, young lady. Stop encouraging her. This wedding will be good for both the manor and the local economy. Just you wait and see. Now if you'll excuse me, I'll pay my respects and be off."

"Well done, George," Colleen said, accompanying him to the sitting room. "We can take him off our list of suspects, Simon. Those three, too, I would imagine," she added, nodding at her great-grandsons. They were still where she'd left them sitting by the fire. It was good to see them together. She stopped and listened in, smiling when she heard Liam and Griffin telling Aidan how to handle Harper from now on. Good, it was about time someone talked to the lad. Colleen never did like Aidan's wife. Told him so the day he'd brought Harper to meet her and Kitty.

Colleen headed for the sitting room. Out of her three great-grandsons, only Liam would care about the conversation in the study. But she knew him well. He wouldn't stoop to eavesdropping. If Liam overheard the conversation, he would have confronted Sophie right then and there. Colleen had a feeling it wouldn't go well for those two when Liam discovered the truth.

Mr. Wilcox left the sitting room and walked straight through Colleen. They both shivered. She was about to apologize then remembered he couldn't hear her. Probably a good thing. He'd have a heart attack and then where would she be? She couldn't remember if she'd made arrangements for another trustee.

Definitely wouldn't have been Sean or Maura, she thought as she entered the room. Her grandson and his wife stood in front of the painting Colleen had commissioned. Maggie had a great talent; she also had a secret. And if someone happened upon Colleen's memoir…

It was bloody annoying that her taped message cut out just before she'd delivered the book's whereabouts. She'd noticed that electronics went haywire when she was close by and shouldn't have touched the television screen. But she'd caught a glimpse of herself in the casket and was so shocked by the sight of her garishly made-up face, she'd leaned on the television for support. Which didn't help because of course she fell through it. She'd haunt the staff at the funeral parlor if she wasn't tied to the manor. Something she'd discovered when she'd tried to follow Hazel and Paige the day she'd died. She'd wanted to see what they were up to. She knew now, didn't she? Proving it would be another matter.

She went to stand behind Sean and Maura. "A brilliant job you did, Maggie," Colleen murmured, looking at the faces of those she loved in the painted crimson sky. She'd probably be bawling now if she were able to. If things hadn't worked out the way they did, she'd be with them. Ah well, it was looking like her family here and Greystone needed her more.

Which became as clear as crystal when she heard Maura say, "I don't care what George says—there must be a way to contest the will. You're a lawyer, figure it out."

"I've already gone over the will, Maura. George crossed

his t's and dotted his i's, and there's nothing to be gained by tying the will up in the courts."

Maura sighed. "I suppose you're right. It'll be up to Bethany then. The last thing she wants is to be tied to this mausoleum and Michael's cousins forever. Not to mention the money at stake. If Michael hopes to run a successful campaign for political office, he'll need the extra funds. Did Ms. Townsend tell you what that developer offered for Greystone and the estate?" She shook her head. "They'd all be set for life."

"Money isn't everything, Maura."

"It is to Bethany. She's accustomed to a certain lifestyle, you know. I'm sure she expects Michael to provide for her the same way her father did. If he isn't careful, he'll lose her."

"A blessing if you ask me," Sean said under his breath.

"Oh, hush. She'll make a wonderful politician's wife, and our son loves her." She turned to smile at her husband and patted his arm. "Thank you, darling. You always make me feel so much better."

"How? I barely said ten words."

"True, but by talking it out, I realized there's no need to worry after all. Bethany probably convinced Michael to sell on the drive back to Boston. We should leave too. You know how much I hate this place."

Colleen shuddered, and it had nothing to do with Maura passing through her body on her way out of the sitting room. No, it was because Colleen had assumed Michael's love for Greystone could withstand any attack Bethany launched. But he was his father's son, and Sean had never been able to stand up to his wife.

Colleen had to get rid of Bethany. There was only one way she knew how to do that…aside from murdering her, of course. Michael needed to know he was Mia's father now. Colleen had to find her book, but that was proving harder than she'd anticipated. None of the Widows Club had found it either. Then the answer came to her. The private investigator she'd hired to keep track of Sophie in LA years before had sent her a package. She had a copy of Mia's birth certificate in a locked drawer in the study.

"Sorry, Sophie my girl, but it's for your own good. Take it from someone who knows—lying weighs heavy on the soul. It's time for the truth to come out. This truth at least."

It felt like déjà vu. And not in a good way. Sophie was sitting at the kitchen table with her grandmother and Mia when the phone rang. Instead of lunch, they were having breakfast and Mia was drawing a picture of Mistletoe Cottage. "*Sì*. Yes. *Un momento*." Rosa let the phone dangle from the long cord. "Mia, come with Nonna. I'll show you my ticket for the raffle. We'll say a novena."

When Mia skipped off, Rosa whispered the dreaded words, "Protective Services. Her name is Ms. Olivetti. I liked the other one better." She made the sign of the cross.

Sophie's breakfast curdled in her stomach as she picked up the phone. "Sophie DiRossi speaking."

"Ms. Olivetti, the social worker assigned to your case. I have a date for your in-home visit. Do you have a pen?"

"Yes." As if she needed a pen. The date and time would be burned into her brain.

"Friday at nine a.m. sharp."

"Oh, I…my caseworker in LA said I would have at least a month to get settled. Mia and I are moving into our apartment today. I—"

"A matter was brought to our attention, and we've moved you up due to that."

Sophie briefly closed her eyes. She should have been nicer to Aidan's ex-wife. At the very least heard her out. Maybe tried to explain…Sophie frowned, but that was just yesterday. There's no way Harper could have called Protective Services between now and then…unless she knew someone personally. "What matter are you referring to, Ms. Olivetti?"

"There was an article, along with a photo, of you and your daughter in the *Harmony Harbor Gazette*. We, or at the very least, your previous caseworker, should have been made aware of the incident at Greystone Manor. Has the minor child spoken yet?"

Sophie clenched her teeth. "No, *Mia* has not spoken yet, but she's doing better. She no longer has nightmares, and she's acting more like herself." When she isn't crawling under caskets and smiling and waving at imaginary people.

"I'll make my own evaluations, thank you. I'll see you at nine a.m., Ms. DiRossi. We'll schedule follow-up visits at that time."

Follow-up visits? Oh God, she was never going to get rid of them. They'd always be there, watching her every move, judging her. She wouldn't measure up. They'd take Mia away. Her heart pounded so hard she couldn't hear herself think. And she needed to think. As she took slow, deep breaths, the answer came to her. No matter how much the thought of Michael digging into their life terrified her, she didn't have a choice. He was her best hope. "May I have your full name, Ms. Olivetti?"

"Olive Olivetti."

An inappropriate laugh escaped before Sophie managed to stifle it with her hand. The woman's name wasn't that funny. It had to be panic fueling the half-hysterical giggle.

"Goodbye, Ms. DiRossi." The caseworker's sharp tone left no doubt she'd heard Sophie laugh.

She rested her forehead against the phone as she hung up, positive she'd made everything worse. If the woman didn't have it out for her before, she did now.

"What did she say, *bella*?"

Sophie's feet were heavy, her heart filled with dread as she returned to her chair at the table. "There was an article in the *Gazette* about Halloween at Greystone, when Mia got lost in the tunnels. It sent up a red flag, I guess, and they've moved my in-home visit to Friday." She rested her elbows on the table and rubbed her eyes. "One of many from what Ms. Olivetti inferred."

Her grandmother pulled a chair closer and sat down. "These people, I don't trust them. They pick, pick, pick until they find something. You have to call Michael. He's an important man. A lawyer. He'll take care of this Olivetti person."

Her grandmother had questioned Sophie when she came home last night about what had upset her. She'd ended up telling Rosa as a means of distracting her from asking about Liam. Now she was wondering if she'd made a mistake. The way her grandmother was playing with the gold chain around her neck and her refusal to meet Sophie's eyes made her nervous.

"I'd already decided to ask for his help, Nonna. I'll call—"

"If you told him the truth, he'd take care of you and Mia." Rosa rubbed her thumb against her fingers. "He has money. You work too hard. If you married him—"

Stunned, she stared at her grandmother. Sophie opened her mouth and no words came out. They were stuck in her throat.

Her grandmother nodded, looking beyond her. "*Sì*. It would be best for everyone. Mia, she needs a father. She—"

Once her throat unlocked, the words exploded from Sophie's mouth. "Have you lost your mind? The man is getting married in six weeks. At Greystone. On Christmas Eve. You know the high-profile wedding that will save the manor?" What was she saying? Sophie shook her head. She'd lost her mind too. "I don't love him, and he doesn't love me. I don't think he even remembered me."

Rosa crossed her arms. "Once you tell him about his daughter, his memory, it will return."

"No doubt, but this would be far from the happy reunion you obviously think it would be, Nonna." She leaned across the table to ensure her grandmother's bedroom door was closed. It was, but she lowered her voice to be safe. "Have you met his fiancée? Can you imagine her as Mia's stepmother? And Maura? Do you know what would happen if she knew?"

Last night, after she'd left the manor, Sophie had asked herself those exact same questions on the drive home. Her guilt at keeping Mia a secret from Michael had eaten at her while she shared her story with Ava. Things looked different in the cold light of day. While there was a part of her that wanted to tell him—she was tired of the lies—the fear that the situation would play out just as she expected it to outweighed the guilt over keeping her secret.

Her grandmother lifted a shoulder. "We can get rid of the fiancée. Maura...she'd be a pain in the *culo*, but she doesn't live in Harmony Harbor. And Michael will move here once he marries you. It's perfect. He wants to save Greystone, and so do you."

"This is crazy talk. I don't know what's gotten into you."

Her grandmother uncrossed her arms and shuffled her chair closer then took Sophie's hands in hers. "It's time, *bella*. All the lies...they make you sick. They'll keep growing. Mia has to go to school sometime. You see her face when you lie about her age. Your worst fears? They're already coming to pass. If you do not end this now, you will lose your daughter's love."

Sophie closed her eyes. It wasn't fair. No one loved their child more than she did. All she'd ever tried to do was give Mia the best life she could. To make sure her daughter always knew how much she was loved. "I'll…I'll talk to Mia, try to explain. I'll ask Michael for his help, but I can't tell him, not yet. I need to know what kind of man he is. I need to know he'll love and protect Mia. I'll know better once I meet with him and Bethany. But I can't just spring this on them. It wouldn't be fair to either of them. If I'm going to have any chance at all of turning Greystone around, we need their wedding. And we need it to be perfect."

Rosa nodded. "I'll talk to the Widows Club. We'll have our next meeting at the manor and include the local business owners who aren't in the club. *Sì*. Yes, that will work."

Sophie didn't trust the smile on her grandmother's face. She looked a little too pleased with herself. "Nonna, what will—"

She patted Sophie's cheek. "Don't worry, *bella*. Nonna will take care of everything."

That's what Sophie was afraid of.

Every time Sophie looked in the rearview mirror at Mia, she got a painful lump in her throat. She felt like she'd already lost her. Not only because of the lies. Their lives would never be the same after she told Michael. And she would—as she'd promised her grandmother—tell him after his wedding. Even if everything went well and Michael and Mia didn't hate her for keeping them apart, Sophie's relationship with her daughter would change. It wouldn't be just the two of them. They'd have to figure out custody arrangements…

She felt shaky and breathless at the thought of not having her little girl with her, not tucking her in at night, not waking up to her sweet smile in the morning. Even if she hadn't seen that smile for far too long. And Michael would be able to give Mia everything Sophie could only dream of. Snowflakes dotted the windshield, and she thought how this might be the last Christmas she had with her daughter.

She blinked away the moisture welling in her eyes and forced a smile. "Are you excited we're going to live at Greystone and have our very own apartment?"

Mia met her eyes in the rearview mirror and nodded.

"You'll have a room of your own. That's pretty exciting, isn't it?" They'd always shared a bedroom. "As soon as Mommy gets paid, we'll go and buy you some things and decorate however you want. How about pink with purple polka dots?" She caught the small smile tugging on her daughter's lips and her heart lightened. "No? What about purple with pink pigs?"

The hint of a smile still playing on her lips, Mia pulled a folded piece of paper from her red velvet coat, leaning as far forward as the seat belt allowed. Sophie reached back and took it from her. Keeping her eyes on the road, she smoothed the paper open on her knee. Mistletoe Cottage. "You really love this place, don't you, baby? I'll ask Kitty if we can check it out this week. How does that sound?" The smile Mia gave her was wide, warm, and wonderful. Exactly the smile Sophie had been praying for.

She swallowed hard. She didn't want to mess up what she had to say by crying. "I know you've been mad at me for telling people you're six. You don't understand this right now, but I've been doing it to protect you, to protect us.

Really soon, I won't have to. Someday I hope you'll understand why I did what I did, baby. Someday I hope you'll be able to forgive me for everything." Greystone's imposing gates blurred, and Sophie swiped at her eyes.

She drove past the parking lot and the front of the manor before turning onto a loose gravel road. "Here we are. Home sweet home," she said as she pulled in front of the carriage house. The wood on the front and sides of the building was grayish brown while the roof was black with two peaked windows. Four barn doors were painted black and open to what would have been the bays that once housed Ronan Gallagher's impressive car collection. All that remained was a late model estate car in the far bay to the right.

"Okay, let's get you out of here and settled in our new place." Sophie hadn't had a chance to check out the furnished apartment, but Kitty had assured her it was in good shape. She grabbed the small suitcase off the backseat and set it on the road then lifted Mia out of the car and held her in her arms. She needed to hold her close for just a minute more. Mia surprised her by not immediately wriggling to get down. Then shocked her by touching Sophie's face, and when Mia lowered her fingers to lean in and flutter her lashes against Sophie's cheek, she barely kept it together.

"I've missed my butterfly kisses," she said in a strained whisper, holding Mia tight. "I love you, baby. I love you to the moon and back. Don't ever forget that." She set Mia on the ground and took her by the hand. Grabbing the suitcase with her other hand, Sophie led Mia to a set of stairs. Like the landing, they appeared a little rickety. The handrail needed to be tightened too. Thinking of the caseworker's upcoming visit, Sophie realized she had some work to do.

She started compiling a list in her head as she helped Mia up the stairs. Sophie wondered if Liam would mind giv-

ing her a hand. But when just the thought of him caused
her body to go warm and languid, she pushed the man and
his seductive lips and talented hands from her head. She
had to stay focused, and, as she'd discovered, Liam wasn't
conducive to focusing on anything other than being in his
arms. Right now, probably for the foreseeable future, the
only thing she should be thinking about was proving to Olive
Olivetti that she was a good mother.

Sophie put the suitcase on the landing and dug in her
pocket for the key. She handed it to Mia then helped her fit it
in the keyhole to unlock the door. The first thing that hit her
was the smell of dust and mildew. She set the suitcase on the
hardwood floor and closed the door, at the same time taking
in the living room. What looked to be a couch and two chairs
were covered in sheets, and a small TV sat kitty-corner between two white bookshelves.

"Let's see what's under here," Sophie said, lifting one of
the sheets to reveal a white-and-blue striped couch. Then she
walked over and pulled the sheets from two white canvas-
covered armchairs, sneezing as she did. "A little dusty, but
they're pretty. I'll vacuum them later. Let's go check out the
rest of the place."

She took Mia by the hand, and they peeked into the galley
kitchen to the left of the living room. The appliances were
old and could use a scrub. The white cupboards needed a
fresh coat of paint, but otherwise it looked like everything
was in working order. "Nonna won't be impressed, but it'll
work for us. And we can eat at the manor."

At Mia's enthusiastic nod, Sophie raised an eyebrow. "So
you think Helga cooks better than me, do you?"

This time Mia's nod was accompanied by a grin, and for
the first time in weeks, Sophie dared to hope that their relationship was on the mend. "Hey, you're not supposed to

agree with me," she teased, and tickled her daughter. Mia giggled, and it took everything Sophie had not to burst into happy tears. "Okay, let's finish the grand tour, and I'll take you for lunch." She kept her voice light and casual, afraid if Mia saw how deeply affected Sophie was it might spook her.

When they reached a closed door a few feet to the right of the kitchen, Sophie said, "This must be the bathroom. What do you think the chances are that it has a soaker…" She opened the door, and her jaw dropped. Liam stood barefoot and bare-chested with a white towel wrapped around his hips. His hair was wet and slicked back from his face, a razor raised to his foam-covered jaw.

Chapter Thirteen

♥

The door to the bathroom opened. Liam lowered his razor to smile at Mia and Sophie. She slammed the door in his face.

"You stay right where you are," she ordered him from the other side. "Mia baby, let's go check out your bedroom."

He heard the sound of their retreating footsteps and shrugged. He wasn't sure what the problem was. He'd just lifted the razor to his chin when the door reopened and Sophie stepped inside, closing it behind her. Her eyes flitted over him; then she raised her gaze to meet his, a hint of pink coloring her cheeks. He grinned at her reaction. At least he wasn't the only one feeling the attraction.

She glared at him. "If you wanted to give me a welcome-to-the-apartment present, flowers or a plant would have been a better idea than…than this." Her hand fluttered between them.

"You think I'm your welcome-to-the-apartment present?" he said, unable to keep the amusement from his voice.

"It's not funny, Liam. I have an impressionable daughter. You can't just show up at my apartment half naked, expecting to—"

He put the razor down and turned to her, crossing his arms. "Expecting what?"

"Don't do that. It won't work," she said, her eyes landing somewhere between his chest and the towel.

"Soph, you've lost me. I don't have a clue—"

"Please, as if you don't know how sexy you look right now standing there all naked and wet with your muscles on display."

He looked down at himself then raised his gaze to hers while holding back a full-out grin as it hit him what was going on. He didn't plan to enlighten her just yet. He was having too much fun. "You forgot my impressive abs."

Her eyes narrowed. "Where are your clothes? You need to get dressed and…What are you doing?" she asked as he closed the distance between them.

Her palms landed on his chest when he crowded her against the door. "I just thought, since I went to all this trouble to surprise you, you could at least give me a kiss."

"No, Mia is in the next room." She stared at his mouth. "Even if I wanted to kiss you, you have shaving cream on your face."

"Admit it. You like your present. And you really, really want to kiss me."

The corner of her mouth lifted as her hands inched their way up his chest and around his neck. She leaned into him. "Yes, I like my present. But I'd like it a whole lot more if Mia wasn't with me. I might want to kiss you a little."

"A lot," he said, and cupped her face in his hands, lowering his mouth to hers. He wanted to linger, to explore her sweet mouth with a deep, all-consuming kiss. Instead, be-

cause Mia was down the hall, he went with soft and tender
and long enough that she'd feel how much he wanted her.
He pulled back. Her face was tipped up, her eyes closed. He
smiled at the shaving cream covering the lower half of her
face and slowly trailed his finger through it to draw a foamy
line of white down her neck. With her eyes still closed, she
leaned back against the door, a small hum of pleasure escaping from between her parted lips. He ducked his head and
whispered, "You like that, don't you?"

She opened her heavy-lidded eyes and nodded, watching
him as he dipped his fingers beneath the V of her caramel-
colored sweater.

He felt her shiver beneath his fingers and moved her hair
off her shoulders with his other hand before rubbing his
cheek against hers. He'd never look at shaving cream the
same way. He wanted to cover every inch of her...

A knock sounded on the door. She shoved him away. Her
eyes wide and glazed, she wiped frantically at her face. "Be
right there, baby."

He'd gotten so carried away he'd forgotten about Mia.
"Sorry, Soph. Give me a sec, and I'll get some clothes on."
He turned to open the door leading into his apartment.

"You have got to be kidding me."

Liam glanced over his shoulder. "Nope, your apartment
shares a bathroom with mine. Welcome to the neighborhood," he said with a wink.

By the time he'd pulled on jeans and a sweatshirt, Sophie
had let Mia in the bathroom and was trying to explain to her
daughter why she had shaving cream all over her face.

Since she wasn't doing a very good job of it, Liam figured
he'd help her out. "Hey, Mia, you want to play with my
shaving cream like your mommy did?"

Sophie stared at him, and he cleared his throat. "Well,

not exactly like your mommy did…" Maybe he should stop while he was ahead. He lifted Mia onto the counter and grabbed the can. "Hold out your hands." He sprayed a dollop of cream into them. "Okay, go to town."

She grinned and turned to look in the mirror over the sink, patting the foam onto her cheeks. Liam shook the can, spraying some onto the tip of her nose. He caught Sophie's eyes in the mirror. She smiled at him. Mia did too. And just like the night in the tunnels, that smile wrapped around his heart and squeezed. Only this time it wasn't just Mia's; it was her mother's too. A powerful desire to make them smile like that all the time overcame him. It was as though they'd taken a pair of rib shears and opened up his chest and walked right inside past the walls he'd built around his heart. It made him uncomfortable. Maybe even a little panicked, he acknowledged when his exposed heart raced. He met a pair of blue eyes and golden eyes in the mirror, saw the flicker of concern in both, and forced his lips to curve.

"Okay, are you ready for a shave?"

Sophie gasped. "She's a girl. You can't shave her face. She'll have a beard before she hits puberty."

"Hey, I'm an old pro at this. I have a little sis…" He'd *had* a little sister. And it hit him like it sometimes did out of the blue. That deep, suffocating ache that made it difficult to breathe.

Sophie laid her hand on his arm and gave it a gentle squeeze. "Liam?"

He shook off the memories and managed a smile while reaching for his razor. He slid off the blade and handed it to Mia. "Have at it, short stuff."

Looked like today was going to be one of those days where he couldn't escape the memories. He used to call Riley "short stuff." Maybe he'd fallen back on the nickname because there was something about Mia that reminded him of his baby sister. Riley had been around Mia's age with the same wavy hair and blue eyes.

Sophie nudged him and mouthed, *You okay?*

He nodded and smiled at Mia in the mirror. "You missed a spot," he said, and touched his nose. "So, what are you ladies doing to celebrate moving in and having me as a neighbor?"

"You're not joking? You really are living there?" Sophie asked, looking past him into the apartment. Definitely not as happy about the prospect as her daughter, Liam thought, taking in Mia's sunny smile and Sophie's worried frown. "Don't worry. I won't be around for long. I'm starting a four-day stretch at the station later today, and then I'll be heading home to Boston."

"You'll be gone Friday morning by nine?"

Her initial lack of enthusiasm didn't bother him…Okay, after that kiss, it kind of did. But this was more than just a lack of enthusiasm; she almost seemed panicked at the prospect of him being around. "Is there a problem I'm not aware of?"

"I'm sorry. I didn't mean to sound rude. It's just…Mia, how about we tidy up the apartment a bit, and then maybe Liam will come for lunch with us at the manor?" She glanced at him. "Unless you're busy."

"Nope. Lunch sounds good. Shift doesn't start till five." He grabbed a towel and wiped the rest of the shaving cream from Mia's face then lifted her off the counter. He tossed the towel to Sophie. "You might want to…" He gestured to her face. Probably better that she took care of it than him. He didn't seem able to stop himself from kissing and touching her when he got too close.

"Thanks," she said, and wiped her face. "Mia, you can

start unpacking the suitcase. Mommy will be there in a minute."

Her daughter looked from Sophie to Liam then nodded. He caught Mia's grin when she skipped off. The mischievous smile looked familiar. It was one he'd seen on his matchmaking great-grandmother's and grandmother's faces every time they thought they'd found his one. Which inevitably turned out not to be the one. Probably because he didn't want a one. Given that he didn't, Mia's mischievous grin should have made him nervous. It didn't.

"So, are you going to tell me why you want me out of here Friday morning or is it personal?"

She leaned back and pulled the door closed, leaving it open an inch. "The caseworker called this morning to set up the in-home visit. They moved it to Friday morning."

"That was fast. But maybe it's for the best, Soph. You'll get it over with, and you can stop worrying about it."

"It's fast because of an article in the *Gazette* about Halloween at the manor. They red-flagged me. That's not the end of it either. The caseworker is scheduling more visits." She rubbed her wrist. "I should have let them know what happened at Greystone. Now, because I didn't..."

The one visit, other than he knew it upset Sophie, didn't seem like that big a deal given the circumstances. But this...He pulled out his cell phone.

"What are you doing?"

His cousin's voice mail kicked in, and he held up his finger. "Hey, Mike, it's Liam. Give me a call as soon as you get this."

"You didn't have to call Michael for me. I was going to do it myself."

"Good. Now it's done. Just in case my cousin can't charm or browbeat the CPS into dropping your case, let's take a walk through the apartment and see if anything needs to be done before Friday."

"You're a good guy, Liam Gallagher. I wish…" She gave her head a slight shake, and before Liam could ask what she wished, Mia was back with a piece of paper.

"Let me guess—Mistletoe Cottage," he said with a laugh.

Mia smiled and nodded.

Liam crouched in front of her. "You do a lot of nodding and head shaking. Gotta be hard on your neck. Why don't you try mouthing the words? No pressure. Just a thought."

She started to nod then stopped and mouthed, *Okay*.

"Excellent." He put up his fist, and they fist bumped. Then he stood up. "How about I go to Jolly Rogers and pick us up some lunch, and then we'll walk over to Mistletoe Cottage and eat there?"

Mia jumped up and down, mouthing, *Yes, yes*.

"Mom?" Liam raised an eyebrow at Sophie.

She looked torn. "Sure, but I'll have to pay you back once I get—"

He knew how much it cost her to admit that she was broke. Like her brother, Sophie had always been proud. "My treat. You can have me for dinner when I'm back in town."

Sophie tilted her head to look at Mia, who was mouthing, *Bad idea*.

Liam laughed. "I don't believe you. I've never met a DiRossi who couldn't cook."

Mia pointed at her mother.

"I think she inherited her uncle's sense of humor," Liam said. "Let's do that walk-through. That way if I need anything, I can pick it up at the hardware store before I grab our lunch."

It took all of fifteen minutes to check out the place. Liam imagined he could take care of everything that afternoon. Once Mia mouthed what she wanted for lunch, Sophie turned the television on for her.

Liam tightened the knob on a kitchen cabinet. "You need anything else while I'm downtown, Soph?"

"No, you've done too much for us already, Liam. I really appreciate it. And I'm paying for whatever you're picking up at the hardware store, so—"

"I'm happy to help out any way I can. That's what friends do, Soph. You're not paying the bill from the hardware store. I'll put it on the manor's tab." After walking through the apartment and seeing how little they had, he wished she'd let him do more.

"The manor has an account at the hardware store?"

"Old Man O'Malley's been running a tab for Greystone for as long as I can remember. Don't imagine it's changed."

She sighed. "If you don't mind, can you get the outstanding balance?"

"No problem. Have you had a chance to go over the books?" He caught her grimace. "That bad, huh?"

Her chin went up. "Actually, the books are in great shape."

He tapped the tip of her nose. "Careful, it's going to grow. I may not be on Team Greystone, but I am on Team Sophie, so whatever you need…" He frowned. "Hey, what's up with the tears?"

She moved into him and did a face-plant into his chest, wrapping her arms around his waist. "You have to stop doing stuff for us, taking care of us like you do. You make me want things I can't have."

"Like what?" he asked quietly, stroking her hair.

"A man to share my life with. A man like you. I don't have time for a serious relationship."

"Well, you're in luck. I don't do serious," he said, and

kissed the corner of her mouth. He felt someone's eyes on him and looked over to see Mia watching them. She gave him a thumbs-up.

Liam lifted his phone and took a picture of Sophie and Mia twirling under a shower of red and yellow leaves that were substituting for snow. Sophie sang "Let It Go" with Mia mouthing the words.

He held up the bag from Jolly Rogers when they took their bows. "Okay, Elsa and Anna, it's time to go. I'm starved."

If he didn't have to take care of the repairs at the apartment before his shift, he'd be happy to watch them play make-believe for however long they wanted. He loved seeing this side of Sophie. Loved hearing her laugh, watching her face light up when she looked at her daughter. But what was supposed to be a ten-minute walk through the woods to the cottage had already taken an hour.

"Kristoff sounds grumpy, Anna. Should we take him to the cottage and feed him, or make him sing for us first?"

Mia spread her arms wide and tipped her head back.

"Sorry, Kristoff. Looks like you're singing for your lunch."

He shook his head with a laugh then belted out a couple choruses of the song. By now, he knew the words. He should since Sophie had been singing the song for the better part of twenty minutes. Mia clapped and ran to hug his legs.

"Be still, my heart," Sophie said, patting her chest. Then she hugged him too. "Thank you."

"For what?" he asked her when Mia let him go to skip along the path.

"For being you."

He took her hand, reminding himself he didn't do serious.

But like the last six times he'd told himself that in the past hour, it wasn't really working.

Especially when Sophie smiled at him like she was now. "In case you can't tell, we're having fun."

He lifted their joined hands to her face and traced her lips with his thumb. "I got that. I'm glad. It's nice to see you happy. Both of you."

She glanced at Mia, who'd crouched on the path to collect rocks. "You're great with her, you know. I should have thought to tell her to mouth words."

"Forest for the trees, Soph. Sometimes it's hard to see what's right in front of you. Cut yourself some slack. You've had a lot to deal with."

"What about you? All we ever do is talk about me." She gave his hand a gentle squeeze. "How are you doing, Liam?"

"I'm good. Why?"

"Um…shot in the line of duty ring a bell? I heard what happened."

"Of course you did. It's Harmony Harbor." He glanced at her, smiled. "I'm getting there. You don't have to worry about me."

"You don't have to worry about me either, yet you do. So humor me. Tell me what it is you're dealing with. It might help to talk about it, you know."

"What are my chances of you *letting it go*?"

She laughed. "About as good as you think…" She frowned. "Mia, what's wrong?"

Mia stood frozen on the path then slowly turned around, her eyes wide and overly bright. Liam scanned the path up ahead, the woods on either side. "I think we're in trouble," he murmured, but at least he'd gotten a reprieve. "Look." He pointed to the red-tail deer to the right of them.

"If she thinks it's one of Santa's reindeer, we are. But as

long as its brother and sister aren't hanging out at the cottage, we should be good," she whispered.

Handing the bag to Sophie, he walked quietly to Mia and picked her up. "Let's see if we can get a little closer." Her eyes glued to the deer, she nodded. They got within ten feet of the deer when something spooked her.

"Wasn't she beautiful, baby?"

Mia mouthed, *Santa?*

"I'm pretty sure the big guy and his reindeer are too busy at the North Pole to be paying us a visit, sweetheart," Liam said as they walked out of the woods and onto the private dirt road. Across the road behind a low stone fence his grandfather had built, sat the two-story cottage nestled in a stand of trees. Wreaths hung in the two windows and on the white door between them.

Mia stared at the cottage, hands over her heart.

"Looks like Jasper got a fire going for us," Liam said, nodding at the smoke spiraling from the chimney on the left. There was another chimney on the right.

"Should we go inside, baby? Or do you need a minute to take it all in?" Sophie asked, a smile in her voice.

"I think she needs a minute, Mom."

Mia wriggled in his arms, and he put her down. She ran to the white picket gate, pushing it open. "I'll go in and heat up our lunch," Liam said when Mia headed around the side of the cottage.

"Okay, we won't be long." Sophie handed him the bag, hugging herself as she started after her daughter.

"You cold?" She wore a denim jacket over her sweater.

"I'm good."

"Sure you are. Wear this." He shrugged out of his leather jacket and handed it to her.

"You can't help yourself, can you?" she said with a smile.

Once she put on the jacket, she reached up on her toes to kiss his cheek. "Don't think I've forgotten our conversation before the deer interrupted us. I'll be expecting a story when I come in."

"I can do that. How about Rudolph the Red-Nosed Reindeer?"

"Ha-ha. I'll see you in a bit." She tromped off after her daughter.

But Liam got another reprieve. Enchanted with the cottage, mother and daughter explored every inch of every room. He understood the attraction. Over the years, the cottage had been featured in several magazines. The living room and kitchen both had fireplaces and whitewashed stone walls, and honey-colored wood framed the windows and doors, and decorated the ceilings. The furniture wasn't fancy; it was oversized and comfortable. Just like the feather beds in each of the three bedrooms upstairs.

Not surprisingly, Mia had been awed by the Christmas decorations. Especially the decorated tree in the corner of the living room. Once Liam turned on the multicolored Christmas lights, she'd parked herself in front of it and hadn't moved. She'd eaten her lunch there while he and Sophie ate on the floor in front of the fireplace.

"That was so good. Jolly Rogers makes the best clam chowder."

"Really? I couldn't tell if you liked it or not," he said then mimicked the humming sound she'd made through the entire lunch.

She laughed and pushed her plate toward him. "Eat the rest of my fries. I can't eat another bite." She glanced to where Mia played with a stuffed reindeer and an elf then smiled at him. "Thanks for bringing us here and for lunch. It was perfect. I hope Kitty didn't mind us coming."

"Of course she didn't. And you don't have to thank me. I enjoyed the day as much as you. Feel free to come here anytime you want. I'll give you the key."

"Don't let Mia hear you say that. She's been obsessed with this place since she saw it in the flyer for the raffle. Dana did a beautiful job decorating. It looks like it belongs on a Hallmark card."

"Grams tells me it's cottage chic, whatever that's supposed to mean. Place has great bones, though. They don't build homes like this anymore."

"Whoever wins the raffle will have a very merry Christmas. Can you imagine waking up in that feather bed in the master bedroom on Christmas morning? It's huge."

He'd done quite a bit of fantasizing when they'd been checking out the bedrooms and it had nothing to do with Christmas morning. "Soph, Mia knows family and staff can't enter the raffle, doesn't she?"

She nodded. "She's been saying a novena over Rosa's ticket ever since…" She briefly closed her eyes. "My grandmother can't win either, can she?"

" 'Fraid not."

"It's nice to have a dream. I think I'll let Mia hang on to hers a little longer."

"What about you? What about your dreams?"

"I used to have them. Believed they had a chance of coming true, and then they all went up in smoke."

He opened his mouth to tell her she needed a new dream, but his ringing cell stopped him from sharing the thought. Maybe it was a good thing he'd been interrupted. There was something about Mistletoe Cottage that had him thinking about happily-ever-after. "Hey, Mike, thanks for calling me back. Hang on a sec." He motioned for Sophie to follow him to the kitchen. Once they were out of Mia's earshot, he said,

"I've got Sophie with me. Looks like she might be needing your help with CPS after all. Okay. I'll put her on. Thanks, bro."

Sophie turned her back on him while she talked to his cousin on the phone. Liam probably should have given her some privacy, but it wasn't like she'd kept anything from him. He wet a cloth in the white farmer's sink and mopped the crumbs off the counter. Outside the window, gray clouds hung low in the sky and the trees swayed. Snow was on its way. It would be the first snowfall of the season, which usually meant a busy night at the station. He ignored the telling clench in his stomach.

Sophie disconnected and handed him his phone. There was something about the way she was looking at him that made him uneasy. "Everything okay?"

"He's going to see what he can do, but he recognized my caseworker's name. He didn't sound as hopeful as he did the other day. At least about Friday's visit."

"If anyone can help you out with this, it's Mike. He has connections. A lot of them."

"That's what he said. He was very nice. Not so—"

"Arrogant? Full of himself?" His cousin had been an entitled ass in his twenties. "He's not the same guy you remember, Soph. He's a good man. I'd trust him with my life. You can depend on him."

"I…" She gave her head a slight shake then wrapped one arm around her waist while pressing a hand to her mouth, angling her body away from him.

He put a hand on her shoulder. "Hey, what's going on?"

She slowly turned her head and lifted her eyes to his. "He's Mia's father."

At first he wasn't sure he heard her right. Or maybe he was hoping he hadn't. "Come again?"

"Michael, he's Mia's father," she whispered. "Don't look at me like that. I did what I thought was best. You don't know what—"

"All this time…So everything was a lie. The fiancé who died… I thought I knew you. Guess I don't, because the Sophie DiRossi I knew wouldn't keep a secret like this. Not in a million years."

"You have no idea what you're talking about. Try being eighteen and pregnant and alone."

"You didn't have to be. That was your choice. You didn't give your daughter or Mike one. Mia deserved better. So did my cousin. If you don't tell him, I will."

Chapter Fourteen

♥

By the time Sophie and Mia arrived at the manor the next morning, Sophie was fifteen minutes late for her meeting with the Widows Club and local business owners. Given the amount of sleep she'd gotten, she shouldn't have bothered to put her head on the pillow. Liam's accusations, his anger, and his warning played over in her head the entire night. She didn't think anyone could make her feel worse than she already did, but Liam managed to.

He'd accused her of being selfish. Selfish because she'd forced her daughter to live in near poverty instead of in the lap of luxury her father could provide. Maybe the accusations wouldn't have hurt so much if they hadn't come from Liam. A man who'd ignited a spark, a hope, the nugget of a dream in a woman who'd thought she'd given up on them.

She only hoped their afternoon together hadn't sparked one in her daughter. But there'd already been signs that it had. She'd caught Mia listening at the adjoining door in the bathroom last night and this morning. Liam had hidden his anger from Mia when he'd walked them back to the apartment, but he hadn't stuck around to help as he'd promised. Sophie was glad he hadn't. If she never saw him again, it would be too soon.

"Good morning, miss," Jasper said when he met them in the vestibule. Sophie blinked. Other than looking down his nose at her, the stern-faced older man had barely acknowledged her arrival in the past. She glanced over her shoulder, positive someone had come in behind her. There was no one but them. The older man smiled at Mia. "How are you this morning, Miss Mia?"

Sophie pinched herself to make sure she was actually awake. She knew she must be because Mia's hand was in hers and her daughter was mouthing, *Good*. She knew for certain she was awake when Mia mouthed, *Liam*.

Sophie prayed he wasn't there, terrified of the nightmare that would unfold if he was. She had no idea if he'd follow through on his threat and tell Michael. She prayed Liam's friendship with her brother would make him think twice.

"As I understand it, Master Liam is staying at the firehouse." As though sensing Mia's disappointment, Jasper added, "I'm sure you'll see him before he returns to Boston." He glanced at Sophie and cleared his throat. "I hope I haven't overstepped, miss, but I thought perhaps you wouldn't have had the time to buy Miss Mia suitable outerwear." He reached behind him for a large box. Sophie recognized the logo. Guppies was a high-end children's clothing store in town. One Sophie could only dream of shopping in for Mia's clothing.

Ashamed she didn't have the money to provide a new snowsuit for her daughter, Sophie opened her mouth to protest. She'd hoped the cold weather would hold off until she received her first paycheck. It hadn't. She'd dressed Mia in the red velvet coat and her blue rubber boots to make the trek through the snow this morning. When Sophie looked into the older man's eyes and saw only compassion and not judgment, she swallowed her pride and smiled. "That was thoughtful. Thank you. Thank you very much. What do you say to Jasper, Mia?"

Her daughter was too busy opening the box—revealing a gorgeous, puffy pink jacket, a pair of pink snow pants, and furry winter boots that matched the trim on the jacket's hood—to say anything. She held up each item to show Sophie, her eyes shining with excitement.

"They're so beautiful, baby." Sophie was surprised she could get the words past the lump in her throat. "Thank Jasper for your—" She broke off when Mia launched herself at the older man and hugged his legs. Her face tipped up, she mouthed her thanks. Over and over again.

Sophie pressed her lips together to hold back a laugh at the uncomfortable expression on Jasper's face. He awkwardly patted Mia's head. "You're most welcome, Miss Mia. There's a hat, mittens, and scarf under the tissue paper." He turned to Sophie when her daughter let him go to lift the pink paper from the box. "Mrs. Fitzgerald's granddaughter Brie is managing the shop. If you're not happy with anything or something doesn't fit, she said to let her know, and she'll take care of it."

"I have a feeling Mia wouldn't let me take anything back even if I wanted to." She nodded at her daughter, who'd already taken off her coat and rubber boots and was pulling on the snow pants. Sophie wanted Jasper to understand just how much his thoughtful gesture meant to her daughter. She lowered her voice and shared, "Mia's never had anything brand-new before. I hope you know how much we both appreciate what you've done."

He gave her a brisk nod. "Quite. If you'd like, I can take Miss Mia with me when I shovel the walkways."

Mia, who'd overheard his offer, pulled the pink knit hat on her head at the same time nodding enthusiastically.

"She'll be in good hands, miss. I'll watch her like a hawk."

Sophie ignored the anxious flutter in her stomach. There wasn't much the older man missed at Greystone, so she knew he wouldn't let anything happen to her daughter. "Thank you. I'm sure she'd love that. Mia, listen to Jasper."

Jasper reached behind him and then handed Sophie a clipboard. "I've taken the liberty of making you a list of the most reliable vendors, highlighting the ones I'd advise you to stay clear of."

She reached in her purse for her glasses and put them on to scan the precise and detailed list. "This is perfect, Jasper. Thank you."

He nodded. "You'll be pleased to know that Miss Adams's grandmother booked twelve rooms from the twenty-first to the twenty-fourth. She also blocked the remaining rooms from the twenty-second to the twenty-fourth. She's couriered the deposit."

"I can't tell you how much I needed some good news today. We might just pull this off after all, Jasper."

"I see no reason why we won't. But if I may make a suggestion…"

"Please do." From the very beginning, she'd hoped to win the older man's grudging support, but his acceptance of her as a member of the team was more than she'd dreamed possible. So much more that she felt like she'd stepped into an alternate universe.

"I would suggest the possibility of a morning or afternoon wedding to Miss Adams. That way the guests won't miss out on their own holiday celebrations. If you mention that it is an accepted tradition among the British royals, Miss Adams may be more amenable to the idea."

"I didn't like having to ask the staff to work late on Christmas Eve, and a morning or afternoon wedding would solve that problem. And I think you've given me the perfect way to sell Bethany on the idea. I take it you've spent some time with her."

The corner of his mouth twitched. "Quite." He looked down at Mia, who tugged on his hand. "Unless there's anything else, we'll take our leave. The Widows Club and business owners are waiting for you in the dining room."

Sophie gave her daughter a quick kiss, thanked Jasper again, and headed for the meeting.

Kitty emerged from the room, smiling when she caught sight of Sophie. "There you are, my dear. I was getting worried about you." The older woman's forehead creased. "Is everything all right? You don't look well."

"Sorry, I'm late. I didn't get much sleep last night. But Jasper just gave me some wonderful news. Did you hear?"

Kitty looped her arm through Sophie's. "Yes, and you don't have to pretend with me. I know this is difficult for you. But we're going to do everything we can to make it as easy as possible."

Sophie froze. "I don't understand—"

"I overheard Rosa talking about it with some of the Widows Club. I'd forgotten you dated Michael. Don't mind me saying so, but I always thought you and Liam…" She waved her hand. "It's neither here nor there. We'll find you a nice young man to get your mind off Michael."

"I'm not sure what my grandmother said, but my mind isn't on—"

Kitty continued as though Sophie hadn't spoken. "Now

that we've solved that problem, I think we may have a bigger one. Your grandmother went quiet when she caught me listening in, but she can't fool me. She's up to something. I'm afraid she might try to sabotage the wedding."

"I'll speak to her, Kitty. But she knows what's at stake and how important the wedding is to Greystone's future. She wants the manor to stay in the family as much as we do."

"Oh, yes, I know that, my dear. Everyone in that room does." She wrinkled her nose. "Except Hazel and Paige. It's just that your grandmother's plan to save the manor and ours are at cross-purposes. She wants a wedding all right. Only with a different bride. You."

All Sophie wanted was twenty minutes, even fifteen would have been great, to savor Jasper's good news. After yesterday, she didn't think it was too much to ask. But thanks to her grandmother, she was lucky if she got two.

"Don't worry, Kitty. I'll take care of my grandmother. And just so you know, I have no romantic interest in Michael. None whatsoever. I want his and Bethany's wedding to be as perfect as you do."

"It's for the best, my dear. It truly is. I'm something of a matchmaker, you know. You and Michael, you're not a good fit. Now you and Liam—"

"Trust me. Liam and I aren't a good fit either. And I'm honestly not looking for a relationship right now. I have to focus all my energy on Greystone. And Mia, of course."

"You're right. We can't have anything distracting you from the job at hand. Leave your grandmother to me. Since Colleen's passed, the Widows Club's loyalties have been divided. Half want me to take over, the other half your grandmother, but I'm gaining momentum."

If Kitty was trying to make Sophie feel better, it wasn't working. "We should probably focus on the meeting for now. Is there anything I need to know? Jasper gave me a list of reliable vendors." Sophie raised the clipboard.

Kitty angled her head to look at the list. "Hmm, I wonder why he highlighted Charlie Angel's name. He owns the Salty Dog, you know. He's not what I'd call reliable. Truth be told, he's something of a scoundrel. Rumor has it he's into something illegal." Far from looking scandalized, Kitty looked intrigued.

"Sorry, I forgot to mention the highlighted names are the ones to avoid."

"I should have realized Jasper would never recommend Charlie. They have a long-standing feud."

"There seems to be a lot of those in town." Sophie prayed that, once her secret was revealed, she wouldn't start another one.

Kitty gave her an impish grin. "Yes, it's quite fun. There's never a dull moment in Harmony Harbor."

After her conversation with Kitty, the meeting went much better than Sophie expected. Though the divide between the members of the Widows Club was somewhat worrisome. Half of the women sat with Rosa on one side of the room, the other half with Kitty. Anytime Rosa or Kitty offered a suggestion, her supporters cheered while her opponents booed.

However, Sophie's biggest concern, at least for now, was Helga. The sandwiches she'd served were unpalatable at best. And Ava, whom Sophie had asked to assist in the kitchen today, was nowhere in sight. Sophie drew her gaze from the kitchen door as Dana Templeton approached.

Sophie smiled. Although she wasn't exactly sure why, she felt sorry for the beautiful redhead. She seemed incredibly lonely and sad.

Dana gave her a small smile in return. "If you need

any help, Sophie, you can add me to your list." Her well-modulated voice bespoke wealth and privilege. Everything about her did, from her conservative, tailored clothing, to her hair and manicure.

"I'd love to have your help, Dana. I was at Mistletoe Cottage yesterday. You did an incredible job. Are you an interior designer?"

"Thank you. No, I'm…I'm not qualified to do anything really."

"Don't sell yourself short. It takes more than just a good eye and exquisite taste to do what you did." She studied the woman, getting the sense that Dana was carrying a heavy burden. As a woman who knew the feeling only too well, Sophie was moved to try and help. At the very least, offer her friendship. "If you have the time and are interested, I could really use an assistant. Something of an event planner. There's not a lot of money in the budget, but I'll speak to Mr. Wilcox and Kitty about working out an arrangement for free room and board." Now that Sophie had made the offer, she really hoped Dana would take the job. Because the more she thought about it, adding wedding planner to the already overlong list of things she needed to accomplish in the next few weeks was overwhelming.

"Money isn't an issue, Sophie. I have all the time in the world too. I'd be more than happy to be your assistant."

"Change of plans, you're no longer my assistant. You're the official event planner-slash-wedding coordinator. And it's only fair that you be compensated. I have a meeting with Kitty and Mr. Wilcox this week."

"I don't know what to say."

"Please say you'll take the job. I"—she glanced at the women clustered into small groups talking before turning back to Dana—"I have some personal issues I have to deal with in the next few days, and I'm afraid they might complicate my interactions with Bethany and Michael."

"I need something to keep myself occupied, Sophie. I'm more than happy to take the job. If you can give me an idea what you had in mind, I can get started right away."

"That would be great. Why don't we go to the study and we can look at what I have so far? Then we'll set you up in an office of your own," Sophie said as she gathered her things.

"I just have to get something from my room. I'll meet you in your office."

"Okay. I'll see you in a few minutes." Sophie went to each group of women to say her goodbyes before heading to the study. A pretty blonde caught up to her as she left the dining room.

"Sophie, I'm Brie Fitzgerald. I'm managing Guppies for my grandmother." The woman offered her hand. "I just wanted to check and make sure everything fit."

"Yes, perfectly. My daughter loved everything."

Brie smiled. "I'm sure Jasper was relieved. It took him two hours to find what he wanted. It had to be the best."

Once again Sophie was touched by the thought and care he'd taken to choose Mia's snowsuit. "It was very kind of him."

"Our holiday wear just came in. We're hosting an event to reveal the line to our customers next weekend. Be sure to stop by with your daughter." Something caught her attention, and she smiled and waved. "I see someone I know. Nice meeting you, Sophie. I'll e-mail you an invitation to the event."

"Nice meeting you, too, Brie. Thanks for the…" Sophie didn't bother finishing the sentence because Brie was already halfway across the lobby. Curious to see who put the flirty smile on the woman's face, Sophie glanced at the entrance. The man the manager of Guppies was obviously anxious to see, and interested in, was none other than Liam Gallagher—looking ridiculously hot in his firefighter's uniform.

Liam kept his smile in place and returned the blonde's wave. He'd always had a good head for names, but for the life of him, he couldn't remember the name of the pretty woman walking his way. Probably because he was focused on Sophie and caught the moment her eyes lifted in his direction. Saw the panic come over her face. She looked exhausted. No doubt his threat had kept her up last night. She wasn't the only one who hadn't gotten any sleep. When he wasn't responding to calls—there'd been two minor pileups and a chimney fire—he'd been thinking of Sophie. Sophie and Michael. At least they'd distracted Liam from his own problems. He'd been fine for the first two calls, but had another flashback when they'd responded to the chimney fire.

Sophie backtracked and took the back hall. He didn't blame her for wanting to avoid him. He'd been angry yesterday. For the most part, in his opinion, rightly so. He'd been angry on his cousin's behalf and Mia's. They both deserved to know the truth. Part of his anger was fueled by jealousy too. He was jealous that Mia and Sophie would now be tied to his cousin forever. They'd share a bond and connection that Liam never would. One that he'd finally admitted to himself that maybe, just maybe, he wanted. Or at the very least thought he might. That's why the news had hit him so hard and he'd said things he regretted. He planned to apologize to her and withdraw his threat. He still expected her to tell his cousin, but it would be on her timeline, not his.

He smiled at the blonde when she reached him. He'd

met her when her nephew and niece escaped from the house up the street to get an early start trick-or-treating. The little boy had been dressed as a fireman. "Hey there, how's your nephew?"

"Still wearing his uniform around the house." She grinned. "You don't remember my name, do you?"

"Sure I do. Bad habit, I always call pretty women *there*."

"I'll put you out of your misery, but only because you complimented me. It's Brie."

He leaned back and gave her a distracted smile. He had a clear line of sight to the study. He had a feeling that's where Sophie was headed. "I won't forget again. Have you taken your nephew for a visit to the station yet?"

"No, but now that you're working there, I'll be sure to bring him by. Maybe we can grab that coffee."

"I'm just helping my dad out for a couple days. I'm heading back to Boston Friday." He glanced toward the study again. Sophie was there and caught his eye then quickly looked away. "Brie, I have something I need to do."

"No problem. How about—"

Liam heard Sophie cry out as she opened the door to the study. He ran toward her, belatedly realizing he'd cut off Brie. "Sorry, another time," he called over his shoulder.

"Soph, what's…What the hell happened in here?" It looked like a tornado had blown through the study. Papers were strewn from one end of the room to the other. All the desk drawers were pulled out, two of them lying on the floor.

"I don't know. It looks like someone broke in. Maybe they were looking for Colleen's…" As though just realizing who she was talking to, her expression closed off, and she gestured to the door. "I'll take care of it."

"Look, I know you're mad, Soph. But—"

"You don't know anything about me, Liam Gallagher. So

just get your sanctimonious self out of here and leave me alone. Go back to your girlfriend."

She turned away from him and put her purse and leather portfolio on the corner of the desk. He shut the door, crossed his arms, and leaned against it. She looked over her shoulder. "I said—"

"I heard what you said. Maybe I overreacted yesterday. It was a shock. I'm not going to tell Michael. You can do it when you're ready. But, Soph, you have to tell him."

She bent over to pick up some papers. "Are you expecting me to thank you? Because if you are, you can forget about it. After what you said to me..." She whirled around and threw a fistful of papers at him. "I didn't deserve that, Liam. I'm a good mother. I did the best I could. Maura would have taken my daughter from me or insisted that I give her up. The Michael I knew then, the Michael he used to be, would have given in to her and you know it."

"Calm down." He moved cautiously toward her. "I should have given you a chance to explain. Will you tell me now?"

She moved away from him. "No, you lost your chance. I have a meeting with Dana in a few minutes. I have to clean this up."

"It'll go faster if you let me help."

"Fine." She turned away to clear off the top of the desk. "Just put them in a pile here, and I'll organize them later."

"Soph?"

"What?"

"Brie isn't my girlfriend," he said, crouching to pick up a file folder filled with documents.

"And I'm supposed to care, why?"

"I didn't want you to think I was seeing someone when I've been making out with you."

"Please, we didn't make out."

He gathered the papers into a pile and straightened to put them on the desk. One fell off. "Really? Maybe you'd like to clue me in to exactly what we were doing then." He scooped the paper off the floor, briefly scanning the document as he returned it to the top of the pile. No, couldn't be. He rubbed his eyes and read the names on the birth certificate again, mother and daughter, the date of birth. His knees went weak.

"What's wrong with you? What are you looking at?"

He raised his gaze to hers. "When was Mia conceived?"

"None of your damn business. Just get out—"

"Sophie, tell me when Mia was conceived," he said through clenched teeth.

"July twenty-eighth. The night of the party at Greystone, okay?"

"Where?"

"Oh my God, I don't know why you think this is any of your—"

His jaw pulsated from clenching it so tight. "Either you tell me or I ask Michael."

She glared at him. "Kismet Cove. Happy now?"

Afraid his legs were going to give out, he pulled the chair over to sit down. He cleared his throat, but his voice still came out a rough rasp. "Mia isn't Michael's, Sophie. She's mine."

Chapter Fifteen

♥

Honorable, honest…virtues Liam's parents had instilled in their sons. Up until that night at Kismet Cove, Liam had done his best to live up to their expectations. It hadn't been difficult. His father modeled the attributes every day and ingrained them in Liam and his brothers. He'd made a drunken mistake, but it had been an honest one. Silence had seemed the better part of valor. He'd been protecting Sophie, Michael, and in the end, he acknowledged, himself.

He'd never intended to go to the party. Couldn't stand seeing his cousin with Sophie. He'd done his best to avoid them that summer. But the day of the party at Greystone, his cousin started asking him questions, and Liam knew he was close to figuring it out. So he went. And like pretty much everyone there, he had too much to drink…

Liam's T-shirt stuck to his skin. The night was hot and sultry and smelled of salt water and roses. He stretched out on the damp grass and tracked the clouds moving across the moon. He closed his eyes when everything started to spin. It didn't help, and he staggered to his feet.

"Hey, lightweight," Marco called out to him. "Where you going? Get over here and meet my new friend. She's got a cousin."

He waved him off. "I'm gonna crash at the manor. Have fun." The word cousin *left a bitter taste in his mouth. He pretty much hated his right now. Hated what Michael was doing behind Sophie's back.*

As Liam made his way to the trash can to toss his half-full bottle of beer, he saw Sophie staring at a couple making out under a tree. It was Michael and Shay Angel. Standing in her white string bikini with her long hair streaming down her back, Sophie was so beautiful it hurt to look at her. He wanted to go to her, take the wine bottle from her hand, and tell her to forget about his asshole cousin. Tell her she'd picked the wrong Gallagher; she should have picked him.

He headed for the manor. She wouldn't listen to him. Wouldn't care that he'd been in love with her for years. He heard the sound of a bottle breaking, a muffled cry, and turned to see Sophie running for the beach. He called out to her. She was drunk, upset, and heading for Kismet Cove. It was dark and dangerous. He started to run, tripped over a rock, and landed on his knees. Shit, he was wasted too. He pushed himself to his feet, calling out to her as he ran across the grass to the beach. He jumped from a boulder into the cold sand. He heard her crying, the sound muffled by the waves rolling onto shore. A few feet to his right he saw a flash of white and went to her, kneeling at her side. "Soph—"

She threw herself into his arms, nearly knocking him on his ass. "I'm sorry—" He started to apologize for his cousin being a jerk, but she shut him up with a kiss. He tasted the wine on her lips, in her warm mouth when she opened and touched her tongue to his. He groaned as he pulled back. No matter how much he wanted Sophie, he wouldn't let her use him to forget about Michael. "You've had too much to drink. You're upset."

"No, I want you. I want this," *she said, pieces of white cloth flying over his head. She took his hands and placed them on her full, bare breasts. Breasts he'd fantasized about. He'd spent two years fantasizing about her naked and under him, and then she was. She stripped off his shirt and tugged down his shorts. He couldn't resist anymore. He wanted her, and she finally wanted him.* "I love you. I've always loved you," *he whispered in her ear as he buried himself inside her. She wrapped her legs around him, taking him deeper, rocking against him. He worshipped her with his hands and his mouth. She moaned and writhed beneath him. He wasn't going to last much...* "Soph, I don't have a condom on. I have to pull—"

She giggled. "You know I'm on the pill, silly. You...yes, yes." *She lifted her hips, her legs tightening around his waist.*

"You know." *The words dropped into his head like a stone in the ocean. Ripples of shock crashed over him as they sank in. She didn't know. She didn't know it was him. His heart raced and his stomach turned. He had to stop. He had to stop now. Panicked, he struggled for control.* "Sophie, we have to stop. You have to let me..." *She moved her hands to his ass, deepening the connection.* "Jesus, no, don't..." *He trailed off on a groan as he shuddered his release.*

She stroked his hair. "Oh, Michael, that was so good. I love you. I love you too."

He shouldn't have gone after her. Ah, but he was the gallant Gallagher, wasn't he? He'd helped her back into her bathing suit and got dressed without saying a word. Smiled when she said something she thought to be funny. Turned his head when she tried to kiss him again, took her hand so she'd stop touching him, and walked her back to the manor.

He couldn't find his cousin. Later he found out that Michael had taken off with Shay. Liam had dragged a lounge chair over to Sophie, sat her down on it, and went in search of Marco. He'd told his best friend that Michael had to take off and Sophie was drunk, and he should take her home. Liam never told anyone about the night Sophie had broken his heart. He didn't want to ruin his friendship with her, Marco, or Michael. No matter that his cousin was an idiot, he was still family. Michael left Harmony Harbor two days later. Three days later, Liam headed out West to fight a wildfire.

He felt Sophie staring at him and scrubbed his hands over his face. "Soph, I can explain—"

"I think I know who I slept with, Liam," she snapped; then her eyes went wide and filled with concern. "You're delusional. Should I call a doctor? No, that wouldn't be good, would it? For your job, I mean. I'll call your dad."

"What are you talking about? I'm not delusional."

"It's all right. Your grandmother explained what happened to you. That you've had problems since the warehouse fire."

For a split second, he was tempted to let it go at that. It would be easier than telling her what he had to. But he had a daughter. Mia was his. All he'd been thinking about was how to tell Sophie what he'd done without her hating him. He'd forgotten the most important person in all of this. Their little girl. Maybe somewhere deep inside him he'd already known she was his, sensed the connection.

"Come here, Soph. Come here and sit down." She did as he asked, taking the seat across from him. He moved his chair closer and took her hands in his. "I'm not delusional. Mia is mine." She tried to pull her hands from his, and he tightened his grip. "No, you have to hear me out. I didn't mean for it to happen, Soph. You have to believe me. I thought you knew it was me."

He saw it was starting to sink in and knew he had to talk fast, try to explain his side. He told her everything, barely taking a breath between words. "I'm sorry. I should have told you the next day. I loved you, Soph. I never would have done anything to hurt you. Please tell me you believe me."

She ripped her hands from his and jumped to her feet. The chair fell backward with the force of her movement. "You took advantage of me. I was drunk, and you took advantage of me!"

He stood up. "Hold it right there. That's not true. At the beginning, I tried to tell—" He broke off and took a second to calm himself down. He'd been living with the memory of that night for eight years. She was only hearing about it now. He had to give her time to digest this. She knew him. She knew he would never take advantage of her or any other woman. He wouldn't remind her that she threw herself at him. Stripped off her own clothes, and his. They'd been willing participants. Both of them. "I thought you knew it was me. It was only near the end when you said Michael's name. Told him that you loved him." *Loved him too.* In response to Liam's earlier *I love you.*

She slapped him across the face, her eyes sparking with anger in her bleached white face. "I hate you. I hate you for keeping this from me. I stayed away because I thought Mia was Michael's. Everything I suffered, everything she suffered, was because of you, Liam Gallagher."

"I'm sorry. Tell me what I can do to make it right, and I will."

"Stay away from me and my daughter."

"I don't know if I can do that. She needs—"

Sophie put her hands on his chest and shoved him back. "Don't you dare tell me what she needs. Where have you been for the last seven years? I've been the one who raised her, who was there for her when she was sick and scared. I was the one, not you."

"If you'd just give me a chance—"

"No. You may be Mia's biological father, but you will never be her father. You didn't earn that right."

Someone cleared their throat. Liam's eyes shot to the door. Jasper stood there with his hands resting on Mia's shoulders. "I'm sorry. Miss Fitzgerald said that you'd cried out, Sophie. I was worried something had happened."

Sophie stood in the bathroom adjoining Liam's apartment and checked the lock. She'd heard him pull up to the carriage house an hour earlier. She turned on the cold water and splashed her face. Her eyes were bloodshot and swollen from another sleepless night, thanks to him. The past three nights had been worse than the first one because she had a daughter who knew she had a father. A man Mia had been intrigued with from the moment she met him. It was as though she'd sensed the connection. Or maybe like her mother, she recognized a good man when she saw him.

Sophie lifted her eyes and looked at herself in the mirror. Looked past the hurt and anger to see the truth. She knew it was there, lurking beneath the ugly emotions and accusations. He hadn't taken advantage of her. They were equally responsible for what had happened that night. Equally irresponsible. Their daughter was the one who'd paid the price.

Liam should have told her. At the thought, self-pity and anger rose up inside her once again.

Hypocrite.

The word came at her hard and fast. It was true. She'd done the same thing when she thought Michael was Mia's father. She'd convinced herself she was protecting her daughter. It had never been about Mia; it had always been about her. She couldn't bear the thought of losing her daughter.

And Liam, who had he been afraid of losing? Her? Marco? His cousin? All three of them if he was to be believed. There was part of her that wished she didn't believe him. It would be so much easier to just shut him out of their lives completely. From past experience, though, she knew he didn't lie. She gave her head a slight shake. *Right.* It may have been a lie of omission, but it was still a lie. Knowing Liam like she did, she imagined the guilt had eaten at him. She knew only too well what that was like. But she couldn't work up any sympathy for him. Not with Ms. Olivetti scheduled to arrive in three hours.

There was a knock on the bathroom door. She shut off the water and stayed quiet. She didn't want to see him.

"I know you're in there, Soph. We have to talk."

For the past three days and nights, he'd repeatedly texted her, tried calling her. She couldn't bring herself to respond. Not with the memory of her daughter's face that day burned into her brain. She'd practically dragged Mia from the manor with Jasper assuring Sophie he would keep what he'd heard to himself. He was actually the one who'd suggested she take a couple days off and work from home. Without his help, she didn't think she would have gotten Mia out the door.

"Will you at least tell me that you and Mia are okay?"

No matter how much Sophie wanted to keep him out of their lives, she had to face reality. Liam wouldn't walk away now that he knew he had a daughter. She unlocked and opened the door. He was in his navy dress uniform, his hands above his head gripping the door frame, his head bowed. He raised his head and searched her face. "I'm sorry," he said as he slowly lowered his hands and straightened.

She didn't doubt that he was. "I know you are."

"Can you forgive me?"

"We both made mistakes. We're equally at fault."

"That's not what I asked."

"I know. It's too soon. I need time."

"What did you tell Mia?"

"That you're her father and that I was young and scared when I found out I was pregnant and that I didn't tell you until the other day."

"I'm pretty sure she heard you tell me that I wasn't welcome in her life. That I hadn't earned the right to be her father."

"You think you have?"

His jaw tightened under the inch of scruff. "I would have taken responsibility if I'd known she was mine."

"And maybe I would have allowed you to had I known there was the slightest possibility you were her father."

"All right, this isn't getting us anywhere. I've got the stuff from the hardware store. I thought I'd take care of everything for you before the caseworker showed up. And I, uh, thought maybe it would help if I was there for the meeting. Present a united front. Let her know Mia has a father who's willing to help out and support you both."

Sophie stiffened at what he seemed to be implying. "I've supported my daughter on my own for more than seven years. I don't need or want your money."

"Too bad, you're taking it. It's time I paid my share." He reached in his back pocket and pulled out his wallet. He handed her a check.

"You don't…" She stared at the amount and closed her eyes before looking again, positive it couldn't be…"Fifty thousand dollars? Are you out of your mind? I'm not taking this." She tried to give it back to him, but he kept his hands in his pockets. "You can't afford to give us this kind of money. It's not necessary. You don't need to buy my forgiveness."

"I wasn't trying to. It works out to be five hundred a month plus interest. I'll be giving you at least that monthly from now on. It's not going to break me, Soph. I had money saved for a house. I don't need—"

"What was I thinking? This will be pocket change once you sell Greystone."

"Really? You don't think we have enough to deal with without you putting that between us too?"

"There is no us." There could have been. It had started to feel like there was. Kissing him, fantasizing about him, had been fun, made her feel like the girl she used to be. It had been simple. Now it was complicated. He had the power to destroy her world.

"Figured that out already, but thanks for the reminder."

The door opened behind her, and Mia peeked her head around. A shy smile tipped up her lips when she saw Liam. He crouched down, his Gallagher-blue eyes shining. He had eyes only for her daughter. Mia had eyes only for him.

"Hey there, sweetheart," he said, his handsome face lit up with a smile when Mia ran to him and threw herself into his arms.

It was like Sophie had disappeared for both of them.

* * *

Liam sat on one end of the blue-and-white striped couch. Sophie sat at the other end. Mia was in her bedroom coloring. Ms. Olivetti had moved the armchair to sit directly across from them. It felt like they'd been hauled into the principal's office. The sixtysomething stern-faced woman could give Jasper lessons on intimidation, and that was saying something. With her salt-and-pepper hair pulled back in a tight bun that looked almost painful, she peered at Liam over her horn-rimmed glasses.

"When exactly was it that Mia became aware you were her father, Mr. Gallagher?"

"Three...days." He stumbled at the death glare Sophie shot his way. What the hell did she want him to say? Maybe if she'd said two words to him between his and Mia's first hug as father and daughter and Olive Olivetti's arrival, he would have known what was off-limits.

"I see." She turned that glacial stare on Sophie. "Is there a reason why Mia wasn't made aware Mr. Gallagher was her father before now, Ms. DiRossi?"

That earned him another death glare from Sophie. Okay, so he should have thought before he blurted out his answer. But he was nervous. Nervous he'd screw up for Sophie's sake and Mia's. If he ever wanted his daughter's mother to speak to him again, he had to make this right. Sophie wouldn't talk to him before the caseworker arrived, but Michael had. Olive Olivetti had a reputation, and in this case, apparently an agenda since his cousin going over her head had ticked her off. Michael warned him not to let her gain the upper hand. It was time for Liam to take back the conversation. Thanks to Jeeves, he had some game.

"Like most twenty-three-year-olds, Ms. Olivetti, I was

immature and stupid. When Sophie told me she was pregnant just before she moved to LA, I hurt her, said and did some things I shouldn't. I had no interest in being a father. I do now. I plan to make up for lost time. I take my responsibilities seriously, ma'am." He gritted his teeth. He really didn't want to do this, but Michael told him it would play in their favor. It's why he wore his uniform. "As you can see from my record with the BFD."

She moved her finger over the tablet's screen. "Impressive, very impressive, Mr. Gallagher."

Liam relaxed for the first time since he'd sat down. He owed his cousin a beer. Or maybe he didn't, Liam thought when Olive narrowed her probing gaze at him. "But you work and reside in Boston, which would preclude you from having the time I believe is required to establish a relationship with your daughter. Unless you plan to move back to Harmony Harbor. As I understand it, your father is the fire chief here. Would it be possible for you to find a position with HHFD?"

"He is, and yes, there's a position available if I want it." The caseworker smiled. Sophie looked like she'd turned to stone. "But I've been with BFD for six years, and I'm..." Beside him, Sophie exhaled and relaxed. Across from him, Olive's forehead furrowed.

If he decided to take the job at HHFD, Sophie would be ticked and Olive would be pleased. If he did the opposite...Yeah, he was caught between a rock and a hard place. This was why he didn't complicate his life with long-term relationships. But this was about Mia. It wasn't about what he wanted, what Sophie wanted, or what Olive did. It was what was best for his daughter.

"I'll be taking the position with HHFD. I should have everything wrapped up in Boston by Thanksgiving."

"Excellent. I'm very pleased to hear that. In my experience, shared custody—"

"No! God, no!" Sophie gave a frantic shake of her head, her chest heaving. "I won't. I won't do it. I don't care if I have to put up with monthly in-home visits for the next ten years."

Chapter Sixteen

♥

You've made a right hash of it, Liam my boy. That you have," Colleen said from where she stood beside Jasper, looking out the window. Her great-grandson and the lady from Child Protective Services stood talking outside the carriage house. Neither Liam nor the woman appeared happy with the outcome of the visit.

But her great-grandson wasn't the only one who'd made a hash of it. Thanks to listening in on Sophie and Liam's conversation, Colleen had finally remembered what had been bothering her the day of her passing. It had niggled at her that day just as it had from the moment she'd discovered Sophie had Mia.

Colleen had been watching the partygoers from her tower room that long-ago summer night. She'd seen Michael getting up to no good with Shay Angel, and, later, Liam leading Sophie from Kismet Cove. Right or wrong, she'd kept her own counsel. Her meddling had hurt too many people in the past for her to risk interfering. But her family needed her help now. She had to take the risk and make everything right.

Jasper, with his hands clasped behind his back, rocked on his heels.

"I'll need your help with this, my boy. We have to move on it quick before hard feelings settle in too deep." She took in the grimly concerned expression on Jasper's face and smiled. "You have a soft spot for the girl now, don't you? Oh yes, I figured out it was you spying the day Sophie told her story to Ava. Her struggles to raise a child on her own reminded you of your mother's, didn't they? You'd understand why she kept her secret better than most. You'll do well by Sophie, Liam, and Mia. I know you will. Always could depend on you."

She patted Jasper's back, and her hand went through him. He stiffened, looking to where she stood. "It's a right shame you can't see or hear me. I'd share my thoughts on how to go about smoothing things over between Liam and Sophie. For now, you're on your own. I'll work on putting an end to Michael and Bethany's wedding while you take care of them. Mia's the key, my boy."

Lying on the couch and watching cartoons with Mia would have qualified as a perfect day in Sophie's eyes three months earlier. But she and her daughter weren't companionably watching TV, and Sophie could barely keep her eyes open after another sleepless night. So her perfect day was pretty much a nightmare. Which was apropos since yesterday Sophie's worst nightmare had come true.

Thanks to her meltdown, CPS would be dogging her every step, judging her every move. But if that's what she had to put up with to keep Mia with her full-time, she would. She couldn't let her mind go to that place without losing it. To a place where social services would take her daughter away from her.

She glanced at Mia sitting cross-legged on the area rug in front of the TV. When she'd overheard Sophie demand that Liam move out of the neighboring apartment, Mia had silently conveyed her anger for the rest of the day and night. She'd changed tactics this morning. Apparently she was pretending her mother didn't exist.

"You didn't eat all of your scrambled eggs, baby. Would you like some cinnamon toast?" It was her daughter's favorite breakfast treat.

Mia stared at the TV.

"Okay, if you're not hungry, why don't we get started on your letter to Santa?"

Mia turned to give her a pointed stare so sharp it pierced Sophie's heart. For the past two years, a daddy had topped her daughter's Christmas wish list. Keeping Mia from Liam had no doubt cast Sophie as the Grinch in her daughter's eyes. She didn't know what to say to make Mia understand. Maybe when she was older...

A knock on the front door cut off the thought. Hope leaped into her daughter's eyes at the same time Sophie's narrowed with anger. She'd told Liam she'd contact him if and when she wanted to speak to him. She got up and walked to the door, jerking it open to give him hell for going against her wishes. The heated words stalled in her throat. "Oh. Hi, Jasper."

"Miss Sophie." His eyebrows rose almost imperceptibly. But he soldiered on as though her eyes weren't swollen and bloodshot and her hair didn't resemble a rat's nest. She may have coffee stains on her pajamas too. "Since Master Michael and Ms. Adams canceled their meeting with you today, I thought perhaps you and Miss Mia would like to put up the outdoor lights with me."

To think that, a week earlier, Sophie's biggest fear had been meeting with Michael and Bethany. She supposed, if she had to look for some good in all of this, that would be it. She no longer had to worry about Michael and Maura taking Mia away from her or how Bethany would handle her role as Mia's stepmother or that they'd cancel their wedding on account of the news. Yay for the good news, she thought. Only to be faced with the bad. Her daughter who loved all things Christmas hadn't moved her gaze from the TV.

Sophie felt the burn in the back of her eyes. If Ms. Olivetti had evaluated Mia today, Sophie might have lost her daughter for good. It had been obvious the older woman thought the heroic firefighter would be a much better role model and parent than Sophie. She wondered if Jasper felt the same.

"Thanks, Jasper, but..." Sophie trailed off when he stepped inside, shut the door behind him, and took off his boots.

"Television off, Miss Mia," he ordered in his familiar, brisk manner. "We have to get the decorations up before two. Helga is serving Christmas cookies with tea today."

When her daughter didn't respond or move, he walked to the TV, turned it off, and lifted Mia off the floor. Mia looked to Sophie as though expecting her to intervene.

But her daughter wasn't the only one being managed by Jasper today. "Off you go, Miss Sophie. You have twenty-five minutes to get ready. The fresh air will do you good."

By the time Sophie had showered and made herself somewhat presentable, Jasper had tidied the apartment and Mia was dressed and ready to head outside. Looking slightly less grumpy.

Sophie didn't have much in the way of outdoor clothing and had layered a sweater beneath her black sweatshirt. She'd have to make do with her black rubber boots for footwear. She pulled them on and set off after Jasper and Mia. The air was cold and crisp. The sun sat high in the cloudless blue sky. Its warm rays melting the snow from the other day. Four large boxes awaited them on the front steps of the manor.

"Jasper, are you sure Kitty doesn't mind us putting up the Christmas lights?" As far as Sophie knew, they hadn't decorated for the holidays since Mary, Riley, and Ronan died.

"She understands that, with the manor hosting a wedding on Christmas Eve and Miss Mia in residence, compromises must be made."

It kind of felt like his compromises comment was meant for her too. If she had any doubts, his raised eyebrows cleared them up. She ignored him and opened a box, forcing a bright smile for Mia. "Wow, look at all these lights, baby. We better…" A car door slammed and a familiar, deep male voice called, "Miller, get back here."

Her eyes shot to Jasper when a barking golden retriever raced toward them followed by Liam. Jasper held her gaze and nodded at Mia. A wide smile lit up her daughter's face, only to disappear when she glanced at Sophie. Stuffing her mittened hands in her pockets, Mia looked down at her feet and kicked at the melting snow.

Liam looked like she'd kicked him in the stomach. Then he turned his furious gaze on Sophie. In all the years she'd known Liam, she'd never seen him this angry. He was easygoing, charming, and calm. He was none of those things now.

He reached for the retriever's leash when the dog went to jump on Mia. "Settle down, Miller." Liam crouched in front of Mia. "Are you afraid of dogs, sweetheart?"

She shook her head without raising it.

"Perhaps you and Miss Sophie could go to O'Malley's and pick up some lights for the carriage house. We only have clear bulbs to decorate the shrubs and trees at the front of the manor. I'm sure the little miss would prefer something more colorful."

"Clear lights are—" Sophie began before Liam cut her off.

"Mia, your mommy and I are going to the hardware store. Will you look after Miller for me?"

Mia went to nod; then an anxious expression crossed her face when Sophie snapped, "Wait a minute. I never said—"

Liam stood up and took Sophie by the arm, talking over her. "We won't be long, Mia. Your mom and I need to work some stuff out. It's okay, sweetheart." His quietly confident voice calmed the anxious look on Mia's face. "Everything will be better when we get back."

"How dare you promise her something like that," Sophie said under her breath as Liam none too gently guided her to the parking lot.

"Have a care, Master Liam," Jasper called after them.

"Always do, Jeeves." Liam looked down at her as he beeped the unlock button on his key fob. "One way or another, this is getting settled today, Sophie. I don't care if it takes all day and night. I won't have Mia put in the middle of this."

"Who do you think—"

He looked at her across the roof of the Jeep. "Her father. Get in."

As much as she hated to admit it, Liam was right. Mia obviously felt the tension between them, and it was having a negative impact on her. Sophie got in the Jeep and buckled up. "I can't do shared custody, Liam. And I don't think it's fair I'm being made out to be the bad guy in this because I'm unwilling to—"

"I'm not asking for shared custody," he said as he started the engine.

"It's obviously what Ms. Olivetti wanted me to agree to." But the caseworker was wrong. Liam didn't need time to build a relationship with Mia; he already had one. And it was better than her own with her daughter. "Because of how I reacted, I'm going to have CPS breathing down my neck for the next ten years."

"No, you're not. If you would have taken my texts or picked up your damn phone, you would have known that."

"How do you not get that this has been really difficult for me, Liam?"

"Hate to break it to you, babe, but you're not the only one having a difficult time. I just found out I had a daughter, Soph. I've missed out on the first seven years of her life. And my mom and sister, they never got the chance to meet her."

"Oh God," she whispered, her voice breaking on a sob. Of all the things he could have said to her, nothing hurt as much as that. Knowing that unintentionally she'd stolen something precious from him, from his mother and sister, broke her heart. She didn't know how he could forgive her. If she could forgive herself. "I'm sorry. I'm sorry—"

He reached over and took her hand, giving it a gentle squeeze. "You didn't know. I shouldn't have said that. Blame it on a lack of sleep." His big hands twisted around the steering wheel; then he glanced at her, hesitating a moment before he asked, "Soph, what would have happened if, instead of assuming you knew it was me when you kissed me that night, I told you it was?"

"I would have…" The answer should have been simple, but it wasn't. Her memory of that night had faded over time and was impaired by the amount of wine she'd drunk, but the next morning when she'd woken up, she remembered smiling. Unlike the first time she'd had sex with Michael, that night she'd felt like she'd been made love to. And remembering how much she'd once loved Liam…"If you told me it was you, I might have…It wouldn't have changed anything. I would have had sex with you."

He nodded, a muscle bunching in his jaw. "I should have told you, and that's on me. But I did tell you I didn't have a condom. You said you were on the pill."

"I was. Sort of. I was embarrassed to go to Dr. Bishop for a prescription. I didn't want Nonna and Tina to find out. So my girlfriend gave me some of hers. Michael and I only had sex the one time, and I..." It was unfair to Michael to tell his cousin that first-time sex hadn't been all it was cracked up to be, and she hadn't been anxious for a repeat. "I didn't take them consistently. So that's on me."

"We're not keeping track. We both made mistakes. But Mia isn't one of them. She's an amazing little girl who doesn't deserve to be caught in the middle. I've seen what Aidan and Harper's custody battle is doing to Ella Rose. I don't want that for Mia."

"Neither do I. I've never once thought of Mia as a mistake. She's the best thing that ever happened to me. That's why this is so hard, Liam. I just need a little time. Can we take it slow?"

"I don't want to make this hard for either of you. I thought we'd take our cue from Mia. Let her decide how much time she wants to spend with me and when. At least in the beginning, and then we can work out a more formal arrangement."

"Do you think CPS will be okay with that?"

"They're not involved anymore, Soph. At least not formally. That's what I was trying to get in touch with you about. Olive and I worked it out. I told her you'd had a rough couple of days, but that we'd figure out what was best for Mia together, and I'd let her know as soon as we have a plan in place. Other than that, all she wants is to be kept apprised of Mia's progress."

Sophie had spent the entire night worrying for nothing. All she'd had to do was pick up her phone. "I don't know what to say. Thank you."

"Thank Michael. He coached me on how to handle her. She wasn't all that bad. She takes her job seriously. Can't fault her for that." He pulled into a parking spot half a block from the hardware store. Once he shut off the engine, he shifted in his seat to look at her. "She actually said something pretty interesting about Mia."

"Good or bad?"

"Interesting. Now don't take this as a criticism..." He gave his head a slight shake when she crossed her arms. "Soph, come on. Don't get defensive. No one is doubting that you're a good mother, but Olive had a case similar to Mia's where the little girl wouldn't speak. Like Mia, there was no medical reason, and it wasn't psychosomatic."

"Post-traumatic stress. Ever hear of it?"

"Living with it, babe," he said, a sarcastic edge in his voice.

She briefly closed her eyes then reached out to touch his hand. "Sorry. I'm sorry. I'm just…Please, tell me what Olive thinks is the problem."

"Because you were as traumatized as Mia and blamed yourself, you were…are overcompensating. You're smothering her, babying her, and she's your sole focus."

"So I'm feeding into it?" she asked, forcing herself not to get defensive.

"More or less. And so is Mia. She likes having all your attention and having you around twenty-four-seven. She's smart enough to put two and two together. Is she stubborn?"

Sophie laughed. "Mia? Big-time. She inherited it from Rosa."

His mouth twitched. "I was going to say she inherited that particular trait from her mother."

She rolled her eyes. "So what did she suggest I...we do?"

He smiled. "She's going to recommend a child psychologist. She also suggested registering her in school. I think it's a good idea."

"I know. It's just hard for me to be away from her for that long. I get panicky. I'm afraid the kids are going to be mean to her because she won't speak." She looked down at her hand, twisting the seat belt between her fingers. "I really am part of the problem, aren't I?"

"My bet is, as soon as your lives get back to normal, Mia will start talking. It hasn't been that long. You're just getting settled here."

"But we're not settled. Not really. And now, finding out you're her father and how I've been acting, I've made it worse."

"It'll get better." He lifted his chin at O'Malley's. "Come on, let's beat the rush."

She looked at the sidewalk crowded with Saturday shoppers. "I'm not sure this is a good idea." She pulled down the visor and made a face at herself in the mirror. "Now I know it isn't. I'll stay here."

He leaned across her and opened the glove box, handing her a pair of aviators. "Wear these. They'll think you've gone Hollywood."

"Yeah, until they get a look at my rubber boots and sweatshirt."

"You're not in LA anymore. People around here don't care what you wear."

He may have a point, Sophie thought as they walked into the store. The elder Mr. O'Malley stood behind the counter wearing a Santa's hat and a flashing red bow tie that matched his suspenders. With his tufts of white hair at his ears and his mischievous grin, the diminutive Mr. O'Malley had always reminded Sophie of a leprechaun. The hardware-slash-general store had been one of her favorite places to visit as a little girl. It was just as crammed with a hodgepodge of merchandise as it had been back then. Its warm, honey-colored wood floors, shelves, and walls gave it a homey feel. The pot-bellied stove sitting in the middle of the floor scented the air, bringing back happy memories. As did the jars of old-fashioned candy beside the ornate silver cash register.

"Now there's a sight I haven't seen in a good long while. Sophie DiRossi and Liam Gallagher back together again. Where's your sidekick?"

Liam and Marco used to bring Sophie in to spend her weekly allowance. "Hi, Mr. O'Malley. Marco's working at the deli." She glanced around and smiled. "Nothing's changed. O'Malley's looks as wonderful as it always did."

He chuckled. "There's been a few changes. Look, I still have your favorite." He lifted the lid of a jar and dug inside to hold up a package of Wild Berry Pop Rocks.

"I haven't had these in…wow, twelve years." Feeling a little emotional, her smile wobbled as she took the candy from his gnarled hand. Life had been so simple back then.

"I heard you were back in town and brought them in just for you."

Touched, she leaned across the counter and gave him a hug. "Thank you. I'll be in once a week from now on. I'll bring my little girl with me. She'll love it here."

"Better give us ten of them, Mr. O'Malley. If Mia's anything like her mother, she won't want to share."

"A mini Sophie DiRossi...Now that'll be a sight for sore eyes. You call ahead, make sure I'm here. Don't have as much pep in my step as I used to."

"Dad, are you flirting with the customers again?" A tall, handsome man wearing a white shirt with a black vest and pants carried a box to the counter. It was John, Mr. O'Malley's eldest son.

"Why do you think all the ladies keep coming in? It's not to look at your grumpy face," Mr. O'Malley senior said to his son. "I'd have some competition if I could convince my grandsons to come back home." He eyed Liam. "You should give Reece a call. Tell him you've moved back home. You and Sophie."

John rolled his eyes. "Give it up, Dad." Then he smiled at her. "Good to see you, Sophie. Folks in town are happy to have you home."

"Thanks, Mr. O'Malley. I'm glad to be back." And despite the past few days, she was. The O'Malleys' warm welcome reminded her what she loved most about her hometown—feeling like she belonged, being part of a community.

Bells chimed over the door as three older women walked into the store. Mr. O'Malley straightened his bow tie and winked at Sophie before he turned his grin on them. "The good Lord's smiling down on me today, bringing ladies as lovely as yourselves into my humble establishment," he said, as he walked around the counter to greet the women.

John watched his father, an indulgent smile tipping up his lips. "The tourists love him. In about five minutes, he'll be laying on the brogue so thick you won't be able to understand him." He glanced at Liam. "Don't tell me Jasper sent you for more white lights. He cleaned me out this morning."

Sophie shared a look with Liam. He smiled and gave his head a slight shake. Obviously he thought Jasper had set them up too. Since he was in only hours ago, he could have just as easily picked up the lights for Mia then.

"No, we're here for colored lights," he told John.

"I can help you out with that." John lifted his chin. "Far end to the back. Give a shout if you need a hand. I've gotta keep an eye on the old man."

It took a few minutes to make their way past the boxes and merchandise piled on the floor to the Christmas decorations.

"Big or small, twinkle or static?" Liam asked, holding up two boxes in each hand.

Sophie pushed the aviators on top of her head and leaned in. "Small and twinkle?"

He smiled; then his eyes narrowed at something on the shelf. "Isn't this the elf Mia was playing with at the cottage?"

Sophie nodded. "She used to have one just like her. Do you think John would mind putting it on hold for…" She sighed when Liam added it to his growing pile. "You're going to spoil her, aren't you?"

"Me? Never."

"Right…Hey, look at this. Mia would love it, and we wouldn't have to put up a bunch of lights." She held up a package that contained an eight-foot blow-up Olaf.

Liam frowned. "He's kind of an odd-looking snowman, don't you think?"

"It's Olaf."

"Is that supposed to mean something to me?"

"From *Frozen*. Remember, 'Let It Go'?"

He laughed. "How could I forget?" Then his laughter faded, and a pained expression crossed his face as though he was thinking about their day at Mistletoe Cottage.

It had been an amazing day. Until it wasn't. Then it hit Sophie that maybe "letting it go" was exactly what she had to do for all of them to move forward. She leaned into Liam and whispered, "I forgive you."

A slow smile curved his lips. It wasn't his *you're cute but annoying* smile or his charmingly wicked smile. It was warm and wonderful and made her remember how much she'd once loved him. "I forgive you too," he said.

Chapter Seventeen

♥

Sophie sat in the chair behind the desk, chewing her thumb-nail. Her cousin was making her nervous. If she hadn't al-ready told Ava that Michael was Mia's father, Sophie would have kept her mouth shut. But she and Liam had agreed to tell their families. He'd taken Mia to the fire station today to share the news with his father. Sophie thought she'd start with a more reasonable DiRossi before telling her grand-mother. It wasn't exactly working out as she'd planned. "Um, are you going to say anything or just keep staring at me like I've grown two heads?"

She'd done it now. Ava started spewing Italian curse words faster than Sophie could keep track, her hands moving as fast as her mouth. Sophie lunged for the coffee cup on the edge of the desk and moved it out of the way. Passionate and hot-tempered, this was the cousin Sophie remembered, but she would have appreciated it more if all that fire wasn't be-ing directed at her. Or more accurately…Liam. "*Bastardo!* The bastard took advantage of you! I'll castrate him! I'll—"

"Ava, no. Calm down and keep your voice down. It wasn't like that. He thought I knew it was him and—"

Ava stabbed a finger in Sophie's direction. "No. Do not justify what he did to you. He took advantage of you. You were *ubriaca*!"

"Yes, I was drunk, but so was he. He loved me, Ava. He told me that night." And she'd told him she loved his cousin. She'd hurt him, but he didn't lash out or embarrass her. Didn't make her pay or suffer by telling his cousin. "He didn't mean to hurt me. He thought he was taking care of me, protecting me."

Ava's chest was heaving, her face flushed, and in her green eyes there was something dark and haunted. This wasn't about Sophie; it was about Ava. "What happened to you? Who hurt you?"

A flash of panic crossed Ava's face before her expression went carefully blank. "Nothing. Nothing happened. I was upset for you." She tilted her head to the side and shrugged. "But if you're okay—if you and Liam are okay—that's good. I'm glad."

They were good, she supposed. At least better than they had been. After they'd gotten back from O'Malley's, they'd had tea at the manor before setting up Olaf outside the carriage house. Mia had seemed happier, more like herself. They hadn't seen Liam yesterday because he had to work, but this morning reality set in for Sophie when he asked to take Mia to the fire station. "We're getting there. We—" She was interrupted by a knock on the door. "It's probably Dana."

"I'll go then." Ava started to get up from the chair.

"Come in," Sophie called out, gesturing for her cousin to sit down. "Stay. I want your opinion about an idea I have. Hi, Dana." She smiled at the woman who'd entered the study.

Dana offered Ava a tentative smile then looked at Sophie. "I'm not interrupting anything, am I?"

Sophie prayed the stone walls had provided a sound barrier against her cousin's vitriol. "Not at all." She gestured to the boards with swatches of fabric on them and a file folder in Dana's elegant hands. "Looks like you've been busy. Sorry I had to postpone our meeting. Sit down. I'm anxious to see what you've come up with. Dana's agreed to take on the role as event planner. She'll be helping to coordinate Michael and Bethany's wedding," she explained to her cousin.

"Ah, I see. Well, if you don't need me, I'll—"

"If we're going to pull off this wedding, I don't just need you. I desperately need you. Helga can't handle this without your help, Ava."

Dana looked relieved. "I'm so glad you brought that up, Sophie. I didn't know how to approach you about Helga. Lately my meals have been so bad, I've been going into town to eat. Sorry, I know that's not what you need to hear right now."

"It's exactly what I need to hear, and why I want Ava to take over the restaurant."

"Helga chased me out of the kitchen with a butcher knife the morning the Widows Club met here. I'm the last person she wants in her kitchen."

"I'd wondered where you were. You should have come to me." The old Ava wouldn't have needed Sophie to defend her. Sophie would have ended up having to protect Helga instead. "Or maybe you should have yelled at her like you just did me," she said, secretly pleased when her cousin shot her a narrow-eyed look.

"I wasn't yelling at you."

Since they both knew she had, Sophie ignored her. "I'll talk to Kitty and Jasper. They should be able to make Helga see reason. Between us, though, I'm hoping she'll retire. Because what I'd really like to do is have someone lease the dining room."

"Sophie, I've seen that look in your eyes before. Do not aim it at me. I can't do it. I can't take over the restaurant."

"If it makes you feel better, Ava, I didn't think I could do this either." Dana held up the swatches and files. "But I've enjoyed it more than I've enjoyed anything in a long time. And the meal you and your cousin prepared for the reception was fantastic."

"*Grazie.* But even if I wanted to, I couldn't. I have my father to care for."

"We can talk about it at another time. Right now, my sole focus is this wedding. We need it to be fabulous, a wedding that gets future brides dreaming of holding theirs here. I have a list of wedding planners on the East Coast that I'll be reaching out to early next week. So the food for Michael and Bethany's wedding has to be amazing. Which means, unless we outsource, which will cut into our profits, I need you, Ava. Not tomorrow, today. We have to design a menu. I have a feeling Bethany will require several tastings before making a decision."

"I wouldn't know the first thing about designing a menu for—"

"You don't have to. All you have to do is cook." Dana pulled some papers from her file folder and handed them to Ava. While her cousin perused the menus, Dana continued. "I've already dropped off three alternate designs for the wedding cake to Truly Scrumptious. They've promised to have a quote to us by tomorrow. The tasting samples will be ready for your meeting Saturday morning, Sophie. In Bloom will have quotes for the floral arrangements to you by then too. And so will Tie the Knot. The owner, Arianna Summers, is a designer. Her line of bridal gowns is fabulous, and she also carries bridesmaid dresses and tuxes. I'm sure Bethany's ordered hers months ago, but Arianna's sisters design one-of-a-kind invitations, programs, and guest books. Their wedding favors are super cute and unique too."

Sophie stared at the woman, stunned. "I never expected you to have done so much in such a short time, Dana. You're amazing."

"Thank you, but I can't take all the credit. You wouldn't believe how excited everyone is. They made my job easy. I was actually pretty shocked that I didn't have to order online or make a trip to New York. The stores here are unbelievable. There's this candy shop on Main Street—A Spoonful of Sugar—and they make the most adorable teaspoons coated in just about anything you can imagine. And they have these lollipops…" She released a self-conscious laugh. "Sorry, I'm getting a little carried away."

"Don't apologize. I'm as excited as you are. I forgot how much the town has to offer. I didn't realize till now what this could mean for the local business owners. Especially…" An idea hit her. If they cut out the wedding planners and advertised directly to newly engaged couples, they could…

"Oh no, she's got that look in her eyes again. Hurry up, Dana, and show us your ideas for Michael and Bethany before she turns Harmony Harbor into Wedding Town," Ava said.

"Wedding Town." Sophie nodded. "I like it. That would be the perfect way to market—" Ava cut her off with a groan. "Okay, you're right. One thing at a time." But the idea was definitely going on Sophie's list.

Dana reached down and picked up the boards to place them on Sophie's desk. "Here's what I've come up with so far. I thought it would be best to have a few ideas for

Bethany to choose from. If she isn't happy with them, I'll go back to the drawing board."

"I don't know how she couldn't be. These are amazing. Are you sure we can pull them off?"

"Absolutely. All I need is their budget, and I'll go from there."

"This one is fabulous," Sophie said, indicating the ice-blue-and-white theme. "But this one is my favorite." She tapped the board with the red-and-gold theme.

Ava moved to the edge of her chair. "You're very talented, Dana. All three are beautiful. Myself, I like the black and white." She held up the sample menus. "I might make a couple of suggestions, but otherwise, I like how you coordinated the food to each theme." Her cousin made a face at Sophie. "You think you're so smart. This, I will do, because it's good for Greystone. The other, no."

Dana shared a smile with Sophie then said to Ava, "If you do decide to lease the space, I know exactly how to update it without a heavy outlay of cash and in a short turnaround time. I'd love to do it. I'd do it for free just to—"

"*Pazza*. Now I have two crazy ladies to deal with."

The phone on Sophie's desk rang. "Greystone Manor, Sophie DiRossi speaking."

"Hey, Sophie, it's Michael." She mouthed who it was to Dana and Ava.

"Hi, we were just talking about your wedding. I think you and Bethany will be pleased."

"About that, we have to cancel again. Something's come up, and we're not going to make it next Saturday. Any chance you can fit us in around Thanksgiving? My mother and Bethany's mother and grandmother want to be there. We figured we'd stay a couple nights and get everything nailed down then. Work for you?"

She widened her eyes at Ava and Dana. "Of course, we'll make it work. I'm just a little concerned about the timeline. It's cutting it close."

"Bethany will be in touch with you today, and you can go over the colors and whatever else you need a decision on with her. That way, all we'll have to do when we're there is finalize last-minute details."

"All right, that sounds"—she glanced at an incoming text, and then another, and another—"great. Just get back to me with dates and times and how many rooms you'd like booked." She reached across the desk to hand her phone to Dana as two more texts came in.

Dana's eyes widened. Ava leaned in to read over the redhead's shoulder. "*Pazza*. The woman is *pazza*," her cousin muttered.

"Will do. How did your meeting with Olive go?" Michael asked.

"Good." She glanced at Ava and Dana, who were looking over the menus, talking quietly. "No more in-home visits to worry about. Liam tells me that's thanks to you. I appreciate all your help with this, Michael."

"Just gave Boy Wonder a few tips." He cleared his throat. "From what Liam told me, I owe you an apology, Sophie. I was a grade-A asshole that summer. Even though it turns out I'm not your daughter's father, I can't say I would have behaved any better if you told me back then that I was. If it makes you feel better, I got what was coming to me. Karma's a bitch, and she bit me good."

"Sounds interesting. You know my deep, dark secret. Seems only fair you share yours. Does karma have a name?"

He gave a dry laugh. "You probably do deserve to know since she was the girl I was cheating on you with. Shay Angel."

"It couldn't have been Shay. She was arrested that summer for grand theft auto."

"And that's a story for another time. I'll see you in a couple of weeks. And, Sophie, you and Mia got lucky. Liam is the best man I know. He'll be an incredible father."

"I'm sure he will be. Thanks again, Michael." She disconnected, feeling like she'd closed a chapter on her past. Like the choices she'd made back then had been the right ones. Even if she'd made them for the wrong reasons, Michael's validation was somewhat freeing.

She looked at the two women with their heads bent over Dana's file. "Please tell me Bethany's texts weren't as bad as they looked at first glance."

"Worse," Dana and Ava said at almost the same time.

"That woman is going to be a nightmare to work with. She's already sent five more texts that contradict the first ones. Oh, and her mother sent two, and so did Michael's," Dana said.

"She has a grandmother. Hopefully she doesn't know how to text," Sophie got out just before there was another ping from an incoming text.

"She does." Dana sighed as the phone kept pinging.

"Okay. We'll write them all down and see if there's something we can work with to—" Sophie was interrupted by a knock on the study door.

Jasper peeked his head in. "Sorry to disturb you, miss, but you need to see this right away." He walked in and handed her a copy of the *Harmony Harbor Gazette*. She stared at the front-page headline: BOSTON SOCIALITE BETHANY ADAMS IS HOLDING HER WEDDING HERE? Several unflattering photos of Greystone Manor accompanied the article. Sophie opened her mouth to curse out the publishers of the *Gazette* in Italian, and the lights went out.

Chapter Eighteen

♥

Sophie was tired of taking on the chin whatever life had to throw at her. Every time she took one step forward, she took two steps back. Thanks to Byron and Poppy Harte, the publishers of the *Harmony Harbor Gazette*, and Greystone's outdated circuit breaker box that needed to be replaced ASAP, those last two steps might as well have been made by a giant. From where she was standing, they seemed insurmountable.

Her cell phone pinged with an incoming text as she pulled into a parking space half a block from the *Harmony Harbor Gazette*. To add to her already craptastic day, it had started snowing on the drive there, and all she had on over her uniform of a white blouse and black skirt was her suit jacket, and no boots, just shoes.

She picked up her phone and was about to put it in her purse when it started to ring. She'd been forwarding Bethany's texts to Dana without reading them. Well, at least no farther than the first line or two. So far there'd been no mention of the article in the *Gazette*. But given the state of Sophie's luck these days, she didn't count on that being the case for long. Hopefully by then, the *Gazette* would have printed the retraction Sophie planned to insist upon.

She glanced at her phone. It wasn't Bethany.

"Hi, Mom. Do you mind if I call you back? I'm a little busy right now." She'd spoken to her mother only once since she'd arrived in Harmony Harbor. Tina had wanted to make sure Sophie knew that she'd given a glowing report to her previous caseworker.

"This'll just take a second. I'm on my way into my yoga class, and I can't be late. Oh, did I tell you I'm teaching now?"

Sophie bowed her head and took a couple deep breaths before saying tightly, "No, you didn't. Congratulations on the job."

"Thanks, baby. I don't have to work, you know. Larry takes such good care of me. But it's just so much fun and, wink wink, it keeps me flexible, if you know what I mean."

Her fifty-four-year-old mother had left her father and turned into an incense-burning, om-chanting, tantra-practicing nymphomaniac who thought her twenty-six-year-old daughter, who probably requalified as a virgin, was her best friend.

Thanks for asking, Mom. Your granddaughter and I are doing great. You remember Mia, right? The seven-year-old you thought was capable of babysitting herself. No, she's still not talking. But guess what? She has a father. That's right, Liam Gallagher, the boy I thought was God's gift to womankind. Oh, and I got my dream job even without my degree. I'm managing Greystone Manor. Now if I can just keep it from falling apart around us, prevent the local newspaper from sabotaging the wedding of the century, and satisfy a

woman who gives bridezillas everywhere a bad name, every-
thing will be just peachy keen.

"Sophie, did you hear me?"

"Yes, I'm sure Larry's thrilled by how flexible you are. I really have to—"

"You know it, girlfriend. That's not what I was talking about, though. He wants to know when you'll get the Cadillac back to him. You know how the man loves his babies. Wink, wink. How does a week sound?"

"I thought you said I could keep the car for as long as I needed it."

"I was overwrought and feeling guilty—"

"Gee, you got over that pretty quick. Glad to hear it."

"Thanks, baby, I knew you'd understand. I gotta get to my class. Larry has a big night planned. Text me the deets on where and when the car will arrive. *Ciao, bella.*"

Pow, another one right on the chin. And one more gigantic step back. But Sophie didn't have time to worry about how she was going to get the car back to Larry and how much that would cost. She had to convince Byron and Poppy Harte to print a retraction or, better yet, do another piece on Greystone highlighting the manor's history and the fabulous architectural features and views.

Sophie got out of the car and was about to lock the door when she thought back to her earlier conversation with Michael. She opened the door, put the keys back in the ignition then closed the driver's door without locking it in hopes someone would steal the car and save her the trouble and cost of sending it back. She bowed her head against the biting wind coming off the harbor and slipped and slid the half block to the *Gazette.*

By the time she reached the white Colonial with its black door and shutters, she was shivering. Her skirt and jacket were molded to her body, her shoes soaked, and her hair plastered to her face. She swiped a finger under her eye to check for mascara. Surprise, surprise, her finger came away covered with it. She faced the wall, licked her fingers and rubbed them under her eyes and over her cheeks then pushed her hair from her face. Turning, she straightened and opened the door with a professional smile on her face. A pile of snow fell off the overhang and onto her head.

"Say cheese," a man said with a smirk in his voice.

Sophie shook off the snow in time to see the flash go off. When her vision cleared, she noted the man at a desk with his feet up and a camera in his hand. His blond hair was slicked back from his angular face. He had a Hollywood tan and movie-star teeth. "If it isn't Sophie DiRossi, Greystone's esteemed manager."

Sophie assumed he must be Byron. She didn't know the Harte grandchildren well. They only spent summers with their grandmother and were older than Sophie.

"Byron, I told you snow was building up on the roof." A tall, attractive blonde hurried over to Sophie with a towel in her hand. "I'm so sorry. Are you all right? Please, come and sit down."

"It's just a little snow, Pop Tart. I doubt she'll sue. You know what, on second thought, please do."

"Just ignore him. Byron, go get Ms. DiRossi a coffee from Books and Beans, or do you prefer tea?"

"A coffee would be great, thanks. And it's Sophie," she said as she towel-dried her hair and took the seat Poppy pulled out for her.

"Any excuse to stop by and chat up the lovely Julia," Byron said as he walked to the coat rack and grabbed a jacket and scarf.

His sister sighed when the door closed behind him. "I'm

sorry, you'll have to excuse Byron. He just found out our brother's latest book sold for millions at auction." She made a face. "You're probably here about today's edition, aren't you?"

"Yes, it's not exactly a flattering piece about the manor. And, as you probably know, we need all the good publicity we can get."

"I do, and believe me, I did everything in my power to talk them out of running it, but Hazel's our landlord and Paige paid a premium for the front page. We need the revenue."

"Wait a minute. You didn't write the article?"

"No, Paige did, with some help from Byron, and she took the photos. The majority of people in town want Greystone to succeed, Sophie. It's good for all of us if it does. But Paige has managed to convince Hazel, and a few other people, to back the condo development. They're willing to do anything to make it happen."

"So you won't print a retraction?"

"I can't. I fact-checked the article. There's nothing she said that wasn't true."

"What if you wrote one from another angle? In the past the manor has hosted several high-profile weddings. You could do a feature—"

Poppy tapped her finger on her lips. "Why don't we save that for the spring? I'm thinking more Christmas at the manor. We'll do a big spread."

"That would be great, but we need this wedding, and I'm afraid our bride-to-be will be second-guessing her choice of venue after reading the article."

"I see what you mean. Okay, if you can get me names of couples who had winter weddings at the manor, I'll interview them for a piece. I'll come by and take some photos next week that will show the manor in the best possible light. But, Sophie, I stopped by after Mrs. Gallagher's funeral and

Greystone is looking more shabby than chic. There's lots of tricks I can do with lighting and such, but it would help if you spruced it up a bit. Even decorating for the holidays would make a difference."

"Are you a professional photographer?"

She scratched her flushed neck. "I'm just picking it up again. I have a website." She rummaged around her desk and picked up a card, handing it to Sophie.

"Great. I'll check out your site. I'm not sure if Michael and Bethany have a photographer already, but we're hoping to make Greystone a full-service event destination. I'd like to use local talent whenever possible."

"I really hope you can make this work, Sophie. It would be great for Harmony Harbor. Byron was such a jerk, you probably wouldn't want to work with him, but if you're looking for someone to consult about marketing and publicity, he owned a big ad agency. He wasn't always this way. He's had a lot to deal with recently."

Haven't we all. But something Poppy said was nagging at Sophie. "You mentioned that your brother helped Paige with the article. Is it possible there's more to it?"

"They have gone out together, but I don't think it's anything serious." She looked at Sophie. "There is a lot of money on the table, though. If she offered Byron...I'm sorry, I can't say for certain that he isn't more involved with Paige than I realize."

"Thanks for being honest with me. I know this is asking a lot, but until you're sure your brother isn't backing the condo development, I'd appreciate it if you keep anything we talk about between us."

"It won't be easy, but I'll keep as much from him as I can."

"Thank you. I really do have to get going." She extended

her hand. "It was nice meeting you, Poppy. I look forward to working with you. I haven't gotten up to speed yet, but we will be sponsoring local events. So if you have anything you think might be worthwhile, let me know."

"I still have spots available to sponsor the annual Christmas parade. I think Greystone used to host an event after the parade and provide hot chocolate. If you're planning on starting up the tradition again, we'll be happy to publicize it."

Sophie remembered attending the event herself. However, she had a feeling many of Greystone's traditions had died along with Mary, Riley, and Ronan. "I'll talk to Kitty and let you know."

Byron was coming in just as Sophie was leaving. "Not leaving on my account, I hope," he said.

"Sorry you had to go out on mine. Thanks," she said when he handed her the coffee.

He held on to the to-go cup. "So tell me, is there any truth to the rumor that Colleen wrote a memoir that exposes the secrets of everyone in town?"

Sophie thought of her torn-apart office, and her stomach jittered. "Not that I'm aware of. Enjoy your coffee."

"You too. By the way, you might want to stop by Books and Beans yourself." He held the door open for her. Just before it closed behind her, Sophie heard him say, "Pop Tart, we should do a piece on Ms. DiRossi. I think it would make for a fascinating read."

Her stomach, which moments ago had been treading water, did a nosedive. Byron Harte knew something, and that something had to do with Books and Beans. Sophie looked up Main Street and saw a brown-and-pink sign featuring an open book and coffee cup. She'd passed it on her way to the *Gazette*. She didn't know much about the owner, Julia Landon, other than that she'd been engaged to the mayor's son.

Sophie's phone pinged in her purse. She couldn't look at another message from Bethany. After talking to Poppy, Sophie was already overwhelmed with everything she had to do. Not to mention worrying about what Byron and Paige might be up to. Maybe having Liam help out with Mia wasn't such a bad thing after all. The thought had barely passed through her mind when she saw them.

Mia and Liam were leaving Books and Beans with Brie Fitzgerald and two children. Sophie was positive the couple was behind Byron's innuendo. He wanted her to see Liam with Brie. While there may have been a small stab of jealousy seeing the couple laughing together, it was the thought that Byron meant to exploit her daughter in a piece featuring Sophie that set off the panicked jump in her pulse. All she could think of was getting Mia as far away from Byron as possible.

Which may have been why, when she called out to Liam, she sounded furious and frantic. He looked up at the same time Sophie hit a patch of ice.

Liam was trying to figure out what had warranted Sophie yelling at him when her feet flew out from under her and she landed flat on her back, her coffee flying. He heard the dull thud of her head hitting the ice as he ran toward her, and his stomach turned. He'd barely knelt at her side when she jerked upright. He placed a hand on her shoulder. "Take it easy. Sit still for a minute. You took a bad fall."

Mia, Brie, and her nephew and niece gathered around Sophie on the ground.

"I'm okay, baby," Sophie said, and pushed herself to her feet, ignoring him because obviously she was more concerned about upsetting her daughter than for herself.

Placing his hands on her shoulders, he carefully turned

Sophie to face him. He looked into her eyes. "Are you dizzy?"

"No," she snapped, and started to shake her head. She pressed her fingertips to her temple. "A little."

He gently probed the back of her skull. "Blurred vision?"

"No, I...um...my vision seems fine, but I may be hallucinating. I see Cinderella standing in the doorway over there." She gestured at Books and Beans.

Liam smiled. "You're not hallucinating. Julia, the owner, dresses up for the kids' story hour."

"You took Mia to story hour?" She frowned. "You told me you were just taking her to the station."

"I texted—"

"It's my fault, Sophie. Liam took us on a tour of the station, and the girls were having so much fun together, I suggested we take them to story hour. I hope that's okay."

Sophie gave Brie a forced smile and nodded. "It's fine."

Yeah, not so fine, Liam thought. He got it, though. She was overprotective of Mia to begin with, and now she had to deal with him being part of her daughter's life. Mia came to stand beside him, looking up at her mother with a worried expression on her face. Sophie crouched in front of her. Liam watched her as she did. Her balance seemed to be good.

"I'm not lying, baby. I'm okay." She smiled and straightened Mia's hat. "I should have put on a pair of boots before I left the manor."

Liam frowned as he took in what she was wearing. Her hair and clothes were soaked. "You should have put on a lot more than boots. What were you thinking coming out dressed like that?"

Other than the hardening of her delicate jaw, she ignored

him. "What's this?" She smiled, touching the Elsa backpack Mia clutched to her chest.

Liam didn't have to worry about his daughter keeping quiet, but he did have to worry about Brie. Since Sophie hadn't been responding to his texts, he obviously had some explaining to do. He sent Brie a warning glance before he said to Sophie, "We should get you to Doc—"

"Isn't it the cutest? We just got them in. I made Liam buy one for Mia. Amanda, my niece"—she gestured to the little girl standing beside her—"has one, too. She and Mia are BFFs. We're so lucky the principal agreed to put them in the same class. Amanda was really nervous about going to school, but now that Mia's in her class, she's not, are you, honey?" Amanda smiled shyly at Mia, who smiled back. "We better get going. Don't forget our playdate tomorrow, you two. I hope you feel better, Sophie."

"Thank you. We have to get going too. Mia, come on." Sophie reached for her daughter's hand, her face frozen in fury. Brie wouldn't notice, but Liam did. This was a train wreck of epic proportions, and he had no idea how he was going to make it right. He knew she was nervous about Mia attending school, and he'd gone ahead and registered her anyway. And not because he felt it was his right to make those kinds of decisions as her father. It just happened. Brie practically dragged him to the school. Her excitement was infectious. The girls got caught up in it, and Liam had ended up going along for the ride.

Mia shook her head and refused to take Sophie's hand, wrapping her arms around Liam's legs instead.

Aw hell. Now on top of him overstepping, Mia had just chosen him over her mother. At least that's how he imagined Sophie saw it. If he had any doubts, the expression on her face cleared them up. She looked heartbroken.

"So cute. She's her daddy's girl, isn't she?"

Sophie walked away without saying a word.

"Did I say something wrong?" Brie asked, blinking her guileless blue eyes.

"It's okay, Brie." He lifted Mia into his arms. "I think we better postpone that playdate for another time, though. Sophie, hold up."

When he caught up to her, she was standing in front of an empty space between two parked cars. "At least something went right today," he thought he heard her say, but must have been mistaken because…

"Did you park here?" he asked warily, not sure what to expect from her.

She shot him a sideways glance. "Yes, and someone stole my car. I'll report it…later. When I'm feeling up to it."

He cleared his throat because there was no way in hell he was going to laugh after what had just gone down. "I'm pretty sure it was towed, not stolen. You were parked in a no-parking zone."

The only time she spoke the entire drive to Greystone was when he suggested he take her to Doc Bishop. She'd responded with a flat, lifeless *no*. When he stopped the Jeep in front of the carriage house, she turned to Mia before she got out. "You should probably stay with your daddy tonight, baby. Mommy isn't feeling so good. I love you to the moon and back." She kissed the tips of her fingers and leaned over the seat to press them to Mia's cheek.

She got out of the Jeep and walked up the stairs to the apartment without looking back. She didn't see Mia pressing her small hand against the glass and her bottom lip quivering.

Chapter Nineteen

♥

Sophie sat on the shower's tiled floor with her knees pressed to her chest while the scalding hot water beat down on her. Steam and heat filled the small bathroom, but it did nothing to banish the cold that seeped into her bones and heart. She was like Humpty Dumpty. She was broken, and nothing could put her back together again. She'd lost Mia to Liam.

"Sophie," her grandmother's voice came through the door at the same time she knocked. She heard her talking to someone in anxious, rapid-fire Italian.

"Chunk, get your ass out of the shower."

Two women swore at Marco in Italian, and then her cousin's voice came through the door. "Sophie, we're not leaving until you come out. We need to know you're okay."

Instead of all the king's horses and all the king's men, Sophie got the DiRossis.

"Move aside. I'll break the door down," her brother said.

Sophie turned off the shower.

"Told you it would work," Marco said in a voice smug

with the knowledge he knew exactly how to get through to his baby sister. "She'll be out in a minute. Go put the soup on, Ma. Ava, give her a hand." She heard the sound of retreating footsteps. "So, sister mine, how do you want me to handle this? Kill him quickly or torture him? If it were me, I'd pick slow torture. Maybe a horse head in his bed to start with."

She grimaced at the gory image and got out of the shower, reaching for a towel. Her brother loved *The Godfather*. He used to embarrass Sophie and Lucas by telling his friends outlandish tales about their great-grandfather who Marco claimed was a member of the Cosa Nostra. Sophie wrapped the towel around her, not quite ready to face her family, and rested her cheek against the door. "Mia would never forgive us if you hurt her father. She loves him," she whispered.

"He called me, Soph. Nonna and Ava too. He's worried about you," he whispered back.

"You love him too," she said, realizing he'd been teasing her, trying to make her laugh.

"Like a brother. But if I thought he'd done anything to intentionally hurt you, sister mine, he would be a dead man. Can you come out? I think I got a sliver in my lip from talking to you through the door. Ouch. Jesus, Ma, would you quit whacking me upside the head?"

Ten minutes later, Sophie sat in bed with four pillows stacked behind her back, an ice pack on her head, and a cup of chicken soup in her hand. Her brother and cousin lay on either side of her while her grandmother sat on the end of the bed rubbing Sophie's feet. "*Stupida* going out with no clothes on."

"Wait…No one said anything about her streaking down Main Street. I'm sure I would have heard about it."

Sophie pursed her lips at her brother. "I'd just seen the article in the *Gazette*, and then half the manor's lights went out when a bunch of fuses blew on the circuit panel. The electrician is replacing it as we speak and will be dropping off his five-thousand-dollar bill when he's done. So I was a little scattered. And it wasn't snowing when I left." She told them about the article in the *Gazette* and why she was in such a hurry to get to their offices. Then, because the three of them didn't seem upset with Liam, she told them everything that had happened. About Liam registering Mia in school without consulting her. About Mia choosing her father over her.

Ava and Marco looked at Rosa instead of Sophie. Her grandmother made an *eh* gesture with her hands. "It's for the best. It's time for Mia to make friends her own age. He texted you, *bella*. Mia's just trying to find her way. Open the cage door, let her fly. She'll come back to you. Just like you came back to us, *sì?*"

Ava touched her hand. "Sophie, you were a baby yourself when you had Mia. For seven years, your life's revolved around your daughter. She was your sole responsibility. Now you have someone to share that with. Maybe, for a change, you can take some time for you."

"Ava's right. It's time for you to have some fun. Get your groove on." Marco frowned when the three of them stared at him. "What?"

Before they could respond, there was a knock at the front door. Rosa got up to answer. Marco's phone pinged. He looked at his cell and rolled his eyes. "He's worse than a woman. Would you respond to his texts already...Wait a minute, I have to check you over before you do or I'll never hear the end of it."

Her brother took the mug from her hands and made her sit on the edge of the bed. She was touching the tip of her finger to her nose when Kitty and Jasper entered the room. They each carried a bag with a logo Sophie recognized—Ship to Shore, an exclusive women's clothing store on Main Street. Behind them, Rosa rolled her eyes. Ava got up from the bed, gave Jasper and Kitty a self-conscious smile, and took Rosa by the arm, dragging her from the room.

"Sophie dear, are you all right? We were so worried when Liam called to tell us about your fall." Kitty put down the bag and came to sit at Sophie's side. "You don't have to worry about Mia. Maggie's over there giving the boys a hand. How's your poor head?"

Sophie didn't know Maggie well, but there was a certain level of comfort knowing the woman was with Mia. "It's fine, thank you. Just a little dizzy when I move too fast."

Jasper thrust the bag at her. "You'd do well to wear these next time you go out in the snow, miss. I should have gone to the *Gazette* and taken care of the matter myself."

"It's my job to handle negative publicity. You didn't have to do this," she said as she pulled the white-and-blue striped tissue paper from the bag to reveal a pair of red boots with white snowflakes. "They're adorable. Thank you." She smiled, holding the boots to her chest.

Jasper gestured to the bag. "There's traction cleats in there too."

Sophie caught her brother struggling not to laugh and surreptitiously kicked him in the shin. Marco grimaced then lightly stepped on her toes. "I'll heat up your soup," he said.

"Here, dear, there's a warm coat to go with the boots. We can't have you coming down with pneumonia." Kitty handed her the other bag.

Sophie lifted a long, puffy red coat with a white fur-trimmed hood from the bag. "Thank you both. They're beautiful and much warmer than anything I have."

"It was our pleasure. But, Sophie, Jasper's right. You can't take everything on yourself."

"Dana's helping me with the wedding and so is Ava." Sophie paused, remembering how overwhelmed she'd felt leaving the *Gazette*. Trusting someone else to handle things had never been her strong suit. She'd have to learn to do that with Liam, and maybe she had to stop thinking it was a sign of weakness to ask for help. "We need to have a meeting with Mr. Wilcox. We have to keep our eyes and ears open. There's more than Paige and Hazel interested in seeing us fail." She told them what Poppy had said.

Kitty stood up and patted Sophie's shoulder. "Don't you worry. We'll find out soon enough who else is involved with Paige and Hazel and put a stop to it. For tonight, you rest. We'll figure out everything in the morning."

Jasper stayed behind when Kitty left the room. "Master Liam is a good man, miss. You have nothing to fear from him. For either yourself or the little miss. The family has withstood more than their fair share of sorrow these past several years. They deserve some happiness, as do you and your daughter."

"I know they have, and I do know Liam is a good man. So are you, Jasper. Thank you for everything you've done for me and Mia."

Obviously not a man comfortable with gratitude or praise, he gave her a clipped nod and left the room. Sophie heard the low hum of conversation from the kitchen and picked up her phone from the nightstand. She scrolled through all the texts. Liam had been telling the truth. He'd texted her about registering Mia at school. Twice.

"Hi. It's me."

"How are you feeling?" he asked, his voice deep and rough.

"I'm okay. Better. How's Mia?"

"Worried about her mother. So am I. You have to believe me, Soph. This is the last thing I wanted."

"Makes two of us. I didn't see your texts," she said, explaining why she'd missed them.

"So what you're telling me is you were already having a crappy day, and I made it worse. You have to believe me, Soph, the only reason I went ahead without hearing back from you is because I knew you were worried about Mia making friends. She and Amanda really hit it off, so I thought—"

"No, you were right. It's just…" She swallowed past the lump in her throat. "When she picked you instead of me…It was hard. I've never had to share her before. I've never been away from her overnight. When she was in the hospital, they let me stay too."

"I'll come and get you. You can stay here. She's asleep or I'd bring her back."

"It's probably better if I stay here. I have to get used to it. She's going to want to spend time with you."

"I'll bring her home as soon as she gets up. I'm heading to Boston tomorrow. I'll be back for Thanksgiving."

"Are you leaving because of me?"

"No, I have things to take care of. When I get back, I was hoping you'd let me take you to dinner and we can talk, get to know each other again as adults. We used to be friends, Soph. I know you're not exactly thrilled with me at the moment, but I could kinda use your help. This is all new to me. It's…well, to be honest, it's terrifying. I don't know how you did it."

"Welcome to parenthood. And honestly, these past few weeks, I wouldn't win an award for Mother of the Year. I'm pretty sure Mia wouldn't have voted for me."

"Don't do that. You're a great mother, and she's a great kid."

"She's amazing. I just wish she would start talking again, and you'd see what I mean."

"I already know she'll be amazing. She's just like her mother."

"That's not fair. You can't say things like that to me after I was such a witch." She fell back against the pillows before she realized what she was doing. She must have made a noise because Liam said, "What's wrong?"

"Just a little dizzy."

"Okay, I'm hanging up now. You need your rest. Make sure someone stays with you tonight. If Mia wakes up and needs you, I'll bring her home. I'm sending you a picture of her sleeping. Please tell me it's okay that Miller's sleeping with her. I'm worried he's going to roll over on her. But every time I try to take him out, Mia scowls and Miller growls at me."

He sounded so panicked that she started to laugh. "It's fine. She's always wanted a dog, and a daddy. I get this is all new to you, Liam, but I think both Mia and I got lucky that you're her father."

"Don't say things like that to me, Soph. I might have to come over there and kiss you. Get some sleep."

So maybe it didn't take just the DiRossis to put her back together again...maybe she needed the Gallaghers too. She wondered what her grandmother would think of that.

Colleen sat in the back corner of the sitting room taking in the drama unfolding before her. She'd never thought she'd live to see the day. She laughed, reminding herself that she was, apparently, neither alive nor dead. Still, it was a grand thing she was witnessing. After fifty years of carrying on a bitter feud—though it hadn't been nearly as acrimonious since Ronan's death—Kitty and Rosa were forced to work together for the benefit of their grandchildren and Greystone. Colleen couldn't have planned it better herself.

Maybe the end of their feud would wipe another sin from her eternal soul. If it wasn't for her meddling, the once best friends' lives would have turned out differently.

Rosa slashed her hand through the air, interrupting the members of the Widows Club's chatter. "*Silenzio.* We have work to do. If we want to save Greystone, we must join forces. No more of this pick, pick, pick. We—"

"Rosa is right," Kitty said, cutting off the other woman and earning herself a raised eyebrow from Rosa.

"Good to see you have some backbone, Kitty my girl," Colleen murmured. "It's about time you stood up to Rosa." Colleen had always been fond of Sophie's grandmother, but the woman was about as subtle as a steamroller.

A small frown pleated Kitty's forehead as she cast a sidelong glance at Rosa.

"Oh no, you don't. Give that one an inch, and she'll take a mile. You've lived with me long enough. You can handle her," Colleen encouraged her daughter-in-law, even though she couldn't hear her.

She smiled when Kitty squared her shoulders and continued. "Well, now, as you all know, one of my grandchildren is on board to save the manor. We need all ten—"

"*Sì. Sì.* They know that already. But they don't know we have half of one more. We just need to give him a little nudge, and then we have two."

"You mean Liam?"

Rosa nodded her head. "*Sì.* Liam is Mia's father. He marries my *bella*. She says sign, he says *sì. Capisci?*"

Ida Fitzgerald stood up. "I'm looking for a husband for

my granddaughter. She likes Liam, and Greystone, too, for that matter. Why can't—"

"No. Liam and Sophie are meant to be together. I have other grandsons. Let's focus on one at a time."

Rosa smiled. "*Grazie*, Kitty."

"You're welcome, Rosa."

"Jesus, Mary, and Joseph, at the rate you two are going, you'll be dead before you get this over with," Colleen muttered, and moved behind the two women. She blew on the papers on the lectern. They fluttered, drawing Rosa's and Kitty's attention to the meeting's agenda. The two women looked at each other and frowned, and then thankfully remembered what they were there for.

"Evelyn, you need to take back control of the *Gazette*. Paige and Hazel are wielding their influence over your grandchildren," Kitty informed the woman.

Evelyn muttered something about kissing her month in Florida goodbye then reluctantly agreed. She'd write an article to counter Paige's.

"Our most difficult job will be spiffing up the manor before Michael and his fiancée arrive for Thanksgiving. Sophie and I had a meeting with Mr. Wilcox this morning, and he's releasing some funds—not much, mind you—but Dana, you all know Dana Templeton"—Kitty pointed at the woman at the back of the room—"says she can work with it. We'll be breaking up in groups, and each team will be responsible for specific rooms."

Colleen smiled when Dana stood up and handed out her plans for the manor with Ava's help. She was pleased to see the two girls together. They'd be good for each other. This was working out better than she'd hoped.

"All right, Simon. Time to get back to work. We have to find the book before it falls into the wrong hands." Colleen started to walk away when Simon's insistent meow drew her attention. He looked from her to the women then back at her. She frowned when he did it again. "Bejaysus, are you telling me one of them has the book?" She could have sworn he nodded. Well now, that would explain why she hadn't found it yet. "A change of tactics then. We'll keep a close eye on this lot, Simon. One of them will let it slip."

Colleen walked through the door, and through Jasper, who had his ear pressed against it. She shivered. Jasper did, too, and then he looked to where she stood. Like the other day in the study, she didn't think he could see her, but she was beginning to wonder if he sensed her presence.

"I shouldn't be surprised. You always were a canny one, Jasper my boy. A fine and loyal man you grew up to be. And you had good reason not to. None of them know you have more right to Greystone than they do. You're another sin on my eternal soul. I'll do right by you. You have my word. Come, Simon." The cat meowed at the women again, but thinking of how well Jasper knew her, Colleen wondered if Simon was mistaken. "You'd have your own reasons for not wanting that book to be seen, wouldn't you, Jasper my boy? I wouldn't worry so much if it was in your hands. But until I'm sure, I'll be keeping a close eye on all of you."

Chapter Twenty

♥

Liam searched the rows of chairs in the school gymnasium for Sophie. The white walls were plastered with colorful fall leaves and equally colorful turkeys. Brie stood up in the second row and waved him over. He walked toward the front of the gym, nodding at several familiar faces. He did his best to ignore the leaden weight in his chest. The last time he'd been at the school was for Riley's Christmas pageant.

He'd been feeling the same uncomfortable pressure in his chest for the past two weeks in Boston. He'd convinced himself he'd gotten his head back in the game, but the flashbacks had come back worse than before as soon as he walked through the doors of Ladder Company 39. The picture of Billy with his turnout gear and helmet hanging on the wall beside it reminded Liam of that night every time he walked by. The station wasn't the same without his friend. Liam had spent his last days with his old unit riding a desk and going out with EMS.

He'd looked forward to coming home to Harmony Harbor.

Something he'd never dreamed possible a couple months before. But he'd missed his daughter...and Sophie. She'd called him with daily updates, acting as Mia's translator.

After a particularly trying day, Sophie had finally opened up to him, and their conversations had become longer, more personal. They'd talked about what had been happening in their lives since they'd left Harmony Harbor. He'd gotten to know the woman she'd become. And he liked that woman, a lot. What he hadn't liked as much was Sophie's insistence that he talk about the warehouse fire and Billy. He'd realized then that the trait he'd admired most when she was younger—her need to step in and fix everyone's problems—was annoying when applied to him. Annoying or not, she somehow got him to open up.

It was the first time he'd talked about that night to anyone. It wasn't easy reliving the nightmare or admitting that he still suffered from his own. In the end, he supposed it had been helpful. He'd felt surprisingly lighter after talking to Sophie.

He looked over his shoulder before taking a seat beside Brie. He was surprised Sophie wasn't here. She'd told him she would be.

"Welcome back, stranger." Brie smiled up at him.

"Hey, Brie, thanks for saving me a seat. Have you seen Sophie?"

"According to my grandmother, all hell broke loose at Greystone this morning. They had a flood in the bridal suite, and the water leaked into the dining room. The Widows Club is on the warpath. They think Paige Townsend had something to do with it. Anyway, I guess they're scrambling because Michael and his fiancée arrive tomorrow. I hope Sophie doesn't miss the pageant. Mia will be disappointed. They've been practicing all week."

He pulled out his phone to check for messages. His last one from Sophie had come late yesterday afternoon. It was a picture of Mia in her pilgrim costume. His chest tightened, no longer uncomfortable; it was suffocating. He was worried about Sophie, afraid someone was going to come through that door and tell him he'd lost her too. His reaction, he knew, was over-the-top, and there was no reason for him to be jumping to the worst-case scenario. He knew the why and how of it, but he couldn't seem to convince his brain or body that he was overreacting, that she was okay.

It was the same fight-or-flight response he'd been dealing with since the warehouse fire. But with Sophie, and Mia, he didn't have a choice. He had to fight. Deep down he'd known the moment Sophie'd walked toward him through the smoke at Greystone, the moment Mia gave him her mother's smile, that his days of running were over. The pages from his playbook tossed out the window—no more simple and easy for him.

Just as he was about to text Sophie, she burst through the gymnasium doors wearing a red coat and boots. The muscles in his chest loosened and relaxed, and he half rose from his chair and waved. She fast-walked toward him, her face flushed, her hair windblown and wild, with a smile he hadn't seen in a long time. Brie moved over and Liam had to remind himself to do the same. He'd forgotten how having that smile aimed at him made him feel. How Sophie made his head spin and stole his breath.

"Hi," she said with that smile still on her face.

But it was her breathy voice that got to him now. "Hi," he said, looking into her eyes. "I missed you." Yeah, that smile and voice were definitely doing a number on him because he hadn't meant to tell her. They were doing better, but he

didn't think she was open to considering a relationship with
him yet.

"I missed you too."

"Yeah?"

"Yeah. I really could have used you and your toolbelt."

"I love when you talk dirty. Feel free to use me anytime."

She rolled her eyes and leaned forward. "Hi, Brie."

Brie waved her hand with a smile. "Don't mind me. Keep
flirting."

"We're not—"

"We kinda are."

"You probably were, but I wasn't. It's been one disaster
after another at the manor." She narrowed her eyes at him as
she shrugged out of her coat. "Do not say I told you so."

"You just did, so I don't have to." He helped her out of
her coat. "But if you'll come to dinner with me, I'm all yours
tonight. Sounds like the ceiling in the dining room is going
to need some patchwork."

"You heard." She sighed then lowered her voice as the
kids filed in. "I could really use your help, but Mia's been
counting down the days until you come home. She has her
suitcase packed."

He tucked her hair behind her ear so she couldn't hide behind it. "You don't mind?"

"No…" She smiled when he raised his eyebrows.
"Maybe just a little, but with Michael and Bethany arriving
tomorrow, it's probably for the best." He lost her attention
when Mia's class walked by. Sophie twisted at the waist,
waving as Mia appeared wearing her pilgrim's costume. His
heart gave an unsteady thump when his daughter spotted
him and her face lit up with a smile. *Oh hell,* he thought
when his eyes welled up. He returned her smile, gave her a
thumbs-up then looked at the ceiling once she'd walked by.

Sophie tipped her head back. "Anything interesting up there?" He heard the smile in her voice.

"Heating duct needs to be cleaned out."

She slipped her hand into his and leaned against him. "It's nice to have someone to share this with. My friends used to come to some of Mia's school events, but it's not the same as having someone who loves her like I do." She tipped her head back again and blinked her eyes.

"Heating vent on the far right." He gently squeezed her fingers. "I'm glad I could be here for you, and Mia. Now stop looking at me like that or I'll kiss you and embarrass our daughter," he said when she turned her head and gave him a watery smile.

By the end of the pageant, Liam figured he and Sophie had inspected every inch of the gymnasium's ceiling. "I'm wrecked," he admitted once they'd finished clapping and all the kids had filed by on the way back to their classrooms.

"It would have been worse if you heard her sing. She has the voice of an angel." She reached for her coat and glanced at him. "Just like her father. I should have known she was yours."

He helped her into her coat and whispered in her ear, "Wanna check out the equipment room with me?"

She laughed. "You have a one-track mind. Come on." She reached for his hand. "Family are invited back to the class-rooms for a snack."

Brie joined them as they walked down the hall. "Did you see the boy mocking Mia when she was mouthing the words to the songs and pulling the feathers off Amanda's headdress? He's such a bully. I'm going to talk to Ms. O'Meara."

"Yep, caught that, and also caught my angelic daughter kick him in the shin when she thought no one was looking."

He'd been feeling exactly like Brie until he saw Mia defending her friend.

"I see you're having a proud papa moment," Sophie said. "When we get our first phone call from the principal's office, I'll let you handle it."

"I wish Amanda would stand up for herself. Thank God she has Mia in her class. Did Mia tell you…" Brie grimaced. "Right. But she probably wouldn't have anyway. Two of the girls in class were making fun of Amanda's pigtails the other day, and Mia *accidently* got glue in their hair during craft time."

Liam laughed. "No doubt about it, she's a DiRossi."

Sophie nudged him. "It's not funny. I wonder why Ms. O'Meara didn't call."

"Probably because no one would tell on Mia. She might not talk, but she's really popular," Brie said.

"More likely they're afraid what she'll do to them," Sophie grumbled.

"Honestly, Sophie, I would tell you if you had anything to worry about. I volunteer in their class a couple times a week. Mia's a sweet, outgoing kid. She just doesn't take crap off anyone."

"Thanks, that makes me feel better. I wish I had more time to volunteer in their class. Maybe in the new year, once things settle down."

Liam was about to offer to volunteer in her place, but things were going well, and he didn't want to blow it. If she wanted him to, she'd ask.

"What did you have to make, Sophie? I got popcorn balls."

"Turkey cupcakes."

"Oh cute!"

"Well, they were. I had the first dozen made when Mia

reminded me I couldn't use miniature peanut butter cups for their faces. I went with blobs of icing instead. I hope they taste better than they look," she said, sounding concerned.

Liam thought back to his daughter's comical reaction to her mother's cooking and had his doubts. "I'm sure the kids will love them."

As soon as they walked into the classroom, they found out that wasn't the case. Their daughter sat on the bench in the cloakroom, a mutinous expression on her angelic face.

Ms. O'Meara, who looked like a high school student, broke off her conversation with another parent to meet them at the door. "I'm so sorry. I didn't want to put Mia in a time-out, but I didn't really have a choice."

Sophie crossed her arms. "What happened?"

The teacher looked embarrassed. "Well, one of the boys made an unkind remark about your cupcakes, and, ah, Mia pushed him."

Liam held back a laugh when Sophie beamed at their daughter.

Michael, Bethany, and their entourage had arrived. Bethany had brought her maid of honor along with her mother and grandmother and mother-in-law–to-be. When four of the women gave Sophie up-and-down looks, she was grateful she had Dana and Ava at her back. Sophie swallowed her nerves and introduced the women to each other.

Mrs. Adams, Bethany's mother, tilted her head. "Have we met?" she asked Dana.

"I don't believe so. I'm from the South and, other than Greystone, have never been to Massachusetts," Dana said with a light Southern drawl.

Ava gave Sophie an I-told-you-so nudge from behind. Her cousin was right; Dana Templeton was hiding from someone or something. Before now, Sophie had never heard a hint of the South in Dana's voice. She also had blue eyes today, not her usual green. They were overshadowed by a pair of thick, black-framed glasses. But the one thing Dana couldn't conceal was that she'd dealt with women like the Adamses and Maura before, and they didn't intimidate her one little bit.

Sophie was so relieved that she was tempted to give Dana a fist bump.

"I'll let you ladies get on with it. I have work to do," Michael said.

Bethany pouted. "But, darling, this is your wedding too. I need your opinion. It won't feel like *our* wedding without it."

"Michael, really dear, this is important to Bethany. Surely you can—" Maura began before Bethany's grandmother cut her off.

"Since when do you listen to anyone's opinion but your own? Go on, Michael. It's bad enough they dragged me along. If I didn't want to get a look at the place, I would have stayed home. Have a drink at the bar for me."

Bethany glared at her grandmother at the same time her mother said, "If you felt that way, perhaps you shouldn't have come, Mother Adams."

Michael shared a conspirator's wink with Bethany's grandmother. Obviously they'd worked this out beforehand. Sophie was a little disappointed Michael wouldn't be there to run interference, but she had a feeling they had an ally in the senior Mrs. Adams.

"I'm the one paying for this little shindig. I want to see what I'm getting for my money." The woman thumped her cane. "I haven't got all day. Let's get the show on the road."

"I like her," Ava whispered to Sophie as they followed the group of women Dana led through the lobby. "She reminds me of Colleen."

"Me too." Sophie looked around and frowned. "Where's Jasper and Kitty? I thought they'd be here to…No, no, do not tell me there's another problem," she said when her cousin grimaced.

"It's under control. Someone called Truly Scrumptious and told them we needed the sample cakes next Wednesday and not today. I ran into Mackenzie on my way to work this morning, and they started making them right away. Kitty's at the bakery to make sure nothing else goes wrong. And, um, Jasper's at In Bloom doing the same. It's okay. Lily called to double-check the order Monday morning. She was able to get what she needed."

"Right about now I wish we did have mob connections. I'd take a hit out on Paige Townsend."

"I'd take one out on Helga," her cousin muttered. "Don't worry. Everything is prepared, and I put a padlock on the cooler just in case. Kitty and Jasper are going to come up with an excuse to get Helga out of the kitchen when it's time for the tasting. Marco's coming to help, and Erin will be here. So we're good."

"I thought Nonna—"

"She's busy standing guard with the rest of the Widows Club. I'm surprised you haven't seen them. They have every point of entry covered." Ava's mouth tipped up at the corner. "Who needs the mob when we have the Widows Club."

"They're not armed, are they?"

"Don't ask questions you don't want the answer to is what I always say."

They joined the women in the atrium. "You'll exchange vows under the arbor," Dana said, indicating the white arbor that was decorated with tulle and tiny crystal snowflakes and stood in front of the bank of windows with a view of Kismet Cove and the red-roofed lighthouse on Starlight Pointe. It was a scene off a postcard. "I've incorporated the ice-blue-and-white theme just so you have a visual, but there's photos of all three in your packets. If you go with the red-and-gold theme, the Christmas tree will stay as is." She gestured to the elegantly decorated tree to the right of the room, its twinkling red lights reflected in the window. "As you can see, each of the three tables and the chairs have been decorated according to theme."

The sun glinted off the snow covering the rocks at Kismet Cove, and Sophie found herself smiling, thinking about the night her daughter was conceived, and the man she'd conceived her with. Liam…A small gasp cut her off mid-thought. Beside her, Ava widened her eyes and looked at the hardwood floor polished to a high sheen…and the mice scurrying across it. In all her time at Greystone, Sophie had seen one mouse. And it wasn't white or huge like these three were. She had to think of something fast. They were headed to where the women were standing. She looked up to meet the senior Mrs. Adams's twinkling eyes.

Lifting her cane, the older woman turned to tap it on the window, drawing the other women's attention. "Now, what did you have in mind for here?"

At the same time Mrs. Adams asked her question, Simon padded into the room with what sounded like a low, menacing growl coming from his throat. Sophie and Ava moved to block the women's view. Sophie coughed to cover a squeak. Mrs. Adams raised her voice to cover another.

"Simon's getting liver pâté for dinner," Ava whispered.

"I think he'll be full," Sophie whispered back with a grimace, forcing a smile for the women when they turned her way. "Why don't we go to the dining room? You can have a cup of tea or coffee while you discuss your options."

The senior Mrs. Adams hung back while the other women followed Dana. "Put a little nip of brandy in my coffee, will you? Don't let my daughter-in-law see you do it, though."

"I'll be circumspect." Sophie smiled. "Thank you so much for covering for us. We never had a problem with mice—"

"Place as old as this and on the water, I'd be more surprised if you didn't. But not the ones that were running around in there. Those were someone's pets, and my guess, given your troubles of late, they were let loose on purpose."

"How do you know—"

"Michael. He knows of my interest in Greystone. I've been meaning to come for years. I consider myself something of an amateur historian. I attended several of Ronan Gallagher's lectures over the years. Handsome man. His grandsons take after him." She looked around as they walked through the lobby to the dining room. "Magnificent place. I look forward to spending some time here. By the by, do you know who your ghost is?"

Sophie shared a look with Ava. "Ghost?" they said at almost the same time.

Mrs. Adams grinned. "Oh yes, you have a ghost all right. If I had to take a guess, I'd say it's a woman." She nodded. "Yes, definitely a woman. Set your mind at ease, you have nothing to fear from her. She's looking out for the manor and, I think, all of you. Who have we here?" she said, looking down at Simon, who stared up at her. "Interesting," she murmured. "Very interesting indeed."

They were met at the entrance to the dining room by three older women wearing fur coats and outlandish hats decorated in flowers. *Oh dear, Lord,* Sophie thought, *what are they up to now?* It became clear as soon as her grandmother opened her mouth. They were pretending to be high-society ladies who do lunch and extolling the virtues of the manor.

"*Magnifico,* the food here is *magnifico,*" Rosa said in a thickly accented voice.

"Very." Her grandmother nudged the woman. "*Très.* Very *très bonne.*"

"*Sì.*" Rosa nudged that woman too. "*Oui—*"

Mrs. Adams chuckled. "I really do like this place. I do indeed," she said as she walked away.

"Poor Dana. Did you see her face when Bethany decided she wanted to be married outside instead?" Sophie asked her cousin, who sat in the passenger side of the estate car. Liam had insisted Sophie use some of the money he'd given her for Mia to send the Cadillac on a train back to California.

"Yes, but it wasn't as bad as when Bethany decided none of Dana's ideas worked for her, and the other three agreed."

"Thank God for the senior Mrs. Adams. Now let's hope Michael can convince his fiancée to make a decision before they leave. We're already pushing it. At least they agreed on the menu. You did an amazing job, Ava. Even Maura couldn't find anything bad to say."

"She's an awful woman. I feel sorry for Michael. He's turned out to be a pretty nice guy."

"He has, and I have to admit, if we didn't need this wedding, I'd tell him to dump Bethany. She's a Maura clone."

"Her best friend and mother are no better. I don't even want to think what it will be like having them all under one roof for a few days." She ducked her head and looked out the windshield. "You can let me out here, Sophie." It was a dead-end street a block from Ava's house. "You'll get stuck in traffic on the South Shore. It's busy Wednesday nights. There's a pathway. I'll be fine," she added when Sophie hesitated.

"I don't mind, Ava. I haven't seen Uncle Gino since I've been home. I—"

"He's not been feeling like himself. Come another time."

"Well, take the cake samples at least. The white chocolate and raspberry was amazing."

"So was the red velvet. You should consider contracting out the desserts to them. It would be worth it."

"Or you could." Her cousin pursed her lips at Sophie's suggestion. "Just think about it, Ava. Dana did a fabulous job updating the dining room." With the help of pretty much everyone at Greystone, Dana had lifted the Persian rug and stripped and refurbished the hardwood floors, removing the wallpaper and painting the walls a soft white and the wood panels gray-blue. She used accents of burnished gold throughout the room. "Between that and your food, you'd do really well. I guarantee you'd make a lot more money than you do now."

"I can't, Sophie, but I appreciate you thinking about me. I really do." Ava leaned across the console to hug her. "It's good having you home. Now why don't you take those cake samples and spend the evening with Liam and Mia?"

"I can't spend the night with him, Ava."

"I said spend the evening with him, not the night." Ava shook her head with a laugh. "Don't look so disappointed. You're an adult; you can do whatever you want. Just make sure this is what you want. Because, Sophie, I think Liam Gallagher is a man who plays for keeps."

With her cousin's words in her head, Sophie drove around the block twice before pulling in front of the Gallaghers' sandstone brick two-story. It was a pretty house with a red front door, its landscape carefully tended to. It looked much the same as the other homes on Breakwater Way. Nothing ostentatious or impressive like the McMansions on Ocean Drive or like the down-on-their-luck bungalows where her cousin lived along the South Shore. But she imagined to Mia, who never lived anywhere other than a cramped apartment, the Gallaghers' home on Breakwater Way was as impressive as the homes on Ocean Drive.

Sophie reached for the boxed cakes and got out of the car. Liam's Jeep and his father's Durango were parked in the driveway. She'd been rehearsing what she'd say when Liam answered the door, but she hadn't thought about what she'd say to Colin. Halfway up the driveway, she turned around and headed for her car then stopped, turned around again, and started back up the driveway. She wasn't fifteen, and Colin had always been nice to her. Just because she'd unintentionally kept his granddaughter from him for seven years wouldn't change…She groaned and walked back to her car and got inside. She drove to the end of the street and was about to head toward Main Street when she glanced to her right and caught the lights of Harbor Front.

She hadn't been down there since she'd been home. She'd been meaning to bring Mia. Sophie stopped and parked the car at the end of Breakwater Way. Huddling deeper inside her coat, she walked the short distance down to the docks. There was a brisk wind coming off the Atlantic with the smell of snow in the air.

She put her hands in her pockets, enjoying the cold against her cheeks, the breeze whipping around her hair. She'd missed the change of seasons. Missed being able to afford to live close to the sea. She walked to the end of the well-lit wharf and leaned against the rail.

If she stretched far enough to her left, she could see the

Outer Harbor and the lighthouse on Starlight Pointe. The waters of Harmony Harbor encompassed more than thirty miles of rugged coastline. Along with sandy beaches, inlets, and coves, there were at least a dozen wharves and private docks. The marina was on the South Shore and provided dockage for several hundred commercial and recreational boats, while the commercial fishing fleet docked in the Inner Harbor.

In the spring and summer months, the area would be a hub of activity. Local artisans would be selling their wares out of the brightly colored fishing shacks a short walk to her right at the end of Main Street. But it was quiet now, and she was enjoying the solitude. It was like she'd been living at a theme park, riding a roller coaster since she'd arrived.

Even with all the craziness of the past few weeks, she'd fallen in love with the manor all over again. For the first time since she'd come home, she could honestly say she was happy to be back. Admittedly the change in her relationship with Liam played a big part in that.

She glanced at the homes lining the ridge and picked out the Gallaghers. The big picture window looked out over the bay. She wondered how many times Colin and Mary had stood there watching their sons surf the wild waves that crashed against the rocks.

All four of them were adrenaline junkies. Griffin the Navy SEAL, Aidan the DEA agent, Finn with Doctors Without Borders, Liam the firefighter who'd gone out West to fight wildfires at twenty-three. Because of her, she now knew.

He'd run from her the same way he'd run from Harmony Harbor when his mother and sister died. Sophie understood why. She'd done the same herself, only for different reasons. Maybe that's why she couldn't work up the nerve to walk up their driveway. If she did, there'd be no turning back. She'd be all in. Because while her cousin thought Liam was a man who played for keeps, Sophie was beginning to think she was a woman who did too.

"Are you ready to concede?" a deep voice asked from behind her.

The wind blew Liam's black hair from his stubbled face, a glint in those Gallagher-blue eyes, a sexy flash of white teeth. He reminded her of a modern-day pirate. She wondered if he'd come to ravish her. She kind of hoped that he had. She wanted to be ravished by him. No, she acknowledged, she wanted more. She wanted to be loved by him.

"Concede to what?"

He walked toward her. The wind tugged at the open brown leather bomber jacket he wore over a cable-knit cream sweater. His well-worn jeans hugged his powerful legs as his steel-toe boots thudded against the boards. "To the inevitable." He leaned against the rail, his eyes moving over her face. "I saw you walking up and down the driveway. You were talking to yourself. You didn't get far."

Embarrassed that he'd been watching her, she gave a self-conscious shrug. "I haven't been down here since I've been home. It's still as beautiful as I remember."

"So are you." He moved in behind her and wrapped his arms around her, his cold, stubbled cheek pressed to hers. "You didn't answer my question."

"By the inevitable, do you mean—"

"Me. Us. I want you, Soph. Same as I always did."

Forever and for always? she wanted to ask, because that's what she wanted. "It's not just you and me. I don't want to confuse Mia. Set her up for disappointment."

"I wouldn't do that. I've never been in a long-term relationship before. I've never wanted one. With you I do. But, Soph, we can't know how it's going to turn out. Look at Aidan and Griffin. Your mom and dad."

"Maybe they just gave up too easily."

"I won't," he said.

"Promise?"

He smiled against her cheek. "Promise." Then he turned her in his arms, before lifting her off her feet and carrying her to the other side of the dock. "Didn't think you'd want an audience when we sealed the deal," he said in response to her raised eyebrows.

"You mean just a kiss, right? Because it's too—"

"For now," he said, and then her pirate ravished her mouth.

Liam's kiss had banished the cold and her doubts, at least where they were concerned. But her stomach gurgled with nerves when they entered the house on Breakwater Way. Liam wasn't helping matters by refusing to let go of her hand. Every time she tried to pull free, he'd tighten his grip and grin.

Colin Gallagher straightened from where he'd been looking in a mirror over a console table to smile. "Good to see you, Sophie. I've stopped by the manor a couple times and keep missing you."

Her stomach knotted. "Is there a problem, Mr. Gallagher?"

"Colin. No, I just wanted to"—he rubbed his jaw and glanced at his son, who seemed to be enjoying his father's obvious discomfort—"welcome you to the family. And to thank you for sharing Mia with us."

The knot left her stomach to settle in her throat. "Thank you. She loves spending time with you and Liam. Miller too.

She draws pictures of the three of you every day. I can't see my fridge anymore."

"She's working on doing the same to ours. Take your coat off, Soph."

"Maybe if you'd let go of her hand, she would." Colin winked at Sophie and then fidgeted with the knot in his blue tie.

"You think you would have learned to tie a tie by now," Liam said, moving his father's hand to straighten the knot for him. "You look good for an old guy. Maggie's unveiling my dad's naked painting at the gallery tonight," Liam told Sophie, his eyes glinting with amusement.

"How many times do I have to tell you I'm not…" Colin glanced at Sophie, a rosy flush coloring his cheeks. "I'm fully clothed."

"The painting Colleen commissioned Maggie to do was incredible. I'm sure yours will be too." He looked so uncomfortable about it, Sophie thought she better give him a heads-up. "Kitty's bringing Michael, Maura, and Bethany and her family to the showing tonight." He stared at her, and she grimaced. "The Widows Club are going too."

Liam ducked his head to look at her. "We actually want him to go, sweetheart. So could you maybe—"

"Who else, Sophie?" his father asked.

"All the staff at Greystone who aren't on duty tonight. Dana and Jasper too. You're a very popular man in town, Colin."

"Okay, Dad. Time to go. You don't want to keep your fans waiting."

"The three of you should come. Maggie will be disappointed if you don't show."

"Come on, Dad. We're not going to expose our seven-year-old daughter to a naked painting of her grandfather."

Colin scowled at Liam and walked to the hall closet. "Mia mine, come kiss your granddad good night," Colin called as he shrugged into his coat.

Mia came running down the stairs with Miller galloping after her. She stopped in her tracks when she saw Sophie. *Maybe this wasn't a good idea after all.* Liam, who apparently could read their daughter as well as Sophie, said, "Look who came for a visit. Your mom brought us cake."

Mia gave Sophie a tentative smile then ran to her grandfather, who swung her up in his arms and gave her a kiss. "I'll see you in the morning. You be good for your mommy and daddy." He put her down and came to Sophie. Cupping the back of her head, he kissed her forehead. "I'm glad you're here." As much for her daughter's benefit she thought as for hers.

The to-serve-and-protect Gallaghers were always on the job. Sophie got the warm fuzzies knowing that they considered her worthy of their protection.

Chapter Twenty-One

♥

The next morning Sophie arrived at Greystone eager to get to work. She felt revitalized, invigorated, ready to take on Bethany, her mother, and Maura. One way or another, Sophie was determined to nail down the plans for Bethany and Michael's wedding today. She had Liam and the best sleep she'd gotten in months to thank for her newfound energy. Even knowing Mia wanted to stay with Liam didn't dampen her spirits...much. At least they'd be having Thanksgiving dinner together at the manor. If Sophie and Liam's relationship was headed in the direction it seemed to be, it wouldn't be long before they were living together as a family.

She powered up the computer with a smile on her face then rolled her eyes at herself. She needed to get her mind off her future and concentrate on the present. She had to approve the changes to the manor's website and reconfirm the times for her conference calls tomorrow with three wedding planners and two bridal magazines.

But, she admitted, having a future as bright as the one she was imagining would be enough to throw off anyone's concentration. Especially someone like her, who not that long ago had given up on dreaming.

The door to the study opened, and the man who played the starring role in Sophie's dreams walked in. So much for concentrating on work. Liam wore jeans and a long-sleeved gray thermal T-shirt that hugged his impressive shoulders, chest, and arms. It was the toolbelt at his waist that held her attention, though.

"You really do have a thing for my tools, don't you?"

Thanks to his teasing remark, her eyes dropped to the front of his jeans. He laughed, and she jerked her gaze to his face. His gorgeous face that was just as distracting as the rest of him.

"What are you doing here? Where's Mia?"

"Hi to you too. Are you always this grumpy in the morning?"

She made a face. "Sorry, I'm just surprised to see you."

"Good surprised?"

"Good because I'm happy to see you. Bad if you plan on sticking around and distracting me. I have a lot to do today." She sighed when he put his cup of coffee on her desk and moved to take her face in his hands. "You're going to distract me, aren't you?" she said, looking into his beautiful eyes.

"Yeah, but I promise you'll like it." He held her gaze and pressed a soft kiss to the corner of her mouth. "You shouldn't have left before Mia went to bed. I didn't get the time I wanted with you." She didn't get a chance to respond. He gave her a closed-mouth kiss, his lips warm and firm. She could smell his spicy aftershave, his minty breath. He slowly pulled back, his fingers caressing her face.

"I didn't want to intrude on Mia's time with you."

"I got that," he said as he kissed her again. Only this time, he let his lips linger a little longer before pulling back. "I appreciate it, but I want to spend time with you too."

"We need to take it slow," she murmured, sinking into her chair when he kissed her just below her ear.

"Not sure I can." As though to prove that to be true, he gently tilted her head and slanted his lips over hers, taking her mouth in a breath-stealing kiss. She fisted her hands in his T-shirt to keep from sliding off the chair, drawing him closer. His powerful arms caged her in, the heat and friction of his chest against hers making her moan. Taking advantage of her parted lips, he delved deeper, exploring her mouth with his tongue. By the time he slowly pulled away, they were both panting. "No way are we taking this slow, babe." Removing his hands from her face, he straightened.

"Then why did you stop?" she asked, as her body thrummed with want and need.

He raised his eyebrows and pointed at the door when someone knocked. Obviously, by his reaction, not for the first time.

"Just a minute," she called out, finger-combing her hair and then smoothing her rumpled jacket and skirt.

Liam smiled and gently rubbed his thumb over her bottom lip. "I'll stop by and see you later, and maybe we can take up where we left off."

She pretended she didn't hear him, ignoring her body's reaction to the promise in his voice. "You didn't tell me what you're doing here or where Mia is."

There was another light knock on the door. "Sophie, I forgot something in my room. I'll be back in five minutes," Dana said through the door.

"Guess we weren't as quiet as I thought," he said with a grin then turned to her. "Kitty called me at seven this morning with a list of crap she needed done. First of which was to bring you your morning coffee. Mia, Amanda, and my dad were playing Barbie when I left."

She waited for her chest to tighten, the sudden drop of her stomach at the news Mia wasn't at the manor. Nothing happened. She wasn't overcome with a rush of panic. It felt good to be free of the worry, the thought that she was the only one who could keep her daughter safe. "Your dad's sweet with her. How did his night go?"

"Turns out we had nothing to worry about." He swiped his phone and handed it to her.

A picture of the painting showed Colin sitting on the rocks. He wore a faded denim shirt and jeans with Miller resting his head on Colin's thigh. It looked like the wind was blowing through their hair, sea foam on the waves rolling onto shore, a seagull pinwheeling overhead. Looking down on them from the window of the Gallaghers' dining room were Colin's four handsome sons, his wife, and daughter. "She did it again. I bet there wasn't a dry eye at the showing," Sophie said, swiping under her own. "It's heartbreaking and beautiful at the same time. How did your dad handle it?"

"Mixed feelings, I think. He didn't say much."

"And you?"

"Same as the old man, I guess. I feel bad for Maggie. I think she may have been expecting a different reaction."

"She's in love with your dad, isn't she?" You could almost feel Maggie's emotions—passion and desire mixed with heartache—through the painting. Like Colin was just out of reach. Caught between her and his family.

"Yeah, and I'm pretty sure it isn't one-sided. But lately he's been pulling away from her. Having Mia around, staying in Riley's room, I think he's reminded of all that he's lost. Of what he and my mom had."

"Has it been hard on you too?"

"It's different, right?" He gave her his quiet smile. "I've got my daughter, and I've got you."

"Kitty, Mrs. Fitzgerald said you needed—" Sophie looked up to where Liam stood on the ladder in the middle of the library fixing a loose wire in the chandelier. "They're driving me insane. They're worse than Bethany and her mother and Maura, and let me tell you, they're really bad."

His matchmaking grandmother and the Widows Club had been making up any excuse they could think of to get Sophie alone with him. "I told you what they're doing and how to stop it, but you won't listen to me."

"I'm not telling them we're together yet. Not before we've given Mia time to adjust to the idea."

Since they'd had this conversation three times in the past four hours with the same result, he went back to what he was doing.

"Are you ignoring me?"

"Yep. Go nail down Bethany's wedding plans so we don't have to hear about it all through Thanksgiving dinner," Liam said.

"Easy for you to say." She threw open the door that had inexplicably closed behind her when she'd walked into the library. "Men have no idea the work that goes into planning a wedding. It would be a lot easier to *nail* Bethany down if we could find her husband-to-be. He's a pain in the *culo*."

"Soph," he called out just before she shut the door.

"What?" she snapped.

He held back a grin at her show of temper. "I'm heading up to the bridal suite next to fix the tiles in the en suite. So if the Widows Club sends you up there, don't refuse."

"Even if I had the time, which I don't, I have no idea how to lay tiles, Liam."

"Who said anything about laying tiles. I thought we'd check out the king-sized mattress."

She swore in Italian and slammed the door.

He laughed when it opened a few minutes later. "Change of heart, babe?"

"How did you know, darling?" his cousin said, ducking his head outside the door to look down the hall before shutting it. Michael looked up at him. "Can you remind me why I thought this was a good idea?"

"Getting married or having your wedding at Greystone?"

"Having it at Greystone was a good idea. I know where to hide. It's the planning-the-wedding part."

Liam wondered if it was more the marrying Bethany part. That, he could understand. "You've got cold feet. I hear it goes with the territory."

"Nope, they're pretty much frozen." Michael sat in their grandfather's leather wingback chair and placed his elbows on his thighs, rubbing his fingers on his forehead.

"What's really going on?"

"I feel like I don't know Bethany anymore. I know she can be difficult and demanding, but she has good qualities, too, and I was able to look past that. But now I'm not sure we want the same thing. The wedding has kinda been an eye-opener. I'd be happy with something small and intimate, but Bethany, along with her mother and mine, insist we have to have this huge spectacle. And you know why? Because of my political career. A political career I no longer want, and I don't have the balls to tell Bethany or my mother."

Liam nearly dropped the chandelier. His aunt had been grooming his cousin to be in politics for as long as Liam could remember. "That's huge, Mike. I have to admit I'm kind of shocked."

"Just imagine how my mother and Bethany will feel."

"What brought this on?"

"The case I'm prosecuting. Actually, it's one of many. The guy's guilty, and he's going to walk because the cops bungled the investigation, and there's not a damn thing I can do about it. I want to make a difference, and lately, on the job, I feel like my hands are tied."

"Sounds like you're thinking about more than giving up on running for political office."

He nodded. "I talked to Aidan at GG's funeral. I'm thinking about going into law enforcement."

Whoa. Aunt Maura would have a coronary. And Liam didn't think Bethany would react any better to the news. He couldn't imagine the woman living on a cop's salary. "That's quite the career change. Are you sure it's not the stress of the job and wedding getting to you?"

"No. I've been thinking about it for a while now. Just didn't know how to break the news to Bethany and my mother. Then Bethany decided she didn't want to wait until next summer to get married because two of her friends did the unforgivable and are getting married next spring. I don't understand women, I really don't." He rubbed his stomach. "I'm thirty-three and have an ulcer and high blood pressure."

"My advice, cancel the wedding until you…" He frowned. His cousin was looking past him with an oh-shit expression on his face. Liam turned to see Sophie staring at him. "Soph, I can ex—"

"All this time we've been worrying about Paige and Hazel and their evil minions sabotaging the wedding, and the person we should have been worrying about is the man that I…my daughter's father."

"Sophie, put the knife down. You're making Dana nervous," Ava said.

Sophie looked down at the butcher knife clutched in her hand. She hadn't realized she'd been waving it around. They were in the kitchen at the manor, cleaning up after the Thanksgiving dinner that, according to Kitty, had been an unmitigated success. For Sophie, it had been a disaster.

Mia had sensed that Sophie was mad at Liam, probably because she hadn't done a very good job hiding her anger, and now her daughter wanted nothing to do with her. The one positive of the day had been that Helga had stormed out earlier that morning, leaving Ava responsible for the Thanksgiving meal. Though Ava would probably disagree.

Sophie was exhausted. All she wanted to do was go home and crawl into bed. Dana looked like she wanted to do the same.

"I understand you're mad at Liam, Sophie. But I didn't see any sign at dinner that they were calling off the wedding. Michael was being very sweet and solicitous to Bethany. He agreed to everything she wanted." Dana's narrow shoulders rose beneath her silk blouse. "Even to holding the first dance on the pond. Michael can skate, but Bethany can't, so I have to book lessons for her. You may want to look into the manor's insurance policy."

Ava turned from where she stood at the sink and took the knife from Sophie's hand. "Stop looking like you want to murder someone. Everything will be fine. Just because Liam suggested that Michael cancel the wedding doesn't mean that he will. He looked as nervous as Liam did every time you came out to serve the table. I'm sure he was worried you'd spill the beans to his fiancée."

"Either that or he was afraid she was going to spill hot gravy on his lap like she did Liam," Dana said, sounding as though she was trying not to laugh.

Sophie narrowed her eyes at the statuesque redhead. "That was an accident. I can't help that I haven't waited tables in years." Not that she'd share with her cousin and Dana, but she'd been embarrassed having to wait on Mia and her daughter's new family. But they were short-staffed, and she didn't have a choice.

"Sophie, you can stop worrying, right, Dana? They've signed off on the plans, and the senior Mrs. Adams gave you the deposit."

"But if we order everything and we get a phone call from Michael three weeks from now canceling the wedding, the deposit won't cover our expenses," Sophie said.

Kitty walked into the kitchen. "We have a problem, ladies. I overheard Michael and Liam. They're meeting up at the Salty Dog. Liam will probably ply his cousin with alcohol and convince him to cancel the wedding. You have to get over there and put a stop to this once and for all, Sophie. Stop Liam in his tracks or, the next thing we know, he'll convince Michael to sell Greystone, and then we're doomed. Doomed, I tell you."

Sophie imagined the bottle of brandy she'd caught Kitty and the senior Mrs. Adams sharing was behind the older woman's prediction of doom. But Sophie had to admit she wasn't exactly thrilled to hear Michael and Liam were going off alone to the Salty Dog. If Michael was getting cold feet, it wouldn't do for him to meet up with his old girlfriend, the owner of the Salty Dog's niece—Shay Angel.

When she caught the silent exchange between the three women, she crossed her arms. "You're setting me up again, aren't you?"

"Why would we do that?" Ava asked.

"Because you're all members of the Widows Club, and you probably took an oath when you joined. All for one and one for all and all that jazz. They've been trying to set me up with Liam all day."

"You're a member too," Dana reminded her.

"No, we revoked her membership. Sorry, dear, but you're neither widowed nor divorced. Shouldn't you be leaving for the bar now? I don't like to think what Liam will get up to with Michael. I truly don't."

"I agree with Kitty. It's probably best if you go, Sophie," Dana said.

"So do I. It's the perfect opportunity to confront Michael without Bethany and Maura around," Ava added.

"Fine. I'll go, but you two are coming with me."

It took some convincing, but Dana and Ava finally agreed to go along. An hour later, they parked across from the bar. Kitty wouldn't let them leave until they'd changed and freshened up. Since neither Sophie nor her cousin had much in the way of a wardrobe, Dana had insisted they take advantage of her extensive one. She'd turned the second bedroom of Liam's old apartment into a closet. She'd moved in the day before Michael and the Adamses arrived.

Sophie had agreed to borrow a cream sweater and black boots but wore her own jeans. Ava wore a pair of Dana's skinny jeans, black half-boots, a black sweater, and a leather fur-lined bomber jacket. With her hair loose and falling to her waist, her cousin looked gorgeous. So did Dana in a short, fake fur jacket over her black jeans and white shirt.

The bar was on the corner of Main Street and South Shore Road. A twenty-foot wooden sailboat mast was secured to the brick building and decorated in red and green Christmas lights. In the crow's nest overhead sat a fiberglass bulldog. Sophie opened the door and was hit with a wave of warm air and the sounds of laughter and people talking. The bar was packed. Every stool was occupied, and people were squeezing between them to lean onto the bar and yell their orders at Charlie Angel and another man.

Sophie scanned the bar for Liam and Michael. The tables on either side of the room were all taken, wooden barrels serving as chairs. Barmaids dressed as serving wenches carried trays over their heads, weaving through the people crowded on the dance floor. Drinking beer and talking, they waited for the band tuning up on the raised stage. When she was younger, Sophie had snuck into the bar a couple times to hear Liam and his brothers' band. Charlie had always spotted her and thrown her out for being underage.

"Get up there, Gallagher," several people called out.

Sophie heard a familiar, deep laugh and went up on her tiptoes, following it to a table a few feet to the right of the stage where Liam and Michael sat. Michael banged his beer on the table, chanting, "Liam, Liam." A chant that was taken up by the surrounding tables. Sophie was about to turn to Ava and Dana and point out where the two men were sitting when she felt herself being maneuvered through the crowd toward the stage.

"You have got to be kidding me," she yelled to be heard. "You set me up!"

"You were always trying to sneak in to hear him sing. Now's your chance. He wasn't trying to sabotage the wedding, but you were being stubborn and wouldn't hear him out. So…" Ava shrugged.

"You know what they say about payback, right?" But she wasn't thinking about payback when Liam got on the stage and accepted a guitar from a bearded man. She heard Dana and Ava talking behind her, and then they were tugging on the sleeves of Sophie's coat.

"What do you think you're doing?"

"You're looking a little warm," Dana said.

Sophie sighed. Dana was right. She let them take off her coat. "Michael," Ava yelled, and tossed it in his direction. He grinned and raised his hands to catch it, but something caught his eye and the coat landed on the table. Sophie turned to see what he was looking at. A woman in black leather pants and jacket carrying a motorcycle helmet in her hand had just walked into the bar. Her long, black hair was pulled into a severe ponytail. She was stunning and fierce-looking, and Sophie knew who it was right away. Shay Angel. Maybe it was a good thing she'd been set up after all. She could make sure Michael and Shay didn't spend any time together.

Then the band started to play and Sophie only had eyes for the man center stage. He was looking right at her with a smile on his face. A smile she'd always dreamed would one day be directed at her. Sexy, hot, and filled with promises. Just like his voice when he started singing "Galway Girl," only he changed black hair to brown, blue eyes to brown, Galway girl to Gallagher girl.

Dana leaned into her when he came down off the stage. "It's like that scene in *P.S. I Love You*."

Sophie couldn't respond even if she wanted to. Liam was in front of her, singing to her while the crowd sang along and clapped, stomping their feet in time to the music. Liam was a born performer. He played to the crowd, his voice deep and raspy. He circled her, moving closer each time. Then, just as the song ended, he cupped the back of her head and kissed her long and hard before saying to her in a thick Irish brogue, "Are you going to take me back to your room, my Gallagher girl?"

Sophie lay beside Liam in a blissed-out state. "If that was makeup sex, I think we should fight every day," she murmured, trailing her fingers up and down his bare chest.

"Making love with you every day is on the top of my wish list, babe. Fighting…not so much." He had his arm around her and gently tugged on her hair. "I was looking out for Michael when I suggested he cancel the wedding, not trying to sabotage you. If you—"

"I know you weren't." She kissed the underside of his stubbled jaw. "I'm sorry I shut you down and didn't give you a chance to explain. The past couple of days have been crazy stressful, and you were on the receiving end of that, I guess. It doesn't help that I'm stubborn."

He looked down at her with an amused smile. "Really? You're stubborn?" He laughed when she lightly pinched him then lifted her hand to his mouth and kissed her fingers. "I can handle you being stubborn. It's the shutting me out I don't like. You don't have to do everything on your own, Soph. If we're going to make this work, you've gotta trust that I'm here for you. You and Mia are my priority."

"It's not easy for me, the trust thing, I mean. But I'm working on it."

"I get it. After Mom and Riley died, I didn't want to let anyone in. I closed myself off, and then you and Mia came along and knocked down my walls. Let me do that for you. I won't let you down."

"In my heart, I know that. It's my head that's the problem. When things get crazy, I revert back to the LA me. I guess it's a control thing."

"Single mom on her own in a big city? You needed to be

that woman. I like the woman you've become. I just need you to let me in."

She knew what she needed; she just wasn't sure she could ask for it, and she didn't want him to say something he didn't mean. But he wanted her to open up to him, so she would. Lifting his arm from her shoulder, she moved on top of him and looked into his eyes. "I might not remember everything about that night at Kismet Cove, but the one thing I do know is I felt loved."

He smiled, lifted his hand to stroke her face. "That's because you were. You are."

"You love me?"

"Ah, yeah. I told you I did when…" The confusion on his face cleared, and he wrapped his arms around her, rolling her under him. "Guess you didn't hear me. I should have waited until you stopped moaning."

"I wasn't that loud."

"Yeah, you were. And I loved it. I love you, Soph. Always have and always will. You're it for me."

"I loved you as a boy, but I love the man you've become even more." She took his face between her hands and kissed him then whispered, "Stay the night with me, my Gallagher guy."

Chapter Twenty-Two

♥

Two weeks after that night at the Salty Dog, everyone in Harmony Harbor knew Sophie DiRossi was Liam's girl. Including their daughter. Liam let Mia sound the siren as he stopped the engine in front of Greystone. Sophie stood in the open doors to the manor in a red dress with a welcoming smile on her gorgeous face. He'd seen her standing along the Christmas parade route with Kitty, Ava, and Dana before they'd hurried back to get ready for the onslaught. After seven years, at Sophie's instigation, Greystone was reviving its long-standing tradition and opening its doors to the people in town. There'd be hot chocolate and cookies and a visit from Santa. Fergus had been about as thrilled as Liam to learn about the event. In the end, Mia's and Sophie's enthusiasm won Liam over. Fergus, who'd been assigned the role of Santa, not so much.

"Okay, guys, we better get in there before Sophie freezes to death. Leave the helmets and jackets on the seats." As Marco helped Mia and Amanda out of their gear, Brie's nephew Zach stared longingly at the siren. "Okay, buddy, give it a go," Liam told the little boy, laughing when Sophie stepped inside the manor with her hands over her ears and closed the door.

He jumped out of the rig to help the kids down. "Did you have fun, sweetheart?" He didn't have to ask. Mia had been grinning from ear to ear the entire parade route. But Liam was getting frustrated with her unwillingness to talk and had been trying to get her to speak.

She gave him an enthusiastic nod and mouthed, *Yes*.

"Sorry, couldn't make it out. How about telling me with words?"

She gave him a look, pressed her lips together, and reached for Amanda's hand. The two little girls set off for the manor.

"It's scary how much she looks like her mother sometimes. In case you didn't get it, she just flipped you off with her eyes," Marco said.

"I got it, all right, and I've been getting it for the past week. She's been playing Sophie and me off each other too."

Marco slung his arm over Liam's shoulders. "Still find it hard to believe my baby sis is a mom and that you're a dad. It seems so...grown up."

Liam understood what his best friend meant. Every once in a while, it hit him how much his life had changed the past month. It was nothing like he'd envisioned. It was so much better, he thought as Sophie ushered Mia, Amanda, and Zach inside and her eyes met his.

"Hey, beautiful," Liam walked up to her, kissing her temple. "I missed you." He dropped by whenever he had the chance, but he was just coming off a four-day rotation. Which meant he'd been sleeping at the firehouse when he'd rather be sleeping with her. They had some catching up to do, and he planned to do it tonight.

"I missed you, too, handsome." She kissed him on the jaw.

"Seriously? I don't think I can be friends with you anymore." Marco looked down at Mia. "You have to put up with these two making goo-goo eyes at each other all the time, *cara*?"

Mia gave her uncle a woe-is-me look and nodded.

"I feel for you, kid. I really do." He took her hand. "Come on, I'll get you a hot chocolate. You too," Marco said to Amanda and Zach.

"Just when I'm tempted to whack him, he does something sweet. I guess I shouldn't be surprised. He's really good with Mia."

"Hate to break it to you, babe, but your brother isn't doing it out of the goodness of his heart. In his mind, the kids are chick magnets."

She raised an eyebrow. "From what I saw and heard at the parade, all you guys at HHFD are chick magnets."

"It's the uniform. Speaking of which, I'm going to get out of my gear."

"I was kind of hoping you'd stay in it."

"I'll wear it for you later when we're alone," he said with a wink. "Did you leave my stuff in the study?"

"Yes, but your dad and Kitty are in there getting Fergus ready. I'm serious about you staying in uniform. I was hoping you'd man the raffle table and charm all the ladies into buying tickets."

"You're joking." He sighed when she fluttered her eyelashes at him. "You're serious. You're lucky I love you. Tell me where you want me."

She gave him a wicked grin.

"Don't tease me," he said, taking her by the hand. "I

know you too well. I won't get five minutes alone with you until this thing is over." It was true. Sophie had an incredible work ethic. In the short time she'd been at Greystone, she'd made huge changes to the manor. All for the better. He was beginning to believe what everyone else did, that she could turn Greystone around. She'd already booked five weddings and two conferences for the new year. Over the past couple of weeks, people had been stopping him on the street to tell him to pass on their messages of support to Kitty and Sophie. The town's economy had taken a lot of hits over the past several years, and they saw Greystone's survival as a sign of hope for the future. Liam figured it was about time he got on board and let his daughter's mother know he was not only Team Sophie but he was Team Greystone too.

"I'll make it up to you tonight," she promised as she led him across the lobby that had been decked out for the holidays. Beside the roaring fire in the stone fireplace stood a sixteen-foot tree decorated in multicolored Christmas lights. A red velvet wingback chair sat in front of the tree waiting for Santa.

"Something to think about while I'm twiddling my thumbs in the corner."

"You won't sell many tickets with that attitude."

"I didn't think you had that many left. Grams said sales have been great."

"That was before we got the estimate for the new generator and an estimate from the plumber you recommended. Anything extra will help."

"Right. Forgot about that. I'll go over the plumber's estimate and see if I can save you on labor. I can work with him on my days off," he said as they walked past the staircase with gold pots of poinsettias lining either side of the red runner to the table set up beside it.

"I was wondering how you'd feel about me contributing some of the money you gave me for Mia." He looked at her, and she winced. "I guess that's a no. I probably shouldn't have asked. It's just that Greystone is Mia's legacy too."

He pulled out the chair behind the table. "It's not a no. But how about we save this conversation for tonight, okay?"

She nodded, looking relieved. "Are we staying at the apartment or at your dad's place?"

They'd been basically living together since the night at the Salty Dog. "Dad's not working tonight, so we'll be staying at the apartment." He opened the cash box and leafed through the tickets. "How many do you want me to sell?"

"Twenty would be great."

"Okay, I'll see what I can…" He noted the Widows Club walking his way. They wore long red dresses, white fur shawls, and wide-brimmed bonnets. "Ah, Soph, why are your grandmother and the members of the Widows Club dressed like that?"

"They're our entertainment. They're singing carols."

"Where are they…Hi, Mrs. DiRossi, Maggie, Mrs. Fitzgerald." When he'd finally finished saying hello to all the women who were currently taking their places on the stairs, he looked at Sophie. "I'm moving the table."

"You can't. It'll be great for business."

It was good for business, but hell on his ears. The owner of Books and Beans approached his table. She was dressed as an elf and had been helping Fergus with the kids. "Hey, Julia. How's Santa doing? Has he made any kids cry yet?"

She grinned. "Only two." She looked over at the Widows Club, who were singing "God Bless Ye Merry Gentlemen." "They're very—"

"Bad, and loud."

"I was going to say enthusiastic."

"That's 'cause you're nicer than me. Can I interest you in a couple of tickets?" He'd sold fifteen so far. He was hitting up the carolers when they took a break. He figured they owed him.

"I'll take twenty-five," she said just as the Widows Club started singing "Jingle Bells" and shaking bells.

He put two fingers behind his ear. "Sorry, I don't think I heard you right," he yelled, and got shushed by Rosa.

Julia blushed and pulled a check from the pocket of her red apron. "Twenty-five tickets, please."

Liam looked from the check for twenty-five hundred dollars to the woman in front of him. "You sure?"

She nodded. "It's for a good cause."

"Okay, great." He was so getting lucky tonight. He handed Julia a pen, and she got started filling out the tickets. She'd just finished signing the last one when a cold blast of air blew them off the table.

Liam frowned, wondering where the draft had come from. "Someone must have left the doors open. I've got them." He moved around the table to help her pick them off the floor. Simon padded over and pawed at the tickets, leaving muddy prints on a couple of them. Liam nudged the cat aside to pick them up. "Do you want new ones?"

"No, that's fine." Julia glanced over her shoulder. "This elf better get back to work. There's a line."

He tore off the stubs from her tickets. "Here you go. Thanks for your support. Good luck." As Julia headed off to help Santa, Liam spotted Mia in line. She was giggling and waving. At first he thought it was at him, but when he waved back, she looked like she'd just noticed him sitting there. He had to admit, like her still not talking, it worried him. But he wasn't sure how Sophie would react to him suggesting Mia see a therapist.

Liam sold the last ticket just as Mia was about to sit on Fergus's knee. He hurried his customer along so he could get over there in time to take a picture. Sophie joined him. "She wouldn't let me help her with her list. Kitty and Jasper have been working on it with her."

"I'll get it from Fergus," he said, watching his father's best friend with his daughter. Mia shyly nodded at something Fergus said and handed him her letter. It made Liam think of all the Christmases he'd missed. Sophie had shared enough about her years in LA that he knew the holidays had been especially tough for her. Struggling to get by, she'd scrimped and saved to make Christmas special for their daughter. As his eyes welled with emotion, he looked up at the ceiling and vowed to make this a Christmas they'd never forget.

"Are the beams as dusty as I think they are?" Sophie asked, her voice husky.

"Yeah, I'll need an extension ladder to get to them."

"I'm not sure it will reach, son," his father said from where he stood on the other side of Sophie, looking at the ceiling, his voice gruff.

"Perhaps a pole would help, Master Liam," Jasper's equally gruff voice came from behind them.

Liam smiled, wondering what the people filling up the manor thought of the four of them staring up at the ceiling. In that moment, he realized how much he'd missed his family. How much he'd missed out on by staying away from Harmony Harbor.

Liam tightened his grip on Miller's leash and jogged around the pond before heading into the woods. The light from his flashlight bounced along the path to Mistletoe Cottage. If GG was here, she'd tell him he'd made a hash of it. And she'd be right.

As soon as the Christmas party at the manor had ended a couple hours ago, he'd brought Mia and Sophie to Mistletoe Cottage. He'd thought his daughter would be thrilled at the prospect of staying there for the weekend. She was until he had to explain that no, they weren't moving in as she seemed to think. Then he'd made it worse by adding that it would be their last chance to spend time there because of the raffle.

He'd gone home to pick up Miller in hopes he'd bail Liam out. If anyone could smooth things over with his daughter, it would be the loveable retriever, who had a way with women. Until Mia and Sophie, Liam used to think he did too.

Something ran across the dark path ahead of them and cut through the woods. It was black and bigger than a rat. Miller took off, ripping the leash from Liam's hand. "Miller!" he yelled, panicked. All he needed to do now was lose the dog. He chased after Miller, calling out to him as he ran. Up ahead he heard Miller yelping, and then he came running back to Liam with his tail between his legs. Liam knelt on the snow-covered ground to check over the trembling dog. "Something gave you a fright, didn't it, boy? You're okay." He gave the retriever a rubdown before rising to his feet.

A few minutes later, they reached the stone cottage in the woods. Colored lights from the Christmas tree twinkled in the front window, the welcoming smell of wood smoke in the air. Liam had barely gotten the front door open when Miller bounded past him, galloping up the stairs. It was like he had Mia radar.

Sophie's eyes went wide when she saw the dog. He hadn't told her he was going to get Miller, just that he had a plan to cheer up their daughter. "Liam—"

She didn't get anything else out because Miller had

jumped into bed with Mia. Liam heard a hiss, and then Simon was flying at Miller. The dog yapped, batting at the cat with their daughter lying in the middle of the fight. Liam launched himself across the room and onto the bed. "Miller, down," he said, shielding his daughter with his body. He pushed on Miller's chest at the same time he raised his arm to block Simon's flying leap. Both the dog and cat fell off the bed. Mia looked at Liam and started to cry.

"I didn't mean to hurt—" As Liam attempted to defend himself, both the cat and dog made dramatic whining sounds from the floor. Mia sobbed harder, and Liam got to his feet. He'd messed up again.

Sophie rushed over to the bed and took Mia into her arms. "It's okay, baby. Daddy was just protecting you. Miller and Simon are"—she craned her neck to look over the side of the bed—"um, they'll be fine." Both animals looked up at Liam and gave themselves a shake then jumped back onto the bed. "All right, you two, if you want to be with Mia, you have to learn to share her," Sophie said sternly, looking from Simon to Miller then asked Mia, "Do you want them to stay?"

She gave her mother a watery smile and nodded. When the animals lay on either side of her, Mia put an arm around each of their necks. Sophie tucked the covers under Mia's chin and gave the animals another stern look, wagging her finger at them. "Behave, or you're out of here." Miller whined, and Simon gave what could only be described as a haughty twitch of his ears.

Sophie turned off the light and followed Liam out of the room. He glanced at her as she closed the door. "Looks like I can't do anything right tonight."

"Don't say—" She broke off with a smile and nodded behind him. He turned. Mia, wearing her *Frozen* nightgown, was standing in the doorway. She crooked her finger at him. He went down on one knee, and she wrapped her arms around his neck and gave him a butterfly kiss on his cheek. "Thank you, sweetheart," he said, stroking her hair. "I'm sorry I made you sad. I thought staying here for the weekend would be fun. I'll make it up to you tomorrow, okay? I checked out the pond. We'll go skating."

She rewarded him with a wide smile, nodded, and went back to her bed. Neither Miller nor Simon yelped or hissed when she climbed over them to get under the covers. They settled in beside her.

"How did Simon get here?" Liam asked as they headed downstairs.

"I have no idea. Not long before you arrived with Miller, I heard scratching at the bedroom window."

Liam had a fairly good idea who'd darted past them on the path now. "Poor Miller, I think Simon terrified him."

Sophie laughed. "Miller outweighs him by a hundred pounds."

"I outweigh Mia by at least a hundred and fifty pounds, and she terrifies me."

"She does not." Sophie joined him on the couch in front of the fire. "You're wonderful with her, and she adores you. Stop beating yourself up over tonight. It was a sweet gesture. She's just weirdly attached to this place. It doesn't help that she's convinced she has a chance to win. Nonna isn't helping matters. I explained to her about the rules, but every time we go over to her place, she insists on taking out the ticket and the two of them do another novena."

"Do you think it would help if we started looking for a place of our own?"

"I don't want you to rush into something just because—"

He lightly pressed a finger to her lips. "Stop. You know I

want to be with you and Mia. Going back and forth between my dad's place and the apartment might be confusing her. Once she feels more settled, maybe she'll start talking…and, ah, stop waving and smiling at imaginary people."

She stiffened. "It's not uncommon for children to have imaginary friends, Liam."

"Yeah, I know that, babe. But you have to admit…" He took in the defensive jut of her chin. He had to switch gears if he didn't want to ruin his plans for the night completely. "You know what? Why don't we just forget about everything and enjoy our weekend together?"

She drew her feet up on the couch and snuggled against him, wrapping an arm around his waist. "Good idea. We won't have a lot of time alone together once all the wedding craziness begins."

He stroked her hair. "Bethany still driving you nuts?"

Sophie nodded. "She calls at least five times a day with something else she wants to change or add. It's like talking to a wall. She won't listen to reason. I actually had to call Michael yesterday and explain that it's too late to make more changes. I felt kind of bad, but I didn't know what else to do. I was afraid Dana was going to quit if I didn't intervene. Michael sounded stressed."

"No doubt. I don't know why he…Probably should keep that to myself if I want to get lucky tonight."

She lifted her arm and moved over him, sitting up to straddle him. "Oh, you're getting lucky tonight, handsome," she said with a smile, and undid the top two buttons of his shirt. She pressed her lips to the skin she revealed. "So, are you going to tell me how you charmed all those women out of their hard-earned dollars?"

"You keep moving around like that on my lap and kissing me, this conversation will be over before it starts."

"Talking's overrated," she whispered in his ear, and added another torturous wiggle.

He wrapped an arm around her and rolled her beneath him. Covering her with his body, he gave her a long, passionate kiss before raising himself on his elbows to look down at her beautiful, flushed face. "I've got something else that I think will ensure I get really, really lucky tonight, and maybe first thing in the morning too." He reached under the couch and pulled out the document he'd signed with Mr. Wilcox this afternoon, confirming his vote to keep Greystone and the estate in the family. He handed the paper to Sophie.

She frowned then took it from him to read. She slowly raised her eyes to his. "You're on Team Greysto—" She couldn't finish because she was crying. Liam rested his forehead on hers and groaned.

Liam sat on the jump seat across from Marco, feeling pretty good, all things considered. They'd just responded to a call; a Christmas tree had caught fire at the town hall. No one was injured, and apart from being unable to save the tree, there wasn't any damage to the premises. For Liam, it also marked his third week on the job without a flashback.

"Hazel was a little testy considering we saved the town hall from burning down," Marco said.

"Probably because her and Paige's latest attempt to shut down Greystone failed." Sophie had been fielding visits from health and safety inspectors for the past week. "Last I heard they've been reaching out to my cousins, so hopefully that'll keep them busy, and Sophie won't have to deal with anything other than the wedding party this week. They start arriving tomorrow."

"I'll be glad when this wedding is over. Rosa is practically living at the manor, so she's hardly working at the deli. Our payroll doubled last month. And Ava and Sophie roped me into cooking for the wedding."

"You and me both. Bethany, her mother, and Maura are already running your sister off her feet. She'll probably sleep through Christmas."

"Your cousin should—" Marco broke off when Liam held up a finger and answered his phone.

"Hey, Soph, we were just talking about—"

"D-Daddy."

Hearing his daughter's voice for the first time, Liam's eyes welled up. It took some effort to be able to say, "Mia. Sweetheart, you don't know how happy I am to hear you say my name—"

"Are you kidding me? She's talking? Let me hear." Marco reached across to hit speaker on Liam's phone.

"Daddy, there's a fire. I can't wake Mommy up."

Chapter Twenty-Three

♥

Liam felt the darkness closing in around him and pushed it back. He met Fergus's eyes in the rearview mirror as he put in the call to the station and saw his own fear reflected there. And in Marco's eyes as his best friend lifted his cell phone to his ear. Liam shut down everything that was going on around him and forced his voice to remain calm and even. "Okay, sweetheart, you hear that? You hear the siren? Daddy's on his way. Where are you?"

"In my bedroom. Daddy, I'm scared," she whispered.

"I know you are, but everything's gonna be all right. Where's Mommy?"

"Right here, on the floor. She fell. She won't get up."

Liam's jaw clenched so tight he felt it pop. "She will. I'll take care of her as soon as I get there. Mia, I need you to tell Daddy if you see any fire or is there just smoke?"

"Fire," she said, her voice small and terrified. "It's in the living room. There's smoke too."

"It's okay. We're almost there. I need you to shut the door

to your bedroom, sweetheart. Stay on the line with me and do that for Daddy, okay?"

" 'Kay." He heard her moving around, and then the sound of the door shutting.

"Good girl. You should hear the sirens anytime now. Can you hear them?"

"Hurry, Daddy."

"No one's picking up at Greystone," Marco said, his voice tight.

"Fergus is driving as fast as he can. Your uncle Marco is with me too."

"Hang in there, *cara*. We're almost there," Marco said, holding Liam's gaze as he tried the manor again.

"Is Mommy on her back or her tummy?"

"Her—" There was a crash, and Mia screamed. "Daddy, Daddy, hurry, hurry!"

"Mia, it's okay, baby. Come here. Mommy's got you. Give me the phone. Liam," Sophie's voice came over the line. She sounded groggy.

There was so much he wanted to say to her, but now wasn't the time. "Soph, how bad are you hurt?"

"The smoke detector went off, and I ran to get Mia. It was dark. I tripped and hit my head on the dresser."

"You're bleeding, Mommy. There's blood on you," Mia whimpered.

"It's just a little cut. It's fine. Don't cry, baby."

His fingers tightened around the phone.

"Almost there, son. We're almost there," Fergus murmured.

"Soph, you were out for a bit, so take your time standing up. But I need to know if you can walk. Hold on to the bed and try to get up."

He heard movement then. "Good. I'm good. I hear the sirens," Sophie said.

"You're gonna see me in about four minutes. Soph, is Dana in the apartment next door?"

"I think so. I'm not sure."

"Baby, I've gotta go. I'm coming to get you." He wanted to tell her he loved her, that he loved them both, but the words got stuck in his throat. If he said them, it felt like he was saying goodbye.

Sophie sat on the bed and pulled Mia onto her lap. She cupped her daughter's face, looking into her tear-filled, Gallagher-blue eyes. "I'm so proud of you." Mia had found her voice, and in all likelihood had saved their lives. "Daddy's coming. You don't have to be afraid." She tried to ignore the sounds outside the door—the hiss and pop of the fire spreading through the apartment. She thought of Mia alone, curled up in the closet of the bedroom they once shared in LA, and held back a sob, holding her tighter. "Mommy's not going to let anything happen to you. Not this time, baby. I promise."

"What if Daddy doesn't come before the fire—"

Sophie glanced at the base of the door, her heart pounding faster at the sight of the faint glow beneath it. The temptation to pick up Mia and make a run for the window in her bedroom all but overwhelmed Sophie. She forced herself to stay where she was. She trusted Liam. There was no one she trusted more. "Nothing will stop your daddy from getting us out. You know that."

There was the sound of wood splintering at the front of the apartment. She heard men's voices, heavy footfalls in the hall, and then the door opened and Liam was there. She held back a sob at the sight of him filling the doorway with an ax in his hand, smoke and the yellow glow of the fire behind him.

He rested the ax against the wall and came to them, lifting his visor to kiss them both. His eyes held Sophie's for a brief moment before he said, "Okay, let's get you out of here." He lifted Mia into his arms. Shifting their daughter to his hip, he helped Sophie to her feet, wrapping his other arm around her. "We have to go through to the apartment next door." There was a low groan from the front of the apartment and it felt as though the whole building heaved. Liam shot a look to his right, and then he lifted Sophie off her feet, running toward the bathroom. He angled them through the doorway then kicked the door shut behind them then did the same to the other door.

There was so much smoke, the flames hissing and licking up the walls, that she shuddered, fighting against panic. Reaching a hand across him to hold Mia's, she buried her face in Liam's shoulder. She jolted as he kicked another door shut. When he set her on her feet, she was surprised they were in a bedroom. Colin stood on a ladder outside the window, pulling off the screen. Sophie saw the two men's eyes meet as Liam passed Mia through the window to his father. Colin hugged Mia tight before handing her to someone below him. As Liam lifted Sophie and turned her back to the window, hands wrapped around her ankles and placed her feet on the rungs of the ladder. Liam held on to her arms to steady her.

"Got her," his father said.

Liam briefly stroked her cheek and then turned and ran toward the door, throwing it open. He disappeared into the smoke and fire. "No! Liam!" She struggled against his father's tightening grip as he half dragged her down the ladder.

Hands reached up, and she found herself in Fergus's arms. As he carried her from the burning building toward the crowd gathered outside Greystone, firefighters raced past them. "They've got Dana," Fergus told her. "She's going to be okay."

Sophie's body sagged against the barrel-chested man with relief. Dana was okay. They were all going to be okay. Fergus set her on her feet beside the back of the ambulance where the paramedics checked Mia over. Kitty and Jasper were at her side.

"Mommy, where's Daddy?"

"Don't worry, baby. He'll be here in a minute." She saw a flicker of emotion cross Fergus's face before he turned away and headed for the men readying the hoses.

"Fergus." She ran to him and tugged on his arm. "What is it? Why isn't Liam out by now?" she asked when another fire-fighter jogged toward the ambulance with Dana in his arms.

"It's Marco, Sophie. Liam—" Fergus broke off when Colin yelled.

"Out, everyone out now! The roof isn't going to hold for much longer."

Liam checked the second bedroom. Johnny was lowering Dana out the window. Marco had been right behind Liam. It should have been Marco who had gotten to Dana first, not Johnny. "Johnny, where's Marco?"

"I thought he was with you."

"No. Chief, we've got a man missing," Liam informed his father over the radio as he ran back through the bathroom to Sophie's apartment. He grabbed his ax from the floor of Mia's bedroom and headed for the front of the apartment. The roof wasn't going to hold much longer, and if Liam's suspicions were correct, a portion had already fallen. As he moved past the kitchen, he saw that he'd been right. He carefully worked his way to the far side of what had once been the living room. Part of the roof had collapsed. Somewhere underneath the burning beams and debris, he knew he'd find his best friend. "Marco," Liam repeatedly called out as he shoved the plywood and tiles out of the way.

"Liam."

He quickly moved to where he heard Marco's muffled voice and pushed aside a chair, sheetrock, and two-by-fours to reveal a hole in the floor to the level beneath them. His best friend lay on the dirt floor with a wooden beam across his lower legs. Several of their fellow firefighters raced into the apartment. "Don't come any farther!" Liam yelled. "It won't hold your weight."

"Out, everyone out now! The roof's not going to hold for much longer," his father's urgent command came over the radio.

Marco looked up at him. "Do as he says—get the hell out of here."

Liam stretched out on the floor and carefully dropped his ax a few feet from Marco. "No man left behind," Liam reminded his best friend, and lowered himself into the hole, jumping to land on his feet. Overhead, he heard what sounded like a freight train. Liam grabbed the end of the beam and lifted it off Marco's legs to toss it aside. He'd barely gotten his friend to the far corner of the storage room before the rest of the roof collapsed above them.

When the building stopped shaking and the dirt and smoke and debris settled around them, Liam tried his radio. All he got was static. He started searching for the weakest point, a way to get out. He heard a cat meowing and squinted. A small section of the brick wall had collapsed. Simon was there, showing him the way out.

"I never liked cats, but I'm growing fond of that one," Marco said.

"Me too." It took about ten minutes for Liam to make a

hole big enough for him to pull Marco through. Once he'd gotten them both out of there, Marco complained the entire time Liam positioned him across his shoulders.

"This is just embarrassing. Put me down, and I'll lean on you and walk." Marco groaned as Liam carefully looped his arm around his leg. "Or hop."

"Your left knee is dislocated, and you have a compound fracture in your right. You're not walking or hopping anywhere for at least a couple months. Better start laying off the pasta, buddy."

Marco snorted as Liam headed away from the burning building, taking a circuitous route back to the manor to avoid burning debris. His radio crackled, and then he heard his father's voice, calling out orders, gruff and heavy with emotion. "Chief." To hell with it. "Dad, we're out. Marco and I are out of the building, and we're okay."

"Thank God. Thank God. I thought…It's good to hear your voice, son." Cheers erupted in the background as word went out over the radio.

"I wouldn't be if you hadn't risked your life for me," Marco said, his voice serious and quiet. "I love you, bro."

"You would have done—"

Fergus's voice came over the radio, cutting Liam off. "Don't want to interrupt your bromance, boys, but would you two get your asses back here before…Sophie. Sophie, get back…Grab that kid. Mia…"

Sophie and Mia, both wrapped in blankets, ran toward them, repeatedly calling out, "Liam" and "Daddy" simultaneously.

"Hey, what about me? I'm the one who's injured," Marco said.

An hour later, Liam's hero status had diminished in one of his girls' eyes. Sophie sat on the stretcher at the hospital with her arms crossed, eight stitches on her forehead, and a mutinous expression on her face. "I heard you talking to the doctor, Liam. I don't need a head X-ray. I need—"

"Humor me, okay?" He framed her face with his hands. "You have no idea what it was like not knowing if I'd get to you and Mia in time, Soph."

She raised an eyebrow then winced when the action tugged on her stitches. "I think I do since I spent twenty excruciating minutes not knowing whether you were dead or alive."

The curtain separating the emergency room beds slid across the rod. "I'm seriously starting to get a complex. Do you not care that I nearly died? I am also the only one who was *really* injured," Marco said.

A curtain on the other side of Marco slid across a rod. "I do. I'm sorry you were hurt trying to rescue me, Marco," Dana said from where she lay on the stretcher, her arm in a sling, her blond hair brushed back from her pale face. "If there's anything I can do for you, just let me know."

Marco grinned and closed the curtain between his sister's bed and his. "Now that you mention it…"

A nurse entered the room and glanced at her chart. "Sophie and Marco DiRossi, time to take you both for X-rays."

Two days later, Sophie was sitting at her desk when Mia skipped into the study. "Hi, Auntie Ava." She gave Sophie's cousin a big smile then leaned in to peer at Sophie's face.

"What are you doing, baby?"

"Daddy sent me to check on you. He said if you're pale, you need to take a break."

Her cousin held back a laugh. Probably because Liam had checked on Sophie fifteen minutes ago trying to get her to go lie down. "You tell Daddy that Mommy can't take a break because he made her take yesterday off."

"Okay," she said, and skipped out the door.

"You must love that she's talking again, Soph. She has the sweetest voice."

"Yes, when she's not parroting her father." Sophie clicked through computer screens. The rehearsal party was tonight, and she needed everything to go perfectly. When Maura had heard about the fire, and then had seen the burned-out shell of the carriage house, she'd done her best to convince the bridal party to stay at the hotel in Bridgeport, declaring the manor unsafe. Liam, Colin, Michael, and surprisingly Maura's husband, had all weighed in, managing to stave off a mass exodus.

Maura had demanded a safety audit by an outside party. The fire chief from Bridgeport, an old friend of Colin's, had conducted it yesterday. As they already knew, the wiring would eventually need to be replaced, but there was no immediate cause for concern. It was more an efficiency issue rather than a safety one. But faulty wiring had been ruled the cause for the fire at the carriage house, so Maura hadn't been totally pacified. Sophie had no doubt Michael's mother would share her safety concerns with the other guests. In Sophie's mind, it was just one more reason the wedding had to go off without a hitch.

She went over the list for the rehearsal dinner with Ava, relieved when every item was checked and accounted for. But four hours later, Sophie discovered that something could always go wrong despite the best-laid plans.

She now stood unobtrusively in the corner of the dining room wearing a black dress. Jasper was on one side of her wearing a black tux and white gloves while Dana stood on the other side in a black pantsuit with wide legs, her hand in a cast. She was no longer a redhead or a blonde; she was a brunette. Since Sophie had had her own secrets, and she had no doubt her cousin did, too, they didn't push Dana about hers. But because she'd become a good friend, they both made sure she knew they were there for her whenever she wanted to talk.

Picking up on the guests practically humming through their meal of pork roast stuffed with dried fruit and corn bread and served with garlic-whipped potatoes, gravy, and roasted fall vegetables, Sophie whispered, "Ava's entrée is a hit."

"I believe you're right, Miss Sophie," Jasper said with a twitch of his lips.

"Wait until they taste her crème caramel," Dana added.

As though sensing her eyes on the table, Liam looked up. He was Michael's best man. Mia, whom Michael had asked to stand in for their flower girl who'd canceled last minute, sat beside her father. Looking at them both, so beautiful and happy, Sophie's heart expanded with love. Liam held up ten fingers, and Mia did the same.

"See that? They gave the dinner a ten, and I can barely get Mia to eat anything other than pizza and pasta."

Liam grinned and shook his head, mouthing, *You.* Mia rolled her eyes.

Michael pushed back his chair and stood up, tapping his wine glass lightly with his fork. The bridal party went quiet and looked at him expectantly. "I have an announcement to make. As most of you know, Greystone had some excitement this week. Thanks to the heroics of my cousin and best man, everyone got out alive. So let's raise a glass to Liam."

"Hear, hear," everyone at the table cheered, as did Sophie, Jasper, and Dana. Maura and Bethany were notably silent.

"He's my daddy," Mia announced proudly.

"We're well aware of that, dear," Maura said snidely, and Bethany tittered.

"Miss Sophie, perhaps Miss Dana and I should serve the coffee," Jasper murmured with a hint of nerves in his voice.

Michael's father leaned into his wife and said something that caused her to purse her lips and lift her shoulders.

Bethany smiled expectantly at her husband-to-be. "Do go on, darling."

Michael looked from his mother to his fiancée, rolling the stem of his wine glass between his fingers. He cleared his throat. "I brought up my cousin's heroics not only because he's the best man I know, but also because he makes me want to be a better man."

"Oh, darling, please. You are the best man at this table, bar none. Wealthy and an accomplished lawyer, soon to be the next governor of—"

"Bethany," Michael said, his voice tinged with exasperation. "I don't want to be governor, and I don't want to be a lawyer anymore. I've handed in my notice, and I've signed up for the police academy."

His mother jumped from her chair. "Over my dead body! Do you know how hard I've worked to get you to where you are today? Do you?"

"Maura, sit down. You're making a spectacle of yourself," his father said then raised his glass. "Good for you, son. I'm proud of you." Maura took her husband's glass from him and poured the red wine onto his head.

"Yes, I do indeed love this place," the senior Mrs. Adams said.

"Oh, Mother Adams, would you just shut up for once."

"Shut the front door," the senior Mrs. Adams said to her daughter-in-law.

Sophie slapped a hand over her mouth to keep the half-hysterical giggle from escaping. The rehearsal party was imploding before her eyes.

"Bethany, do you have anything to say?" Michael nervously asked his fiancée, who'd been staring at him the entire time. She looked to be trembling with fury.

"How dare you, Michael. How dare you decide something like this without consulting me first. If you intend to throw your life away to become an...an underpaid, blue-collar worker, you better start looking for another wife because it won't be me!" She dramatically tugged on her engagement ring then narrowed her eyes at Michael. "Well, aren't you going to say something?"

He lifted a shoulder. "Guess it's better that we found out now instead of after we married and had children."

"Children? Who said anything about having children?" She pushed back her chair and threw her engagement ring at him.

Chapter Twenty-Four

♥

Sophie stood huddled in her coat under the arbor over-looking Kismet Cove. Lights from the Christmas tree in the atrium danced in the snow. Everything was bright and beautiful and ready for the wedding that wouldn't happen now. She looked up at the stars winking overhead, the moon peeking playfully above the wisps of clouds in the night sky. Somehow it reminded her of Colleen. How happy the older woman had been at the thought of her great-grandson being married at Greystone. "Sorry, Colleen," Sophie whispered. "We did our best. We really did."

At the crunch of footsteps in the snow, she turned. Liam walked toward her, a black dress coat over his dark suit, the light wind off the water ruffling his hair. "Hey, handsome."

"Hey, beautiful, why are you looking so sad?" he asked, coming to stand behind her. He wrapped his arms around her. "Mrs. Adams paid the rooms in full, and Michael's covering whatever the deposit doesn't. You're going to end up making money even with the wedding being canceled."

She rested her head against his shoulder. "I know, but we're not going to get the positive publicity we were hoping for, or the referrals."

"I don't know about that. The senior Mrs. Adams is a fan. She was talking about booking the manor for an historical conference in March."

"I like her. Colleen would have liked her too. She's the real reason I feel bad."

"Babe, you don't have to feel bad. She told Michael he got off lucky and congratulated him."

Sophie laughed. "Poor Michael. I don't think he expected Bethany to dump him. But I wasn't talking about Mrs. Adams. I was talking about Colleen. She was excited about the wedding. In a way, it feels like I let her down. Her and everyone else. They all worked so hard the past few weeks to get the manor ready and make sure everything was perfect."

"No one worked harder than you. And Soph"—he stepped back and turned her to face him—"GG would probably be telling Michael he got off lucky too. She'd be as proud of what you've accomplished as I am. But if it makes you feel better, we could go ahead with the wedding just as planned."

"Did something happen that I—" She broke off as he went down on bended knee.

"Marry me, Sophie DiRossi. And make our daughter's Christmas wish come true."

Mia bounded into Sophie's bedroom at Greystone and jumped on the bed. "Merry Christmas Eve day, Mommy and Daddy. Santa's coming tonight." Her daughter's bright smile faded as she searched the bed and room. "Where's Daddy?"

"He stayed at Grandpa Colin's last night."

Mia's bottom lip quivered. "How come?"

"Because it's bad luck for him to see the bride before the wedding." Sophie watched her daughter absorb what she'd said. She knew the moment Mia understood when her face lit up brighter than a Christmas tree.

"We're getting married! We're getting married!" She jumped up and down on the bed. "That's the best Christmas present ever, isn't it, Mommy?"

"It is. The very best. But we have lots to do to get ready, and I need your help with something. I need your advice."

"Okay. I can do that," she said, and sat cross-legged on the bed, an earnest expression on her sweet face.

"Well, I need to pick a maid of honor. It's an important job, and it can only go to someone very special. It has to be someone who's been with me through the good times and bad, someone I love most in the world and who loves me, too, someone who—"

"Is it okay if the maid made you cry sometimes and hurt your feelings?"

"Yes, because none of us are perfect, baby. Mommy probably did some things that made the maid angry and hurt her feelings too. But the most important thing is that the maid and Mommy always, always loved each other."

"Then it's me, silly. I'm your maid of honor," she said, and threw herself into Sophie's arms.

And Sophie's maid of honor took her job very seriously. The first thing she did was announce to everyone in the manor at the top of her lungs that they had a wedding to get ready for. For the past six hours, Greystone and Sophie's bedroom were a hub of activity. Dana, who was also one of Sophie's bridesmaids, took care of the only detail that they hadn't looked after for Michael and Bethany's wedding. Tie the Knot sent over a romantic, ruffled gown with a red satin belt and fitted bodice that fit Sophie to perfection, as well as red satin bridesmaids' dresses for Dana, Ava, and Mia. Her daughter's was ankle length, Ava and Dana's cocktail length with long sleeves.

Mia ran into the bedroom with Miller following behind her. "Mommy, Daddy's here with Granddad, Uncle Griffin, Uncle Aidan, and Uncle Marco." She grabbed a red basket filled with white rose petals off the dressing table. "Come here, Miller. You can be the flower girl. Miller?" The dog hightailed it out of the room, and Mia chased after him.

Ava, whom her grandmother had just forcibly sat in front of the dressing table to do her makeup, looked at Sophie in the mirror.

She winced. "Sorry, I guess I forgot to tell you that you'd be standing with Griffin. But we weren't sure he was going to make it on such short notice."

"I can't…" Ava began then looked at Sophie and shrugged. "What are you going to do."

Rosa paced behind Ava, tapping her lips. "Something is wrong. Ah, I know what it is. Your hair, *cara*. You look like an old lady because it's too long. We cut it, *sì*?"

Ava put her hand to her head. "No, we don't cut it. It's fine."

Rosa was right. Not that Ava looked old—it was just that her overlong hair dragged down her face and had no life, no bounce. "Maybe just a trim, Ava. You're practically sitting on it."

"I agree with Rosa and Sophie," Dana said, and walked behind Ava to lift her hair, folding it to the middle of her back. "This would be the perfect length for you."

It was exactly the length Ava used to wear her hair.

"Pain in the *culo*, that's what the three of you are. Cut it then. I don't care."

It was going to be a difficult enough day for Ava, and Sophie didn't want to make it worse. "Maybe another—" She was too late. Her grandmother had already grabbed a pair of scissors off the dressing table and was starting to cut Ava's hair when Sophie realized they were the same scissors Dana had used for the ribbons. "Nonna, no! They're pinking shears!"

"Oh, *accidente*. Don't worry, I fix it."

"Here, Rosa. I'll do it," Dana said, and grabbed another pair of scissors. Ten minutes later, she stood back.

"*Sei bellissima tesoro*. You are so beautiful, *cara*. Look, look at your hair, your curls have come back." Rosa pressed her hands to her chest, staring at Ava with shiny eyes.

Ava waved her hand. "It's just hair."

But Sophie caught her cousin staring at herself in the mirror with what looked to be a small hint of pleasure and surprise in her eyes.

Kitty walked in and did a double take. "Ava?"

"*Sì*. Look." Rosa held up the long hank of hair. "We'll donate to charity. The one that makes wigs."

Kitty smiled then said, "Poppy Harte has arrived to take pictures. I don't imagine she has ever had a more beautiful bridal party. You all look absolutely stunning." She walked over to Sophie. "I have something for you, my dear. It's a small token of our appreciation for all you've done and to welcome you to the family. It was Colleen's," she said, holding up a gold charm bracelet. "I know she would have very much wanted you to have it. May I?"

"Yes, please." Sophie held out her arm, the heavy gold bracelet covering the faded scar on her wrist. "It's beautiful. Thank you, Kitty."

Liam's grandmother kissed her cheek. "Now what can I do? Do you need anything?"

"Oh," Sophie gasped. "I need…I'll be right back." She lifted her skirts and ran from the room, racing down the hall in her red shoes. She ducked when she reached the landing and hid behind a potted plant. She heard Liam's and his brothers' voices near the bar. The man she was looking for was seeing to the guests. "Jasper," Sophie called out, trying to keep her voice low. His head came up, and his gaze shot to the bar.

He hurried to the stairs. "Miss Sophie, what are you doing? It's bad luck for the groom to see the bride." He bounded up the stairs to stand in front of her, blocking her from view.

She looked up and smiled at him. "My parents can't be here to give me away, and my brother is standing, well, sitting for Liam, so I was hoping you would."

He gave her a clipped nod. "I would be most honored, miss."

Liam stood beside Sophie by the fireplace. He pulled a sprig of mistletoe from his pocket and held it over her head. His brother Griffin rolled his eyes. "You've kissed her at least twenty times already. Leave the poor girl alone."

"Ten. I instigated the rest," she admitted, and reached up to press her lips to the corner of Liam's mouth.

He wrapped his arms around her and looked at their guests. "Shouldn't everyone be leaving soon?" He'd been asking the question as often as he'd kissed her. "Maybe I should tell them that NORAD just announced Santa has been spotted flying this way."

"It's only five o'clock."

"Can you blame a guy for wanting to be alone with his wife?"

"No, because your wife wants to alone with you. All we

have left to do is draw the raffle winner, I'll throw my bouquet, and then—"

He smiled down at her. "Make my Christmas wish come true. I love you, Mrs. Gallagher."

"I love you, too, Mr. Gallagher." She gave him a quick kiss. "Now let's make someone else's Christmas wish come true."

Liam looked around as they walked toward the big plastic ball on the stand by the grand staircase. "Maybe a good thing Mia isn't around. This is going to be tough on her."

Sophie frowned. "Where is—" She broke off when Mia appeared at their sides with Miller, Zach, and Amanda. The four of them were covered in dirt. "Mia, what happened?"

Their daughter slipped her hand in her father's. "We were hunting for treasure like Daddy used to when he was a little boy."

"You were in the tunnels?" Liam asked, and she nodded. "Sweetheart, next time you want to play down there, you have to tell us. You need to have an adult—"

"But we did…" She looked beyond them as a cold draft caused Sophie to rub her arms; then Mia giggled and nodded, placing a finger on her lips.

Liam and Sophie shared a look. They had hoped now that they were married Mia wouldn't need her imaginary friend. It looked like they were wrong. "Why don't you guys go and get some cake in the dining room?" Sophie suggested, hoping to distract Mia while they picked the winner. Jasper had just made the announcement, and people were walking their way.

"Oh no, Mommy. I have to pick the winner. It's my job."

Before Sophie had a chance to gauge if doing so would, in the end, make the situation better or worse, Simon jumped onto the table, batting at the plastic ball. It started spinning on the stand, the tickets flying around inside. Mia pressed a hand to her mouth, giggling behind it.

Liam whispered in Sophie's ear, "Is she hysterical or happy?"

"I'm not sure, but Simon's going to flip over the ball if we don't do this now."

Liam grabbed Simon, and put out his hand to stop the ball. "All right, everyone. Here's what you've all been waiting for. Mia, give us our winner, sweetheart."

"Baby, you, um, can't look through the tickets. You have to pick just one," Sophie said as her daughter, a small furrow on her forehead, tossed one ticket after another aside.

"Got it," Mia said then winked at her imaginary friend and held up a ticket with a paw print on it.

Liam took the ticket from her and smiled. "Our winner is…Julia Landon." There were whistles and cheers for the beautiful brunette. She was obviously well liked in Harmony Harbor. "Come on up and get the key to your new home, Julia."

Mia shifted nervously, looking expectantly at the woman when Liam handed her the gold key with a sprig of mistletoe attached to it. "Thank you." Julia smiled and clutched the key to her chest.

Mia's smile dimmed. Then she glanced to Sophie's right and nodded, the smile reappearing on her face.

"Don't doubt me now, child. I know what I'm about," Colleen murmured, watching as Julia accepted everyone's congratulations. Though some of her confidence faded when Julia slipped away and disappeared into the crowd. Colleen had picked her for a reason. She knew the young woman well. Her secrets too.

Simon gave Colleen a testy meow. "After all this, you're

doubting me now? Give the girl a chance. It's a hard thing she's dealing with. And don't think you're out of my bad book just because I'm talking to you. I haven't completely forgiven you for eating Mr. Lancaster's pet mice. You'll have to earn my trust back after ruining my plan to get rid of Bethany. You're lucky it all turned out in the end. Though I doubt Mr. Lancaster will be staying with us again. Oh well, he was a bit of an odd duck."

Colleen looked at Mia and held up five fingers. The child nodded, nibbling on her bottom lip. Liam picked her up, and he and Sophie did their best to cheer Mia up.

Colleen smiled. "Now that's a beautiful sight, isn't it, Simon?" But she'd lost the cat's attention. He was looking at something behind her. Colleen turned to see Paige and Hazel and growled low in her throat. Oh, but she'd love to give those two a fright.

"Faulty wiring, my eye. I know it was one of you who set fire to the carriage house," she said. They wouldn't have known Mia, Sophie, and Dana were there. Somehow Colleen would find a way to get the proof she needed, and when she did…

Julia reappeared wearing her red hat and coat, distracting Colleen from her thoughts.

"There's been a mistake," the young woman said as she approached Mia and her parents.

Colleen smiled. "You're a fine girl, Julia. You are indeed. Paying for a sin that was not of your making. You'll get your reward, of that you can be certain. I promise you that."

Liam frowned. "What's wrong?"

"There's a note attached to the key." Julia held it up. "It's from Santa to Mia. Mistletoe Cottage was meant to be hers."

"Julia—" Liam and Sophie started to protest at almost the same time.

"I'm one of Santa's helpers, remember? I've sworn an oath to do his bidding. If this is what Santa wants, who are we to say otherwise?"

Liam brought up the rules of the raffle, one being that the winner can't sell the house. "No, but there's nothing in the rules that says a winner can't gift it to whomever she chooses." She handed Mia the key. "Merry Christmas."

Mia wriggled out of her father's arms and went to Julia. She crooked her finger. When Julia bent down, Mia kissed her cheek and then whispered in her ear. They both turned to look up at the landing.

"Well, I'll be," Colleen murmured.

Julia muffled a sob with her hand, and Mia once again whispered in her ear. The woman nodded, touched a finger to her lips, and then to Mia's cheek. Julia stood, wished everyone a Merry Christmas then hurried from the great room.

Colleen listened to everyone's theories with a knowing smile. The majority believed that Julia was attempting to make up for the trouble Hazel Winters had caused the Gallaghers. But one day, the truth would come out. It always does. And when it was revealed…

Kitty and Rosa came to stand beside Colleen, interrupting her thoughts.

"She's here, isn't she?" Rosa said to Kitty.

"I believe so. She never did trust me to take care of the manor and the family on my own. I can see her standing at the pearly gates, telling them to kiss her behind. That she wasn't ready yet and had things left to do."

Colleen chuckled despite herself. However, she felt a twinge of guilt knowing there was some truth to what her daughter-in-law said. She had doubted Kitty's ability to look after things without her. But she had to give credit where it was due. It had been Kitty's idea to raffle off the cottage and look how well that had turned out. Given her ghostly circumstances, Colleen would need all the help she could get. Especially with Paige and Hazel upping their game. Too bad no one could hear her.

Rosa crossed herself and brought her crucifix to her lips. "*Sì.* I do too." Rosa moved her head in something of a figure eight as though searching for Colleen's whereabouts. "If you are here, my Ava and Griffin, they should be next."

"I promised Ida that we'd match Brie with one of my grandsons. I thought maybe she and Griffin—" Kitty began.

"No, it must be Ava and Griffin." Rosa did that odd thing with her head again. "You do this, and I will forgive you, *sì*?"

It was true. Colleen needed Rosa's forgiveness to wipe another sin from her eternal soul. So she supposed it worked to her advantage that she'd already chosen Ava and Griffin. Though she had a feeling they wouldn't be as easy as Sophie and Liam. Ava's secrets were dark and deep. It would be painful for all involved when they came to light.

She looked up to see Liam, Sophie, and Mia at the top of the grand staircase. The single women of Harmony Harbor were gathered below them. Including a reluctant Ava, who'd been dragged to the front of the semicircle by Dana.

No time like the present, Colleen thought, and wove her way to the bottom of the stairs. Mia waved at Colleen, and all the women waved up at Mia. "Can I throw the bouquet, Mommy?" She smiled when Sophie complied and threw the bouquet at Colleen, who batted it directly at Ava. If it wasn't for Dana, the woman would have let it drop at her feet.

And so it begins, Colleen thought as she walked to the chair by the fire and took a seat. Simon leaped onto her lap,

and Jasper came to stand by the fire, clasping his hands behind his back. "It's good to have you home, Madame. I take
it you have plans for all of us here in Harmony Harbor."

Colleen chuckled. "Right you are, dear boy. Right you
are."

About the Author

DEBBIE MASON is the *USA Today* bestselling author of the Highland Falls, Harmony Harbor, and Christmas, Colorado series. The first book in her Christmas, Colorado series, *The Trouble with Christmas*, was the inspiration for the Hallmark movie *Welcome to Christmas*. Her books have been praised by *RT Book Reviews* for their "likable characters, clever dialogue, and juicy plots." When Debbie isn't writing, she enjoys spending time with her family in Ottawa, Canada.

You can learn more at:
AuthorDebbieMason.com
Twitter @AuthorDebMason
Facebook.com/DebbieMasonBooks
Instagram @AuthorDebMason

For a bonus story from another author that you'll love, please turn the page to read "A Forever Home" by Annie Rains.

As Della Rose chats with the handsome man seated next to her on the plane home, she forgets all about her fear of flying. Roman Everson wants his conversation with the optimistic woman to continue as they are forced to share the only rental car left at the airport. Picking up a stray dog along the way was not part of the plan, but newly named Jingle Bell may be just the canine to make Christmas complete!

FOREVER

Chapter One

❄

Planes made Della Rose nervous. They always had. She guessed that's why she was talking her seatmate's ear off, much to his obvious disdain.

She couldn't help it. Every time there was the slightest turbulence, her adrenaline spiked. There was also the fact that the guy sitting beside her could pass for George Clooney's younger brother. He had dark hair and darker eyes. He'd only looked over a couple times to meet her gaze, but she'd forgotten all about her plane anxiety during those brief moments.

"I have to get home in time for my sons' recital. They're performing tonight," she told him.

He was only halfway participating in the conversation. She didn't think he was unfriendly. Maybe just uninterested. Or perhaps planes made him nervous too, and he was doing his best not to find a paper bag to breathe into, like her. "Where do you live?" he asked, half-heartedly.

"Somerset Lake. I'll be catching another flight once we

land in Charlotte and taking one of those smaller planes." Just thinking about that prospect made her heartbeat quicken. She'd had to take the smaller plane when she'd headed out of town. In her meager experience, smaller planes equaled more turbulence. And she doubted there'd be a George Clooney clone on that trip to ease her nerves. "What about you?" she asked.

He kept his gaze forward as he answered. "I've lined up a rental car for when we land. I'm heading three hours north."

"What's there?" she asked. Not that it was any of her business.

The man seemed to hesitate.

"I'm sorry. I'm a ball of nerves, I guess. I don't mean to pry. I'm just trying not to—" The plane dipped and righted. Della's whole body stiffened as she pressed back into her seat and clutched the armrests. Her fingers brushed against the stranger's hand resting on the middle armrest, the feel of his skin against hers creating a zinging sensation that made her heart and breath quicken. She removed her hand and patted her chest as a high-pitched giggle bubbled over her lips. "I'm sorry," she said again. Her voice quivered this time, though.

The stranger must have taken pity on her, because he started talking. "I'm going home for the first time in over a year. I'm from Sweetwater Springs. It's in the Blue Ridge Mountains."

Her lips parted. Where did she know that town from? She searched her brain, pleased that the answer came quickly although she was such a mess right now. "I have a friend from Sweetwater Springs. She just moved to Somerset Lake this spring. Trisha Langly. Do you know her?"

This was the first time the stranger smiled. "Yeah. She was younger than me, but everyone knows each other in my hometown."

Della offered a small laugh. "Yeah, I know what you mean. Mine is the same way."

"You sound about as thrilled about that aspect as me," he noted.

She waved a dismissive hand. "Oh, it's fine." She was never going to see this guy again after they landed, so why not spill her own life story? Or at least the last twelve months of it. "Or it was fine until my husband cheated on me and everyone seemed to know my marriage was over before me. I found out that his new wife was having a baby through the town's blogger."

The stranger grimaced. Unless she was imagining it, sympathy flashed in his dark brown eyes. "That's rough."

"Yes, it was." She had been through a lot this past year. Her divorce was finalized last month, and her ex had already given his girlfriend a diamond twice as big as the one he'd once given Della. They'd married in a private ceremony. "I'm a mom, though," Della said with resolve. "I have twin boys who keep me focused. I can't just fall apart the way I want to. They need me to be strong, so that's what I'll be." She blew out a breath and looked over. "I'm Della, by the way," she said, offering her hand.

The man slipped his palm against hers. "I'm Roman. Nice to meet you, Della."

They held each other's hands and shook briefly. Then the plane dipped again. She sucked in a little breath but kept her gaze locked with Roman's. Her focus was trained there and not on the possibility that they'd crash before Christmas, which was only five days away. This was going to be a different kind of Christmas, and Della wanted so badly for her boys to have a good one, regardless of their parents' messes.

Once the plane had righted again, Roman pulled his hand from hers and continued talking. "I haven't been home in

over a year because my dad and I bump heads whenever
we're together."

"You let a few disagreements keep you estranged from
your family?" Della didn't intend any judgment in her voice,
but if the stranger's reaction was any indication, it came
through. "It's just, family is everything to me. I can't imagine not going home for that long, no matter how mad my
folks make me."

"Well, our relationship is complicated," he said. "I respect my brother, though. He's the mayor of Sweetwater
Springs and a force to be reckoned with. He's been in a
wheelchair since his senior year of high school, but he's
never let that slow him down. He's getting an award this
afternoon. That's why I'm going home."

Della smiled. "That's nice. Maybe you'll make up with
your parents too. 'Tis the season for new beginnings, right?"

Roman shook his head. "What's the good in a new beginning when the ending will always be the same?"

Della settled back into her seat. When she wasn't talking,
her focus stayed on every bump the plane made, so she ignored the stranger's pessimism. "My boys are nine. It's a big
deal for Jett to be in a recital this evening. He's the shy one.
I promised I'd be in the front row to cheer him on."

"You're cutting it close, don't you think?" Roman asked.

She frowned at him. "I'll be home hours before the
recital."

"Assuming that the plane will leave and land when it's
supposed to. I never count on my flight schedule to be accu-
rate. It rarely ever is, in my experience."

Della's anxiety rose for a whole different reason now.
Was this just more of the stranger's glass-half-empty attitude? "I don't fly much, so I guess I don't have a lot of
experience. You don't think I'll make it home in time? Be-

cause my boys would be a mess without me. Their new stepmom will be there, of course." Della felt every muscle in her body tense. "But a stepmom is not the same as having your real mother there."

Roman looked at her with interest. "No, it's not. Don't worry. I'm sure you'll get to Somerset Lake in plenty of time to nab the front row seat for your boys' recital."

Della wasn't as confident of that fact anymore, thanks to Roman. "And I'm sure you'll have a better time than you bargained for in Sweetwater Springs," she said.

Roman glanced over, looking equally doubtful.

* * *

Roman was trying not to notice how Della was white-knuckling the armrest between them on the plane. Some primal part of him wanted to reach over and take her hand to comfort her. The other part, the one that won out, looked forward. He had enough on his mind without having to worry that the woman beside him was about to have a panic attack.

The pilot announced that it was time to take a seat, fasten your belt, and prepare for landing.

"Oh, thank goodness." Della blew out a breath beside him. "That's good news."

"You know those smaller planes have a lot more turbulence than this, right?" Roman looked over. "It'll be a bumpier ride."

Her face blanched. "I'm trying not to think about that."

"The good news is that it'll be a shorter trip. You'll get through it," he told her. Some part of him wished he'd be sitting there with her to help ease her mind. He felt a bit sorry for the woman. And, if he was honest, he was attracted to her too. She had high cheekbones, a friendly smile, and pale

green eyes that struck him every time he met her gaze. She
had on jade stud earrings that were almost a perfect match to
the verdant shade of her irises. He thought maybe she was a
couple years younger than him, but it was hard to tell. She
had two kids, which in his experience could either age you
beyond your years or keep you young.

"Are you okay?" he finally asked the woman.

"Yeah." She nodded too quickly for that to be the truth.

Roman could feel the plane descending. Out of pity, and
maybe something more, he started talking to distract her.
"I've never been to Somerset Lake. Is it a nice place?"

"Oh yes. I'm a real estate agent there. I don't even have
to sell most of the places I show. The homes sell themselves
because every square inch of Somerset Lake is to die for."

He could hear the shallowness of her breathing beside
him. "I'm sold already," he said with a forced smile. He had
a lot on his mind today, and none of it was smile-worthy. The
stiffness of her body seemed to relax, though.

"The town is on the lake," she told him. "You've never
seen a lake until you've seen Somerset. It's a little slice of
blue heaven on earth." She went on to talk about the shops
on Hannigan Street, which was apparently the main downtown stretch. She told him about the bookstore her friend
owned, the new B&B another friend of hers was starting up,
and a place that catered to chocolate lovers.

"I don't like chocolate myself," he said.

Della looked at him. "I don't believe you. Everyone likes
chocolate."

"Not me."

She narrowed those beautiful green eyes of hers. "You
must. Hot cocoa?"

"Only when coffee isn't an option."

"Chocolate-covered strawberries?" she asked.

He chuckled softly. It felt surprisingly good. When was the last time he'd laughed? He lived a serious existence in Dayton, the hours of his days revolving around his work as the lead commercial contractor for the company he worked for. With a shrug, he said, "I'm an oddball, I guess."

"Well, if we were going to spend any more time together, I'd take that statement as a challenge," she said. "I would prove to you that there is some sort of chocolate you would like."

From the corner of his eye, Roman saw the plane's landing gear lower. Without thinking, he reached for Della's hand. Her eyes subtly widened. "Here we go," he said. "We're about to hit the ground rolling."

She didn't yank her hand away. Instead, she squeezed his hand and shut her eyes. Roman couldn't help but admire her beauty when she wasn't looking. She had smooth, supple skin with a natural pink blush on the apples of her cheeks. Her hair was a dark blond, pulled back to the nape of her neck, but a few short pieces curled at her ears.

As the plane bumped forcefully along the ground and shot forward on the runway, Roman heard Della's sharp intake of breath, and then she seemed to stop breathing altogether. He still held her hand as the plane's speed began to decrease.

"You can open your eyes now," he said quietly, pulling his hand back once the plane had stopped.

Della's eyes fluttered open. She looked at him, a timid smile curling at the corners of her lips. They were a pretty pink hue that grabbed his attention and didn't let go. "Thank you. One more plane trip, and then I can see my boys perform tonight."

"What instruments do they play?" Roman asked. He wasn't trying to distract Della anymore. Instead, he was genuinely interested.

"Both play guitar. They're very much beginners, but I'm so proud of them."

"I can tell just looking at you." A mother should be proud of her children. Roman tried not to make the comparison between Della and his own parents, who were the opposite of proud when it came to him. Growing up, he could do no right, whereas his brother, Brian, could do nothing wrong. Roman could trace that sentiment back to the Christmas he'd singlehandedly ruined. He could also trace his dislike for the holiday to that year.

When it was time to stand, Roman stepped into the aisle and allowed Della to go ahead of him. They left the plane and walked down a long corridor into the airport terminal. Then she turned back to him and offered her hand.

"It was nice meeting you, Roman."

Roman shook her hand, feeling something warm in his chest along with a sense of regret that he'd probably never see this woman again. "You too, Della. Enjoy your sons' recitals. Wish them luck for me."

"Thank you. I will. And I hope you have a Merry Christmas," she said cheerfully. Now that she was off a moving plane, she looked much calmer.

"Merry Christmas to you as well," he said, meaning it. As for him, the thing that would make this Christmas the merriest would be skipping it altogether.

* * *

Della hurried through the airport, her carry-on bag flopping against her left hip while her purse swung off her right shoulder. She'd booked the flights close together to ensure she'd make it home in time. What kind of mom missed her children's first recital? Not this one. Especially since their new stepmom, Sofia, would be there cheering them on.

Della didn't want to feel jealous, but she couldn't help it. She didn't want to share the boys with the woman who'd stolen her husband. They were Della's kids. She'd gained fifty pounds during her pregnancy with them and had suffered morning sickness for the first two trimesters. She had loved them since the moment she'd found out she was pregnant, had changed their diapers, and cleaned up after them nearly every day of their lives.

Della stepped into the short line in front of the gate attendant for the small airplane she was about to board. She took a few calming breaths. An hour from now, she'd be landing at the pint-sized airport right outside her hometown of Somerset Lake. Her car was parked there. If things went as planned, she'd be home by mid-morning. She could unpack and relax before heading out to the church this evening. She might even do some last-minute online Christmas shopping.

"Yes ma'am?" the attendant said as Della stepped to the front of the line.

"Hi." Della laid her ticket down. There wasn't a boarding line right now, which surprised her. "Is this flight running on time?"

The woman picked up the ticket and looked at it, her over-tweezed brows furrowing. "It should be. But we won't know until closer to your flight tomorrow."

Della laughed because that was absurd. "No, my flight is today. Right now actually." She glanced at the nonexistent boarding line again.

"No, it's tomorrow," the woman reiterated, handing the ticket back.

Della looked at the paper in her hand, and instead of laughing, she felt like dissolving into a puddle of tears. "But

I booked it for today. I know I did. I need to get home this afternoon, not tomorrow," she said, her voice rising a panicky octave. "Can you change it for today? I have plans for tonight that I can't miss." Because she didn't want to let her boys down. They needed her, not some stepmother who could never take the place of the real thing.

The gate attendant looked sympathetic. "I'm sorry, ma'am, but there are no more flights going out this afternoon. The next one isn't until tomorrow at nine a.m."

Della's heart sank as she let go of her carry-on bag, dropping it to the floor. She didn't even know what to do right now. Wait here at the airport until tomorrow? Get a cab to take her to a hotel?

"But you could rent a car and drive, if your plans are that important," the attendant suggested. "I don't know how far you've got to go."

Della blinked. She could have flown into the Asheville Regional Airport, closer to home, but there was no flight availability that would get her home by this evening. Flying into the Charlotte airport left her with a two-hour drive. Maybe three depending on traffic. "Yes, I could rent a car. That would work. Thank you." She grabbed her bag from the floor and turned. If she hurried, she'd still have plenty of time to freshen up at home before going to the church. Everything would work out just fine.

She sprinted through the airport, eager to get a car. She was also well aware that Roman had been on his way to get a vehicle that he'd reserved to drive to his hometown. Maybe she'd get to say hello to him again. She hoped so.

When Roman had first sat beside her on the plane, he'd been closed off. He'd warmed up, though, and he'd helped her get through her flying anxiety. There was also the fact that he was perhaps the most attractive man she'd ever laid eyes on. Not every woman would agree, but Della had always liked his type. He had skin that was tanned from the sun, like he worked outside. He also had intense eyes, the color of dark chocolate. Maybe he didn't like chocolate, but it was her favorite food group.

She rushed toward the car rental section of the airport and pushed through a set of double doors, looking around the room. There were no George Clooney lookalikes in sight. Just a wary reservations clerk behind the counter, who didn't look all that excited to see Della.

"If you're looking for a rental car, I just handed out keys for the last one," the young woman said. "Sorry, but you're out of luck."

Chapter Two

❄

While his cell phone was in airplane mode, Roman had dodged all the angry calls and texts from his former employee's wife. As soon as he'd landed, the notifications had started piling up, though. He dreaded looking at them.

He wasn't the owner of the construction company where he worked, but he was the manager of the crew. If the guys didn't pull their weight, they were let go. The owner was adamant about that fact, and he didn't care what the reasons might be. So Roman had the hard job of letting Bob Coker go yesterday.

Bob had missed several days for a few months in a row due to a sick child at home. Roman wasn't really sure what exactly was wrong with the child, but he thought it might be serious. Bob had rarely missed a day of work before his son had fallen ill. It wasn't Bob's style. If Bob was calling out, Roman guessed it was out of necessity. Even so, Roman had been ordered by his boss to call Bob into his office and break the news—less than a week before Christmas.

Roman felt like a jerk. It wasn't his decision, of course. But he'd been the one to hand down the news. He'd argued with the company's owner, but Mr. Wilcox wouldn't hear of giving Bob any more grace period. He was costing the company money, so he had to be let go.

Bob was too humble to do anything but accept the decision and leave. Bob's wife, however, was more vocal about her anger.

Roman's phone buzzed in his hand as he walked down the hall that led away from the public restroom. Without thinking, he checked the screen and saw the wife's latest text pop up.

You are despicable. It's Christmas! How could you fire a family man with mouths to feed?

Guilt sucker-punched Roman in the gut. He shoved his phone into his coat pocket. Bob was a good worker with a good heart, and Christmas or not, he didn't deserve the financial stress this would cause his family.

Roman pushed through the door into the main waiting area of the rental place. A couple hours from now, he'd be pulling up to Sweetwater Springs and seeing his family, who, except for pictures on Facebook, he hadn't laid eyes on in over a year. No part of him wanted to go, but Brian would appreciate having Roman there.

A familiar-looking person caught Roman's eye. She sat crumpled in one of the waiting room chairs as he started to pass by. Her head was down, but he recognized the blond hair cascading toward her lap as she leaned forward. She was wearing dark-rinse jeans and a soft pink cotton top—just like Della had been wearing on the plane beside him. "Della?"

She lifted her head. "Roman. You're still here."

"Barely. I'm on my way out. Shouldn't you be on a plane?"

She grimaced. "I got the plane reservations wrong. I don't know what I was thinking. I don't fly that often."

"You don't say," he teased.

She gave him a half-hearted glare. "My ticket is for a flight tomorrow, so I was going to miss my sons' recitals. I thought I could rent a car and just drive back to Somerset Lake, but the woman at the desk said she just handed out the keys for the last car." Della narrowed her eyes at Roman.

He held up a set of keys and jingled them. "Guess that would be me. Sorry."

"Don't be. You reserved that car ahead of time. It's rightfully yours. I just don't know what I'm going to do. Getting home by tonight is so important to me." Her eyes grew shiny, and Roman suspected she was on the verge of tears.

Roman felt the buzz of his cell phone in his pocket again. It was no doubt another angry message from Bob's wife. Maybe one good deed would cancel out the bad one he'd done on his boss's behalf. He could only hope. "I have to go to Sweetwater Springs. I'll be there for at least an hour and a half. Probably more like two," he said.

Della looked up at him.

"Somerset Lake is about two hours from Sweetwater Springs. By my calculations, we could drive to my hometown, stay a couple hours, and head straight to your town, having you at that recital just in time to see your boys' performance."

Della's lips parted. "Really?"

He nodded. "We'd really be cutting it close, but you'd be there in time. If you don't mind sharing a car with me and humoring my relatives."

"I don't mind at all." She stood quickly and threw her arms around him, surprising him. His arms reflexively locked around her to keep them both balanced.

"Thank you so much. I hate to impose, but I don't really have any other options right now." She pulled back, her face close to his.

He didn't breathe for a moment. He'd been out of a relationship for over a year now. It'd been that long since he'd held a woman in his arms for any kind of reason.

She took a small step back until the backs of her knees touched the chair behind her. "Well, we better go. We have a lot of ground to cover today, don't we?"

"I guess we do," he said, ignoring the buzz of his cell phone again. As well as the unwanted buzz of attraction now zipping through him. He picked up his carry-on bag from where it was lying at his feet and headed toward the exit, leading the way. He opened the door for Della and waited for her to pass. Then he headed toward the parking lot, where a blue sedan was waiting to take them both on a Christmas road trip. First stop, Sweetwater Springs. Last stop, Somerset Lake.

* * *

Della was tired of hearing herself speak, and Roman wasn't really helping carry the conversation. Either he was shy, which she didn't really think so, or he didn't like her, which she didn't believe was true either. He could just have things on his mind. Judging by his deeply furrowed brow and serious expression as he drove, she suspected that was the reason for his silence.

"Going home really makes you nervous, huh?" she asked.

He glanced over but didn't answer as he returned his gaze to the road.

"If I'm being too nosy, just tell me so. You won't hurt my feelings." She looked out the passenger-side window. "I used to say it was pretty hard to hurt my feelings, but my ex succeeded to the point that I might have bruised emotions for the rest of my life."

Roman glanced over again. She could feel his eyes on her. "Time will heal."

She released a soft sigh that fogged the window she was staring out. "So I've been told. Right now, it's hard to believe."

"You told me that your ex was unfaithful," Roman said.

Della faced forward. Jerome's unfaithfulness hadn't just hurt her feelings, it had also hurt her pride. What was wrong with her that her husband had to find someone much younger and, some estimated, more beautiful? "I thought we were happily married. We had a great house and twin boys, and our lives seemed to be on autopilot. He was working late a lot, to provide for the family." She laughed humorlessly because she felt foolish now for believing that lie. "Or so he said."

"He wasn't working late?" Roman asked.

Della was glad that he was at least participating in the conversation now, even if it was at her expense. "He was really with a woman ten years younger than me. She's prettier and more successful, and she doesn't have the body of a woman who's carried not one but two kids at the same time."

"I don't think you're giving yourself enough credit. You're a very beautiful woman," he said, lowering his gaze as he looked at her before returning his focus to the road.

She tried not to pay attention to the little thrill that ran through her. "Thank you for saying so. I thought it was just a fling. Just a phase. I still would have left him, but somehow that would have made it better than the fact that Jerome was in love with her."

"Really?"

Della shrugged. "It was more than physical. It was an emotional affair too. He wanted our marriage to end. Our divorce was finalized this year, and he didn't waste any time proposing to Sofia and getting her pregnant." Della felt the familiar sting in her eyes. "At first, I was secretly hoping Sofia was carrying twins. Maybe even triplets. Not because children are a blessing—which they are, of course—but because it would give her stretch marks and all the things I was always so proud of until my husband cheated on me."

"You should be proud of who you are. You're a mom, and that's incredibly attractive, if you ask me."

She cleared her throat, feeling her cheeks flush again. "Um, thank you. I guess it's hard to feel that way when my ex went behind my back the way he did."

"Men can be stupid."

Della laughed unexpectedly. "You're a man."

"I know. I can be stupid too." He slid his gaze toward her, and her body warmed. "I'm not the kind of guy who would do what your ex did. I like to think I'm pretty loyal." He cleared his throat. "When I can be."

Della heard his phone buzzing in his pocket. "So, if that's true, who are you working so hard to ignore on this trip? A girlfriend?"

Roman frowned. "I haven't had one of those in over a year."

And that fact shouldn't make Della feel a small sense of relief. There were no romantic possibilities between her and Roman. "Then who is so desperate to talk to you?" she asked.

He blew out a breath as they drove under an overpass. She watched the lights flicker across his face, highlighting fine crow's feet and laugh lines. He was so serious; she couldn't imagine he'd earned those laugh lines with actual laughter. "The wife of one of my former employees."

Della felt her mouth drop. "Why is his wife calling you?" And did she really want to know the answer? Roman seemed like a nice guy, but looks could be deceiving. Was he in a relationship with a married woman?

Roman glanced over. "It's not what you're thinking. It's because I fired her husband. At Christmas. When their child is sick."

That might be even worse than Della was imagining. "You what?" She blinked and shook her head.

Roman held up a hand. "It wasn't my decision. The owner of the business I work for asked me to do his bidding. I tried to convince my boss to give Bob another chance, but he wouldn't hear of it. He wanted me to fire him and set an example of work expectations." Roman ran a hand through his dark waves of hair. Della's fingers curled into her thighs because she wanted to do the same.

"What did he do that was so wrong?" she asked.

"He took off work to care for his sick kid." Roman shrugged. "I would have done the same. But his family won't be able to afford to eat or keep a roof over their heads without this job. To be honest, I think my boss didn't want to foot the insurance bill for Bob and his family. I'm guessing the kid's illness might be making the premiums spike."

"That's awful. How can you work for a person like that?"

Roman's frown deepened. "I like what I do. We build the best buildings in the Dayton area. I'm proud of our work."

"Just not proud of how the crew is cared for," she said quietly.

Roman tapped his phone. "She's left me at least a dozen messages, calling me everything under the sun. I'd change the circumstances if I could, but I can't."

"So you're just not going to answer?"

"There's nothing I can say." His fingers tightened around the steering wheel.

"You could tell her the same thing you just told me."

Roman shook his head. "I have a job, and her husband doesn't. She's going to be mad no matter what I tell her."

"That's a bad situation."

"It is," Roman agreed. He put his blinker on and started maneuvering to the far right lane. "Our exit is coming up. I guess I should probably warn you."

Della stiffened. She didn't like the sound of that. "Warn me?"

"My family can be hard to bear. They'll ask you a million and one questions. Feel free to tell them to mind their own business."

"They sound like my kind of people." She wondered why Roman didn't seem to get along with his parents. That really was none of her business. Some families just weren't close.

Della had always been close to her own parents. They lived in Somerset Lake, and she saw them a couple times a week. They watched the boys as often as they could and always acted like Della was doing them a favor by allowing them to.

"We'll just attend the ceremony for my brother and leave. That's the plan," Roman said as they drove past a large carved wood sign that read WELCOME TO SWEETWATER SPRINGS. "You're a good excuse not to be here too long."

"I'm your excuse?" Della said with a small laugh, taking in the town as he drove. In some ways, it reminded her of where she lived. All the shops on Main Street begged her to stop and go inside. There were folks on the sidewalks chatting merrily with one another. All the streetlamps were decorated with holly leaves for the season.

"You want to get home to your boys' recital, don't you?" Roman asked.

Della nodded. "More than anything."

"Then I'm using you as my ticket out. We'll get in, get out, and get you to Somerset Lake for your boys' performance, Cinderella."

* * *

Roman not only had a cell phone vibrating obnoxiously in his pocket, but his nerves were also amplified. Every time he saw his dad, they ended up fighting about something. Roman was never good enough, in his dad's view, starting with his middle and high school years, when he decided not to play sports.

His dad was a huge football fanatic, and his brother, Brian, had been on track to go to the Olympics before the accident that paralyzed him. Roman, on the other hand, didn't want to play or participate in any kind of athletics. He still didn't. His idea of exercise was cutting wood, carrying it to and fro, hammering beams into place, and building something from nothing.

"Well?" Della said, reminding Roman that he wasn't alone. "Are we getting out?"

Roman had parked but hadn't moved to open his door yet. He'd needed a minute to collect himself. If he and his father argued, it wouldn't be on him. He planned to smile and be easygoing while he was here. He didn't want any trouble; all he wanted was to support his brother.

Della reached out and touched Roman's shoulder. "Hey. You've got me beside you. I'm your excuse, remember? That goes for awkward conversations too. If you need saving, give me a sign. I'll demand food or that you help me find a bathroom. You're not going into this situation alone."

Roman looked over at her. She was a very beautiful woman. He'd thought so the first time he'd seen her on the plane. Getting to know her had only made her more attractive in his mind. She was kind and generous, and he was going to take her up on that offer. "Okay. I like that plan. What's the sign?"

She lifted her eyes up as she seemed to think for a moment. "We'll do code words instead of a sign. The code words are 'I need hot cocoa!'"

Roman couldn't help but smile. "You want me to say 'I need hot cocoa' when I want out of a situation?"

"Yes. Then we'll have to extract ourselves from whatever situation we're in and go find some."

"I don't even like chocolate, remember?" he said playfully.

"I remember you saying so, but I still don't believe it." She winked at him and pushed open her passenger-side door.

She seemed confident about this choice in code phrases, so he nodded. Then he reached for the door handle and pushed his door open as well. Della met him in front of the car, bundled up in her heavy coat. "I'm actually looking forward to this. I love small-town gatherings. And your brother is a celebrity here. This will be fun."

Roman wished he had her enthusiasm. "The event will be held on Main Street. There's a large angel tree that gets decorated and lit up this time of year. I think they're setting up a stage around there."

"An angel tree? How fun is that? Somerset Lake has a town Christmas tree too. Seeing it get lit up every year is one of my favorite moments of the season."

"Sounds nice." One thing Roman did miss about his

hometown was how enthusiastic about the holidays everyone got here. There was something going on every weekend during the month of December.

"Roman Everson? Is that you?" a woman's voice asked.

Roman spun on his heel to see Emma Hershey walking toward him. "Hey, Em. I thought you'd be running the café today."

"And miss your brother's big moment? No way. Brian does so much for the people here. I want to be up front and center when he gets that award." She smiled wide and looked from him to Della. "You brought someone?"

Roman cleared his throat. "This is Della," he said, realizing he didn't know Della's last name. It was odd that he and Della had only known each other half a day but had already spent the amount of time one would across two dates. But since their plane and car rides weren't actual dates, they'd felt free to share things about themselves that they might not otherwise. Like the fact that Roman had fired a family man with a sick child. That certainly didn't cast him in a good light.

"Nice to meet you, Della," Emma said, reaching out her hand.

Della shook it. "And you as well. You own a café?"

"The Sweetwater Café." Emma pointed. "It's farther down Main Street. You'll have to stop in. Nina is running the shop today," she told Roman. "You remember her, right?"

Roman squinted his eyes as he tried to place the face. "I'm not sure."

"Well, that's because you've been gone too long," Emma said good-spiritedly.

"Does your café sell hot chocolate?" Della asked.

Emma grinned. "Of course it does. Although, I'll be honest. If you want cocoa, I'd go to Dawanda's Fudge Shop. Hers is the best."

"Good to know." Della cast Roman a conspiratorial look. "I don't think we're quite ready for hot cocoa just yet."

"No," he agreed. "Not yet."

Jack Hershey stepped up to Emma and put his arm around her. "Hey, Roman," he said. Kaitlyn and Mitch Hargrove walked over to say hello as well.

Roman shook their hands. As much as he told himself he didn't, he'd missed these faces. Once upon a time, he'd hung out with this crowd, with the exception of Kaitlyn, who had moved to Sweetwater Springs a few years ago. Roman, Mitch, Emma, and Jack had all been friends, roaming around the town and growing up together. He knew their pasts, and they knew his. He guessed that's what made him so uncomfortable.

"Roman was just introducing me to his girlfriend, Della," Emma told the group.

Roman started to object, but Brenna McConnell squealed as she joined them as well. "Roman has a girlfriend?" From what Roman had seen on Facebook, Brenna was a teacher now and dating the town's fire chief—a newcomer to Sweetwater Springs. "You must be something special to nab Roman's attention," Brenna told Della. "He's always been a guy to go on a couple dates but never get serious with anyone."

Roman couldn't argue that point. He needed to set the record straight, though. He and Della were here together, but they weren't romantically involved.

"So how did you two meet?" Kaitlyn asked. "I love stories about how couples found each other." She beamed as she glanced between him and Della.

Roman started to respond, but Della reached for his hand, surprising him.

"Well, I guess it was fate," Della said. "Wouldn't you say so, Roman?"

Roman felt his lips part, but no words came out.

"We found ourselves sitting next to each other on a plane. I'm terrified of planes, and Roman helped me keep my sanity." She cast him another conspiratorial look. "We've been together ever since."

She failed to mention that the story she told had happened only a few hours before. Or that they weren't a real couple.

Even so, Roman didn't pull his hand away. His palm resting against hers felt nice, and it was working to calm him. Being in his hometown, surrounded by the people of his past, wasn't easy. "That's right," he agreed, looking at Della. "I think I could use some hot cocoa."

Della's green eyes subtly widened. "I hear Dawanda's Fudge Shop has the best around."

Chapter Three

❄

When they walked through the door of Dawanda's Fudge Shop, Della was accosted by the aroma of chocolate, cinnamon, nutmeg, and every other sweet-smelling spice.

The woman behind the counter waved cheerily. She had bright red hair that poked in various directions off her head, and she wore purple glasses that rested low on her nose.

"Roman Everson? Is that you?" she asked.

"The one and only," he said, breaking into what looked like a sincere smile.

Della still didn't know Roman very well, but she started to understand when he was faking a smile, like he'd done on the plane when she'd gone on and on about her boys, and when he was being authentic. She liked this look on him. Relaxed. Easygoing. He almost appeared to be enjoying himself.

"Well, wonders never cease. It's good to see you home," Dawanda told Roman.

"It's good to see you too, Dawanda," he said.

Dawanda looked between him and Della expectantly, no doubt waiting for Roman to introduce them.

Della wasn't sure how Roman would react when she pretended to be his girlfriend earlier. She hadn't really thought it through. The poor guy just seemed to need someone on his side. His friends seemed nice enough, but Della could feel the anxiety radiating off him. She wanted to be there for him. She wanted to be a friend. And somehow she'd become more than a friend. At least that's what she'd led his friends to believe.

Roman glanced over at her, the corners of his mouth quirking softly. "This is Della," he told the fudge store owner. "She's my…" He hesitated. "She's my, uh…"

Della understood his dilemma. If he called her a mere friend now, he'd look like a liar to the friends she'd just met. They had to keep the charade up.

"Girlfriend," Della supplied, looking at Dawanda.

"Girlfriend?" The fudge shop owner looked absolutely thrilled by the news.

He cleared his throat and looked down for a moment. He didn't confirm or deny Della's declaration.

"Well, in that case, your fudge today is on the house," Dawanda said. "And I can give you a cappuccino reading if you want," she said, her voice lifting hopefully.

Roman shook his head quickly. "No, that won't be necessary."

"What's a cappuccino reading?" Della asked.

Roman looked over at her. "Dawanda is famous for sitting people down and reading their fortune in the foam of a cappuccino."

Della's lips formed a little *o*. "That sounds fun."

"But," Roman interjected, holding up his pointer finger, "we don't have time for that today. We're in a hurry."

Dawanda nodded. "Yes, I know. Your brother is getting an award today. You don't want to miss that. I'm guessing that's why you traveled all this way."

"It is," he confirmed. "And as soon as the ceremony is over, I'm taking Della to her hometown of Somerset Lake."

Dawanda's brows rose high on her forehead. "Is that where Trisha Langly moved this past year?"

"Yes, it is," Della said. "I've become friends with Trisha since she's moved to the lake. We're in a book club together."

"Well, isn't that wonderful?" Dawanda said. "It's such a small world, isn't it?"

Della nodded. "My nana always said so. Then again, she never ventured past the town line, so it was true for her."

Dawanda pointed at Della. "She sounds like my kind of woman."

"We'll also have two cups of hot cocoa, if you don't mind," Roman said, giving Della a look. "And I'm afraid we'll have to take it to go, because we don't want to miss the ceremony for Brian."

For a moment, Della thought she saw sadness sweep over Dawanda's face. She gave Roman a look that said volumes. But since Della didn't know the backstory, she couldn't read the unspoken things between them.

Dawanda set to work placing two fudge squares for Roman and two for Della on a piece of wax paper. She wrapped them up, slid them across the counter, and then poured two cups of hot chocolate. "Here you go!" She looked at Roman again. "I understand you're in a hurry today, but please don't stay away too long. I miss seeing your face around here, and I know your parents do too. Your mom comes in here often and speaks about you all the time."

"She does?" Roman asked.

"Oh, yes. I ask her how you are, and she tells me all about the work you're doing in Ohio. We're all so proud of you here," she told Roman.

"Thank you. It's nothing award-worthy like Brian."

"Don't compare yourself to your brother. Or anyone else for that matter. You are your own man," Dawanda said. "And in my opinion, you're a stand-up one."

Della and Roman said goodbye to Dawanda and walked out side by side.

Della didn't say anything to Roman at first. She didn't want to pry or ask too many questions. Instead, she sipped on her hot chocolate thoughtfully and enjoyed the environment of Sweetwater Springs. Maybe she'd come back here one day to shop and get more fudge from Dawanda. Della looked over at Roman. "Have you ever had one of Dawanda's cappuccino readings?"

He laughed. "Yes, I have. I venture to say anyone who grew up in this town has been subjected to one of her readings."

"What did she tell you?"

He shoved his hands in his jeans pockets. Della had always loved a man in jeans. Some women liked a guy in uniform, but a man in denim had always caught her eye. "It was a long time ago. I don't really remember, to tell you the truth."

"So you don't know if her predictions came true or not?" Della asked.

Roman narrowed his eyes. "Don't tell me you believe in that kind of stuff."

"What stuff?"

He circled his hand in front of him. "Fortunes and psychics."

She burrowed deeper into her coat to block the winter air. Even though Sweetwater Springs was only a couple of hours from where she lived, the temperature seemed to be several degrees lower here. "I don't know. Maybe. I do believe in fate, so perhaps there are people out there who sense what's in store for us."

"Fate, huh? Don't tell me I'm fake-dating a romantic."

When she looked over at him, he winked. The gesture made her heart skip a beat. She was very much a romantic, even now, despite what her ex-husband had done to her. She wanted to believe in that one person out there in the world who would stay true forever.

But not Roman, she told herself in case her romantic heart got any ideas. He was just a fake boyfriend for the next two hours, and that was all.

* * *

Roman found seats for him and Della and looked around the growing crowd, recognizing most of the faces. Some folks recognized him too and hurried over to say hello. Della was a social butterfly. She seemed to make fast friends with everyone she met, which he admired about her. His brother, Brian, was the same way.

Roman's gaze caught on an older couple weaving through the crowd, and Roman stiffened.

"What?" Della asked, seeming to notice how tense he'd become.

"My parents are heading this way," he said quietly. "I apologize in advance."

Della let out a startled-sounding laugh. She probably thought he was joking, but he wasn't. "Oh, come on. It can't be that bad," she said.

Roman lifted his gaze as his parents approached.

"Roman, you came after all," his mother said. She was

dressed to the nines as usual with her hair and makeup done up perfectly.

Roman stood and gave her a hug and a kiss on the cheek. He was a good foot and a half taller than her, so he had to dip down. "Hi, Mom. I wouldn't miss Brian's big day."

"You've always been such a wonderful big brother," she said affectionately.

"Roman," his dad said once he'd pulled back from his mom's embrace. "Good to see you."

Roman didn't believe his father was sincere in saying that for a second. "You too, Dad." He stepped forward and hugged his dad even though he suspected his father would be fine with forgoing that gesture. His dad wore a long-sleeved polo shirt that probably cost as much as Roman's monthly truck payment. He had on a sport coat and wore a pair of dark navy pants with loafers.

The Everson family was one of the richest in town. Roman had never cared about appearances, but his dad did. Roman guessed that was one reason why Brian was his father's favorite son. Brian, while humble, was an overachiever. He thrived in the spotlight, and everyone adored him, including Roman.

"And who have you brought with you?" his mom asked, looking at Della. Roman loved his mother dearly, but he guessed she was probably trying to figure out what brand of clothing Della had on and whether it came from an expensive boutique or a department store.

Della stood and shook his mother's hand. "Hello. I'm Della Rose. Roman was so nice as to invite me to come with him today."

"Do you live in the Dayton area?" she asked. Roman could tell his mom was now trying to figure out who Della Rose was to him.

Della shook her head. "No, I live in Somerset Lake. It's a little lakeside town a couple hours from here."

"Yes, I've heard of it," his mother said on a warm smile. That was the thing about Roman's mom. She was superficial with all her fancy clothes and focus on outward appearances, but when she smiled, it was authentic. Even if she determined that Della's wardrobe was unbearable, she wouldn't hold it against her. His mom valued material things, but she put more value on the traits that went deeper than what a person looked like on the outside. "I think one of our town residents moved there."

"Trisha Langly," Della confirmed for the third time in the last hour.

Roman watched as Della and his mom chatted back and forth while he and his dad said nothing to each other. What more could be said? His dad had blamed him for his brother's accident. Yeah, his dad blamed several people, primarily Mitch Hargrove, the driver who'd hit Brian's vehicle one winter night. Mitch had walked away from that wreck, while Brian had never walked again.

But his father blamed Roman too. Roman was at that party with Brian. He was supposed to make sure his brother didn't drink too much, which Brian never did. Then Roman was supposed to drive Brian home. They were each other's buddy system. Needless to say, Roman had failed as a big brother that night. He'd met a girl, and he'd wanted to stay at the party longer to flirt and maybe get her number. Brian, being the rule follower he was, had been adamant about keeping curfew. He left while Roman had stayed behind.

Ten minutes after Brian had gone, rumors of an accident began to circulate. Roman had heard that it was Mitch. He was friends with Mitch, so he'd been a little worried. Soon there was news that the other driver was Brian.

Roman should have been there. He should have been driving. He should have been the one in that wheelchair.

Roman met his father's gaze now. If looks could talk, that's exactly what his dad's eyes were saying. Still, after all this time.

"Oh, the ceremony is about to begin," his mother said, glancing back at the flurry of activity on the makeshift stage. "We're sitting in the front row. Come join us," she told Roman.

Roman shook his head. "We'll stay back here. I'll tell Brian hello before I go."

"How soon do you have to leave town?" his mother asked.

"As soon as it's over, I'm afraid. Della has an event of her own in Somerset Lake. We can't be late."

His mom looked disappointed. "Well, you know what time we're having Christmas dinner. We always set a spot for you, should you want to come."

Roman didn't attend anymore. He hadn't in years.

"Should we set a spot for Della too?" she asked, looking between them. Roman could see his father's impatience creeping into the edges of his serious expression.

"Oh, that's so kind of you to ask," Della said, "but I'll be spending Christmas with my two sons."

"You have two sons?" his mom asked. Roman suspected she was worrying what he was getting himself into by dating a single mother of two.

"Twin boys," Della said. "They are the apples of my eye."

"As are all my children," his mom said, giving Roman a meaningful look. "I hope you'll be home for Christmas. It would mean the world to me. I love you."

"You too, Mom." He gave her another hug but spared his father this time. Then he took his seat and watched his parents navigate through the crowd toward the front row.

"They seem so nice," Della said, tapping her elbow into his arm to get his attention. "What do you have against them?"

Roman inhaled deeply as Brian, the mayor of the town, rolled onto the stage in a wheelchair. "It's what they have against me. See that man up there? That's my brother, Brian."

Della followed his gaze.

"He's in a wheelchair for the rest of his life," Roman told her. "And I'm partly responsible for that."

* * *

Della's heart had been breaking for Roman since he'd shared his story with her. They'd watched the ceremony, and afterward, she and Roman had said hello to Brian and his wife, Jessica. Roman had made it a quick exchange, offering his congratulations and his regrets that they had to leave so soon. Then he and Della had climbed back in the rental car and driven silently out of town.

"We need gas," Della pointed out, leaning across the center console to check the dashboard. She couldn't help but catch the scent of Roman's cologne as she got close. Judging by how perfect it was, she guessed it was expensive. If he had money, he wasn't showy about it. Unlike his parents.

"I'll stop at the next gas station before getting back on the highway," Roman said.

Della nibbled at her lower lip as she returned to her upright position in the passenger seat. "Your brother and his wife seemed great."

"Yeah." Roman nodded.

She wanted to ask for more details about his family situation, but it wasn't any of her business. So instead, she continued to nibble her lip, a bad habit she'd had since child-hood. She'd managed to nix biting her nails and twirling her finger in her hair, but she'd never been able to stop chewing softly on her lip when her nerves were overfiring.

Five minutes down the road, Roman pulled the car into a gas station. He parked and got out to fuel up.

Della pushed open her car door as well to get some air. It wasn't all that fresh. Instead, it was tinged with gasoline and cigarettes. She coughed, preparing to close the door again when a dog came dashing toward her with a friendly bark.

"Well, hello to you as well." Della didn't stick her hand out immediately because the furry canine might be rabid. It timidly approached her with a wagging tail, panting softly as its tongue lopped out of its mouth. There was no collar on the dog's neck, and it appeared to be thin and dirty. "Where's your owner?" Della asked.

The dog took another step closer.

"Are you hungry?" She turned back toward the center console, where she had a piece of bread she'd pulled out of her bag. It was homemade bread that she'd packed for her trip. She broke off a piece and held it out to the stray. It stepped closer, sniffed, and then pulled it into its mouth quickly, eyes trained on her the entire time.

"It's okay. I'm not going to hurt you," Della said quietly.

"There you are!" a man said, taking quick steps toward the car. He was wearing a shirt with the gas station's logo. "I'm sorry if the dog is bothering you, ma'am," he told Della.

"Oh, he's not bothering me at all."

"Well, she's been bothering me for about two weeks now. Every time I call the animal shelter to come get her, that ras-cally stray is MIA." The man addressed the dog, pointing his finger. "Not this time, girl. They'll be here any minute, and then you are going to doggy jail." The man laughed like that was funny.

Della didn't find the humor in that prospect, though. She looked into the dog's sad eyes. "She's been hanging out here for two weeks?" she asked the gas station attendant.

"Maybe longer than that."

"Where's her owner?"

"Don't know," the man said. "Whoever it is must not care too much if they didn't even put a collar on her. I've searched the local message boards to see if anyone's missing her. Nothing." He pointed at the dog a second time. "Enjoy your freedom while you can, sweetheart. Because in a few minutes, you're gonna be locked up." He laughed again and then waved at Della as he headed back inside the gas station.

Della flicked her gaze up to see Roman exiting the station. She nibbled her lower lip some more. Then, on an inhale, she stepped out of the car, opened the back passenger-side door, and whispered to the dog, "Hop in, girl."

The dog didn't waste any time. It jumped in the back seat and settled on the floorboard. Della closed the door and plopped back into her seat. She closed her own door behind her and faced forward. When Roman took the driver's seat, he was all business.

He glanced over. "You okay?"

She nodded quickly, hoping he wouldn't see the dog until they had at least left the gas station parking lot. She couldn't stand the thought of the poor thing being hauled away to a shelter, where it would likely go unadopted and might even be put down. "Yep." She rolled her lip between her teeth.

"All right," Roman said, setting the car into motion. "Next stop Somerset Lake."

Chapter Four

❄

Della broke off a piece of her bread and glanced over at Roman. He seemed to be lost in thought, so she reached behind her seat and handed off the bread.

The dog was surprisingly quiet. It sniffed and took the bread. The poor thing was starving. And scared. All alone. What was she to do?

"My boys have asking for a dog for Christmas," she told Roman.

He glanced over. "A dog? That's a pretty big request. Are you getting them one?"

Della shrugged. "Maybe so."

"What kind of dog?" he asked.

"Oh, probably a rescue of some sort. Maybe a brown one with a white patch of fur on its forehead."

He gave her a humorous look. "That's pretty specific."

"Do you like dogs?" she asked, resisting pulling her lip between her teeth. That was a sure telltale that she was hiding something.

"I like them well enough. I don't have one of my own. I agree that finding a dog in need of a home is the way to go. I'm sure your boys would be happy if you got them a pet." His cell phone buzzed again, and Roman looked unnerved.

Della held out her hand. "Mind if I talk to her?"

Roman gave her an are-you-crazy look. "What?"

"Well, you're apparently not going to. She needs to vent her frustrations to someone. Let me be that person. Maybe I can help."

Roman didn't look so sure. Even so, he pulled his cell phone out and placed it in Della's palm, his fingers brushing against her skin as he released it. Della ignored the little buzz that zipped from his touch to her toes.

She tapped the screen to connect the call and held the phone to her ear. "Hello?"

"Who is this?" the woman snapped on the other line. Only three words, but her anger was evident.

"I'm Della Rose. Are you Bob's wife?" Della could feel Roman watching her from the corner of his eye, possibly regretting his decision to allow her to speak to this woman.

"Yes, I'm Marie Coker," the woman huffed. "I want to speak to Roman Everson."

"I'm afraid he's busy right now," Della said. Roman was busy helping Della get home so that she wouldn't miss her boys' recital. He was her hero today, even if he was the very opposite of that for Mrs. Coker. "But I have plenty of time if you want to talk to me," Della told Marie. "You can tell me what's on your mind."

"Your boyfriend is on my mind. He fired my husband a couple days before Christmas," Marie said.

Why did everyone keep assuming that Della was Roman's girlfriend? Okay, well, Della was responsible for the folks in Sweetwater Springs believing that. There was no reason for

Marie to jump to that conclusion, though. "I'm very sorry about your husband's job, but it wasn't Roman's decision. It was his boss's. Roman was just the bearer of the bad news."

"Well, if he can dish it out, he should be able to take it," Marie said. "Bob is the breadwinner in our family. I have to take care of the kids. And one of our children, Tim, is sick right now. Bob can't afford to be out of work. What kind of man fires another one at Christmas?"

Della nibbled on her lower lip as her gaze slid over to catch Roman's. He was a good man in her estimation. Then again, she'd thought her ex, Jerome, was better than he was. No one was perfect; some were far from it. An idea came to Della's mind. "I think I can help you, Marie," she said.

"You?"

"Yes. What if I set up a GoFundMe page for you and your family? I can explain your story, how your husband is out of work and that you have a sick child. I've set one up before for a lady in my church," Della explained. "That GoFundMe raised almost ten thousand dollars."

"Wow," Marie said quietly. "Even a quarter of that would allow Bob to stay home and search for a job that he likes."

"And he could be there for you and Tim. Wouldn't that be amazing?" Della asked. "I can set the page up over the next hour and a half. I'm on a long car ride, so I have time on my hands, and I want to help."

"Thank you," Marie said, her tone notably softening. "That's really nice of you."

"You're welcome. I can help your husband with a job search too. I'm great with navigating searches online. I'm a real estate agent in my town, but people come to me and need other areas of their lives worked out in order to find the perfect home," Della explained. "They want to know about schools for their kids or jobs close to the neighborhood that they're looking at. If you tell me what Bob wants to do for employment, I can send a few searches to him."

"But you don't even know us," Marie said.

Della looked out the passenger-side window as the world passed by. "My nana used to say that if you've ever been on the receiving end of someone else's help, you recognize another person in need. There are no strangers, just friends waiting to make your acquaintance."

Della stayed on the line a while longer, collecting the Coker family's information so that she could put up the GoFundMe. Then she promised she'd email Marie when she was done so that Marie could share the link with friends and family. Della would be sharing with hers as well. "The folks in Somerset Lake, where I live, love to help another in need. This awful thing is going to turn out to be something good. Just wait and see."

"You're amazing," Marie said. "Thank you."

"You're very welcome. I'll be in touch." Della disconnected the call and sucked in a startled breath when Roman reached for her hand. He glanced over, taking his eyes from the road for just a moment.

"You are an amazing woman, Della. Thank you for that," he said, voice low.

"It's the least I could do, considering what you're doing for me today. You're driving out of your way to make sure I get home in time for my boys. One might argue that you're pretty amazing yourself. Not Marie, of course," she teased.

"No, she'd argue otherwise. But you are turning things around for them. I appreciate that."

Della swallowed, noticing that Roman hadn't removed his hand from hers yet. His skin was warm and welcome. "I better get started on that GoFundMe page. People love a good cause."

Roman pulled his hand back to the steering wheel. "Maybe you can help me find another job too. I don't want to be the bad guy anymore."

"Sure. I can do that. That'll mean you don't get rid of me after dropping me off in Somerset Lake, though."

"Fine by me," Roman said.

*   *   *

Roman had felt something when he'd touched Della's hand. A spark somewhere deep inside his chest. He wanted to ignore it, but some part of him was thinking that he'd be making a huge mistake if he dropped Della off, turned around, and didn't make arrangements to see her again.

There was something about her that soothed the deep ache that resonated within his heart. He hadn't realized how lonely he was until the last few hours. Hearing Della talk about her life and family made him realize that he wanted that for himself. Seeing his family and the folks in Sweetwater Springs again made him regret how long he'd stayed away—even if his father still blamed him for Brian's accident.

He was serious about looking for another job. His position was a good one—a dream job on paper. But he missed getting his hands dirty. He loved drawing his own designs and being involved with every aspect of building. He didn't enjoy doing someone else's dirty work for them. He'd helped ruin the Cokers' holiday while Della had just singlehandedly saved it.

Woof!

Roman tapped the brakes. "What was that?"

He glanced over at Della, who didn't look shocked at all. Instead, she looked sheepish as she nibbled on her bottom lip.

Woof!

Roman glanced in the back seat and saw a brown dog with a patch of white fur between its eyes. He looked at the road again and took a breath. "Della, where did the dog come from?"

"The gas station attendant had already called animal control. He said that the dog had been hanging out there for weeks. It doesn't have any tags, and I mean, look at the poor thing. Obviously, it has no owner. I couldn't just allow it to get hauled off to the shelter. What if no one adopted it? You know what happens in places like that."

Roman pressed his lips together for a moment. "You don't know if it's rabid."

Della rolled her eyes as a nervous-sounding laugh tumbled off her lips. "She's not Cujo."

"She? Have you named her yet? Are you keeping her?"

"My boys want a dog, remember? Maybe we can keep this one. And as far as names go, I think a Christmassy name would be fitting, since it's the holidays. Have any suggestions?"

Roman frowned. He still didn't think bringing home an unknown dog was a fantastic idea. "What if it bites?"

Della reached around to the back seat to pet the dog's head. "I've a good read on people and animals. This dog is harmless. I'm thinking Jingle. Or what about Bell? Jingle Bell?"

"A first and last name. I guess you're serious about keeping her," he said, wondering at the warmness inside his chest over a practical stranger rescuing a down-on-its-luck dog from an uncertain fate. "Jingle Bell is a good name." When he glanced over again, Della looked pleased.

She reached for a piece of bread that Roman had seen her pinching off for the last hour and handed it back to the canine. "Here you go, Jingle. Eat up. It's going to be an exciting night for you. My boys are a handful," she told the dog. "I hope you're prepared for a new family."

Roman felt that comment in his chest too. Instead of warmness, it stung. "My family seemed to like you," he said.

"They were nice. I'm sorry about all the difficulties you've had with them." Della reached for his arm.

"Thanks. I guess I can't complain. My brother is the one in the wheelchair."

"He looks happy."

"More so than me, I guess," Roman agreed.

They grew quiet for a long time as Della focused on making the GoFundMe page for the Coker family. An hour later, Roman pointed.

"Here we are. Welcome to Somerset Lake."

Della looked up and cheered while Jingle Bell barked excitedly. Roman started to laugh, but then the car spun out on a patch of black ice. He gripped the steering wheel, held his breath, and prayed that all would be calm when the spinning stopped.

After long seconds that seemed to defy time, Roman looked over at Della.

"Are you okay?" he asked breathlessly.

She seemed to relax, then blinked and looked around. "That was terrifying."

"Yeah." Roman checked on Jingle Bell, who was cowering on the back floorboard. Then he surveyed the car, which had landed at the bottom of the slope off the shoulder. "There's no way I can push this thing up onto the road."

Della's eyes widened as she seemed to process what that meant. "Oh, no. We're not going to make it to my sons' recital." Her eyes quickly teared up. She looked down at her folded hands in her lap and remained quiet for a moment.

"Yes, you are making it to your sons' recital," Roman finally said. "I'll just call an Uber to come get you and take you there."

She shook her head. "There aren't Ubers in Somerset Lake. The recital starts in half an hour. What am I going to do?"

Roman pulled out his phone, tapped into the browser, and connected with the number of the first tow truck listed in the area. "Hello, I'm looking for a tow on the edge of town…Yes, I realize it's after hours, but I'll make it worth your while. But first I need you to drive my friend to the church in town. After that, I'll need help getting my car out of this ditch."

The man on the other line objected until Roman doubled the normal fee. It was Christmas, after all—who couldn't use a little extra cash during the holidays? He gave the man the location and disconnected the call before looking at Della. "Your ride will be here in ten minutes or less."

Her lips were parted. "Thank you for arranging the tow truck. I'll pay, of course."

"No, you won't. This is my Christmas gift to you. Just enjoy your family tonight."

Her eyes were still shiny, but she was smiling. Then, surprising him, she crossed the center console and threw her arms around his neck. "Thank you, Roman. Thank you so much."

His arms closed in around her, and he breathed in her sweet scent. "I should be thanking you." How was it possible that they were only strangers? He felt like he knew this woman.

She pulled back and looked at him, her face only inches from his. "Why would you thank me? You've gone out of your way for me. Twice now."

"You made me realize that I want a change in my life. A new job for starters. Maybe I want a closer relationship with my family too." And maybe he wanted more than a pretend girlfriend. He didn't tell Della that, though. She wasn't an option, because they lived too far apart. It would never work. Some changes would be good, but he didn't plan on changing his zip code for someone he'd known less than a day.

The tow truck's headlights flashed as it approached.

"There's your ride," Roman said quietly.

Della suddenly looked sad. "Come with me."

"I need to stay with the car. Besides, it's your family. Your kids might not understand why their mom is attending their recital with a strange man."

Della offered a faint smile. "True. It's much more complicated when kids are involved."

As opposed to when he'd introduced Della to his family.

"Will we ever see each other again?" she asked.

Roman shrugged, his shoulders feeling like lead. "I hope so."

The tow truck flashed its lights again.

"You better go. After all this, it would be a shame if you were late to the church."

She nodded. Then she leaned forward, gave him one more quick hug, and pulled away. She opened the back passenger-side door, retrieved her things from the back, along with the dog, and looked at Roman. "Goodbye, Roman. Merry Christmas."

"Merry Christmas, Della Rose." He lowered his gaze to the scrawny dog who'd managed to find herself a home tonight. "Merry Christmas, Jingle Bell."

* * *

Della felt awkward walking into a church with an overnight bag and a dog. Even though she'd promised Jett she would be sitting front and center, she took the back pew to go unnoticed with Jingle Bell at her side.

Jingle was a good dog so far. She kept still and quiet and continually looked over at Della with soulful, sad eyes. Was she sad to see Roman go as well? Probably not, but that's why Della's mood felt deflated.

She and Roman had made a connection of some sort. They'd only known each other a day, but it felt like they had unfinished business. Della was tempted to pull out her cell phone and text him to make sure the tow truck had come back to get him, but the lights in the church dimmed and the first child for tonight's performance walked out. Della absently petted Jingle's head and watched, her thoughts on Roman until her own boys came out to perform a duet. She saw Jett search the audience for her. Della raised her arm to show him she was there. She would always be there no matter what happened, including divorce and delayed flight plans, a minor road accident, or a handsome stranger who might have become more.

Jett smiled and returned his focus to his acoustic guitar.

Della beamed with pride as she watched their festive song. Then the boys bowed and walked off stage with their instruments. She'd traveled all day to make sure she was here for those two very important minutes, and she would do it all over again if she had to.

When the recital was over, Della hurried out of the church with Jingle Bell and her overnight bag to avoid making a scene. She waited for her ex and his new wife to walk out with the kids. When Jett and Justin saw her, they came running.

"Mom!" Jett said.

Della noticed the moment he saw the dog in her arms.

His feet slowed, and his mouth dropped open. "A dog? Is that our dog?" he asked hopefully.

Justin clapped his hands. "Are we getting a dog?"

Della laughed. "It's a she. And she's getting us for Christmas too. Win-win, I think." Della looked past her boys to see Jerome and Sofia heading toward her. She smiled politely.

"I'm glad you made it," Jerome said.

Della nodded. "It was iffy for a moment there, but I'm glad I made it too. I wouldn't miss my boys' recital for the world." Or for a mysterious and handsome stranger she'd felt an unexpected connection with today.

"So I guess the boys will be riding home with you?" he asked.

That was the original arrangement. Della would be keeping the boys until Christmas night. Then Jerome would have his turn with them again.

"Actually, I don't have a car at the moment. Long story. Do you think you can give us all a ride home?" she asked.

Jerome looked over from her to their boys and the dog in their arms. Then he looked back at Della. "Of course. We're parked over there." He pointed at the large SUV in the far lot.

Della and the boys followed him, and they all climbed inside. The boys were chattering excitedly about the dog and their performance.

"Did we do a great job, Mom?"

Della nodded. "Oh, yes. You two were amazing."

Justin grinned ear to ear over her compliment.

It took ten minutes to make it home. When Jerome pulled into her driveway, Della helped the boys and dog get out. They waved goodbye to their dad and Sofia. Then Della pointed toward the house. "Go wait for me on the porch. I want to talk to your dad for a minute."

The boys dutifully raced ahead with Jingle Bell at their heels.

Once they were out of earshot, Della headed to Jerome's window. She was still thinking about Roman and his family. It was best for families to work through their differences sooner than later. Time could drive a wedge, and Della didn't want that for herself, her boys, or for Jerome and his new wife. No matter what their family looked like, they were still a family.

Della leaned inside his open window. "If we're going to continue to be good parents to the boys, we need to be on the same page. There can't be secrets, lies, or even just awkwardness."

The skin between Jerome's eyes pinched softly. "I agree, and I want that too. More than anything, I want for us to be friends, Della."

"I'm not sure I'm ready to be friends yet. But friendly is a good starting place," Della said, looking past him to Sofia. She was going to be in the boys' lives whether Della wanted her to be or not. They needed to be able to talk and work toward providing them with the happy family they deserved. "So," she said, taking a breath and looking at Jerome, "Christmas breakfast is at eight. I know it's early, but the boys wake at six on Christmas day."

Jerome chuckled. "Oh, I know."

"If you want to come, you're welcome to," Della added. "You and Sofia, of course," she said, looking past him to Jerome's new wife. "I know the kids would enjoy having all of their family there."

Jerome's eyes narrowed. "Really?"

"It's Christmas, and more importantly, it's family. They can show you their presents, and we'll have breakfast together. And then lunch if you're still around."

Jerome cleared his throat, looking emotional for a moment. "Thank you, Della. That would mean a lot to me."

"The more the merrier, right?" That's what they always used to say. She had just never thought it would apply to Jerome's new wife. Della didn't want him back. She was over him, and for the most part, she was also over what he'd done to her. Now all she wanted was to provide a stable family environment for her boys to grow up in.

She said goodbye to Jerome and Sofia, feeling good about the conversation she'd just had as she went inside to get acquainted with their new dog. That involved a bath, a bowl of chicken she cooked up, and water. By the time they were done, Jingle Bell looked and acted like a brand-new dog.

"Tomorrow, we'll go get her a bed and some toys," Della said. "For tonight, I'll make her an area with some old blankets."

"Can she sleep in our room?" the boys wanted to know.

"Not just yet," Della told them. "While she's getting settled in, it's probably best that she sleeps where I am."

By the time Della climbed into her own bed, she was exhausted. It was five days before Christmas. For the most part, she'd already gotten everything she could possibly want. She reached over and grabbed her cell phone, hesitating before tapping out a quick text to Roman.

I hope you got back on the road okay.

She imagined he was back at the Charlotte airport by now and waiting for his flight home to Dayton. What a long day for him.

The dots on her screen started bouncing as Roman responded to her.

I'm sitting outside the terminal, waiting to board.

Della smiled as she lay in bed. *Good*, she texted back.

How was the boys' performance? he asked.

Amazing, she told him. *The best two minutes of my year.*
And Jingle Bell? he asked.

Della shone the light from her phone to the corner of her room where Jingle was already sleeping. Then she tapped out another text. *She's already a member of our family.*

Della nibbled at her lower lip. *Thank you for today, Roman.*

I should be thanking you. Mrs. Coker didn't feel the need to keep calling me after you talked to her.

Glad I could help, Della texted. *Last I checked, her GoFundMe page already has $900.*

Wow. That'll be helpful for their family.

Yes, it will.

Della waited for Roman to text more, but more never came. Maybe his plane was boarding. Or perhaps that was all they had to say to each other. She laid the phone back on her nightstand and closed her eyes. At some point, she drifted off to sleep, exhausted from the long day she'd had and the road trip adventure she'd been on with a stranger who had quickly become a friend. She didn't wake up until morning, when the boys barreled into her room to check on Jingle Bell. Then the day snowballed forward with retrieving her car, shopping for their new pet, and preparing for Christmas.

Before heading home afterward, Della stopped at Hannigan's Market. She was pushing a buggy when her phone vibrated with a new text. She pulled it out and laughed at the screen, where a text from Roman was waiting.

I made it to Dayton, but I'm missing my pretend girlfriend.

"Who is it from, Mom?" Justin asked, tugging on Della's sweater.

"The man who helped me get home for your recital. He made it back to his home as well," she told her son.

"Hooray!" Jett said. "Everyone made it home for Christmas."

"Yes, they did." Della tapped out another text to Roman. *Who needs the real thing when you have the pretend?*

Not me, Roman texted back.

The texts continued sporadically that evening and the next day, coming in at random times and making Della smile. Her heart began to skip every time Roman's name popped onscreen. It was foolish, because he lived in a whole other state. But it was making her happy.

Show me a pic of Jingle Bell, he texted the following night.

Della did one better and took a selfie of herself and Jingle together.

There they are. The two girls who stole my heart this Christmas.

Della's smile crashed into a frown. What was she doing? She couldn't allow herself to fall for a guy that she might never see again. She was heading for another heartbreak that she didn't need. She was a mother. Her boys needed her focus to be on them, not in Dayton, Ohio.

She laid her phone down without texting Roman back. It vibrated a few more times with incoming messages and then fell silent. Their time together had been brief and fun. She didn't regret it by any means. But if she continued to allow this thing between them to go on, she might.

Her mind was set; her resolve solidified. It was time to say goodbye to Roman Everson.

Chapter Five

❄

Roman hadn't heard from Della since last night. He missed her much more than he was expecting. He didn't date often because he didn't feel that spark with most dates. But he'd felt a spark with Della. It appeared she was done with him, however.

He pulled up their thread of texts and looked at the picture of her and Jingle Bell for a long moment, missing Della's face. A memory came to mind of the mischievous sparkle she got in her green eyes. He liked that look best of all. He also liked the way she nibbled on that lower lip of hers. He'd thought about doing the same more than a few times.

As he held his phone, it started to ring. For a moment, he hoped it was Della. Instead, his mom's number flashed onscreen. He tapped to connect and held the phone to his ear. "Hey, Mom."

"Roman," his father's voice said.

Roman stilled for a moment.

"I figured you wouldn't answer if I called from my phone," his dad explained. "I, uh, just wanted to tell you that it was good to see you the other day."

"Okay," Roman said, for lack of anything better to say. He was waiting for the *but*. *It was good to see you, but you can stay away for another year. The visit was good, but you're to blame for my bad mood over the last forty-eight hours.*

His father cleared his throat. "I also wanted to tell you that, if you've stayed away on my account, I'm sorry." His father groaned softly. "No, that wasn't a great apology, was it? Let me try that again. Roman, I know what I said to you was wrong. I was out of line to blame Brian's accident on you all those years ago. I was hurt, and I lashed out. I know that's not an excuse. I guess I just felt embarrassed and ashamed for what I said. I let those feelings come between us when I should have just apologized."

Roman was barely breathing as he listened to his father. He could hardly believe his ears. Where was this coming from?

"Roman, I am truly, sincerely sorry. I've been sorry since I said those words, but I guess I wasn't strong enough to take them back."

"You can't just take something like what you said back. Those words changed me. They hurt me." His eyes stung as he waded through his emotions. He didn't want to be bitter; all he wanted was to move on. "But I know it took a lot for you to say you're sorry."

"It took about six months of talking to a therapist," his father said. "I've been working on myself behind the scenes. I want to be a better man. I want to be a better father. To all my children."

Roman swallowed past the swell of emotions clogging

his throat. "It'll take time, but I think we can work on re-building our relationship," he finally said.

"I really hope so." His father's voice cracked suspiciously. "You're a bigger man than me, son."

Once upon a time, Roman's father had been his hero. No one was perfect, and some were far from it. Roman had never wanted to be the guy who fired another at Christmas, even if it hadn't been his decision. He wanted to brighten people's lives—like Della—not make them harder.

"Anyway, your mom would really like for you to come home for Christmas," his father added.

"I see," Roman said, still processing all his thoughts and emotions.

"And so would I," his father said. "It's not Christmas without you here, son. Just think about it, okay?"

It was the eve of Christmas Eve. Roman would need to book a flight today and another rental car to get to Sweet-water Springs. "I'll consider it," he said. They shared a few more awkward exchanges, and then Roman said goodbye. When the call had ended, the phone's screen returned to the picture of Della and Jingle.

Roman blew out a breath. Going home for Christmas would be preferable to spending it alone here. He didn't have anything tying him to Ohio except a job he didn't even like anymore. He could see his family and maybe take a short road trip to Somerset Lake to wish Della a Merry Christmas in person.

The idea was appealing. He mulled it over a bit longer, and it only grew on him. Then he grabbed his laptop and pulled up a browser, hoping there'd be flights home.

His hope dissipated as he looked at the screen. There were no flights going out until Christmas night. He'd miss dinner at his family's home and Della's face on Christmas.

So there it was. This holiday was destined to be a lonely one after all.

*   *   *

Della waved as she watched Jerome's SUV pull out of her driveway with Jett and Justin on Christmas night. They'd spent the day at her home, which hadn't been part of the plan until Roman.

She put her hands in the deep pockets of her coat, and her fingers wrapped around her cell phone. She wanted so badly to text Roman and wish him a Merry Christmas. Every time she thought about him, though, her heart ached a little bit. She'd fallen for him fast and quick, which was so unlike her. And if she was never going to see him again, she needed to cut ties for her heart's sake.

She turned and walked inside the house, where Jingle Bell was standing behind the glass door watching her. She stepped inside and petted Jingle's head as she propped her front paws on Della's thighs. "It's just you and me now, girl," she told the dog. "I'm so glad to have you here keeping me company."

Jingle panted happily. Then she returned to four paws and jogged into the kitchen. Della followed. There was a countertop full of dirty dishes from all today's cooking and eating. Della was tempted to prepare herself another plate. Instead, she opened the fridge and eyed the bottle of holiday-flavored wine from the Duplin Winery, a favorite in North Carolina. It was a gift from Jerome and Sofia.

Della pulled out the bottle, set it on the counter, and grabbed a glass from the cabinet. She poured herself a nice serving and sat on the barstool. Her cell phone sat on the counter in front of her. Roman had texted earlier to say

Merry Christmas. She could at least return that sentiment, she thought after half a glass of wine. She picked up her phone and started to text when her doorbell rang.

Jingle Bell took off running toward the door, barking excitedly. Della put her glass down and headed to see who her Christmas visitor was. When she opened the door, her friend Lucy Hannigan waved from the porch. She had her new boyfriend Miles beside her.

"Merry Christmas!" Lucy said.

"Merry Christmas to you too. Do you want to come inside?" Della asked.

Lucy shook her head. "Oh, we can't stay but for a minute. Miles and I were just driving around to look at all the beautiful Christmas lights on your street, and we thought we'd stop by to give you a holiday hug."

"Well, I do love holiday hugs," Della said, wrapping Lucy in a tight embrace first. Afterward, she gave Miles a hug.

"Is this your new dog?" Lucy bent to pet Jingle for a moment. Miles petted Jingle too.

"Yes, this is Jingle Bell. We rescued her from a gas station," Della told them.

Lucy straightened. "You and the guy who gave you a ride home the other night?"

Della looked down for a moment. Just thinking about Roman made her feel bittersweet emotion. "Yes."

Della had told Lucy all about the shared ride with Roman on the phone the other night.

"Have you spoken to him lately?" Lucy asked.

"Not for a couple days," Della said. "He texted me earlier, but I haven't responded."

Lucy narrowed her eyes. "Hmm."

"What?" Della asked, noticing the shared look between Lucy and Miles.

Lucy shrugged. "Oh, nothing. Just, you must really like this guy if you're too afraid to even respond to a Merry Christmas text for fear of falling even harder for him."

Della shook her head on a nervous laugh. "You can't fall for someone you only met for a day."

Miles raised his hand. "I beg to differ. I fell for Lucy the first moment I saw her. I still fall for her every time I see her."

"Aww," Lucy said on a sigh as she looked over at him. Then she looked at Della again. "Text him back. A heart is a resilient thing. Even if you fall for this guy and your heart gets hurt, you'll be okay. It's Christmas, and you said he's all alone, right?"

Della nodded. "His family lives in Sweetwater Springs, but he doesn't go home for the holidays."

"So he could probably use a little Christmas cheering up." Lucy stepped in and gave Della another hug. "It's supposed to snow some more tonight, so we should probably get home."

"Thank you for stopping by," Della told Lucy and Miles. "Merry Christmas." She shut the door behind her and headed back to her glass of wine. Then she picked up her cell phone again, gathering her courage to text Roman. She pulled up their thread of messages, and her heart skipped at just the sight of his name. She started to tap out a message, but her doorbell rang again.

Jingle Bell took off running toward the front door once more, barking all the way.

Della set her phone down and headed in that direction. She opened the door, expecting to see Lucy and Miles standing there again. Instead, her heart lifted high at the man who'd been just a stranger a few days ago. "Roman. What are you doing here?"

He was wearing a heavy coat dusted in small white snowflakes. It was snowing! And Roman was standing on her doorstep.

"I was in the area," he said with a shrug and a smile. "Well, in Sweetwater Springs anyway. I spent the day with my family."

Della's mouth dropped open. "You did?"

He nodded. "I did. My dad called to invite me, and he also apologized."

"Wow," Della said. "That's amazing. And you forgave him?"

Roman nodded. "Someone taught me earlier this week that you only get one family."

"I thought you taught me that," she said, leaning against the doorway.

"I guess we taught each other. Anyway, since you won't return my texts, I thought I'd drive down here to wish you a Merry Christmas in person."

Della nibbled at her lower lip. "I was just working up the nerve to text you back, actually."

"You had to work up the nerve to do it?" he asked, brows softly pinching.

"Well, I don't want to risk falling for my pretend boyfriend." She looked away for a moment. Maybe she'd said too much. She could blame it on that Christmas wine.

"Ah, I see. Yes, that was a concern of mine as I drove down here. Falling for my pretend girlfriend might be complicated."

She looked at him, finding him even more handsome than she remembered.

"But I was thinking, maybe we could go on a real date sometime," he said.

Della folded her arms around herself. "That might be hard, considering that you live so far away."

"There were no flights," Roman said. "So I drove from Dayton all the way to Sweetwater Springs. Then I drove here."

Della grimaced. "That's a long way to drive for a date."

"It is. But I'll be spending a lot more time in Sweetwater Springs. I agreed to work on a job there with some guys I know. We're building a house for a family who lost theirs in a fire."

"Your current job will allow you to take that much time off?" Della asked.

"No. I quit that job this morning. I am currently unemployed." He narrowed his brown eyes. "Maybe that doesn't exactly make me real boyfriend material. An unemployed contractor who doesn't exactly have a home."

Della furrowed her brow. "You don't have a home?"

"Well, I'm planning to sell my place in Dayton. Without the job, there's not much holding me there. I'm not really sure about moving back to Sweetwater Springs, but I wouldn't mind being closer to my family."

"So you're jobless and homeless?"

"You'd be crazy to agree to a date with me, huh?" he asked. The snow was making a fine layer of white on his coat and hair.

Della's eyes burned but not because of the cold. This was the sting of happy tears rushing to the surface. She wasn't going to cry, but she easily could. This was so unexpected and also exactly what she'd been secretly wishing for. "I happen to be great at finding jobs and homes for people. It's a talent of mine."

Roman's gaze was steady on hers. "So I've heard."

"Maybe I could help," she offered.

"I'd be indebted to you."

She looked at the beautiful man in front of her. She still didn't know everything about him, but she knew him. She recognized something inside him as if they'd been friends forever. "I've lost track of who is indebted to who. Maybe we can just call it even." Della nibbled her lip and glanced over her shoulder. "I was just about to have a glass of wine. Would you like to come inside?"

Roman looked past her for a moment as he seemed to weigh his answer. Then he shook his head. "I would love to, Della. But I don't want to mess things up with you, because I have a feeling about us."

"You do?"

One corner of his mouth quirked up. "And I want to do this right. That means we need to start with a first date. When are you free?"

She thought for a moment. "My kids are with their father for the next two days."

"Can I take you out to dinner tomorrow, then?" he asked.

Della hugged her arms around herself as warm fuzzies floated around in her chest like winter snowflakes. "I know a good restaurant here in town."

"Perfect." His breath came out in white puffs as he looked at her. "I like to do things in order so the first date comes before the first kiss."

Her heart skipped a beat. "That's where we differ. I kind of like to mix things up and do what I want, when I want."

His half smile dropped as she stepped toward him and went up on her toes. She paused just a few inches from his lips. Then her gaze flicked up to meet his, silently asking for permission. "And I want to kiss you right now."

He scratched his chin thoughtfully. "I suppose we could count our airplane ride as our first date."

"And Sweetwater Springs as our second," she agreed.

"In which case, this is our third date," he determined. "We're overdue for some kissing."

"Yes, we are." Her smile grew as she waited for him to make his move.

He smiled as well. Then he dipped his head to meet her lips. All the sensations of the night swirled together. The cold snow. His warm mouth. Her racing heart and the aching slowness of the kiss that made time stand still.

When she pulled back to look at him, Roman was still smiling. "I still can't come inside. Not even for a glass of wine. That's definitely fifth date for me."

Della leaned into him, pressing another kiss to his lips. "Dinner tomorrow, then. Merry Christmas, Roman."

"Merry Christmas, Della Rose."

Jingle Bell barked at their feet.

Roman looked down and petted the dog's head. "And Merry Christmas to you, Jingle." He looked at Della. "I don't know about you, but I got everything I didn't know I wanted this year. And more."

"Same," Della said. "Well…" She paused. "There is one more thing I want."

"Oh? What's that?"

She leaned back toward him, bracing her hands on his chest. "One more Christmas kiss."

Roman wrapped his arms around her and held her against him. Then he fulfilled her final Christmas wish this year, leaving Della's heart full of warmth and something that felt a lot like hope and the beginning of love.

About the Author

ANNIE RAINS is a *USA Today* bestselling contemporary romance author who writes small-town love stories set in fictional places in her home state of North Carolina. When Annie isn't writing, she's living out her own happily-ever-after with her husband and three children.

Learn more at:

AnnieRains.com
Twitter @AnnieRainsBooks
Facebook.com/AnnieRainsBooks

Can't get enough of that small-town charm?
Forever has you covered with these
heartwarming contemporary romances!

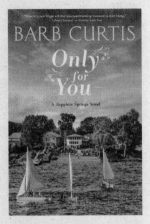

ONLY FOR YOU
by Barb Curtis

After Emily Holland's friend gets his heart broken on national TV, he proposes a plan to stop town gossip: a fake relationship with *her*. Emily has secretly wanted Tim Fraser for years, but pretending her feelings are only for show never factored into her fantasy. Still, her long-standing crush makes it impossible to say no. But with each date, the lines between pretend and reality blur, giving Tim and Emily a tantalizing taste of life outside the friend zone...Can they find the courage to give *real* love a real chance?

THE HOUSE ON SUNSHINE CORNER
by Phoebe Mills

Abby Engel has a great life. She's the owner of Sunshine Corner, the daycare she runs with her girlfriends; she has the most adoring grandmother (aka the Baby Whisperer); and she lives in a hidden gem of a town. All that's missing is love. Then her ex returns home to win back the one woman he's never been able to forget. But after breaking her heart years ago, can Carter convince Abby that he's her happily-ever-after?

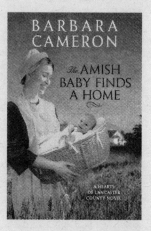

THE AMISH BABY FINDS A HOME
by Barbara Cameron

Amish woodworker Gideon Troyer is ready to share his full life with someone special. And his friendship with Hannah Stoltzfus, the lovely owner of a quilt shop, is growing into something deeper. But before Gideon can tell Hannah how he feels, she makes a discovery in his shop: a baby... one sharing an unmistakable Troyer family resemblance. As they care for the sweet abandoned *boppli* and search for his family, will they find they're ready for a *familye* of their own?

NO ORDINARY CHRISTMAS
by Belle Calhoune

Mistletoe, Maine, is buzzing, and not just because Christmas is near! Dante West, local cutie turned Hollywood hunk, is returning home to make his next movie. Everyone in town is excited except librarian Lucy Marshall, whose heart was broken when Dante took off for LA. But Dante makes an offer Lucy's struggling library can't refuse: a major donation in exchange for allowing them to film on site. Will this holiday season give their first love a second chance?

THE INN ON SWEETBRIAR LANE
by Jeannie Chin

June Wu is in over her head. Her family's inn is empty, and the surly stranger next door is driving away her last guests! But when ex-soldier Clay Hawthorne asks for June's help, she can't say no. The town leaders are trying to stop his bar from opening, and June thinks his new venture is just what Blue Cedar Falls needs to bring in more tourists. But can two total opposites really learn to meet each other in the middle? Includes a bonus story by Annie Rains!

TO ALL THE DOGS I'VE LOVED BEFORE
by Lizzie Shane

The last person librarian Elinor Rodriguez wants to see at her door is her first love, town sheriff Levi Jackson, but her mischievous rescue dog has other ideas. Without fail, Dory slips from the house whenever Elinor's back is turned—and it's up to Levi to bring her back. The quietly intense lawman broke Elinor's heart years ago, and she's determined to move on, no matter how much she misses him. But will this four-legged friend prove that a second chance is in store? Includes a bonus story by Hope Ramsay!

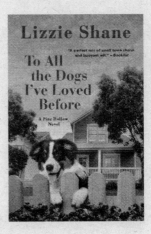

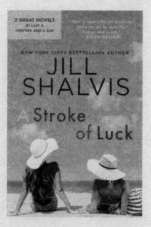